The Kiss of Judas

The Kiss of Judas

by R. A. SCOTTI

DONALD I. FINE, INC.
NEW YORK

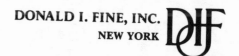

**To my mother and my father,
for the candles and the love**

The major players in *The Kiss of Judas*

MARCUS ANDRESCA, major domo of The Catacomb, the highly sophisticated, highly secret interrogation center of Italy's police forces.

ENRICO BERLINGUER, chief of the PCI, the Italian Communist Party.

ENZIO BERNESCHI, the most skillful art restorer in Italy.

SANDRO BUSCATI, leader of the terrorist *covo*, or cell, an arrogant, young genius behind the operation to ensnare the Fisherman of Souls.

CARLO CARDI, a petty criminal used occasionally in terrorist actions.

MASSIMO CENCI, see Piero Massi.

ANDREA DEL SARTO, general of the carabinieri under whose command comes the antiterrorist squad.

MICHELE DI VOTO, a dangerous, dedicated terrorist since his student days at the University of Bologna.

SANDRA DI VOTO, Michele's doting mother.

LUIGI DOMENICA, Michele's lifelong friend and comrade in the *covo*.

MONICA DOMENICA, Luigi's doting mother.

MARCELLO DONATO, a farmer in the Castel Gandolfo region, who is meanly treated by life and the agents of death.

GUIDO FELICE, the dogged, eminently fallible, and in his fashion heroic, chief of the antiterrorist squad.

PIERO MASSI, a triple agent: a member of the terrorist *covo*, a KGB informer, and under the alias Massimo Cenci, an officer in the antiterrorist ranks of the unsuspecting Detective Guido Felice.

FRANCO MIRABELLA, a naive, young zealot who has abandoned his faith in the Church for his faith in the *covo*.

MARCELLA MIRABELLA, a lifelong friend and disciple of Pope Paul VI.

PAOLA MIRABELLA, Franco's too loving, too trusting sister.

ALDO MORO, the ex-premier of Italy, kidnapped and assassinated by terrorists in May, 1978.

PAUL VI, the elderly, ailing, courageous Supreme Pontiff of the Roman Catholic Church.

MARCUS ROSE, a professor of political science at the University of Rome and founder of the club, *Studenti per una patria libera* (SPL), terrorist breeding ground.

BABE GAYNOR TAGLIA, an American tobacco heiress, divorced wife of an Italian industrialist, and errant mother of a terrorist daughter.

LISA TAGLIA, a sensualist, a killer.

INGRID AND STEVE TAYLOR-MARTIN, sybarites, social leeches who make a career of bleeding the idle rich, such as Babe Gaynor.

VLADIMIR VISHNEVSKY, a KGB colonel and Piero Massi's control.

CARDINAL COSTANTO ZANELLI, an ambitious, conservative Prince of the Church who bears more resemblance to Machiavelli than to Christ.

PROLOGUE

The old man shuffled to his desk, sat down slowly, and pushed off the red suede slippers that had arrived unexpectedly one day from New York City, the gift of an American friend. His life was austere, almost spartan. But the slippers, which fit snugly together in a small matching pouch, were as soft as the finest gloves on sale in the finest shops along Via Condotti. The slippers and the books, row upon row of which lined the walls of the study, were the few luxuries he allowed himself.

He leaned back and flexed his toes, savoring the exquisite freedom of it. Then, clutching the carved arms of the chair, he forced his swollen feet into the white satin shoes of his office. His valet, almost as elderly as he, waited respectfully, an ermine cape draped ceremoniously over his arm. The valet's sharp, hawklike features were fixed in their habitual expression—a mixture of modesty and pride, servitude and honor. But not a movement of his master, not the rare surrender to self-indulgence nor the involuntary flinch of pain, passed unnoticed.

The old man looked up at the valet and smiled. The weariness that had seemed etched in his face softened.

"Not today, Enrico. I will not need a cape today." He held up his hand as he spoke and waved the valet away. "Could you imagine Peter in a fur cape in May—or any other month?" He laughed softly to himself. How far we have come from the rugged Peter, he thought. How would he have faced these desperate children—these killers?

Enrico stood humble but unwavering, his face tense with anxiety. He was a man who took his responsibility gravely, who knew his duty and was determined to see it through. "I beg you, with the utmost respect. It is May, but a very chilly May day, not at all like a true Roman spring. Your doctor insists, your secretary..."

The old man glanced from his valet to the tall, unprepossessing man waiting patiently at the door. Monsignor Pasquale Macchi was more than a secretary; he was a trusted adviser and confidant. Friends said he protected the old man; enemies charged that he isolated him. But none disputed the extent of the secretary's power or the canniness with which he wielded it. Monsignor Macchi had a long, bland face that never betrayed him, but now his head inclined ever so slightly in agreement.

Everything is awry this season, the old man murmured to himself. Where is the resurrection and the light? He leaned heavily on his desk to steady himself as he stood up. A dog-eared copy of Maritain's *Integral Humanism* lay open on the blotter. In the agonizing weeks and months just past, he had returned to it again for inspiration and hope.

"Very well, Enrico, your will be done—and my doctor's and my secretary's."

With an almost imperceptible sigh of relief the valet draped the ermine cape over the stooped shoulders. The old man fastened the gold clasp himself. His hands were not those of a laborer. The smooth, tapered fingers were almost feminine and were weighted by a square amethyst set in a heavy gold ring that gleamed for an instant against the sleeve of the servant's black broadcloth suit.

"You are a good man, Enrico. You care for me too well."

The valet beamed. He would treasure those few words all through the day, caressing them in his mind as one would caress

10

a woman, and repeat them to his wife over their simple midday meal.

The old man moved slowly across the room, each step more painful than the one before. Monsignor Macchi bowed respectfully and opened the door. Together they walked through the wide hallways, tapestried in red damask, past the unblinking guards who snapped to attention.

Five centuries before, Michelangelo had designed their uniforms. The red, yellow and blue striped suits remained unchanged. But in place of the traditional halberds, the Swiss Guards within the Apostolic Palace were now armed with submachine guns. The old man was uneasy at the sight but said nothing. Even here, in these sacred walls, we are creating a fortress of fear, he thought.

Downstairs, a black Mercedes limousine with liveried driver waited at the front gate. Was the driver armed too? Most likely, the old man thought, but he would not inquire. He did not want to be infected by the virus of fear that had spread so close; he did not want it to creep into his own heart.

Monsignor Macchi helped him into the back seat, closed the door firmly and got in front beside the driver. He was disturbed by the old man's silence but did not intrude. After years of service, he knew when to speak and when to keep his own counsel.

The limousine rolled through the manicured gardens, rounded the basilica and crossed St. Peter's Square. Motorcycle police in white helmets revved their engines and pulled out in front of the car as it swung onto the broad Via della Conciliazione.

When the old man first came to Rome in 1920 as a graduate student, this grand boulevard leading from the Tiber to San Pietro was a maze of narrow streets called the Spina di Borgo. One would come through the dark, medieval alleys, where Raphael's studio had been, into the sudden bright expanse of Renaissance. Mussolini tore down those old blocks as a gesture of conciliation with the church. Now there is an imperial parade route from the river to the piazza. But the surprise is lost. The old man preferred the Spina di Borgo. He wondered if the pilgrim, or the prodigal son

11

come home at last, might not have been moved more by the surprise than by this elaborate broadcasting of the grandeur and power of the Roman Church.

He sank deeper into the plush seat. The route had been cleared of all traffic. Heavily armed *polizia,* white bulletproof vests hanging to their waists, stovepipe masks protecting their heads, watched from the rooftops. Their orders were shoot to kill. Nothing could be allowed to mar this final day of national mourning.

The Mercedes limousine, license plate SCV1, glided smoothly, almost soundlessly, over Ponte Vittorio Emmanuele, across the ocher Tiber, yellow and white papal flags snapping above the hood. Enrico was right. The day was unusually cold for May, a fitting climax to a chilling spring. A gray wind had swirled down from the bony Appennines. It entered the city along the Via Flaminia, chased rain across the Piazza del Popolo, curled papers down the Corso. From the terraces of the cafés and trattorias waiters eyed the skies every morning for a sign—should they put out the tables or keep the awnings furled? The Tiber was choppy and ice-edged. In paris it was snowing. So much for April in Paris. The BBC was reporting a blizzard north of London. The weather had been turned upside down, inside out; the climate—natural, political, personal—upside down, inside out. It was a filthy spring in Rome.

In the back seat, alone, the old man watched the flags. He did not lean forward and wave paternally to the women who lined the sidewalks or acknowledge the policemen's salutes. He was wondering how the flags held firm in the wind and why his ermine cape did not protect him from its bite.

The frail, sorrowful Bishop of Rome and Supreme Pontiff was going to celebrate a mass for the murdered Aldo Moro, his friend and the former premier of Italy.

Kidnappings and shootings had punctuated the Roman spring, and it had rained every day. Now, at last, it was over, the old man thought. The mass in the Basilica of San Giovanni in Laterano would mark the end of this season of terror.

Rounding the garish monument to Victor Emmanuel, the late, unlamented king of Italy, which iconoclastic Romans christened "the wedding cake," the motorcade moved onto Via dei Fori Imperiali.

The flowers and trees that lined the stately thoroughfare were beginning to blossom. Beyond them on one side was the Foro Romano, marketplace of the ancient city, funeral pyre of Caesar, cattle pasture of medieval days, now a public park and tourist attraction. On the other side was the Fori Imperiali of the five emperors. And, always clearly in view at the end of the long avenue was the Colosseum, built on the site of an artificial lake. In other times, royal sailors hoisted and lowered awnings like sails from the uppermost tier to protect the noble spectators from the glare of the Roman sun.

Pope Paul VI didn't notice the broken temples of the Forum and only dimly perceived the grayish bulk of the Colosseum, partly draped in scaffolding and green matting where restoration work was proceeding. His lips moved silently, forming the words of the prayer he would deliver at the mass: Oh Lord, grant that our heart be able to forgive the unjust and mortal offense inflicted upon this most dear man and upon those who have suffered the same cruel fate.

The motorcade swung around the Colosseum, where on just such a May day Christian martyrs had served as fodder for lions and entertainment for pagans, and turned down Via di San Giovanni in Laterano, toward the basilica.

BOOK I

The Mass

May 13, 1978

CHAPTER ONE

Long slivers of light like luminescent skeletal arms reached down
from the windows to the marble altar spread with starched linen
and set with gold fixtures. On each side like walls of flames a row
of cardinals, brilliant in crimson cassocks and skull caps, stood in
humble attention. The deacon raised the top of the censer for the
acolyte to spoon in the fragrant powder. Bowing to the celebrant,
he lifted the thurible high and swung it against its chain, three
times, creating a flat chime. Through the sweet haze, the candle-
lights glinted like cats' eyes. He bowed again, and with the sub-
deacons holding the edges of his purple chasuble, proceeded with
grave dignity to swing the censer over the altar, the cardinals and
the congregation.

Wrapped in the clouds of incense, the celebrant bent to kiss the
altar where the severed heads of Saints Peter and Paul were said
to repose in silver reliquaries. The image on the twelve-inch television screen flickered, and the reed-like voice of Paul VI, wavering as if it were caught on the wind, filled the abandoned villa.

"*Introibo ad altare Dei*. I will go to the altar of God."

The silver muzzle of a *P-trent-otto* gleamed like the cyclops eye.

The German-made Walther was pointed directly at the fragile figure, swathed in linens and heavily brocaded purple vestments. Sandro Buscati, watching the television, twirled the P-38 on his index finger and responded aloud.

"*Ad Deum qui laetificat juventutem meam.* To God who gives joy to my youth."

The words echoed eerily in the empty parlor. The house itself resembled a movie set or a once comfortable home from which the family had set out on a Sunday drive and never returned. Everything was exactly as it had been left. The ornate, overstuffed furniture, covered in imitation gold brocade, stood undisturbed in the parlor. Dust thickened on the gilt mirror and family photographs. The antimacassars, once lovingly crocheted by the departed signora, had begun to gray.

The new tenants had brought nothing of themselves to the house, or so it seemed. They could have been phantoms, they'd made so small a mark on the abandoned villa. Only the kitchen showed signs of life. A half-empty bottle of Frascati, two green bottles of mineral water, also empty, and an array of dirty glasses, crumbs of bread, and thin circles of the tough outer skin of a salami littered the table.

Alone in the parlor, Buscati slipped the pistol under his belt and settled back to watch the spectacle unfold. It was theater: the color, the costumes, the intensity, the music, the mesmerized audience, its very attendance a deplorable act of communion, and the single old man drawing them together by the magic he performed, a magic that had held Italy in thrall since Constantine. Beside it Shakespeare and even Pirandello were dwarfed. This was drama like no other. Repeat performances. Encores for centuries. Why, Buscati wondered, didn't the people see it for what it was? Theater, and nothing more.

Even the basilica added to the illusion, he thought. San Giovanni in Laterano was the cathedral of Rome. It contained within its imposing walls all the history of the Eternal City. Fausta brought the land to Constantine as part of her dowry gift and was strangled in the hot room of the bath that had stood there. The basilica that replaced the lethal bath suffered vandals, earthquake and fire before it was rebuilt in the Middle Ages with frescoes by Giotto. When it was again destroyed by fire a new cathedral rose from its ashes with bronze doors from the Curia of Foro Romano, a fourth-century pavement, and sculpture of the Medieval, Renaissance and Baroque periods...

Buscati knew his history. He was not like so many of his comrades from the proletariat. He was a son of the patrician class— educated, cultivated. He constantly had to disavow his background to prove that he belonged with the people. This sense of always being on trial drove him to be more daring, more dangerous than any of them. He couldn't reveal a trace of sympathy without risking the charge of being forever the bourgeois. So he'd become catalyst and executioner, mercilessly emptying his revolver into the pleading prisoner's chest. He wouldn't be any more lenient with the one he'd chosen to follow Moro. After this deed, he could never again be doubted, and never again doubt himself. It would be his catharsis, his act of purification—so perfect, so precise, hanging by threads as fine as the spider spins for its net, yet resilient enough to ensnare the fisherman of souls.

The organ swelled, filling the basilica with the majestic chords of Beethoven's *Missa Solemnis*. The pure soprano voices of little boys with nothing to confess floated above the sonorous baritones chanting the plea of forgiveness.

"*Mea culpa, mea culpa, mea maxima culpa*. Through my fault, through my fault, through my most grievous fault." The words of the Confiteor ran through his mind, one count ahead of the chorus of male voices.

Every Italian knew the liturgy of the mass regardless of political affiliation or ideology, and the courtly, contained head of the Communist Party was no exception. He sat in a place of distinction amid Christian Democratic dignitaries, officials of state and international delegations, his head bowed, lost in dark thoughts.

Am I at fault for this death? The question tormented him. He wasn't a murderer, yet he knew there were those on both sides

19

of the aisle who believed Moro's blood stained his hands.

The Communist chief's position had never been weaker. His power was tentative, his loyal comrades few. But he could think only of the brilliant youth, as much a son as a comrade, whom he'd been grooming to take his place.

He and the boy's father had been as close as brothers. They were fellow-travelers, fighting side-by-side in the Resistance. The boy's mother was a ray of southern sun in those desolate war years.

The sounds of the Confiteor faded. It was 1945 again. He beat his breast in mea culpas and heard instead the boots of the Fascist armies, the relentless chant of *"Du-ce! Du-ce,"* the pounding of artillery.

Alessandro Buscati, fair and imperious even with his face muddied and his torn clothing plastered to his wasted body, crouched by the bank of the Arno, bathing in its muddy water. His wife Claudia lay in the tall grass beside him, inhaling deeply, drinking in the cool air as if she might never be allowed to breathe freely again. Though dirty and half-starved, she was still the most beautiful woman he'd ever seen. It was his last memory of them. Days before the armistice, their bodies were shattered in a freak accident with a hand grenade. Even now, more than thirty years later, the senselessness of their death rankled him. They had risked life so courageously. Outwitted death so many times. It was almost as though their very defiance was a crime that demanded the ultimate payment.

He'd walked for three days to bring news of their death to the Buscati family. He remembered trudging through the vineyards and villages of Tuscany. It was the day after the armistice was announced. With what little was left, each town had prepared a feast to celebrate the end of the bloodletting. The people danced and embraced in the streets. Tears of happiness flowed with the wine. He was like a specter of death passing through the festas, casting a pall wherever he went. He was filled with a desolation as great as the jubilation around him.

The Buscati estate, nestled securely in the hills beyond Fiesole, had hardly been touched by war. There were fewer servants, and small economies had been made, but on the surface the placid life had gone on undisturbed. The spacious stucco villa of burnished orange was built around a square courtyard planted with fragrant fruit trees, oleanders, azaleas and other flowering plants more exotic than any he'd seen before.

It was there in the courtyard that they received him—the haughty, arrogant father, his sallow bloodless daughter, and the boy with golden curls like a cherub. The news he brought was met with dry eyes and resentment. The only son of the family was dead—not nobly cut down, an officer in the line of duty, but blown to bits, shabby and scarecrowish, a foot soldier in the ranks of the Reds.

They didn't thank him for his mission or welcome him into their house. And they asked only one question: "The woman?" They blamed Claudia. She had led Alessandro astray, turned his head with her flashing beauty and filled his mind with heretical ideas.

The Buscatis had received him there in the courtyard, and it was there that he left them standing in stony silence. For them Alessandro had died five years before, when he turned his back on their lives and their faith.

For all its beauty, he was glad to be rid of the Buscati estate and to return to the dusty roads. There was something to be said for order, but nothing for sterility. Even now, though, he couldn't forget the boy without betraying Alessandro's friendship.

Five months had passed since the Communist chief had accepted Moro's plan to share power with the Christian Democrats. And now Moro was dead, executed by persons unknown. And five months had passed since he'd seen or received word from Alessandro's son, Sandro Buscati.

In a modest fourth-floor apartment across the Tiber in Ponte Milvio, Paola Mirabella and her mother slid from the sofa where they'd been sitting, watching the live telecast from San Giovanni, and dropped to their knees. The deacon swung the thurible again

21

enclosing the high altar in a silvery mist. Clouds of incense drifted through the vaulted nave and swirled around the colossal statues of the Apostles, which reposed in niches in the massive pillars. Bells rang out, alerting the faithful. In the next moment, the celebrant would bend low over the sacred table and with the brief words of consecration change the round white wafer into the body of their Savior.

The television camera panned over the congregation before closing in on the altar. Paola covered her mouth, stifling the shock that rose in her throat. The image was gone as quickly as it had appeared, yet she had not been mistaken. For a fraction of a second the dark, solemn face of her missing brother Franco had flashed across the screen. She knew that he wasn't mourning Aldo Moro. Why then was he there—so serious, so intense? She looked anxiously over at her mother, but Signora Mirabella's face was buried in her hands, delivered from all earthly concerns by the electronic miracle she knelt before.

Costanto Cardinal Zanelli, resplendent in his purple robes, leaned forward to accept the pontiff's kiss of peace. As he placed his manicured hands on his bishop's stooped shoulders, he felt Paul's frailty through the brocaded chasuble and noted the deep strain in his eyes.

The cardinal suppressed a smile. He was a man of great personal charm and professional ruthlessness—a classical scholar as familiar with the tongue of Vergil as he was with the labyrinths of the Vatican Curia, a staunch conservative and defender of the faith as he saw it. As head of the Office of Sacred Doctrine, he was one of the most politically powerful and feared men in the Vatican. Only Paul possessed more absolute authority.

When Pope John died, Zanelli should have been a leading *papabile*. But the beloved, foolish Roncalli had inspired such a risorgimento throughout the Church that no arch-conservative had any hope of succeeding him.

The old man now leaning over him, murmuring *"Pax tecum,* peace be with you," had taken the place that Zanelli believed was rightfully his. For fifteen years the cardinal had watched impotently while Paul moved ahead with the reforms of the Vatican Council and rapprochement with the Marxist states of eastern Europe.

As he embraced the pontiff, he realized what a deep toll Moro's ordeal had taken on Paul. The chance Zanelli had waited for so long was close at hand, if only he could seize the opportunity. The *brigadisti* had done what he with all his wiles and all the power at his disposal had failed to accomplish. The elegant, urbane prince of the Church savored the irony of it as he returned the kiss of peace.

The air was heavy with the sacred perfume. Beads of warm wax clung to the blessed candles like icicles. An acolyte, clad in a long, white hooded gown, shifted uncomfortably. Bearing the heavy burden of the cross on top of a tall pole had made his shoulders ache and his fingers stiff. A fine line of sweat glistened on the smooth skin above his lip as the chorus began to chant the third and final *Agnus Dei.*

"*Qui tollis peccata mundi, dona eis requiem, sempiternam.* Lamb of God, who taketh away the sins of the world, grant him eternal rest."

Paul prayed for his friend whose last days had been so agonizing; he prayed for his country, which had lived in shock and fear since March, and for the misguided men and women who had terrorized a nation and tortured its leader. He prayed for his universal flock, so unsure in its faith, and he prayed for himself. He was tired from the long, solemn high mass and, more deeply, from the constant turmoil within his Church and the endless conflicts among his cardinals. He would be eighty-one years old in September. Being pope for fifteen years had drained him.

In 1963, when the stove in the Sistine Chapel was fired with the final ballots of the papal electors and its smoke wafted over the crowd gathered in St. Peter's Square, there was general confusion among the faithful. The smoke appeared to be neither black, signaling a deadlock, nor white, proclaiming a new pope.

In the difficult, lonely years that followed, Paul often wondered if it had been an omen. He'd been a compromise choice, elected in a split between conservative and progressive forces, and had satisfied neither side.

Paul VI inherited a Church in crisis from a predecessor who evoked worldwide affection. In the inevitable comparisons between the two, he was unjustly characterized as remote and cold—an intellectual removed from the people, a politician and diplomat more concerned with global power than the poverty and suffering of his own flock.

Paul bowed his head to receive the gold miter of Peter and extended his left hand to accept the shepherd's crook. It seemed only yesterday that he had been secretary to Pius XII. Within the Vatican then, the young Monsignor Giovanni Battista Montini was labeled a modernist. Now the brightest among his young clergy dismissed him as a hopeless reactionary, and the conservatives denounced him as a dangerous radical.

His encyclical condemning birth control had alienated the left wing of his Church. His insistence on following the dictates of Vatican II and his overtures to the Communist bloc had made him suspect among the traditionalists. He'd pleased no one, and worse, he had failed in the mission he'd set for himself. The pressing problems that divided the Church remained unsolved and his people still went to bed hungry.

When he traveled to India and the Middle East the newspapers called him the "pilgrim pope." But what could his presence or his pilgrimage do for the thousands and thousands of starving children held aloft in their mothers' scrawny arms for his blessing, the faith alive in their haunted eyes, gleaming for a moment with a hope he couldn't answer.

Monsignor Macchi, clad in the robes of a deacon, slipped a supportive hand beneath Paul's elbow and eased him up from the throne. Degenerative arthritis in his hips and knees made every movement painful, yet he had insisted on celebrating this mass for Moro. He leaned heavily on his bishop's crozier and felt the cool of the golden shaft. The crude crook of the shepherd had been transformed through centuries of Christianity into a graceful, glittering symbol of power—temporal as well as spiritual. Clasping it now, he felt impotent. Why hast thou forsaken me?

The feeling lingered as he spoke his pontifical blessing. With it the closing act of the long, terrible spring would be over. He intoned the first words of benediction in a high, quavering voice, and prayed again for eternal peace.

CHAPTER TWO

Guido Felice didn't wait to receive the pope's blessing. He had more immediate needs than a plenary indulgence, the ticket to an eternal reward that a pontifical benediction conferred. Crossing himself quickly, he slipped out a side door of the basilica, stepping from the thickly scented air of the church into the raw May day. Carabinieri, their uniforms as crisp and white as the purest soul, stood guard at each entry with open submachine guns. None of them stopped him as he passed. Across the square thousands of grieving Romans waited in silent mourning. The blue-and-white flags with the cross and shield of the Christian Democrats flickered in the gray morning light beside the scarlet hammer and sickle of the Communists.

Felice positioned himself unobtrusively at the side of the Lateran Palace adjoining the basilica. Until Avignon, the palace had been the residence of the popes. Now it housed the diocesan offices and provided a perfect vantage point to watch the mourners as they poured out of the church.

Middle-aged, with a rapidly expanding paunch and a supply of patience that diminished all too quickly, Felice could have passed for a cartoon waiter or fruit vendor. His eyes, which always seemed on the verge of succumbing to a siesta, were heavy-lidded and as black as the ripest olives of Sicily. His suit was black too, and cheap. It was cut too closely at the waist for his unshapely figure and too sharply at the shoulders for his massive frame, and it pulled uncomfortably under the arms.

Buttoning his topcoat against the chill mist that hung over the city like a shroud, he looked over the crowd in the piazza and thought of the steaming roast potatoes, subtly flavored with rosemary, that were the specialty of the small trattoria across from the Domus Aureus, just above the Colosseum. He would stop for a bite of lunch there, even invite his young assistant to go along with him, before returning to headquarters to make his report.

What was there to say anyway? Certainly nothing of urgency. An orderly crowd of five thousand spectators; dignitaries and politicians looking suitably sober and bereaved. No incidents. Not even a body to guard at this funeral mass.

Moro was already buried, thirty-five miles north of Rome in the village of Torrita Tiberina, where he'd kept a country house. Through fifty-four tense days, the nation had been held paralyzed. Then twelve 9-mm. bullets, emptied into the chest of the handcuffed victim, had brought an end to the drama. Felice despised the cowardice of their methods, the irrationality of their deeds, not to mention the disruption they had caused him personally.

Detective Guido Felice, deputy chief of the Squadra Antiterrorismo, had three loves: his city, Elena, and his dinner. He felt that he'd personally failed Rome by not saving Moro. He'd been forced to work such long hours on the case that he barely had time to think of Elena, and the constant pressure had upset his digestion.

He had stalked terror from one end of the city to the other, always arriving in time to watch the pools of blood widen and feel the anguish of the victims, always too late for anything except impotent rage. It was beginning to affect his performance, not that his wife complained. She was probably grateful, he thought

27

grimly, or was he doing her a disservice? He thought of Elena. She loved it as much as he, although she pretended a certain reluctance, an exciting bashfulness.

Soon he would face the accounting that was sure to come. For now, though, there were the roast potatoes, and tomorrow he would slip away to the mountains with Elena. The day of public reckoning could wait a little longer.

Felice looked across the piazza, scanning the crowd with narrowed eyes. A young man had staked out a prime position for himself by the red granite obelisk that rose in the center of the square. He wore baggy, tan corduroy pants, a blue shirt buttoned at the throat and over it, a heavy maroon sweater patched at the elbows. His black hair needed a trim; his scuffed boots needed a shine. Sun shades were clipped over the lenses of his glasses. Officer Massimo Cenci, Felice's first assistant, blended with the crowd so perfectly that he could have passed for one of the demonstrators waving the hammer and sickle. But even across the square, Felice could see that Cenci's concentration was total. He knew his officer would observe and recall details he himself hadn't even noticed.

Felice sighed. The very vigilance of his assistant wearied him. He seemed more like a computer than anything human. Maybe he would soften over the roast potatoes. But the detective knew Cenci would decline the invitation. He was always rushing off somewhere. Always serious, always in a hurry, each action, each hour rigidly accounted for. Perhaps he has a woman, Felice thought. What else could make a young man in such a hurry...?

The center doors of the basilica swung open. *The mass is ended. Go in peace to the mountains with Elena.* Felice parodied the final words of the mass in his mind. In spite of the gold cross that hung around his neck and tangled in the thick black hairs of his chest, he was not a religious man. He left that to his wife, and yet he meant no disrespect. A few days in the mountains, where the air was clear and the tumult of Rome a distant echo, then he would come back to pick up the jumbled pieces of this national disaster in which he'd seemed to be two steps behind the terrorists all the

28

way along the long, tragic route to this May day.

With this mass the curtain was being drawn on *la cosa di Moro,* the final shovel of dirt was being thrown on the silent tomb. Felice had only to make sure that no incident marred this last homage. He scanned the mourners carefully as they filed out of the basilica, wearing subdued faces and speaking in respectful whispers. But he didn't notice the slight, nervous boy who hesitated at the door of the basilica, squinting furtive eyes to adjust to the sudden light. No one had taken note of Franco Mirabella, except his sister Paola, watching on the television, and Officer Cenci.

CHAPTER THREE

"*In paradisum deducant te Angeli.* May angels attend thee in paradise...and may you have eternal peace with Lazarus, who once was poor."

The last notes of the funeral hymn still hung in the air as Franco Mirabella passed through the cordons of police, by the secret servicemen in plainclothes who blended in with the crowd of onlookers, by the plump detective with the distraught face and drowsy eyes.

His slight shoulders hunched, hands thrust deep in his trouser pockets, Franco hurried down the wide steps, turning a contemptuous glance at the crowds gathered in the piazza. Instead of standing there, wrapped in their piety and grief, they should be rejoicing in the revolutionary act that had been committed in their name.

Fools, he wanted to shout. We did it for you. He wanted to shake them by their shoulders and force them to understand.

He turned up the frayed collar of his jacket and headed south toward the Porta di San Giovanni, studying the pavement as he walked. He knew it had to be done. Anything short of killing would have looked like surrender. Still Franco couldn't suppress the shudder of revulsion that swept over him when he thought of the helpless handcuffed body, studded with a dozen bullets. Moro was a victim. But then, we're all victims, that's why we must fight, he instructed himself.

His dark, haunted eyes lifted only once to dart to the left, where the Scala Santa stood, the twenty-eight marble steps down which the carpenter of Galilee had descended after being condemned to hang from a cross between two thieves at Golgotha. Except for the protective wood boards that covered them, the steps were unchanged since Constantine's mother transported them from the house of Pontius Pilate in Jerusalem. At the foot of the stairs stood two statues, "Ecce Homo" and the "Kiss of Judas."

In other years, when he'd worn short pants and his face was still smooth and scrubbed, Franco and his mother had come to the Scala Santa each Passion Week to climb the holy stairs on their knees. Franco's vocation was unquestioned then. He was going to be a priest. Though the boards made his bare knees red and splintered, he never complained. He bore the pain manfully for Jesus, and his mother gave thanks for such a son. Franco hadn't changed. He still *believed*. Only the object of his faith was different.

Passing through the Porta di San Giovanni, out of the ancient city, he walked slowly down the Via Appia Nuova. Although it was a major thoroughfare out of Rome, the traffic was light, just an occasional Cinquecento heading toward the Alban Hills.

It had been two years since Franco had been to mass, and even longer since he'd seen Pope Paul. The mystery and music of the mass always touched him in a special way. Today, led by the old man whom he remembered as strong and vital, it affected him more than he wanted to admit.

Why had he been sent? What could they hope to gain by having a witness to the last act in the drama they'd orchestrated so brilliantly? Franco kicked a stone. How could they know it would be such a torment? After all, he'd renounced all of that.

The Church had failed him and all the other pious fools who'd looked to it for salvation, for a crust of bread and a shred of

31

decency. And Paul had failed them. He should have stripped away Peter's riches to feed the hungry and clothe the poor instead of parading across the city in a limousine with flags snapping.

Franco quickened his pace, leaving the mourners far behind. He could not be late. It was a critical meeting of the leaders, and the first he'd been invited to attend. He was flattered by the invitation. It was an honor he'd long hoped for, a sign that he was fully accepted in the *primo circo*. But he was nervous about it, and the mass he'd just witnessed hadn't helped. What if he were called on to speak? What would he say? Even in the darkness of the confessional he'd always stumbled over the litany of his failures. How could he address a public group, a *covo* of seasoned revolutionaries? And the girl, Lisa. Her cat eyes would be fixed on him—amused, mocking, wary eyes—waiting for him to speak.

Franco stumbled and cursed. Which of them had sent the bullets ripping through Moro's helpless flesh? Massi? Buscati? Domenica? Di Voto? One of them, two, all of them? Lisa, the beautiful Lisa? He would love more than anything to lie beside her, but whenever she looked at him or spoke to him, he stammered like a pubescent boy, awkward and tongue-tied.

Franco turned into the narrow Via Frangene. The street was empty when he entered the yard of the dilapidated villa. What could he report? He'd seen nothing that could not be viewed as well or better on television. There were hundreds of dignitaries, scores of heavily armed police, and one sunken old man in an ermine cape.

Franco knocked, three staccato raps, then pushed open the back door. The silence in the kitchen was intrusive. The empty bottles and dirty glasses had been cleared away, but the crumbs of bread and remnants of salami still littered the oilcloth-covered table where three men and the girl were seated. She was pushing the bread crumbs together with her thumb and forefinger, constructing a pyramid as carefully as a pharaoh. The men watched, as if mesmerized by her precise, monotonous motion.

"Ah, Franco, at last," Buscati called. With a sweep of his hand he sent the crumbs flying across the room.

The girl stared at him. "Bastard," she whispered under her

breath and started collecting the remaining crumbs for the task of rebuilding.

"*Vieni qui. S'accomoda.*" Buscati gestured expansively to Franco to sit down. "Massi can't be far behind. Caesar had his eyes and ears of Rome, and we have our own, Massimo Cenci."

...Piero Massi, known to his boss Felice on the antiterrorist squad as Massimo Cenci. He worked for the *covo* within the very heart of enemy territory. Massi played out well and bloodily his role as terrorist plant in the ranks of an unsuspecting Detective Guido Felice. What Buscati did not know was that Piero Massi/Massimo Cenci was playing a special game... He was an agent of the KGB who had infiltrated the terrorist cell to gain control of it.

Three more staccato knocks sounded. Massi slipped in, still wearing the baggy tan corduroys and patched maroon sweater, and took the only empty chair. Buscati considered each of them. They were a cell of six—five men and a woman. He needed them all for his plan to succeed, a plan that could determine not only the future of their organization but the future of Italy, and maybe beyond.

Leaning forward as if to draw them closer, he began to speak. "Comrades, we have gotten the attention of the world. We've shocked with our daring, with the boldness of our moves. Now, we must strike again. And our blow must make the Moro slaying seem like an act of mercy.

The five hunched over the oilcloth. He could see the excitement, and hesitation.

"Who next? Who is more important to Italy than Moro?" Buscati's voice sank to a whisper. "There is only one. We must cast our net for the Fisherman Paul."...

Piero Massi/Massimo Cenci thought he was hearing a death sentence. The Soviets would never tolerate this. They had no love for the Papacy, but this new operation would jeopardize their own strategy. They had, after all, spent a dozen years encouraging Paul's rapprochement with their satellites to keep the subjugated countries quiescent. He and he alone would be held responsible if this delicate balance were upset.

BOOK II

La Rete del Pescatore - The Fisherman's Net

CHAPTER FOUR

Signora Mirabella marched down Via di Porta Angelica, claiming the sidewalk as her own with each step. To her right the wall of the Vatican stretched blankly, the only wall in Rome unblemished by graffiti. It was midmorning and the narrow street, which began at Piazza Risorgimento and was stopped a few blocks later by the towering columns of Bernini's colonnade, was shrunken with rows of tourist buses. At the high iron gates of the Apostolic Palace the signora paused to proclaim: "*Questo é il mio figlio*. The Holy Father baptized him personally." Her announcement was dictated by pride, not by any question from the Swiss Guards who stood sentry at the entrance.

Behind her, Franco pawed the cobblestones with the toe of a freshly polished shoe. He was dressed as one rarely saw a youth these days, formally in a white starched shirt, tie and dark suit, too big for his slender frame. Round brown eyes peered out of a small, undistinguished face. The guards clicked their heels and the signora sailed through the gates, Franco bobbing uncertainly in her wake, like a dinghy behind a schooner, bearing the omnipresent string bag.

Signora Mirabella was an engulfing presence. She stood five feet ten inches in her stocking feet and was constructed as solidly as the Arch of Constantine. Her face was a lesson in plane geometry—flat and linear. She came from farming country in the north—Lombardy, the same general area as Giovanni Battista Montini, although she hadn't known him in those early days. Beside her Franco was diminished. He could never escape his filial role.

Signora Mirabella entered the palace with nothing more than a *"buon giorno."* She didn't need to flash impressive papers. She'd enjoyed free access for fifteen years. Before Giovanni's death, it had been simpler. They'd lived directly over the street. From their bedroom window she could look right across at the windows of their dear friend. The signora always checked before she lay down beside her husband to see if il Papa was still up. Invariably she would climb into bed, shaking her head: "The lights are still on. You should make him rest."

"He can't sleep, Marcella. You know that. He's never been a good sleeper and now with so much on his mind he's an insomniac. He won't take the sleeping pills Fontana prescribes."

She would bless herself, pull up the covers and move into her husband's embrace. She was ten years younger than Giovanni Mirabella and still in awe of him. He was a journalist, a poet and a musician; she was only a farm girl. She'd never made many friends in Rome. Giovanni and their two children were her whole life. He was round and ruddy-faced and considerably shorter than she. When he died she gave up the apartment and moved to Ponte Milvio. The old apartment belonged to the Vatican, and although the Pope interceded personally so that she could remain there, it was too full of memories of Giovanni and Franco, and the happier days they'd shared there.

It was more difficult to visit the palace now, but the signora made the trip unfailingly twice or even three times a week if the sisters required a particular favor. She'd walk down the hill to the village of Ponte Milvio and catch the bus that would take her along Lungotevere. She'd watch the ocher water slide by as long as the bus followed the river, before bearing west to Piazza Risorgimento.

Giovanni had owned a car, but she never learned to drive. Although Paola had, the signora gave the car away anyway to her brother when Giovanni died.

Once inside the Apostolic Palace, mother and son didn't follow in the footsteps of the elite visitors admitted for the privilege of attending a coveted private or semiprivate audience with the pope—those handpicked few who, thanks to the intervention of a well-placed churchman or politician, were allowed to meet the pontiff personally, kiss his ring, receive his blessing and even, if you were one of the most fortunate, exchange a word or two of greeting. In the vast, damasked hall, the Mirabellas turned to the right instead of proceeding up the sweeping marble staircase. Franco docilely followed his mother. He wedged himself into the cramped, private elevator beside her, carefully protecting the net bag from being crushed, and leaned back against the smooth paneling. The signora settled herself on the delicate red velvet seat. The attendant had pushed the fourth-floor button as soon as he saw her.

"*Attenzione*, Franco. *Ricorda i fichi*," the signora warned.

"*Sì*, mama." He patted the bag reassuringly.

She reached over and touched his cheek. "You always were a good boy."

"*Basta*, mama." He was only home a few days and already his mother was smothering him again. The elevator door opened before she could respond.

"Come on." She nudged him to follow her. Except for the armed Swiss Guard at the door he could have found his way blindfolded. His mother murmured "*permesso*" as they passed. When he was younger he used to run and slide along the bare, polished floor. His mother's direst threat was not enough to make him overcome the temptation. Even the smells were the same—a combination of floor wax and candle wax, and the pungent fragrance of the basil that Suor Marianna kept growing, even in winter, in earthenware pots in the kitchen window.

Franco smiled to himself. What else could he remember? Suor Marianna was soft and warm, like freshly risen dough, when she embraced him. He'd been in love with her—she was pretty like a madonna with pale blue eyes that shone on him, and she always had something special fixed, as if she'd been waiting especially for him. Just seeing her was soothing, like having his forehead bathed with cool towels. She seemed to know exactly what it was like to be a small boy, what frightened him and what excited him—though, of course, how could she? He knew she would seem different now, although he couldn't imagine what to expect.

Franco felt awkward and apprehensive as they passed through the back hall that led to the kitchen entrance of the private papal apartments. It was a narrow whitewashed hall, bare except for the plain black crucifix with the ivory figure of Christ that hung on one wall. He felt as if a childhood dream was about to dissolve before his eyes, like discovering there was no Babbo di Natale, or no God. Everything else had disappointed him, and at least Suor Marianna had not deceived him intentionally. She was a creation of his childish imagination, innocent of duplicity.

"*Cara* Marcella." His mother's granite back blocked the small nun from view as she enveloped her, kissing her on both cheeks. Only the top of Suor Marianna's veil and her eyes were visible over the signora's shoulder. The eyes were pale blue and shining.

"Francetto! It can't be, little Franco grown to such a man, yet still reluctant, waiting behind his mother." She opened her arms and embraced him, like a black sheep returned to the fold. This is what Holy Mother the Church is supposed to be, he thought, as the familiar aroma of starch and lanolin soap assailed him again. He sank into her embrace.

Suor Marianna's eyes were bright with tears when she finally released him. "*Che bella sorpresa,* what a wonderful surprise," she cried, taking a man-size handkerchief from somewhere deep in her voluminous black skirt and wiping her eyes.

"I told you, Franco, Suor Marianna would be so happy." The signora beamed at the nun. "Your prayers have been answered. Franco has come home to me, and when he goes the next time, it will be with our blessing."

"*Grazie Dio.*" Suor Marianna blessed herself, and wiped her eyes.

"No mother could have a better son. He has friends, things to do—many things—yet he insisted on coming with me today to carry these few packages. So thoughtful, so good to his mother. He won't disappoint us, Suor Marianna. He has come home to do what he was always ordained for. I have a reason to live again."

Suor Marianna's eyes kept straying back to Franco as his mother talked. "What are you going to do now, Franco? Have you finished the university? Your mother told me you were studying medicine."

"Not medicine. How to cure sickness. It's too much to explain, and too dull." He turned away. "You wouldn't want to hear."

"Your mother waited so long for this day," she replied gently.

Franco's voice was gruff. It sounded unfamiliar, even to himself. "We can talk about me later, now look at what my mother has brought for you." He thrust the net bag at the nun. She deposited it on the kitchen table and the two women began emptying its contents.

"*Guarda.* Have you ever seen plumper figs than these?" Signora Mirabella held each of the fragile, green-ribbed fruits up in the air, as if they were jewels, for inspection and admiration. "I know how much il Papa likes fresh figs. His favorite fruit. There are a dozen. I chose each one." She'd wrapped them individually in tissue paper to prevent the possibility of bruising on the trip from Ponte Milvio. "How is he? He looks so tired in all the pictures. On television…"

Suor Marianna shook her head. "He is exhausted and still he forces himself to do more. *La cosa di Moro!*" She was still shaking her head despairingly. "It has been very hard, very hard. He barely sleeps at all now. His eyes are full of sadness and black circles deepen them like echoes. The doctor begs him to rest, but he is up at five, offering mass by five-thirty."

"He hasn't changed in thirty years."

"Enrico cares for him well and the monsignore, such a good man, simpatico. But we are worried, so very worried. He eats like a sparrow. I have tried everything he likes. For breakfast a cornetto and a coffee—not even a piece of fruit. Perhaps these plump figs will tempt him. I have never seen him like this before. His despair is so deep…"

41

Franco looked around the kitchen as the women spoke. It was a large whitewashed room with a reddish-brown tiled floor. A pair of wide uncurtained windows beckoned the sun. The room was an amalgam of the old and the modern. A six-burner stainless steel range faced a black iron wood stove. A gleaming Indesit refrigerator shared space with twin porcelain sinks. A squat blue crockery pot filled with gentian from the Vatican gardens stood on the shelf. Braids of waxy red onions, bouquets of dried herbs tied with thread and globes of cheese hung from the ceiling. Fresh fettucine was drying on a rack. A photograph of Pope Paul hung on the wall above the counter. A votive light burned in front of a shrine to Saint Rita of Cassia, patron saint of the impossible, on an adjacent wall. In the windows pots of basil, sage, parsley and fresh tarragon filled the deep sills.

Franco walked over to the window, picked a basil leaf and crumbled it between his fingers. The smell of the crushed leaf was more intoxicating than a vintage wine. "With Paul in our hands," Buscati had said, "imagine the demands we can insist on. The gold of Peter will be turned into bread for the hungry. The jeweled chalices will clothe the naked. The Church's art treasures will buy all the weapons we need to bring down the state and arm the people."

It was what Franco had always prayed would happen—what he'd once believed Montini would do when he became pope. They'd go through the Borgate giving everything to the poor. The slums that festered in the shadow of the Vatican would shine with gold and silver. It had not happened...He held the basil to his nose and listened closely, trying to remember everything the women were saying.

A steel stock pot was simmering on the stove. There was no mistaking the smell of *bollito*—a dinner of beef, potatoes and vegetables boiled together. The Fisherman didn't care about gourmet meals. He preferred simple food. Franco wondered if he should report that to his leader too. He decided to buy himself a notebook to keep a schedule of Paul's days. He wanted his reports to be absolutely accurate. So much depended on him.

CHAPTER FIVE

In Milan twelve days after the Moro mass, Judge Nicolo Benedetti was driving to his chambers. It had been raining through the night and the streets were still slick. He drove cautiously. Prudence was the virtue he esteemed most highly, and exercised most faithfully.

As presiding justice of the Superior Court, he prudently refrained from making public statements on controversial subjects for fear his personal convictions would be confused with his judicial opinions. He only broke his rule once. After the Moro assassination he denounced the *brigadisti* from the bench.

The judge was a distinguished-looking man, with a deep cleft in his chin and three deep lines in his forehead. Between these two distinguishing marks, the features were regular. A comb of gray in his thick black hair gave a dimension of drama to what otherwise would have been a staid appearance. The son of a Pirelli factory worker, he strove hard to attain the position he enjoyed and strove just as hard to maintain the myth that he was a common man. Nothing could be further from the truth, even though he disdained the chauffered limousine the court provided and drove himself to his chambers each morning in a humble Cinquecento.

On the morning of May 25, 1978, he didn't go directly to the court as was his habit. Instead he parked on Via Monte Napoleone and shopped with judicious restraint for a present for his wife Maria. It was their thirty-first wedding anniversary. It took him no more than twenty minutes to choose the present, have it wrapped and return to the car. As he was unlocking the door four well-dressed and neatly groomed young men approached. They were all wearing raincoats and carrying Russian-made automatic rifles. They reached the car as he opened the door.

"*Permesso,* judge," one of them said. Lisa spoke politely.

Benedetti turned. "*Prego,*" he said, and a Kalishnikov replied.

The big bullets, fired at point-blank range, devoured his body. He fell backward into the car, his guts spilling into the gutter, his face cracking against the steering column, breaking his nose and blackening his eyes. He was clutching his abdomen with both hands.

The four folded their automatic rifles and walked off calmly, disappearing into the crowd of shoppers and office workers. With the metal stocks folded, the weapons were only sixty-three centimeters long and easily concealed under a jacket or coat.

By the time the police arrived, the editorial office of *Il Corriere della Sera* had already received a phone call: The execution was in retaliation for Benedetti's malicious denunciation of the new saviors of Italy. The reporter who received the message described the caller as an impassioned female. "*Vogliamo tutto e subito,*" she shouted as she hung up.

The police removed a small square box from the bloody cavity where Benedetti's stomach had been. After subjecting it to forensic tests, they gave it to the widow.

Maria Benedetti's anniversary present was six days late. She opened it gingerly, not wanting her husband's blood on her hands. Inside was a gold-and-enamel pin showing the twin masks of comedy and tragedy. Though the card was brown and stiff the message was still legible. "To Maria, for all the joy and sorrow of thirty-one years. *Ti abbracio,* Nicco."

Nicolo Benedetti's life had been strictly ordained by the moral principles and personal standards he adhered to. If he had to do it over, his widow said in an interview in *Il Corriere della Sera,* he would still have denounced the terrorists, but, she thought as she said it, his voice might have been better modulated.

The assassination of Judge Benedetti was an end only in the most personal sense. For the nation it was the beginning of a second wave of terror, so virulent that the *fasces* began appearing on walls and monuments, and those old enough to remember began to call openly for a new strong man.

CHAPTER SIX

A northerly wind swept down from the Borghese Gardens. It snapped at the canopies along Via Veneto and whipped the tablecloths at the outdoor cafés. A lone waiter in formal dress rushed to anchor the flying cloths at Harry's Bar. Down the avenue, at the corner kiosk, the news vendor hastily secured the international newspapers and magazines on display.

A gust of wind caught the girl just as she stepped out of the cab, plastering the thin, silky Missoni dress to her hips as if an Impressionist painter had taken a brush to her buttocks. She pulled the collar of her raw silk jacket higher around her neck and leaned in the front window of the cab to pay the driver, not unaware of the picture she was making. She lingered a moment longer than necessary, as if debating the tip, then flicked the impatient driver a thousand lira note. He thanked her unctuously. She could sense the anger behind his words. Although he was hungry for the money she offered, he resented accepting the crumbs thrown so casually at him by the rich—the filthy, idle, presumptuous, arrogant rich like her. A sapphire-and-diamond ring caught the street light and shimmered tantalizingly as she withdrew her manicured hand from the window. She had dressed with the utmost care, spending hours on her appearance, something she had not done in months. The effect was flawless.

Lisa Taglia straightened to her full height. Soon the revolution would come, and then the poor bastard could vent his fury and seize power. She clenched her fist in the pocket of her jacket and inhaled a long draft of the invigorating evening air to fortify herself for the encounter she had to face.

Small round tables with white cloths were set under a brown-and-gold awning. The evenings were still too cool to sit outside and watch the parade of starlets and whores, of gigolos and wealthy old men, peddlers of the flesh, buyers and sellers both. So the tables were deserted, except for the single waiter and two elderly men, mustaches combed to perfection, aristocratic faces intent in conversation over espresso and cognac. Both wore double-breasted blue suits that had lasted for decades and would probably serve as their shrouds. They were museum pieces, with the mien of ancient Romans, untouched by the passing carnival. Where would they go in the revolution? There was no place for them; there was also no place for them in the world they were living in. They had outlasted their era—dinosaurs, aliens, as foreign here in Rome 1978 as Caesar had once been in Gaul. Were they aware that they no longer belonged—that their place had been filled without their noticing?

Lisa shrugged. Some innocents must always be sacrificed. They'd had their turn. They'd enjoyed their world of privilege and class. Now it's our turn, she thought. We can't weep for what was or might have been. Pushing open the dark wood door, she stepped confidently into the dim clamor of Harry's Bar. The small bar to the left was crowded and noisy. The smoke of rich Havana cigars clouded the air, mingling with expensive perfumes. It was warm and secure, a male womb paneled in dark wood. Service de luxe. The larger room to the right of the door was also crowded. It was J-shaped and in the rear were tables for dining.

Harry's Bar in Rome is no relation to Harry's Bar in Venice, but both are American hangouts. It sits at the top of the Via

Veneto, just outside the Porta Pinciana, the main gate to the Borghese Gardens, and across the street from the fading Flora, once a hotel of modest distinction, now scrambling to keep up with the expense-account trade much better handled by the Excelsior down the block. In summer Harry's spreads out onto the sidewalk to become the first in the parade of *dolce vita* terraces that march downhill—Café de la Paix (nothing like its Paris namesake), Donney's (where the waiters are supercilious and the cannoli are poems), and around the bend to the shaky, four-table Campari-umbrella stands at Piazza Barberini. The parade of streetwalkers, too, declines in style and price along with the topography. In the bend of Via Veneto stands Casa Rosa, residence of the U.S. ambassador. Marine guards with light submachine guns had guarded the gates since Moro. For two thousand years there had been B.C. and A.D. to mark time and history. Now in Italy there was *primo di* Moro and *dopo* Moro—before Moro and after Moro.

Once Harry's had been *the* watering place in Rome. But in recent years the Via Veneto was being abandoned for the newly chic cafés of the Piazza del Popolo. Enough remained, though, to keep Harry's humming—curious tourists, assorted businessmen in their discreet pinstripes, and dilettante Romans, always in their uniform of white shirt with wide short collar, black suit and somber tie, always in groups of men only, settling affairs of state and country over American whiskey and brio.

Lisa's eyes turned to gunmetal as they swept across the clamorous room. She was cataloguing each table: the two American businessmen, drinking too much, too fast, faces turning as florid as the lips of the whores they were slavering over; a table of six Italians where the wall turned back, wheeler-dealers from the look of them, and clearly habitués of the place; at the table beside them, a couple, newly discovered lovers, savoring that deceptive happiness before the truth slithered out. At the corner table, a half-empty bottle of champagne in front of them, were three Americans—two women and a man. Lisa waved and sauntered toward them, aware with each step of the impression she was making. She wasn't flaunting her presence, but neither was she making any effort to be inconspicuous. She was tall and willowy, her body saved from boyish slimness by the fullness of her breasts. Her ash-blond hair was cropped dramatically short, making her gray eyes seem even larger than they were. Her makeup was expertly applied to give the impression that she was wearing none. The slight flush on her cheeks looked as if it had been made by the brisk evening breeze, and to all but the best-trained eye the redness of her lips was God-given.

"Darling." Babe Gaynor stood up and opened her arms to embrace the girl. Her gesture was expansive without seeming showy. "You're looking marvelous."

Lisa caught the scent of Joy as her mother kissed her lightly on the cheek. One hundred dollars an ounce and her mother bought it by the pint. It had always been her favorite perfume. Her mother's arms closed around her, pressing her close for a second. Lisa felt the familiar warmth, the smoothness of her silk dress, the softness of her lips, and drew back.

The first contact with her mother was always unsettling. Even now, after so many years and so many meetings, she still wasn't sure how much was sincere, how much was practiced and parceled out to provide exactly the desired effect. She looked at her intently for a moment, determined not to give away any more than Babe did. "You're looking marvelous yourself, but then you always do," she said with a dry laugh.

In the flattering light of the bar her mother might have passed for her sister. They were the same height, and the mother was almost as slim as the daughter. Her hair was kept blond by dint of the most careful work of Carita on the Rue du Faubourg-St. Honoré in Paris. Her skin was kept ageless and wrinkle-free by the Mainboch spa in Zurich, and whenever her body gave a hint of her forty-odd years, she immediately had it dispelled with a few well-placed nips and tucks. Her eyes, her buttocks, her breasts, her chin, her neck—the Swiss were good at more than cuckoo clocks, and Babe Gaynor was proof.

Babe should look marvelous, Lisa thought. She'd devoted thirty years to just that and nothing more, working at it every day with calisthenics and creams and exercises, all in the exact proper proportions. Lisa would probably be looking forward to spending her next thirty years working at that same occupation if she hadn't met Sandro. He'd opened her eyes and her heart, and now though the very thought of him aroused a fury in her, she would never turn back. She was ashamed to remember her shallow life before.

"Lisa, darling, meet my dearest friends, Ingrid and Steve Taylor-Martin," Babe was saying. Even after so many years in Europe, her voice still bore the lilt of her native Virginia. "Ingrid went to Radcliffe with your Aunt Elizabeth."

Ingrid Taylor-Martin smiled warmly and took Lisa's hand. "That's all history," she laughed. "I like to kid myself that it's only medieval history, but meeting you makes me realize how very ancient history it is." Her teeth were small and even. In fact all her features were small and even, like a child's, yet they contained a shrewdness that denied them innocence. She was chicly tailored in a three-piece black pants suit and cream silk ascot shirt; a ruby stickpin held the stock tie at her throat. An aging child; no longer adorable, yet not fully adult. Everything about her was diminutive except her husband.

Steve Taylor-Martin stood over six feet. His face was handsome and curiously bland, with a perpetual tan as deep and rich as his voice. Although he was well into his fifties, his face was as untouched as Dorian Gray's. No tragedies or triumphs, worries or weaknesses were revealed there. It was a tabula rasa, waiting to be filled. He took her hand and drew it to his lips. "It's a pleasure to meet another woman as beautiful as Babe Gaynor."

"You flatter me, and do my mother an injustice." Lisa slipped out of her jacket as she answered. The Missoni, a silk jersey brushed with flowers in varying shades of pink and red and belted at the waist with a braided white cord, clung to her body. From the thrust of her breasts and the vague triangle between her legs, it was clear that she wore nothing under it, except the sheerest stockings. And it was clear from the extra second Steve stared at her that more than his interest was aroused.

Lisa sank into a low leather chair between the two women. She was determined to maintain her composure no matter how many questions her mother fired at her. She'd been uneasy with her mother as far back as she could remember; yet when Babe snapped her fingers, she still came running. Even now she couldn't break the habit.

"Some champagne, Lisa?" she heard Steve ask.

She pushed a smile through her reverie. "No thanks, I'd like an Irish coffee, if you see the waiter. The Irish coffee in Harry's is the best in the world."

"It would be easy to be better than the Irish coffee in Dublin," Ingrid said. "It's quite undrinkable. Strictly for tourists. The Irish stick with their Guinness and Potcheen." Ingrid had an unexpected voice, gravelly and much huskier than her childlike appearance suggested.

They all laughed, and Lisa wondered which of the two, Ingrid or Steve, was her mother's new lover. Ingrid, she suspected, but then one could never be sure. Babe might have taken a yen to both of them.

For as long as she could remember, her mother had had her clothes and her facials; her father had his business and his mistress. When they were finally officially divorced, it was an amicable, if faintly rueful, parting. No one seemed to care except Lisa, and by then she was supposed to be old enough to know better. Now her mother had a mistress and her father had facials, and still Lisa wasn't supposed to care.

"I thought you said you were bringing a friend," Babe said. Her voice was soft, as if she were sharing a confidence with her daughter. In fact, she and Lisa had never shared a secret of any sort. They'd never shared anything more intimate than a chiffon scarf, once tossed to Lisa nonchalantly and probably never thought of again. Lisa still had it. She kept it like a talisman.

"No, mother. I said he'd meet us here. He's the first assistant to the Libyan ambassador."

"The diplomatic type attracts you?" Steve suggested.

"You mean swarthily handsome and infuriatingly tactful? They have certain advantages, especially if they're dripping with oil, too." She hated herself for lapsing back so easily into her pre-scribed role.

The others laughed appreciatively while she sipped her Irish coffee. It was a decadent, bourgeois luxury which she was thor-oughly enjoying and one of which the barman at Harry's could be justly proud.

The barman whipped up the frothy concoction mainly to satisfy his American customers. He couldn't remember a time when there were no Americans at Harry's. He was a large man with gold-rimmed glasses—the type who would be singled out as an insur-ance agent or, even more likely, a pharmacist—and he greeted every customer who came more than once by name. It filled the patron with self-importance. Chests swelled visibly. Camaraderie was a much-desired and rare commodity. Of course, it was nothing more than good business on the barkeep's side.

A short, stocky man unfamiliar to the bartender emerged from the dimness of the bar. He was swarthy and appeared single-minded. His suit, his shoes and his eyes were all as black as his hair. Although his hooded eyes and hawkish nose were unmis-takably Arab, he didn't have the stature of an oil sheik, nor did he possess that Western insolence the sons of the sheiks had adopted along with the leather jackets and silk shirts. The Arab sidled through the room unnoticed and made a line as circuitous as a scimitar toward the table where Lisa sat. She had not been out of his sight since she walked in.

"Excuse me, signorina." He bowed formally. "His Excellency sends his regrets. He is unable to join you tonight. He has been most unfortunately detained. He sends this small gift as a token of his esteem."

The courier opened an attaché case and produced a rectangular box wrapped in gold paper, which he presented with another deep bow.

Lisa inclined her head in reply. "His Excellency is most kind. Please convey my regards and my deep appreciation for this me-mento. Tell His Excellency that I look forward to thanking him personally as soon as it is convenient." She spoke slowly, enunciating each word so that the courier could commit them to memory.

"Your message will be delivered. Signorina, signori." He bowed a third time, then slid away like a serpent to lose himself once again in the crowd of drinkers.

"Well, mother, I guess you're stuck with me alone. Do you think you can bear it?" As she spoke, Lisa slipped the package down the side of the chair so that she could feel its weight against her thigh.

"A memento from an Arab potentate, no less. What do you suppose it could be?" Ingrid's curiosity was too intense to disguise.

"Aren't you even going to open it?" Steve looked incredulous.

"Come on, darling, open it. Ingrid and Steve are almost apoplectic with curiosity. Look at them. They're imagining that your dollar-dripping, polygamous sheik has sent you a little billet-doux—the deed to an oil field, perhaps, or at the very least a chest of gold bullion." Babe's smile could have outdazzled the Koh-i-noor diamond. "Darling, be a good sport and satisfy their curiosity before it chokes them."

"Really, mother, Ingrid and Steve haven't the slightest interest in a little trinket some man they don't even know happened to send me, now have you?"

"Well, maybe the very slightest," Ingrid conceded. She laughed to cover her embarrassment for having shown her eagerness so blatantly.

"What do you want me to do?" Lisa replied too sharply. "Behave like an adolescent schoolgirl with a crush and tear it open right here? I should think nothing would embarrass you more. I know nothing would embarrass *me* more."

"At least tell us who your Arab friend is," Steve urged.

"Yes, who *is* His Excellency?" Babe said.

"His Excellency, if you must know, is tall, dark and filthy rich. You should approve of him, mother—and to my knowledge he has only two wives."

Babe's voice rang like Baccarat. "So all is not lost, my darling. The self-righteous student has found herself an ambassador *and*

53

an Arab to boot. Hallelujah! I must confess I didn't think you had it in you. I thought you were doomed to writhe under the weightlessness of sweaty, pale boys with excess hair on their faces and nothing but fury in their hearts. So much for a mother's intuition." She laughed again, merrily, mocking herself. "This calls for rejoicing. Steve, more champagne."

Lisa threw back her head and laughed with her mother. The package felt snug and secure against her leg. Other drinkers turned enviously toward the table where the two stunning women were so clearly enjoying themselves.

"The paper itself is probably eighteen-karat," Steve said.

Lisa's laughter rippled dangerously. It would almost be worth it to open the box just to see the shock on their self-assured faces.

"Very well, since you're all dying of curiosity, let's see what the ambassador has sent." She tore open one corner of the gold wrapping. "What a disappointment, neither a vial of oil nor a bar of gold. Nothing more exotic than a brass box. Are you terribly disappointed, my darlings?" She mimicked her mother.

"But the box could be full," Ingrid said.

"Dripping with diamonds," Babe whispered wickedly.

"Or stuffed with Arabian knights, each one richer than the next and eager to bestow oil wells on me." Lisa leaned across the table to the Taylor-Martins and lowered her voice in confidence. "You know, don't you, that the Arabs bottle crude for hair oil instead of pomade. That's why their hair is so black."

She weighed the box in her hands. "I hate to disappoint you again. But it's too light to be anything more than meets the eye. A box of beaten brass waiting to be filled with my own modest treasures."

Lisa smiled and tucked the box along the side of the chair where she could feel it yet hide it from view. There had already been too much said about it. All that banal talk was pointless, and dangerous. She turned to her mother to divert their attention. "How long are you in Rome for this time, mother?" She couldn't keep the edge of bitterness out of her voice, even though she'd only asked the question to change the subject.

Babe didn't seem to notice. "Until tomorrow, darling. The Taylor-Martins want to go back to Boston, so I thought I'd just fly over with them. Maybe I'll catch a glimpse of Elizabeth while I'm there."

Ingrid watched Lisa's mouth set in a thin, unyielding line as she listened to her mother. "We've been here since Monday, dear," she said. "I do wish we could have gotten together sooner."

"It doesn't matter. I'm going south for a few days anyway. I hate Rome in the summer, don't you?"

Babe ignored the information. "It would be so much more convenient if you lived in your father's apartment, Lisa. Then I wouldn't have to leave dozens of messages for you every time I pop by to say hello. Why do you think he keeps the place except for you? He rarely comes to Rome and could just as easily stay at the Grand when he does."

"Father hates hotels, you know that."

"That's not the point. It's so childish to live like a pauper, pretending you're less than you are. Really, Lisa, at your age you should be finished with all that romantic nonsense about the noble savage and the poor being better than the rich."

"Mother, I'm sure your friends aren't interested in my living arrangements."

"Where *did* you say you were living now?" Babe asked. She blinked wide, innocent eyes at her daughter.

Lisa couldn't help smiling at her mother's little game. "I don't believe I mentioned where I'm living, or whom I'm living with, to spare you another question."

"You always were thoughtful, darling. Another Irish coffee?"

"Why not, mother. Maybe I can become as decadent as you, and you'll finally approve of me."

"Two Irish coffees hardly qualify as decadence." Ingrid laughed throatily.

Babe reached over and squeezed her daughter's hand. "To Lisa, simply sitting here with her own mother and her two dearest friends is decadence, isn't it, darling?"

"Not if she's a Radcliffe gal, it isn't," Steve announced. "From what I hear, a lot more than panty raids goes on at universities these days. It's enough to make the ivy curl." He beamed, dazzled by his own wit.

"Watch out, Steve. You know how protective I am of my alma mater," Ingrid said brightly. "But tell us, Lisa, how did you like Harvard? I have the fondest memories of my college days."

"I was only there less than a year. I guess it wasn't long enough to discover what makes your Ivy League so special."

"What Lisa is actually saying is that she hated Radcliffe, hated Cambridge, hated her mother's country. She left before the year was through and refused to return, much to the disappointment of both her father and me. Enrico had hoped she'd go from Harvard to the London School of Economics, and then into the company with him. After all, she's his only heir and, hopelessly Italian though he is, his blood is even thicker than his chauvinism. She, of course, refuses even to consider the idea of anything so degrading as joining the family business. Making money to buy Fendi furs and St. Laurent dresses disgusts her. Underneath that expensive little dress you may think she's naked, Steve, but she has swathed herself in the rhetoric of the proletariat and the banner of socialism..."

The smile never left Babe's face. She could have been talking about the latest couture collection she'd seen in Paris as easily as her disappointing daughter. But her modulated bitterness was more disturbing than an angry outburst.

Ingrid and Steve avoided looking at either Lisa or her mother. "Really, Babe, you do paint such a bleak picture of your lovely daughter. To listen to you one would think she was off to Moscow to pay her respects at Lenin's tomb." Steve's humor was forced, and Ingrid followed up too rapidly.

"What are you doing with yourself these days, Lisa, besides looking beautiful?"

"Attending the university."

"Still playing struggling student?" Babe put in.

Lisa tossed her head. "Three weeks from now and you won't have to ask." She bit her tongue the instant the words were out and rushed on to cover up her indiscretion. "Actually I'm studying philosophy—Kierkegaard and Nietzsche."

"Let's drink to them both, men of substance and vision." Babe drained the bottle of champagne into her glass and held up the crystal flute to Steve. "Aren't you going to toast my daughter's new gurus?"

"With pleasure, but you just polished off the last drop of champagne. Shall we order another bottle and another Irish coffee for Lisa?"

Ingrid touched his sleeve as if it were a rein. "Why don't we go over to Jackie O's now. We'll have another bottle when we get there, and another toast to Lisa's men of substance." She exaggerated each word, the way childless people do to coax difficult children. Lisa wasn't quite sure which of the three of them Ingrid was trying to calm down.

"What a marvelous idea, Ingrid." Babe leaned across the table and squeezed her friend's hand. "You always do have such marvelous ideas."

It was after four in the morning when Lisa stripped off her dress and panty hose. She left them on the floor where they dropped, walking over them on her way to the bathroom and stepped into the glass box that served as a shower in her father's apartment. Whenever she used it, she felt like a doll, protected from dust and children's dirty fingers by a plastic dome.

She turned up the water until it was scalding and let it beat down on her. She'd suffered almost eight hours of self-disgust, not only observing but joining in the bourgeois display her mother called fun—gorging on food and drink, toying with sex, playing with psyches, spending in a single evening what most workers didn't bring home in a month.

The hot needles seemed to pierce her, cleansing away Babe's calculated interest and her lover's groping fingers. Steve's hands were soft and white—narrow, useless-looking hands with padded palms and polished nails. Sparse black hairs sprouted above the knuckles. A man's hands were important to Lisa. She remembered

57

the way they looked and felt after the memories of eyes and smiles and of what they may or may not have done together were lost in the novelty of a new body weighing her down.

Sandro Buscati's hands were brown and firm, soothing and exciting at the same time. His touch, however casual, said you were his to have, to hold, or to share as he pleased. Lisa soaped herself between the legs, moving her fingers in slow circles through the light, curly hairs. "Damn him," she muttered, "damn him to hell."

The glass walls that contained her were opaque with steam. One degree more and the water would scorch her. She threw back her head, closing her eyes and letting the hot-water pellets beat on her face and neck, and cradled her breasts with her hands to protect them against the force of the spray. She had passed each test of the *covo* with ease. She could hurl a Molotov cocktail, forge a passport, steal a car, compose a stinging manifesto, fire a Skorpion submachine gun without a moment's compunction and read about the anguish of her victims in the next day's paper with satisfaction. But she could never reconcile herself to the tepid trickle of water that passed for showers and the rough, often soiled towels that never varied from safe house to safe house, and seemed, in fact, to be an integral part of the movement. To step into a steaming shower, suffer willingly its piercing needles against her naked skin, then step out into the embrace of a warm bath sheet... it was one of the privileges of class she found hardest to surrender.

The sun was beginning to rise when she finally wrapped the plush towel around her dripping body, tucking one corner inside to hold it above her breasts, and padded barefoot into her bedroom. The apartment that her father maintained for his occasional trips to Rome was extraordinary; the location, spectacular.

One wall was entirely of glass, and when the curtains were opened, the view through this proscenium arch fell on the Roman Forum, with the broken stones and caverns of the Palatine Hill directly in front. On this hill Augustus lived in imperial majesty and Livia slithered from murder to murder.

Lisa sat on her bed cross-legged and pulled the towel tighter around her, pressing it under her legs to make a flat surface. Then wiping a wisp of damp hair back from her forehead, she began to open the package that the Arab courier had delivered in Harry's. She had declined to dance at Jackie O's, in spite of Babe's continuous chiding, and had not even risked emptying her bladder. She was afraid to let the gift out of her sight, yet she couldn't very well take it with her to the toilet without drawing attention to it again.

Lisa carefully folded the gold paper, then abruptly crumpled it into a ball and aimed it at the wastebasket across the room. She studied the box for a moment. It was a perfectly plain oblong of beaten brass; etched on the lid was a mosaic-like design that rippled out from a small carved flower in the center. The first light of day, creeping in through the sheer curtains, reflected off the gleaming metal. Slowly, almost reverently, Lisa raised the lid. Inside was a dun-colored, claylike substance—enough C-4 *plastique* to turn the imperial ruins to dust. It was the signal she'd been waiting for. The full shipment was ready. By the first of July they should have an arsenal of weapons sophisticated enough to bring mortality to the Eternal City.

Lisa stretched like a cat. Thanks to the generosity and cooperative spirit of Colonel Qaddafi, they were not lone assassins but an international brotherhood of freedom fighters—maiming, bombing, killing for the people. She felt the excitement building between her legs. The act of terror had become more of an aphrodisiac to her than the sexual act. It had happened gradually, sneaking up on her as subtly as love.

She threw herself back on the bed, opening the towel, and ran her hands down her nakedness. The brass box still lay open between her legs. She could feel the sharp edge of its rim against her wrist as she began to masturbate.

CHAPTER SEVEN

Monica Domenica and Sandra Di Voto sat under adjacent hair dryers at the Casa Mara beauty salon in Bologna. They'd driven there separately, but they planned to go home together. Monica Domenica had parked on a side street three blocks away, slipping the keys under the mat in the back seat when she got out. Ten minutes later their sons were driving the forest-green Audi north on the Highway of the Sun.

The women chatted together while their hair dried, their conversation protected by the drone of the machines. They'd been friends for thirty years and had brought up their sons together. They still indulged them as though they were little boys playing grown-up games. And in a way they were.

"The boys need a little holiday," Signora Di Voto said. Signora Domenica agreed. She preferred not to dwell too long or too hard on what they'd be doing. But she breathed easier when she knew they were out of the country, and the official plates would let them cross borders with no questions asked. She'd told her husband she was bringing the car in for servicing and would pick it up the next week when she went to town again. There was no need to worry the senator needlessly.

Luigi Domenica switched on the car radio, flipping the dial from the opera his mother liked until he found some American jazz. Michele Di Voto reached over the seat for his guitar and picked at it, trying to strum along. It was Charlie Parker playing "Cool Blues."

They drove from Bologna to Austria and then straight up the autobahn to Berlin, only stopping to switch drivers and to get gas. They'd brought a loaf of bread, a bag of cherries and three bottles of mineral water with them so they wouldn't have to stop for food, and they urinated by the side of the road when they switched drivers.

In Berlin they parked the Audi in the Tempelhof airport parking lot and crossed into East Berlin at Checkpoint Charlie the next morning. They walked through the bleak streets, passed the towers where the police watched every step and broadcast stern warnings. A bombed-out church, they couldn't tell of what denomination, still stood in its rubble thirty-odd years after the war. A boy playing in the ruins beckoned to them and asked for a cigarette. Domenica took an open pack of Marlboros out of his pocket and tossed it to him. For a second the boy stared at the gift in disbelief, then ran away as fast as he could before they could change their minds. He'd never be as wealthy again.

Domenica and Di Voto knew exactly where to go and whom to see. They were back in the western sector of the city before dark and stayed for four days, not returning to the East again. West Berlin was much more cheerful, and they went around the city like tourists. Their order would be filled at the Omnipol small-arms factory in Czechoslovakia and sent to them within the week: VZ-58 rifles, a much lighter version of the Kalishnikov AK-47; Skorpion VZ-61 machine pistols with silencers; M-52 pistols with the powerful bottleneck cartridges, and thousands of rounds of ammunition.

61

From Berlin they drove north to Hamburg, the infamous port city. Hamburg's red-light district is as blatant as a movie set. Whores of every age, shape, creed and color, their wares amply displayed, beckoned from windows and called from doorways to the two young men. They strolled leisurely, passing house after house, looking over the merchandise on display but not stopping to buy. Although temptation was great, they did not plunge in but chose precisely—a house as garish inside as out, and just as dirty. They asked for Ingrid and were presented to a buxom redhead in a brief coffee-colored slip and red garters. Domenica bought her for the night to share between them.

"We've been friends for years," Domenica told the madam. "We do everything together. Don't worry, she won't feel cheated—and neither will you." He paid double. The madam laughed and put the marks down her bosom. Ingrid sighed, already tired.

They left her early in the morning hours, before their time was over, each weighted down with two heavy valises. They'd slept soundly for a few hours, limiting themselves to one turn each with the fat Ingrid, and then taking her once together, one under her, one over her—she was the salami and they were the bread. She had a fringe of red hair around each nipple and a loaded Mauser in the bureau drawer.

The central office of the French secret police has a terminal air about it. It is housed in an innocuous structure, stuck clandestinely on the eastern outskirts of Paris behind a cemetery on Boulevard Mortier. At SDEDE headquarters, Major Philippe Joncet listened stone-faced. His flat blue eyes, like two disks of lapis lazuli, remained fixed on the sergeant relaying the report.

"At least, we aren't involved. It's the Italians' headache—and the wunderkind Germans'. They deserve it."

The sergeant spoke more guardedly. "It may not be too late. The German border guards have been alerted to search every vehicle for the shipment."

"*Bon.*" Major Joncet's lips pursed in a thin line. It was the closest he ever came to a smile. "They will fail, we can be sure of it. They always do. Get me Detective Guido Felice at the Questura in Rome."

Luigi Domenica and Michele Di Voto drove southwest across Germany, not wanting to take the same route home, and crossed into France at Nancy. At Grenoble they stopped for dinner, then cut back into Italy north of Genoa. They held up their passports when they came to the border check. The guards glanced at the official plates and waved the Audi through.

The next morning the women drove into town together for their usual hairdressing appointment, carefully skirting the topic foremost on their minds. They no longer talked about what their sons were doing, or pressed them to settle down. Once they realized where their boys' sympathies lay, they'd come to the conclusion that the fewer details they knew, the more tranquil their minds would be. Sandra Di Voto and Monica Domenica finished at the beauty parlor, had lunch and shopped. In the afternoon, they drove home in separate cars.

CHAPTER EIGHT

"Where did Franco go so early?" Paola rubbed the sleep from her eyes and sat down at the kitchen table. Pulling her pink quilted bathrobe tighter around her, she studied the basket of fruit before choosing a golden apricot. Everything was conspiring to make her late to work. She'd overslept and the bath water was a cold trickle. She'd have to wait a few minutes until it came back on. That was the worst of living in a postwar apartment house. The hot water supply was erratic, depending on how many neighbors chose to wash at the same time.

Signora Mirabella turned from the sink, soapsuds still clinging to her arms. "He's taking some fresh cornetti to Suor Marianna. I baked them myself for il Papa this morning. Suor Marianna said that he's not eating, and he always liked my sweet rolls."

"What are you thinking of, mama? You can't send Franco to the Vatican."

"He offered to go—such a good boy. Suor Marianna was so happy to see him. Did I tell you? We brought some plump figs."

"But, mama, Franco is a *communista*...he told us so himself."

Signora Mirabella cut two thick slices of bread, put them in front of Paola and filled her cup with inky coffee. "*Basta,* Paola. Franco is your brother."

"How can you close your eyes to what he's become after what he did to *babbo?*" Her voice quavered and she threw the half-eaten apricot down on the table. Her mother possessed a marvelous faculty for ignoring what she didn't want to believe. She might know Franco was a communist but she'd never admit it, even to herself.

"Your father died of heart failure."

"Yes, and why did his heart fail?"

The signora shrugged. "Now I'm expected to be a doctor as well as a cook, a maid, a mother...I thank God my son has come back. He said foolish, childish things he never meant, and now he's sorry for them. That's enough."

"He told you that, mama?"

"There are some things a mother doesn't have to be told. I see it in his eyes. He has come home to us. The rest is over. I never want to hear talk of it again." The signora wiped her hands on her apron as if she could wipe away the past as easily.

"But, mama, *babbo* is dead."

"Yes, and your brother is alive and home again where he belongs." Her voice was stubborn and hard. "Your father would understand even if you can't. Now get dressed or you'll have no job to go to."

Paola pushed her breakfast away untouched. "I'm not going to work, I'm going after Franco."

Paola did not wait for the hot water to come back. She washed in the bathroom sink and dressed quickly. She could hear her mother in the kitchen, clashing dishes and pans. "Ciao, mama," she called as she raced out. She didn't want to face her again that morning.

The day was gloomy and indecisive. Patches of cobalt blue defied a gray slate of clouds, raising hopes that the sun might break through. Paola hurried down the hill to the village, stopping at the *tabaccaio* to call the store and say that she'd be late. Although she had little hope of catching up to Franco, she had to try. Waiting at the bus stop, she thought of the other time she'd gone looking for him...

It was in March—after Moro was kidnapped. She'd searched for him at the university but she couldn't find him there or in the cafés he and his new friends frequented. He'd given up his rented room and dropped out of sight. No one she talked to had any idea where he'd gone. Then in April she'd heard he'd been arrested on Liberation Day with other young communists demonstrating in Piazza della Republica in support of the kidnapping. She'd gone alone to the Questura, taking the D-slash bus from Via Flaminia to Via Nazionale, then going the rest of the way on foot, half-running, half-walking. Stuffed in her notebook had been every lira she'd saved in her twenty-three years, and half of her monthly paycheck from her job selling lingerie at La Standa. She'd given the other half to her mother as she always did. There'd been no point in making her mother suspicious, and the rent had to be paid. Paola hadn't told anyone where she was going. It would be between Franco and her, she'd thought. She'd imagined his dark, sorrowful eyes peering through the bars and the sudden start of recognition; then the cell door would open and he'd rush into her arms. Paola was a romantic like her father. Franco was more rigid, like his mother, although he'd be quick to deny the similarity. The police were more rigid yet. Her reception at the Questura had been as cold and unyielding as the building itself. No information was available about the incident or the demonstrators arrested. The name Mirabella had meant nothing to the curt desk officer. Giovanni Mirabella had been dead two years, and outside of Vatican City, official doors no longer slid open at the mention of his name. Paola had continued to search, more frantically than ever, until a week ago when she had spotted her brother at the mass for Moro in San Giovanni. Then, before her fear could crystallize, Franco had come home...

Paola stepped off the sidewalk and strained to see up the long, steep street. There was no bus in sight. A car pulled over to the curb and the beefy man at the wheel offered her a lift. Just behind him was a taxi. Impulsively she hailed it, something she had only done once before in her life. "Piazza Risorgimento, *per favore,*" she said. The cab was already pulling away as she yanked the door shut. She sat on the edge of the seat watching the meter. She'd been too upset with her mother to touch her breakfast, and now she'd have to go without lunch as well to make up for her lateness.

By the time Paola reached the Apostolic Palace, Franco was already coming out the small side door used by Vatican workers and tradesmen. Suddenly she felt ridiculous. What had she thought he'd do—contaminate the Vatican with his adolescent politics? She stepped back against the wall, hoping he wouldn't see her.

Paola wanted to believe that the brother she loved had come home, but the face she'd seen at Moro's mass kept getting in the way.

Franco zigzagged across the street, heading toward Piazza Risorgimento. He walked quickly, purposefully, through the square and down Via Crescenzia. Paola felt uneasy, foolish, still she followed him, curious to know where he was going. At Via Terenzio she lost him. The narrow street was empty. She looked up and down the block. Although Franco neither smoked nor drank, the only place he could have gone was the *birreria.*

Pushing open the door tentatively, Paola stepped into a rough taverna. Clusters of men bent over bare tables, drinking and playing cards, though it was still morning. There were no other women. She glanced around the room in confusion. Franco was approaching a side table where another young man was playing solitaire. He was holding an unplayed card in his hand and staring at her.

Buscati jerked his chin toward the door. "You brought a friend, Mirabella? What were you thinking of?" He slapped the jack of hearts down on the open pile.

Franco looked back, already beginning to deny it. "Paola," he gasped. "How could she find me here?"

"Who is she?" Buscati's eyes had never strayed from the girl.

"My sister!" Franco choked on the words. An angry flush colored his sallow cheeks. His hands were trembling.

Buscati got up and put an arm across his shoulder. "*Calma,*

Franco. I'm happy to meet your family. It was just the surprise."
His voice was soothing. The girl might be useful one day, if Franco's resolve weakened. He was the only untested member of the *covo*.

Buscati was confident of the other four. Luigi Domenica and Michele Di Voto, loyal comrades from the Communist stronghold of Bologna and friends since school days, had proved themselves dangerous and devoted agitators. Whatever was necessary for the revolution they would do. And whatever response the Christian Democrats orchestrated, they would be warned. Piero Massi, too, was a seasoned veteran. His early reservations had been expected and easily deflected. Now he could be counted on to do his part like a professional. Indeed, he was invaluable. Buscati knew of at least ten instances when Massi, from his position, was able to trip off the *covo* to the activities of targets later eliminated. That left only Lisa, so eager to meet—and overcome—any challenge he held out. The rashness of the operation appealed to her. She was impulsive and foolishly brave. The greater the risk, the less able she was to resist. But there was something else as well. She had neither forgotten nor forgiven him for forcing her to submit to their comrades. To each according to his needs, and everyone needed to make love to Lisa.

Watching them coming toward her, Paola wished she had inherited her mother's blind faith.

"What are you doing here?" Franco demanded in a harsh whisper.

"I thought you might need help with the *cornetti*," she stammered.

"You mean you were following me..."

Buscati interrupted, sparing her the embarrassment of a reply. "Aren't you going to introduce me, Franco?"

"My sister, Paola," he muttered.

"*Piacere.*" Buscati inclined his head in a bow. "Would you like to join us?"

"No, *grazie*, I have to get to work." He looked to be thirty-three or -four. The classical features of a Roman patrician were offset by the blond hair and vivid green eyes found sometimes among southern Italians—a relic of incursion from Aechaen to Visgoth. "I'm very late already."

"Where do you work, signorina?"

"La Standa. I'm a salesgirl, at least I was. I may not have a job to go to after this morning." She was already opening the door, anxious to escape from her brother's anger and his friend's disturbing gaze that had never left her for an instant. She felt as though he was waiting for her to explain why she was there, but she didn't know what to say.

"Another time, then, when you're not in such a hurry." He was courteous and correct as he held the door open for her.

Later, when she thought about him, what she especially remembered were his eyes, which were the color of spring leaves, and his hair, fair and curly...

CHAPTER NINE

"Porca troia!" Felice slammed down the phone with a roar. He'd been looking forward to a peaceful lunch and undisturbed siesta. All morning he'd had the subtle taste of spaghetti alla carbonara in his mouth—the small, crisp bits of *pancetta*, oily and pungent; the pasta, round and firm and steaming enough to cook the raw eggs and melt the cheese the instant they were tossed over it. It wasn't enough that they'd called him back from the mountains. Now he'd have to settle for a *panino di mortadella* at his desk. Felice hated to eat at his desk. He considered it a barbaric habit the terrorists had forced on him.

"Cenci," he bellowed, not bothering to turn on the intercom. The door opened and Officer Cenci entered, brusque and self-contained.

"Yes, sir."

"Joncet from SDECE. Another weapons shipment just crossed the border. He thinks it's coming to us. Paris was tipped off by the Landswehr but not in time. Never in time." He tapped the bottom of a fresh pack of Nazionales and extricated a cigarette with his fleshy lips. "Joncet's sending the full report through Criminalpol."

"We should have it in an hour, then."

"One hour, two, three. What will we do with it when it comes? Put it on top of our pile of reports, or on the bottom, or in the middle? What's the difference? While we're studying it, the new guns will be making more cripples and corpses to add to our files."

He studied a small square box with a picture of San Paulo fuori i Muri printed in black and white on the top, as if it held the answer, then opened it and took out a wax match. "The reports are pouring in from all over the country. Day after day it's the same—shootings, kneecappings, sabotage, arson, bombings. Not only from the north, where we expect it, but from the south too. And now a new arms shipment." He struck the match against the box. "What is there to blow up in the Mezzogiorno except the sun and the poverty? And both of them are out of our reach."

Officer Cenci glanced up at his chief. The noonday sun glinted on his glasses, making it impossible for Felice to read his expression with any degree of accuracy. His job was thankless and discouraging enough without having to bear the added cross of a condescending assistant. Felice had cut his teeth on crimes of passion and desperation. Cenci belonged to the new breed of detective who had learned his profession scrutinizing computer reports and battling urban guerrillas. To the older man he seemed as cold and bloodless as his quarry. Still, he shouldn't complain.

In January, stung by charges that he was a Fascist, the one epithet no Italian politician could risk, Premier Moro had given orders to disband the antiterrorist squad. The result was a circular from the Ministry of Defense reshuffling a vast network whose tentacles had spread the length and breadth of the ancient boot. Three hundred key agents were scattered among remote posts up and down the country, their files misplaced or lost. Felice was moved up from routine detective work to take over what little remained of Rome's antiterrorist division. At first he was honored by the promotion. He was second in command to the carabiniere general himself. But he quickly found out that, in its reduced state, his squad couldn't intercept a gunrunner, let alone rescue a kidnapped premier.

The previous two months had been a nightmare—dealing with

an hysterical press and family; with the government pressuring him daily for some progress, however slight, to ease the national humiliation; and with the international egos of the German and American experts who had been flown in to help flush out the terrorists. Moro, the man, was forgotten in the crush, until his bullet-riddled body was dumped in the middle of the city, equidistant from the headquarters of the Communist Party and the Christian Democrats. And no one remembered, or dared to admit, that it was Moro who had signed his own death certificate.

Felice flicked the burnt match across the room and inhaled deeply, holding the acrid smoke in his lungs too long. "Ah, Cenci, what's the use? I'm just back and already I'm tired again. The few days in the mountains with Elena seem like a distant memory. It's just as well the memory dims—the hand of God probably."

He forced a dry laugh. "You should have seen us. We behaved like young lovers, comical young lovers. Hand in hand we hiked up the wooded slopes, me sweating under the load of an over-stuffed picnic basket, Elena stopping every other step to gather the wild poppies that grow like weeds, and to gather enough breath to reach the next crest. She thought I was deceived, but I haven't been a detective for twenty years for nothing.

"The first time we made that climb we ran up the slopes as easily as mountain goats, Elena going ahead, strands of thick black hair escaping from the bun she wore high on her head, and me overtaking her effortlessly, hungry for the pleasures I'd discovered the night before."

Cenci listened impassively, but Felice went on anyway, asking himself how he could expect to understand the minds of a cold-blooded gang of anarchists when he couldn't even communicate with his assistant..."I still remember it clearly. She broke away, laughing and running until she reached the crest of the mountain and went down the other side to a glade, brilliant orange and green from the poppies and tall grass and so silent it seemed not even a bird or cricket had been there before us. That was our true bed, not the lumpy mattress with the springs that creaked in the village inn where the walls were as thin as *capelli d'angeli*, the eyes of the other guests were lewdly knowing and the rough sheets were stained reddish-brown... In the inn our first time, we'd groped awkwardly under the cover of darkness, bed sheets and heavy nightclothes. But when we got to the glade Elena lay on her back in the poppies. She was laughing with anticipation and love. Her face was flushed. I stood over her, not able to believe that she was mine. Still shy, my young Elena unbuttoned her white blouse, sat up and slipped it off her shoulders, then unfastened her brassiere, slipped that off too and lay back again. Her arms and breasts reached up to me. Her skin glowed in the sunlight. I dropped down beside her and kissed her nipples. For us it was an enchanted glade..." The cigarette had formed a precariously long ash, but Felice ignored it..."We ran naked through the grass and made love again. We swam in a clear pool and did things together I'd been ashamed to even dream about. Only there they were beautiful and right and without *vergona*, without shame. When the sun began to fade we dressed and walked slowly through the gathering shadows back to the village inn and our lumpy mattress and constraining room. In the morning we went back to Rome...

"That was fifteen years ago, it seems like a lifetime. This time there was no enchantment. When we finally got to the glade, panting and sweating, we opened the picnic basket and looked at the mounds of prosciutto and goat's cheese, shimmering sardines, bowls of white kidney beans and tuna, and loaves of bread. So what do you think we did? We settled down to our picnic lunch, feeling but not admitting to each other what the years had lost..."

Felice shrugged and ground out the cigarette. "What can I say, Cenci? Appetites change."

Cenci merely looked at him.

CHAPTER TEN

The second-class compartment held four comfortably. Seven overripe bodies were wedged into it. There was no air conditioning, and even with the window open the aroma of sweat and picnic lunches was overpowering. The door was left open to stimulate a crosscurrent, but the aisle outside was even more crowded. What little air there was in the aisle was being sucked up greedily by the less fortunate, who, unable to find seats at all, leaned, crouched and sprawled there in varying degrees of discomfort.

The train from Rome to Naples was passing through the blood-soaked terrain that surrounded the green rock of Monte Cassino. During the war, the British and Americans had butted their heads over and over against that rock, with Monte Cairo in snow miles above, and all along the Rapido River and through the Liri valley the Germans hung on to every inch, fighting over the ancient road to Rome—the Casalina, the consul road. Then the American bombers destroyed the Benedictine Abbey, needlessly as it turned out...German artillery spotters had not used the abbey; their commander was a strict Catholic and had refused to involve holy ground. Beautiful, bloody valley—and no one in the compartment noticed it.

Beside the window a man and his wife sat across from each other, immersing themselves in the lunch the woman had prepared to ensure that they didn't starve between Rome and Naples. The bag seemed bottomless. They'd already gone through cold meat, cheese and a loaf of bread, and were peeling back the brown-spotted skin of an overheated banana. The woman sat, legs planted solidly apart to catch any stray breeze. She wore flesh-colored pants over her corset that came midway down her thick thighs.

Beside her two German students, with the clean Aryan features and blond hair that had marked Hitler Youth a generation before, slept slumped against each other with their backpacks at their feet. Across from them a salesman and a seminarian tried to read. The seminarian, making his annual visit home, still had the high coloring and open face of a boy. He was being ordained in October, quickly before he learned anything about life. The seminarian's eyes kept wandering from the prayers of Saint Francis of Assisi to the expanse of flesh-colored pants revealed across the aisle. He'd never seen, let alone known, a woman. The salesman's head persisted in drooping over his newspaper. He'd jerk it up and start reading again, only to begin the slow, inevitable decline toward sleep. When the train reached Naples he was still on the same article he had begun in Rome.

Lisa was squeezed between the curious seminarian and the insatiable husband. She wore American jeans and a Fruit of the Loom T-shirt, and she held a duffel bag of light gray parachute cloth on her lap. When the train stopped in Capua she leaned out the window and bought a chocolate ice from a vendor on the station platform. She licked it slowly, trying to make it last until the steaming train finally reached Naples, and tried not to think of Babe.

Naples was one of Babe's favorite cities; Lisa never understood why. Her mother seemed as alien there as someone from another planet. The dirty alleys thick with laundry, the black market that flourished like the poverty, the canny urchins, the arrogant preening men, the weary women, and the voluptuous girls who looked old by twenty-five—but Babe loved it all, the haggling, the howling, the high drama and low life, the gorgeous crescent bay.

Slinging her bag over her shoulder, Lisa began walking across the city to the harbor, ignoring the catcalls and kissing sounds directed her way. At the dock she checked the schedule of the ferries to Ischia. There was one at 7:15 that would give her all the time she needed. She walked back by the sumptuous Excelsior Hotel, where Babe always stayed in a suite with a balcony that overlooked the bay. She stopped at the first movie theater she came to and looked up at the marquee. *Pane e Cioccolata* was playing. She and Sandro had seen it together the first time. She bought a ticket and went in. There were only a handful of people in the theater.

Sitting down in the back row, she watched the end of the movie and stayed until the next showing began. As she went into the bathroom and locked the door, Lisa was still smiling about the misfortunes of the hapless Italian waiter who goes to Switzerland to find work. She sat on the toilet and spread the contents of the bag on the floor in front of her. Massi had arranged it all like a prefabricated house. All she had to do was put the pieces together. She worked expertly, connecting the electric egg timer to the 50-volt dry-cell battery. In an hour the egg timer would go off, sending a charge of electricity through the detonator and exploding the bomb. It took her exactly nine minutes to assemble the bomb, empty the wastebasket, set the device in the bottom and put the papers back in. When she was finished she flushed the toilet and ran the water. She did not return to her seat to watch the end of the movie again.

The seminarian wandered around the city listlessly. He knew he should catch the bus home to Portici. The family would be waiting with a feast prepared. Instead he turned in the other direction. Once he was home, they'd never let him stray out of sight. He'd been born a priest. His life had been a matter of waiting until his age matched his destiny. The first son followed his father's trade; the second son went to the seminary. He had been there since he was ten, only coming home for holidays and deaths.

76

At the end of his vacation they would bring him back; in October he would be ordained, all doors closed to him except the sacristy and finally the Gates of Heaven. He would catch the last bus home. Il Signore would forgive him a few hours of freedom, even if his family didn't.

Elated by his daring, the seminarian walked through the noisy, cluttered streets, excited by every odor, every female leg, passing the whores who operated openly. One of them called to him, a free invitation for a man of the cloth. Her hair was black, her lips were red. He felt himself rise to the bait. Confused and embarrassed, he broke into a run. Suddenly he wanted to escape. He kept running for several blocks, thinking he heard the staccato beat of her heels behind him. But when he turned back there were only a couple of boys peddling American cigarettes. He bought a pack of Winstons, his first, but didn't open it. Instead he stopped to look at the pictures in the display windows of a movie house and to catch his breath. He studied each picture, then finally took a black purse out of his skirt pocket and counted the money he had left. Just enough for the bus and the movie with two hundred lire to spare.

He bought a ticket and went inside. He wanted a place of refuge, a womb to retreat to. The credits were just beginning. "Nino Manfredi in *Pane e Cioccolata*." He sat back in a center seat and relaxed for the first time since he had boarded the train.

The theater bombing in Naples was felt as far north as Rome. Random violence was sweeping the country, but the bombing in the Naples movie theater was the worst incident, claiming the highest toll of dead and wounded. In Rome, where the Squadra Anti-terrorismo was centered, General Andrea del Sarto, head of the special unit, conferred long into the night with the minister of defense.

By daybreak they had agreed on a plan that would not only satisfy the political need to show that they were acting decisively, but would also relieve del Sarto of a chronic headache. Detective Guido Felice, deputy chief of the antiterrorist squad, would be given a special assignment: to devise a new plan to counter the blight of urban terror.

The general delegated authority with skill, which was why he had risen to the top of the carabiniere so fast, and he had never liked Guido Felice.

CHAPTER ELEVEN

"Holiness." Costanto Zanelli hurried across the room as the pontiff started toward him. He reached for the hand bearing the amethyst ring. His left knee, bent in the obligatory gesture of genuflection, did not so much as graze the Oriental carpet that covered the parquet floor of the papal study.

"Holiness," he said again, his lips brushing the cool purple stone.

Paul raised him gently and gestured for him to sit down. "We do not wish to be interrupted, monsignor," he said to his secretary. Monsignor Macchi bowed, understanding that the words were a dismissal. The pope wanted to be alone with his dangerous nemesis.

The elegant, urbane cardinal had three weaknesses: electronic gadgets that, it was whispered, he had installed throughout the Vatican and even here in the pope's private apartment; fast cars; and the papacy. The first two were well known, but he took pains to conceal the third.

"As you wish, Your Holiness. I will be outside if you need me." Monsignor Macchi began to back out of the room. If he wondered what the two had to say to each other, if he worried that Paul might be manipulated by this most ruthless of men or that his words said in good faith might be taped, doctored and turned against him, he showed no sign of his concern. Drawing the double doors closed, he left the old men, the two most powerful princes of the Church, alone together.

Cardinal Zanelli had not visited the private apartments that looked out onto Via di Porta Angelica in almost a dozen years. As he and Paul settled themselves in adjacent wing chairs Zanelli scanned the room, considering the changes he would make. First, the decor. Paul had redone his living quarters in the light, off-white shades favored by contemporary decorators and replaced the works of the old masters with modern art. Zanelli preferred the traditional style, the thick damask wall covering and ornate furnishings. Second, the television. It would go. Paul liked to watch it in the late evenings. For years he had been an insomniac, which accounted for the dark circles that seemed to be perpetually drawn under his sunken eyes. Zanelli disdained television. He had a small set in his office on which he watched the *telegiornale* in the early evening. Otherwise it was a waste of time. He neither knew— nor cared to discover—what insipid entertainment enthralled the masses of his countrymen.

He smoothed the skirts of his purple cassock over his lap and considered his pope. Paul had angled himself so as to face his visitor more squarely. His thin frame occupied a small portion of the oversized chair. His hands were clasped together in his lap. "My brother, I need your help," he began.

"It is always an honor to serve you, Your Holiness." The words rolled off his tongue with a resonance that seemed to swell majestically from the depth of his chest.

There were many, Zanelli knew, who would have heard the pontiff's words and been disarmed by their humility. He was not deceived. He had never believed that Paul possessed the virtues of modesty and meekness, if virtues they were. He had too much respect for his resilient, longtime adversary. Paul was shrewd, yes; soft-spoken, yes; diplomatic, most certainly. But he could be stubborn and unyielding, and he valued no man's opinion as highly as his own. He had known Montini since they were monsignors together, the best and the brightest in the Curia. Montini had not survived—and risen to such eminence—by being merely a simple, humble man. And yet, and yet, Zanelli thought, Blessed are the meek, for they shall inherit the earth, and clearly Montini had. Zanelli sat back and waited, curious to know why Paul had summoned him.

They had been allies once, though never friends. When they were young, Montini had been a modernist; Zanelli, a traditionalist. With age and power, Paul had become a conciliator, Zanelli an arch-conservative and intractable foe. He felt justified in his enmity. Throughout his pontificate Paul had done his utmost to truncate the power of the conservatives. By mandating the age of retirement for every bishop of the Church except himself, he'd forced out many of the most influential conservative leaders. Most notable among them was the rotund, byzantine head of the Holy Office, Alfredo Cardinal Ottaviani, a prince, many thought, more on the lines of Machiavelli than of the Church. Under Ottaviani, the Holy Office had earned a reputation for enforcing orthodoxy to the letter, if not the spirit, of the law. He was reactionary or vigilant, depending on one's point of view, and Zanelli was his handpicked successor. With Ottaviani's retirement, Paul had insisted on reorganizing the Holy Office. He hoped to change its image; he succeeded only in changing its name to the Sacred Congregation of Doctrine of the Faith, Zanelli recalled with satisfaction.

Paul leaned forward, closer to the cardinal than their positions dictated, his deep blue eyes fixing Zanelli from their dark cavities. "I shall not be circuitous. The possibility, some would say probability, is great that the Communists will soon become the decisive force in France, Spain and Portugal. Throughout Latin America they pose a constant challenge to the existing institutions, including our own Church. Here in our beloved country the Marxists control thirty-six local governments and have formed a coalition with the Christian Democrats for the first time in history. Catholics and Communists are living side by side in apparent harmony, and the phenomenon is bound to spread further. There is little hope that the Christian Democrats can regain their position or even contain their losses." Zanelli began to demur, but Paul held up a warning hand. "I share your abhorrence of Communism, my brother, but the Church can no longer remain deaf to her children. The vox populi is clear. We ignore the political realities of Euro-Communism at our own peril. Politics is both a science and an art. When we force people to choose between the promise of bread to feed their hungry children and sanctifying grace to nurture their immortal souls, then we drive them from the arms of their Holy Mother the Church."

"Holiness, isn't the Church the teacher of her children, and not the reverse?" Zanelli replied with thinly concealed sarcasm.

"Perhaps we have been too intransigent," Paul urged. "There may be times when we should place the common good above all— even at the risk of cooperating with our Marxist enemies. We must become more sensitive and responsive to political and social evolution, and learn to distinguish between those proposals which have a certain merit and those which are inimical to Christian life. Isn't it better to sit down with our enemies and try to reach an accommodation that will allow our people to practice their faith to the best of their ability than to be righteous in our indignation and cut off our children? Christ himself said, 'Render unto Caesar the things that are Caesar's and to God the things that are God's.'"

Zanelli was shaking his head. "Marxism and Christianity are incompatible philosophies. I—and the Church Magisterum—have never wavered in this belief. I, at least, intend to stand firm."

"In that we will stand firm together. I am not suggesting that we embrace our atheistic brothers, only that we prepare for the inevitable instead of holding implacably to a hopeless cause, as we too often do."

"Faith and hope are virtues which I, for one, cannot abandon so lightly," Zanelli answered stiffly.

"And what of charity?" Paul allowed himself a smile. "You will oppose us then?"

The cardinal hesitated. Was he underestimating Montini? Was

82

Paul pretending to seek his support only to warn him that he would lead the Church intractably to the left rather than hand over the keys of Peter to a conservative like himself? Zanelli sensed that he had been fed the bait by this so-called Fisherman of Souls, and now he was going to be reeled in slowly, skillfully.

Could Paul have learned that he was sending out feelers to other influential conservative cardinals—to Cooke in New York, Hoffner in Cologne, Wyszynski in Warsaw—discreet feelers to test the water, to signal that the day was drawing near when he would be a *papabile* and would need their support? Had he felt the hand of death tightening its grip, squeezing out his life? Or was Paul, in his most diplomatic fashion, telling him not to raise false hopes within himself, that he, Paul, was determined to cling to life and power?

"It was so much simpler in the old days, or so it seems in the memory of an old man." Paul was reminiscing. "When we were young there was one foe—the Fascists. Our enemy united us. Remember the strength, the conviction of the university students? They flocked to our Catholic action groups. They had faith and courage, and perhaps, even more important, they had optimism. They never doubted, at least the best of them, that we would triumph."

"And we did, after a fashion," Zanelli replied.

"Ah yes, one could say we did, if to triumph is to become powerful and envious, consumed by vices, divided by enmities as deep as those that once united us. How did it happen? How did we become so dispersed? Why did we turn against one another? Look at us, look at Italy, look at the student leaders then—Moro, Andreotti, and later Mirabella. Moro is dead, his death a national disgrace, ugly, cowardly—a deed that sickens us and the world. Mirabella is dead too, in circumstances too personally painful to relate, as much a victim as Moro. Only Andreotti is left of them. God protect him. And who are the leaders of today's youth who will become the nation's and the Church's leaders tomorrow? They are the murderers, living like ferrets underground, coming up from their stifling caves only long enough to strike another blow at our soul. Their philosophy is a contradiction. Their faith is in destruction, their future is in chaos... from destruction will come resurrection, renewal? No, it is a resurrection of the Anti-Christ. His resurrection, the one which gives meaning to our Church, was proof to fearful, fallible man that life and hope are indestructible... We are old men, Costanto, old men who have lived too long. Age is a cross we both must bear. But we need not be foolish too. We must all die to live again, even you and I, although we have been fighting the idea with tenacity."

Zanelli thought he detected a trace of exasperation in the pope's voice, but perhaps he was projecting his own feelings. "Your Holiness," he said rising, "we are both servants of Christ and of His Church."

"Yes, yes. But what is His Church, Costanto, that each of us serves? Is it the same Church with different interests? Or do we serve one master in two separate houses?"

"Holiness, I fear time and your memories may be conspiring against you. It is true we shared a common enemy once when we were young. But that is all we shared. We both detested and feared Mussolini. You because you hated Fascism and deplored the man who tried to make it our national religion. And I—I for different reasons. I despised the man. He was a braggadocio, a knave and a sybarite. But I approved the philosophy."

Paul looked at him sadly. "You will persist in denying us then?"

Zanelli could feel more than hear the steel ring in Paul's quiet voice. "It is not Christ I deny. It is Peter."

"And in me Peter denies Christ a fourth time. That is what you think."

"It is you who wears the shoes of the Fisherman—and it is not for us to say how well they fit."

"Costanto, will you do an old man a simple favor?" Paul began with difficulty to push his way out of the chair. "Give us your blessing."

"Holiness," he began to protest, but Paul was already struggling to his knees. Costanto Cardinal Zanelli, angered, embarrassed and disoriented by this strange, painfully personal encounter, brought his hands together. *"Benedictat vos omnipotens Dei, pater et filius et spiritus sanctus."* He formed the sign of the cross over the bowed head of Paul VI.

"Amen," Paul murmured.

"Amen, your Holiness," Cardinal Zanelli muttered in reply. Then, his back straight, only his head inclined in a grudging gesture, the minimal token of respect, he backed out of the august presence. Paul remained kneeling on the floor, his head sunk in his hands.

Once outside the study, Zanelli turned swiftly on his heels, nodded curtly to Monsignor Macchi and strode down the hall, purple moiré robes rustling as he went. If Paul thought he could be turned around with some faded memories, he had either grossly underestimated Costanto Zanelli or he was getting senile. Paul had shrewdly undermined the chance of a conservative succeeding him by forcing the old guard into retirement and filling their places with new Third World cardinals, and by leading the Church to the left with his policy of *ostpolitik* and his Vatican II reforms. But if he tried to carry out his threatened proposal, Zanelli would fight him with his last breath, by whatever means were available to him.

Zanelli could not imagine why Montini would make such an ill-advised bid for support and tip his hand in the process...Yes, clearly, Paul is slipping, he told himself, and every meter he loses is a gain for me...Zanelli had already taken the first step in launching his candidacy for the papacy—a campaign to destroy any possible rivals with innuendoes and rumors. It was the expected practice before a new conclave, and he was proceeding with subtlety and skill. His mind filled with plans to step up his electioneering before it was too late, yet at the same time he felt disquieted. He hurried down the hallway, almost colliding with a young man carrying a white net bag filled with parcels.

"Permesso," Zanelli mumbled.

"Eminenza, mi scusi." The boy flushed, as if his impure thoughts were visible to the prelate's trained eye, and flattened himself against the wall to allow the cardinal a wide passage.

85

"*É niente.* Zanelli dismissed the boy, brushing him aside as if he were a fleck of lint on his cassock.

When the cardinal was out of sight, Franco Mirabella slipped through the back door of the papal apartment and went into the kitchen, where Suor Marianna was waiting for the packages from the signora with a cup of cappuccino and a plate of *strufolo* for him.

CHAPTER TWELVE

"It is senseless, worse than senseless. Imbecilic!" Detective Felice threw up his hands in disgust. "What is it the Americans kept saying when we were for searching for Moro—like looking for a needle in a haystack. But who can say the needle ever was in the hay, Cenci? Answer me that."

Officer Cenci barely glanced up from the stack of files he was combing through. An equally depressing number of files was spread out in front of Felice. They had been poring over the reports for hours, looking for some clue in the sudden flurry of underground activity, a pattern in the rash of violence that was sweeping the country from Turin to Naples. "Is there an alternative?" Cenci replied blandly.

He always spoke blandly. It was impossible to know whether he was merely stating a fact, or jabbing one subtly. Being a Romano di Roma, Felice was prone to believe the worst. His assistant was mocking him, saying, in point of fact, if I were in your position, this wouldn't be happening. Felice pushed the distracting thoughts aside.

"So be it. I will be tough. Everyone insists—the Quirinale, the minister, the generalissimo all cry for decisiveness and the cost be damned. Italy has been bankrupt for years, and still we go on. Nothing changes. So why should I worry about bankrupting her more?"

He pushed back his chair and swiveled around so that he could look down on the street below. "Rome is an archeologist's dream. It's taking forever to build the Metropolitana because every spade of earth turned over reveals yet another temple. A city of temples and forums. Rome is also a textbook. It explains how to build a city well, and how to run it badly. And so, Cenci, that is why I have been invited to address the special meeting of the Consiglio dei Ministri. Invited! What is the good of an invitation if it can't be declined?" Felice had gotten up and was charging around the crowded office like a bull encircled by red capes.

"I've been commanded. The country—the ministers—need a lamb so that when we are embarrassed again they'll have this lamb to put on the spit, baste, turn and roast before the nation in full color on the evening *telegiornale*. Is that any way to run a city?

"I must personally ask for the special powers to be granted, so that I—*io proprio*—can be held responsible when they fail. And they will fail. We can't stop whatever evil is being plotted—probably under our very noses, so close we could smell it if we knew what scent these terrorists use. That's why it is truly an act of terror.

"You know, I know, the ministers know we won't stop them this time. We may make it more difficult, but we won't stop them, except by some lucky break. And so the ministers want a sacrificial lamb, already trimmed and trussed, ready to be thrown on the fire. They don't want to be forced to point fingers at one another again. This time they plan to have their collective *cola* amply covered. And so the minister of defense and the general very thoughtfully provide me. *Scusi ma*...I am not Jesus Christ, and Easter is passed.

"One night the ministers will have me for dinner. Do you care, Cenci? Will you feel the slightest twinge of regret when they put me on the spit, or will you lick your lips. Your chance has come.

You will replace me. That's what you want, isn't it? Well, Cenci, remember, when my bones have been picked clean, the terror will not be over. Then our august ministers will need a new lamb, and whom will they look to then? Have you thought of *that?*

"So today I will stand before them and humbly but firmly propose decisive action. They'll nod their heads solemnly, and their eyes will gleam with anticipation. They have their man. General del Sarto has served them well. He has delivered their dinner, and an ample meal I'll make. Perhaps they'll even give me a new title—something with a ring of authority so that I'll sound like a person of olympic power when my number is called. I must be raised up to fall far enough, don't you think? Otherwise who would believe that a detective with three children and fourteen extra kilos weighing him down, a simple man, a little slow, perhaps a little plodding, who goes to the mountains when he can steal the time and find the money—that it is he who has failed the Republic? That he handed the country over to hoodlums masquerading as political saviors? I ask you, Cenci, is that any way to run a city?"

Officer Cenci listened dutifully—and made no reply. He had heard Felice's laments before. And he had no doubt that he would hear them again, and again. Felice waited too, with mounting exasperation. Was it indifference or condescension Cenci felt for him? Whichever, he was fortunate to have an assistant at all, let alone one as conscientious and clever as Officer Massimo Cenci. Time and again he'd seen an angle in a case that no one else had considered, and more often than not his hunch had proved right. Felice had a high regard for him professionally, but regretted that he wasn't simpatico. He was a compiler, a statistician. There wasn't any flesh and blood in his calculations. He didn't seem to realize that he was dealing with human lives.

Felice said abruptly: "You will drive me to Palazzo Chigi this afternoon. I'll need a friend at my right hand."

"But your chauffeur, sir—"

"Yes, I know, the chauffeur," Felice interrupted. "But I would like you to drive me today. It's an important meeting—for us both. Humor me, Cenci, this once. What time did the general say we should arrive?"

"The meeting is set for three o'clock, sir." Cenci was always precise in his speech. He was as exact and well ordered as the computer printouts he studied so closely.

"Ah, of course." Felice sighed. "Of course. The ministers must be refreshed by their siestas, or by whatever tempting midday morsel they have the balls to sample. But no matter. We will have something to tell them. Something decisive. *Magari.* We will request permission to make preparations for every contingency.

"Airport security must be tightened, your excellencies, to prevent another highjacking. Every major government office and tourist center must be guarded around the clock to prevent bombings." Felice resumed pacing the room, though with a more measured step, rehearsing for Cenci's benefit the performance he would put on two hours later before the cabinet of grave-faced ministers. "The multinationals, particularly the American companies, must be alerted to the escalating danger their executives face. Naturally we can't be expected to ensure their safety ourselves. After all, gentlemen, our resources are limited. But they must be urged to increase their own protection services—attack dogs, bulletproof vests and vehicles for all top-level personnel, armed guards for themselves and their families, et cetera, et cetera. And to prevent another kidnapping, the bodyguards must be tripled on our Christian Democratic leaders—*i signori* Andreotti and Fanfani, and on the chief of the PCI, Berlinguer. I am sure you share my sentiments, gentlemen, Italy cannot risk another *cosa di Moro.*"

Felice stopped in the middle of the room, clasped his hands together at chest level and gesticulated imploringly at his imaginary audience. "Distinguished statesmen, and today perhaps the saviors of our beloved country, I beg you to consider these requests favorably. The life of Italy is in your hands."

Felice threw up his own in disgust. *"Basta,* Felice! *Basta con il pagliaccio!"* He sank into his chair. He was stumped, and not for the first time, by these radical hoodlums.

"Ah, Cenci," he confessed, "it is all an act. Empty posturing.

Sometimes I think our country is composed of nothing but our heritage and our posturing. The substance is all behind us, and ahead...ahead is a black abyss and we are drawing closer with each bombing, each shooting, each senseless new act of violence. They are succeeding, Cenci. I feel it in my soul. They are moving us to the very rim while we gather in ornate palaces and shape speeches to deceive ourselves and satisfy our critics and superiors that something is being done.

"You're clever, Cenci, bright and clever. You've studied all the files. You know every bit of evidence as well or better than I. Tell me, what is your opinion?" Felice waved his hand in the air. "Forget for a moment that I am *il capo* and you are my assistant, forget titles and rank." He brought his open hand down on his desk so hard that he surprised himself with his violence. *"Porca troia,* Cenci, once, just this once, tell me what you think."

When Cenci spoke it was with his customary deference. "You are taking ever precaution, sir. You can't be faulted."

Felice laughed harshly. "Not this time, you mean, not this time. But that's not what I asked. I asked you what you think? Will all our guards prevent a highjacking at Fiumicino? Will all our security prevent a bomb from exploding in the Quirinale, or the Termini, or the American embassy, or God knows where?"

"Sir, our security measures will make it more difficult for the terrorists to operate, and might even deter them." Cenci spoke evenly, correctly.

Of course he was right. Felice didn't have to hear his measured words to know that he was simply stating the obvious. He was sure Cenci didn't respect either him or his intelligence. It was an attitude of deference, required when speaking to a superior. It was infuriating, and worse, it was debilitating. They'd been working together for five months night and day, and he hadn't once seen Cenci drop his professional guise. Maybe that's all there is, Felice thought. He is a modern man—an automaton, thorough, punctual and neat at all times. A machine.

Still, Felice couldn't accept that even if it was true. He was determined to break through to the man somehow. "I have told you about my Elena, Cenci. A man's woman is his most intimate possession, his most precious gift. Now tell me about yours."

"I'm not married, sir."

"Ah!" Felice began to rifle through the stack of fresh reports Cenci had put on his desk that morning. "Then tell me about your girl. Every young man has a girl. Surely you must have at least one." He smiled encouragement.

Cenci hesitated, as if considering the question closely. "No, sir, I have no girl in the way you mean."

Felice slapped the sides of his legs. "Cenci, Cenci, what do you mean, the way I mean? I've lived and made love for forty-five years. *Porca miseria!* There is only one way. It is hopeless, hopeless. My own assistant is a mystery to me so how can I expect to understand the terrorists—urban guerrillas, anarchists, lunatics, whatever they are. We arrest one, two, a dozen. It makes no difference. They go on as if untouched. The bombings, the knee-cappings, the arson. Ah, to have such faith in yourself. To see the right so clearly and follow it so resolutely. It is their certainty I envy. Even if it does come from their myopia."

Felice began walking the floor again, slowly, heavily. "Get out, Cenci. Go home. Take the rest of the day off. Find yourself a girl—*any* girl. Every man needs a girl—yes, the way *I* mean it, goddammit, the way *I* mean it."

"Are you sure there will be nothing else, sir?" Cenci stood at attention, a faithful soldier before a losing general. How well he played his role...

"Nothing, Cenci, nothing."

"You don't need me to drive you to Palazzo Chigi this afternoon?"

"Ah, the Chigi. I'd almost forgotten. No. I'll bear the slings and arrows of our leaders alone." He tried to smile but his face felt as though it were cast in plaster. He patted the younger man's shoulder instead. "You're a good man, Cenci. Forgive me an occasional outburst. We'll have a plate of pasta tomorrow and forget it, eh?"

"As you wish, sir." Cenci gave a curt bow and turned on his heel.

Alone in his office, Detective Felice sighed deeply and glanced at his watch. A fifteen-minute siesta. Better than nothing. He should be rested to meet the ministers. Clearing off the stacks of files, he stretched out on the couch. Am I any better than Cenci, he wondered? He fawns on me and I fawn on General del Sarto. Del Sarto fawns on the minister of defense, the minister fawns on Andreotti, Andreotti on Fanfani—and none of us respects the other. It's all a pretense, a necessity dictated by our inferior position, while secretly each of us believes he is the better man. Only one in all of Italy is beyond such petty politics. The pope, and he probably fawns on il Signore. Amen.

CHAPTER THIRTEEN

Paola was wrapping three flesh-colored utilitarian brassieres with huge cups, each one the size of a soup bowl. The woman making the purchase was as flat as a plate, and clearly embarrassed.

"They're not for me. You can see." She pointed to her own chest. "I don't even wear one. I have no need. They're for my daughter-in-law. She's just had a son and with the milk..." The woman gestured helplessly as if such a blatant display of sexuality was distasteful.

Paola smiled. "Congratulations. I hope he gives you much pleasure."

"He's my fifteenth."

"You are blessed, then."

"One more, one less." She took the package, shaking her head. "The mother is a cow. He'll be at her tit until he's twenty if she has her way."

Buscati fingered the lace edge of a chemise and studied Paola. She wasn't beautiful in the classical sense. Rather, she had that fleeting beauty typical of Roman girls of a certain age—between the onset of puberty and the beginning of maturity...generous, sensual features, clear golden skin tinged with pink, full firm breasts and a narrow waist. She would grow fat. Her legs and breasts would thicken with the first child, and increase with each additional one. Right now though, she was like a fruit at the moment of ripeness, to be plucked from the tree and enjoyed.

Paola tossed her head, shaking back her thick black hair, and looked around to see if any other customers needed assistance. Sandro held up the chemise—a shell-pink, satiny tricot with a deep border of a darker pink lace all around it. "Do you wear these things?"

Paola couldn't think of a clever answer. She couldn't think of anything at all to say. She'd recognized him immediately when he'd come into her department, but she'd thought it was just a coincidence. Handsome, self-assured boys like that never noticed her. She felt awkward and self-conscious. No man had ever spoken to her so boldly before.

He winked at her. "I'll buy it for you, if you promise to model it for me."

Paola blushed several shades pinker than the chemise. "Are you looking for a present for someone? If you tell me the size I'll try to help you." She tried to sound attentive and courteous, the way the training manager had told her she should approach an uncertain customer. Only she was the uncertain one. She sensed that he knew exactly what he wanted. "What were you looking for?"

"I've been looking for you. I think I've been in every department on every floor. I never thought I'd find you in panties and bras." He laughed at her embarrassment and scooped up a handful of pants. "Which do you wear—the plain cotton ones or these lacy things? Shall I guess?"

The other salesgirls were beginning to titter and nudge one another. When a woman bustled up to the counter and asked to look at slips, Paola turned gratefully to help her. Although she tried to concentrate on the new customer, she brought out the wrong size. While she was correcting her error Gabriella, her best friend at work, went over to talk to Buscati. One by one Paola took out every slip in size thirty-eight and stacked them on the counter. The woman unfolded each one, complaining vehemently all the while about the inefficient help. She went away, still complaining, without making a purchase.

Paola made a point of not looking over at Sandro and Gabriella, although from the sounds of his easy laughter and her animated chatter they seemed to be enjoying themselves. She took a long time folding the slips and putting them away. She was still folding when he came over and leaned across the counter so that he could speak to her alone, without the other clerks hearing.

"Don't you ever get out of here? I can't stand around looking at the merchandise forever and not buying something."

"I work until seven every evening," she replied primly.

"In that case I'll take this." He tossed the pink chemise on the counter. "Would you gift wrap it for me please."

Paola was all thumbs as she wrapped it up, even though she tried not to think about whom he was giving it to. He paid in cash and left with the package under his arm. Watching him go, she realized that she didn't even know his name. She'd have to ask Franco that night, not that it would make any difference. It had been a joke, he hadn't meant to be cruel. The other salesgirls were crowding around her, envious, curious, admiring. They didn't believe her when she said that he wasn't her boyfriend.

The rest of the day dragged on interminably. At seven sharp Paola bolted out of the store like an escaping prisoner. Sandro fell into step with her, taking her arm as though they were old friends to steer her through the throng that was spewing out of La Standa. "Do you mind if I walk with you?"

She shook her head. She didn't say that she'd been rushing to the bus. They walked slowly along the Corso, looking in all the shop windows. Although the street was crowded, Paola was aware only of him. He was talking easily about the other salesgirls and about Franco, saying how popular he was at the university and how well respected.

"We were members of the same club—a philosophical group, really—that's where we met. At one of the meetings Franco spoke about your father. The discussion was so interesting, I waited for

96

him afterward and we went on with it until morning. That's how we became friends."

Paola was acutely aware of his arm around hers, and of the package she'd wrapped, which was still tucked under the other one. As he talked, her mind kept drifting back to the girl, his girl. But at the Piazza del Popolo he stopped and gave her the present.

She blushed. "But I thought..."

He laughed. "You really didn't know it was for you?"

She shook her head and blushed deeper.

"Don't forget, it comes with a condition."

"But I don't even know your name?" Her voice was small, and her eyes were lowered, avoiding his.

He brushed her cheek with the back of his hand. "Buscati," he said. "Sandro Buscati."

He left her there at Piazza del Popolo, where she could catch the bus back to Ponte Milvio. For once the ride seemed as smooth as angels' wings and so short that she almost missed her stop. She was still entranced by Sandro. He gave the impression of being older than Franco, and so much more sophisticated. They seemed like incongruous friends, and yet he had praised her brother and spoken about him with such obvious affection it made Paola feel proud. She began to picture Franco in a new light.

When Paola got home her mother was in the window, with her rosary beads in her hand. Franco was trying to calm her, but he looked almost as worried. Paola always came right home after work.

Signora Mirabella burst into tears when she opened the door, alternately hugging and berating her. "Where have you been? It's almost eight o'clock! Look how black it is outside!"

Paola avoided their eyes. "I had to work late. The girl who had the evening shift went home sick. I had to take her place. I didn't get a chance to telephone." The chemise was stuffed in her pocketbook. She hadn't lied to her mother since she was a child.

The next morning Paola put on her best green dress and high-heeled sandals, even though she knew her feet would be aching by the end of the day. She brushed her hair over and over until it shone, pulled it back then let it fall loose and brushed it again. Still not satisfied with the way she looked, she tried a little bit of the makeup she had bought at least a year before but had never dared to use. Although she had gotten up early to allow herself plenty of time, she was late again. She ran through the kitchen, blowing a kiss in her mother's direction as she passed.

"Your breakfast, Paola," the signora called.

"You and Franco eat it for me. I don't have time."

The signora shook her head at her foolish daughter and her wasted breakfast. "*Mangia,* Paola," she shouted. "It's not good to go to work on an empty stomach."

"Don't worry, mama. I'll eat a big lunch."

At the store Paola's hopes surged as each customer approached, and each time she was disappointed. Although Sandro hadn't asked to see her again, she'd felt sure he'd come. But her confidence drained with the day. At the door she glanced around, not really expecting him to be waiting anymore but still hoping, then caught the bus home, thinking she'd been foolish, and wanting to die.

CHAPTER FOURTEEN

At quarter to three the armored cars began turning off the Corso into Piazza Colonna, where the column of Marcus Aurelius stands, erected in the second century to honor the emperor's victories over the Germans and Sarmatians. In a burst of ill-conceived piety some fourteen hundred years later, a statue of Saint Paul was placed on its summit in place of the emperor and his bride Faustina. In imperial times, the Piazza Colonna was the center of Rome; now it is the center for urgent, top-level deliberations.

The bulletproof vehicles circled the fountains where sculpted dolphins leap and drew up in front of the imposing facade of Palazzo Chigi, the official residence of the prime minister. The first car to arrive was a blue Alfetta carrying in its rear seat the minister of defense and General Andrea Del Sarto, chief of the antiterrorism squad. They hurried across the courtyard originally constructed for the Austro-Hungarian ambassador and disappeared inside, wearing faces of studied concern.

Less than a kilometer away a police siren added to the cacophony of horns, but it did nothing to unclog the snarl of traffic coming down from Piazza Barberini into Via del Tritone. Slumped alone in the back seat of his official car, Detective Felice accompanied the deafening siren with a flow of curses. There was no way to break through the congestion. "Del Sarto will see me hang by my feet for this. We were supposed to be the first to arrive—erect, polished, military bearing. Winning is as much appearance as anything. And just look at me."

His rumpled suit looked as if he'd slept in it, which he had. His fifteen-minute siesta had stretched to forty-five, because after he'd dismissed Cenci he'd forgotten to ask one of the secretaries to wake him. Cenci...he always seems to be at the root of my troubles.

"Let me out here, Mario," he said to the chauffeur. "I'll run the rest of the way." He groaned. "Jogging will be good for my waistline, if not for my suit. Go back, and if anyone wants me, I'm taking the rest of the afternoon off. God knows, I'll have earned it after the ministers are through carving me up."

Pushing open the car door, Felice started down Via del Tritone at a trot, painfully aware of the ridiculous picture he was making. He cut through the Galleria Colonna, not even glancing in the windows of the shopping arcade. Perspiration was beginning to dribble from his forehead and form full moons under the arms of his black suit. His breath was coming in shorter and shorter gasps. Still he paused every four or five steps to take a deep drag from the butt of a Nazionale, so short that it singed his lips when he inhaled.

He rushed on, consoling himself with the thought that once this meeting was over he would treat himself to a dish of *more*. Connoisseurs of ice cream invariably claim that the best *gelato* in Rome is at Tre Scalini on the west side of Piazza Navona. But Felice knew better. He'd grant that the ice cream there was very good, if overpriced, as it was at Rosati in Piazza del Popolo. The strawberry there was particularly good; but it didn't compare to the *more* just up the Corso from Piazza Colonna.

Felice smacked his lips in anticipation and stepped off the curb, holding up his right hand to stop the Cinquecenti, Lambrette and taxis whizzing by and behind him, horns blasting him, drivers raining a litany of abuse on him, condemning the misadventures of his daughter, wife, mother and grandmother.

"Permesso, permesso," Felice chanted as he stepped into the traffic. His hand still raised to ward off the speeding vehicles from his person, he proceeded across the street without stopping or slowing his pace. The Corso runs from Piazza Venezia north to Piazza del Popolo and is one of the busiest streets in the city. The big department stores, La Standa and Il Rinascente, are located there, as is the newspaper *Il Tempo* and the telephone company.

Once he had maneuvered safely across, he paused to light a fresh Nazionale with the butt of the exhausted one. In the relative tranquility of Piazza Colonna a line of limousines, with a liveried chauffeur behind the wheel of each, idled. Felice filled his lungs with nicotine and looked up at the column. Unlike Paul, he thought, I haven't come to convert the infidels but to pay homage to the hypocrites.

The frown that creased General del Sarto's face when his deputy chief entered the splendorous cabinet room was a clear statement of disdain. Felice seated himself against a wall, several yards from the gleaming table where the ministers were arrayed, as if he was unworthy to join in the first ring. Head bowed, he listened as the meeting was called to order.

The first to speak was the minister of finance, overseer of the Guarda di Finanze, the fiscal police. The distinguished finance minister never missed an opportunity to point up the ineptitude of the police units not under his control—namely Rome's Criminalpol, the equivalent of the FBI; the *polizia,* a useless law enforcement agency under the aegis of the Interior Department, and the tough, sometimes brutal, paramilitary Carabinieri, which included the Squadra Anti-terrorismo and was overseen by the Defense Department. Rivalry among the police forces virtually insured their ineffectiveness in stopping the spiral of violence fragmenting the country.

The minister of defense directed a grim, warning glance at General del Sarto. The finance minister's attack was a naked act of aggression. It could not go unanswered. The antiterrorist unit must have a strong response. General del Sarto looked in turn at his lieutenant. Detective Felice appeared to be continuing his siesta. His head had dropped and rested on the several chins that formed a cushion against his chest. The general's hands began to tremble with anger, and he clutched the edge of the table to steady them.

Felice was a true Roman—a Romano di Roma, born and bred in the Eternal City, but the general always thought of him as a southerner. Del Sarto didn't understand southerners. They might as well be another race. Like most northerners he referred disparagingly to all of his countrymen born south of Rome as "*i negri*" or "*Africani*." The great Italians were northerners—Michelangelo, Dante, Raphael, Garibaldi, Da Vinci. Southerners were indolent, slothful and infuriatingly slow. All they could do well was eat and make trouble. And that was just what he feared Felice was about to do for him now. Felice was a slogger, doggedly following every clue. But after Moro, it wasn't enough to say with sincerity, "We're working on it, an investigation takes time." Del Sarto prayed to the Holy Ghost to inspire the detective.

The minister of finance was still on the attack. He'd put on a pair of tinted glasses and was reading from an issue of the New York *Times* in the clipped accent of the British:

NEW ITALIAN TERROR SEEMINGLY RANDOM

BOMBINGS AND INDUSTRIAL SABOTAGE— REVENGE MAY BE THE MOTIVE

ROME—Italy has been plagued in recent weeks by a rapidly increasing number of terrorist attacks that follow no discernible pattern and cannot be traced to any known terrorist organization.

Cases of arson, bombings and industrial sabotage are reported daily from various regions. They occur in the normally peaceful south as well as in the industrial cities of the north, where terrorism has been most frequent. The number of incidents reported ranges to 10 or more a day; many, it appears, are not reported.

Last Friday on a busy street near the University of Rome in midafternoon, two young men wearing goggles and riding a motorcycle drew abreast of the car of Professor Silvio Messinetti, a prominent faculty member, and fired two shots at him, missing both times. The attackers followed the professor and, at the next traffic light, fired two more times. Then they disappeared.

Last Wednesday, in the middle of the night, the headquarters of the regional government of Rome was severely damaged in a blast that awakened people throughout the center of the city. Unlike previous terrorist attacks directed against deliberately selected, politically identifiable targets, such as prison wardens, magistrates, politicians and business executives dealing in labor relations, the recent wave of incidents appears to be "spontaneous" actions against targets of convenience that may have been chosen on the basis of whim rather than political doctrine.

"Et cetera, et cetera. And there is more." He squinted behind his violet glasses. "*Vede pagina trent-otto.*" He tossed the newspaper down on the gleaming mahogany table. "This is only one report out of how many? Our failures are broadcast around the world. In the eyes of the international community Italy has become a free-fire zone, a no-man's land. Not one of us is secure in his own home or automobile. We dare not move without a falange of bodyguards. And still we're unsafe. Our firmness gained nothing.

Moro was a beginning—not an end, and we are all his potential successors. Gentlemen, I ask you, was Aldo Moro sacrificed in vain?"

The debate was opened, the sides quickly drawn. Felice listened halfheartedly while the minister of the interior presented his defense, hinting of major arrests that the *polizia* was about to make and, not until the end, somewhat abashed, admitting that a new rash of violence was indeed spreading through Italy like a plague. The minister of defense rose next and presented General Del Sarto so that he could explain what his antiterrorist squad was doing to counter the new surge and, not incidentally, so that he could be held responsible if the measures proved inadequate. General del Sarto, in turn, promptly yielded the floor to Detective Felice.

Felice rose from the shadows, clearing his throat like a transmission that turns over but won't start. If he had any doubts about why he was there, the expressions on the ministers' faces dispelled them. They were appraising him the way a *donna di casa* looked at a freshly slaughtered carcass hanging in the open market. Felice shifted his considerable weight and approached the first circle.

"*Eccellenzi,* our nation is threatened once more. When we buried our beloved leader Aldo Moro, a blessed calm seemed to descend on our city. We Romans let out our breath and turned our attention to our personal preoccupation this time of year—how to escape from the summer sun that grows more relentless each day. Did any one of us suspect that this was an unnatural calm, a prelude to a new epidemic of terror?"

He moved closer to the long polished table. "One week of quiet passed, then a distinguished justice was murdered in Milan and the reports began filtering into the Questura. An intelligence report from the Israeli Mossad relayed word of a movement of arms from Libyan sources known to be sympathetic to terrorist groups. The Mossad has reason to suspect the shipments were earmarked for Italy. And so it goes, gentlemen, from every intelligence agency. Now an outbreak of violence is sweeping the nation—kneecappings, bombings, burnings—from Turin to Naples."

Felice blinked his hooded eyes and with a broad theatrical gesture launched into the speech he had rehearsed with Cenci. He held the ministers' attention—because of what he was saying or because they saw in him a potential scapegoat, he couldn't be sure. Either way, it didn't matter. Only a miracle could stop this reign of terror. His days were numbered, and he knew it. I'm free, he thought, free to be as imprudent as I dare. He took a long stride, which brought him flush with the ministers' table. The supplicant had become a Savonarola.

"Should we declare war?" he demanded. "That is the question this Consiglio dei Ministri has to answer today. If we do, we must fight back with the full power and resources of the state, and risk losing our children. If we don't, we may well lose our country. The choice, gentlemen, is yours: our children or our motherland?"

Felice knew that an Italian man with his back to the wall would always choose his mother. He sat at a small table in the window where he could look out at the shoppers passing by and let a spoonful of *gelato* melt on his tongue, savoring the indescribable flavor of the fresh blackberry ice cream. Only a few years before, this had been an elegant, old-style café, like the Caffe Greco on Via Condotti. The leather banquettes had been ripped out and a modern trattoria installed, better suited to the needs of the salesclerks and office workers who crowded the Corso. The new trattoria had a *tavola calda* with cafeteria-style service for workers rushing to cram as much into their lunch break as possible. For those who still preferred the leisurely, traditional way of taking a meal, there were small round tables served by waiters in long, white aprons and black bow ties. Best of all, the prices were reasonable. A serving of lasagna forno, a breast of chicken in rosemary, a small *salata mista,* a carafe of wine and an espresso *doppio* could be enjoyed for three thousand lire.

Felice took another large spoonful of *more* and closed his eyes. The flavor was exquisite. He was pleased, even a little proud, of his performance. He'd cut through the official rhetoric and stated the case decisively. In the deliberations that followed, the Squadra

Anti-terrorismo was voted every power he had requested. By tomorrow the stepped-up security measures would begin to go into effect. No doubt Officer Cenci would be pleased with the additional work and the authority they would command at least temporarily.

Felice ordered a second dish of ice cream. He knew he shouldn't. Elena would disapprove, but he was celebrating. He put his hand on his gut, as if measuring it. General del Sarto and the minister had both praised his speech. After the meeting had adjourned they'd clasped his shoulder, his tardiness forgotten, and spoken warmly, even fraternally.

Felice tasted his espresso. Everything he'd said was true and necessary, yet he had a nagging feeling that he'd missed a vital point. He had studied the terrorists so long he felt he knew them better than he knew his own children. One thing he was sure of...they wouldn't be content with small targets—not after Moro. The run of kneecappings and bombings, terrible as they were, had to point to something bigger.

Felice attacked his second *gelato* and tried to think like an immature, overconfident zealot, still flush with his first triumphant mission. What could be more devastating to Italy than that audacious kidnapping and brutal slaying? Another kidnapping, perhaps, but whom would they seize? He spooned the *more* slowly. What would the foreign experts do, he wondered, the officious Germans and arrogant Americans who had rushed in with their grand schemes to rescue Moro?

The Italians are different, the outsider says. True, but not very profound. So is everybody. What the outsider means is that Italians are happy-go-lucky macaroni-eaters with a song in their heart and sex on the brain. They're not flesh-and-blood with dreams and troubles, merely cartoon characters. He sipped his coffee and peered into the distance. During the war men were killing each other right outside these windows. American patrols had a sharp exchange with retreating Germans on the Corso. Would I have fought then? Would I have worn the black shirt? If I'd refused, think of the shame to my family, my father's embarrassment—a coward for a son. I wouldn't have the courage to bear that. I was one of the lucky ones. I escaped the decision. I escaped the bullets, the death and decay, because I happened to be born a few years too late. Perhaps that's why I went into the police...to make up, to apologize for my luck, my *buona fortuna*. I only suffered hunger, cold and fear.

I'm not an honest man—not even with myself. I went into the police because I didn't want to wait tables, to be forced to put on a smile and a slavish face every morning with my black coat, starched shirt and bow tie. And for the pay, which I thought a fortune then. He shoveled the blackberry sherbet into his mouth, then sipped the oily coffee. A girl stood on the curb, her back to him, facing the open square and the column of Marcus Aurelius, now usurped by Saint Paul, the slanting sun revealing the outline of her legs through her filmy skirt. Sex on the brain? Well, why not. We're Italians. Outsiders know that. Bring on the pasta and vino! Bring on the legs and ass! "*Cameriere*, bring the check!"

CHAPTER FIFTEEN

The minister of finance wasn't the only one to read the brief one-column article, datelined Rome, in the New York *Times*. At NATO headquarters in Brussels, General Alexander Haig studied it with concern. In Washington, Bonn, London and Paris it was noted with alarm. The New York *Times*—together with *Il Corriere della Sera, Le Monde, The Times of London, Frankfurter Zeitung* and Soviet *Tass*—were digested and fed to every leader in the NATO alliance. Within hours of reading the story the lines began to buzz at the central telephone exchange in EUR, where all calls were recorded. From Casa Rosa, where the American ambassador was pedaling furiously on his exercise bike; from Villa Wolkonsky, where the British ambassador was working the *Times* crossword puzzle; from Palazzo Farnese, where the French ambassador was submitting to his daily manicure, calls were made to the Quirinale, residence of the president of the Republic of Italy. The messages were the same. Behind the diplomatic phrases and offers of assistance was the fear that Italy's internal turmoil posed a threat to NATO, and that if the violence continued unchecked it would foment incidents in their own countries. From the Weathermen to the Baader-

Meinhoff gang, all would feel strengthened. International terrorism could not be contained unless it was dealt a lethal blow in Italy. The president responded with a confidence tinged with smugness, enumerating the emergency measures that even then were being put into operation.

CHAPTER SIXTEEN

Lisa arched her shoulders back and stretched. Her toes dug into the coarse sand. The narrow beach was hemmed in with parasols, cabanas and dark flesh. Her body glistened with sweat and lotion. Four days at Ischia had bleached her hair and turned her skin a golden brown. She picked up the bra of her lavender bikini and put it on as she walked toward the water, wading out until the sea was lapping around her thighs. The Mediterranean stretched around her as far as the eye could see, and straight ahead rose a deserted castle as big as the tiny island it inhabited. Every islander had a story about the castle, and each swore his was the truth. She dove in, swimming underwater as long as she could, then surfaced and floated on her back. She was still far from the castle. Each day she tried to swim out to it, and each day she fell short of her mark.

If paradise had not been located between the Tigris and Euphrates, it might have been a small island in a turquoise sea called Ischia. Vineyards pregnant with golden grapes entwine over terraced hills. Orange and lemon trees shade stucco villas, and all around, on every side the blue-green water laps serenely. Lisa found paradise stifling. She was impatient in the Garden of Eden.

Across the same expanse of sea that separates two continents Luigi Domenica spat the muddy coffee on the ground. Two weeks in the Palestinian refugee camp, cooped up in a filthy tent, had drained his patience.

"You've kept me waiting for that? Two days ago you promised me an arsenal, and now it's a handful of rifles and a few grenades." He flayed at the voracious mosquitoes that circled his head.

Arafat watched, fleshy lips, like overripe persimmons, drawn back in a persistent smile. "Regrettably, it is the best I can do."

"You let me stew in this hellhole you call a refugee camp while you sat in air-conditioned comfort taking orders from the Russian ambassador."

"Of course, if you would say what the operation is you're planning"—Arafat's voice was eminently agreeable—"perhaps later, in a week, a month..."

"I know your game, Arafat. You're nothing but a Kremlin toadie."

"That's the best I can do for you, take it or leave it, my friend."

Domenica lunged at him, grabbing the Bedouin kaffiyeh that had become his trademark around the world. His bodyguards were already rushing into the tent with fixed bayonets and switches cut from palm trees.

"When the true revolution comes, you'll be the first to hang." Domenica spat at him and received a switch across the mouth. The sharp edge of the palm cut through his lower lip. He felt the sting of the white-green palm across his neck and tried to shield himself as the guards went to work on his head, his stomach and his testicles.

Arafat watched impassively. "Whip him well, then let him go. We are all brothers in the struggle."

Although Domenica had been trained in the PFLP camp, a rival to the PLO, in Hamouniya, south of Damascus, he was no match

for the Bedouin guards in size or sadism. They beat him unconscious, and then some more, having nothing better to do. Barefoot
boys, brown with dust, peered under the flaps of the tent and
cheered on the guards.

In the morning Domenica cleaned his wounds as best he could
in a trough of muddy water. He tried to take off his torn clothes,
but blood and pus had welded them to his flesh. He put clean
clothes on over them. Then he left Beirut, renting a helicopter
to fly him to Tripoli to pick up the matériel Lisa had been promised. He did not see Yasir Arafat or his guards again, and no one
tried to stop him.

Qaddafi was praying in the desert. Domenica was met instead
by an American in chinos and an open-neck, short-sleeved shirt
who trained the Libyan forces.

"We were expecting you two days ago."

"As you can probably see, I was detained."

"What happened? You look like you went fifteen rounds with
a tank!"

"I wish I had. A tank wouldn't be as rough as Arafat's boys."
Domenica hadn't seen himself in the mirror, but if he looked half
as bad as he felt, he must be a sight. One eye was swollen shut;
his lip was split; a long straight cut ran the length of his left cheek.
Both sides of his body from his neck to his knees were a mass of
raw flesh.

The American didn't ask any more questions. Lisa's order was
packed and ready for shipment. There was no haggling over num-
bers or prices. He had received the order and filled it exactly.
Domenica went down the invoice, ticking off the contents like a
housewife checking her grocery list: two dozen Kalashnikov AK-
47 rifles; seven Dragunov sniper's rifles; five V-40 Soviet percus-
sion grenades; one hundred Mauser automatics; forty-eight Uzi
submachine guns; fifty pounds of C-4; one hundred pounds of
gelignite...

When he'd finished, the American was shaking his head. "You
can have the stuff tonight, but not looking like that. You're too

112

conspicuous. I'll give you the name of a doctor who won't ask any questions. Just tell him I sent you."

Michele Di Voto, his swarthy skin sunburned black, jackknifed from a 36-foot yacht anchored off the tip of Malta and swam in widening circles off the bow. Two girls in string bikini bottoms and bare breasts tossed purple grapes down at him from the deck. He laughed and swam back, climbing up the rope ladder they dropped over the side.

"I almost drowned," he panted dramatically. "I think I need mouth-to-mouth resuscitation." He fell down on the deck, pulling the girls down with him. He'd brought one along for his friend Domenica. In the meantime, he'd tried her out to make sure she was good enough. They giggled and went to work, one at each end. It was the last time he'd have them both to himself—not that he was selfish...

At dawn a fishing boat with a Libyan crew pulled alongside the yacht. By the time the girls woke up they were already halfway back to Naples. Domenica didn't have the strength for a girl. Di Voto dropped them off at Capri in a flurry of *abbraci,* then went on to Ischia, where Lisa waited impatiently.

She and Di Voto caught the last hydrofoil to the mainland. He stayed in Naples while she returned by train to Rome, going directly from the station to her father's apartment on the Palatine. In the morning she gave the elderly servant couple an extra day off. They kissed her hand in gratitude. They would go to the sanitarium to visit their retarded son as they did every week on their day off. But first the cook insisted on bringing Lisa breakfast in bed, carrying it in already dressed in her street clothes, a once-chic straw hat sitting squarely on her forehead. She beamed when Lisa complimented her on the hat. It was one of Babe's discards with a net veil and jaunty yellow rose that looked ridiculous on the old woman.

Lisa ate the breakfast slowly, then pampered herself with a bubble bath and pedicure while she waited.

* * *

In the waters off Naples a fishing skiff, coming in with the morning catch, paused beside the yacht. The cargo was off-loaded onto the skiff and hidden beneath the fish. At the dock Di Voto waited with a truck rented that same morning and driver to transport the fresh fish to Rome for delivery at the best restaurants. The rest of the cargo would prove less digestible.

CHAPTER SEVENTEEN

Paola wore her comfortable wedges with the rubber platform soles again. She was glad she had because it was the first day of a lingerie sale and the customers streamed in, one more demanding than the next. She was too busy to think about Sandro Buscati, which was just as well because her mother would never allow her to see him. By seven o'clock her feet ached even in the wedges. All she wanted to do was soak in a warm tub. She hurried out, not bothering to look left or right, intent on getting home. Paola didn't so much see as sense him beside her. He was out of breath, as if he'd been running.

"I was afraid I'd miss you." Sandro smiled.

"You almost did," Paola said, and felt foolish for making such a dumb remark. She forgot how tired she was. She even forgot her sore feet.

"Do you have another date?"

She shook her head. "Only with my dinner."

"Good, then you can tell me about yourself. I want to know everything about you." He took her hand as if he'd done it a thousand times before, slipping his fingers between hers, and they started to walk up the Corso toward Piazza del Popolo.

"There's nothing really to tell. I live in Ponte Milvio with my mother and brother and I work at La Standa. I was studying at the university, but my father died two years ago and we needed the extra money." She felt compelled to explain why she was a salesgirl. Sandro, despite his worn jeans and scuffed work boots, was obviously not from the working classes.

"I know, Franco told me. He's bitter and, I think, a little guilty about your father's death."

"We all are. There are things I guess we never get over, and *babbo* was such a mountain of a man—not in physical size. He was actually short and quite round. We always teased him, saying that with his ruddy complexion and round face and belly he looked like a beach ball. But he had a tremendous mind and spirit." Paola found herself unaccountably opening up to Sandro in a way she'd never done with anyone before—except her father—and he was listening closely. It was the first time that she'd been able to talk about her father since his death. "We could almost see him begin to fail the night Franco left home. He was a colossus one day, then all of a sudden he seemed to crumble.

"Until then I'd always thought I was his favorite. He never seemed to pay much attention to Franco. Franco was mama's boy, I was *babbo*'s girl. But that Sunday night after dinner Franco and he argued over politics. He'd never touched either of us before, but he was so angry he hit Franco. After that he became an old man. He shriveled, and in a few months he was dead. The doctors said it was a coronary, but he'd never had any trouble with his heart before."

"He must have been an extraordinary man. I know from his columns in *l'Osservatore Romano* that he was a distinguished journalist, but Franco says he was also one of Pope Paul's friends and advisers for nearly forty years."

Paola nodded. She didn't trust herself to answer, although knowing that Franco had spoken with pride, even affection, about their father eased the pain of loss. She felt guilty that she'd been judging her brother so harshly.

The crowds on the Corso were thinner now. Dusk was settling over the Eternal City, muting its earthen shades. She felt Sandro's gaze on her and looked up to meet his eyes, which held her like a soft caress.

"Is it true, as Franco says, that the Vatican is like a second home to you?"

Paola laughed lightly, pleased to discover that he was impressed. So Franco had even been boasting a little about il Papa! "Everyone is always amazed. But it's nothing really. My father was a friend of Monsignor Montini, and when he became pope their friendship continued. We rarely go to the Vatican now. Still, my mother is always anxious. She stays in touch with her friend Suor Marianna, who keeps il Papa's apartment, and if anything is needed my mother is happy to oblige." She blushed, always a little embarrassed by the awe with which this knowledge was received.

Sandro squeezed her hand tighter. "I envy you and Franco. I never knew either my mother or my father. My father was the last of an old and very proud Tuscan family. My mother was from the south, from Sorrento. Not a typical southern peasant, but a fair beauty who I think must have brought a special sort of exuberance to the restrained character of my father. At least that's what I've always imagined from the browned photograph I have and the few people I've been able to talk to about them." His voice was so low Paola had to strain to hear him, and his eyes, which were as shaded now as the evening, seemed fixed on something distant. "I have no other memories to rely on. I was an infant when they died. They were the last of the underground killed, blown-up by a hand grenade mistakenly thrown by fellow partisans after il Duce had swung by his feet and the Führer had gone to his Götterdämmerung among the petrol cans. I lived with my grandfather when I was a boy...he has little use for me now."

"*Poverino*," Paola said quietly. They seemed sealed in a bond of intimacy and loss.

Sandro walked the rest of the way to Piazza del Popolo in silence. At Rosati he bought strawberry ice cream and they sat outside at one of the tables to eat it.

117

"Do you know how beautiful you are, Paola?" He reached over and wiped a trace of strawberry from the corner of her mouth with his finger.

She shook her head.

"You're very beautiful, as beautiful as a Leonardo madonna."

She knew she looked awful, still for that moment she believed him.

When Paola got home the signora was in the window with her rosary again. Paola told the same lie as before. The next day she would tell it a third time.

CHAPTER EIGHTEEN

It was a perfect Sunday, azure-clear with the sun warm and comforting. The horses pawed the manicured grass, tossing their aristocratic heads impatiently. More than a dozen flags fluttered over the elliptical track: the red, white and green of Italy beside the Union Jack; the emerald green with the golden harp of Ireland alongside the French tricolor; the Canadian maple leaf brushing the red, black and yellow of the Republic of West Germany.

In Piazza di Siena in the Borghese Gardens, just a stone's throw from Porta Pinciana, gateway to the Via Veneto and a kilometer or two from the heart of a city crippled with fear by urban terrorists, the Twenty-fourth International Horse Show, sponsored by Marlboro cigarettes, was under way. The elliptical track looked like a brilliant rendition of a more graceful, mannered era when the only bombs most people knew were rich desserts and guns were aimed mostly at pheasant and fox. The grass was cropped to a velvet carpet and dotted with colorful obstacles: red-and-white-striped poles laid horizontally one on top of the other, shallow pools of green water, blue fences as high as a horse's shoulder. In the grandstands spectators shed their coats and jackets for the first time that year.

Piero Massi sat alone, seemingly intent on the spectacle unfolding in front of him, and waited as he'd done so many times before in different preselected spots in different cities and towns, always following his instructions to the letter. He'd grown accustomed to waiting. But this Sunday noon he was unusually nervous. He twisted the *biglietto di ingresso,* winding it around his fingers until it assumed its own cylindrical shape. He had handed over three one thousand lire bills at the gate for this ticket that assured him entrance to the *settore del recinto tribune raffaello*—the section of reserved seats called Raffaello. We are hopeless, we Italians, he thought, with our illusions of grandeur. Six hundred years later and we're still trying to live off past glories. We even name a section of seats at a horse show Raffaello. Absurd!

The Piazza di Siena is a rustic amphitheater, encircled by a wooden fence lined with pots of coral rose bushes. At the far side of the ring, across from Massi, four patrician cypresses stood in state. Between the center two was a canopied judges' stand. Above it the flags unfurled, and beyond them, dwarfing the national ensigns, towered a spray of umbrella pines.

It was a spectacle of color and order, of rules and etiquette, an anachronism in a Roman season of terror. The horses groomed, trained and bred to their last hair; the riders stiff-backed and immaculate in white jodhpurs, gleaming black knee-high boots, scarlet jackets and hard black velvet hats; the obstacles brightly painted and precisely placed. Piero Massi, catalyst of chaos, admired its order and precision. A different kind of order and precision was required in his work. It was the only way to produce anarchy. The state would trip and fall on the precise obstacles he and his comrades constructed. It didn't possess the wisdom or the discipline of the golden horse that was flying clear of the lattice fence beyond which a neatly trimmed privet hedge was planted. The state had flexed its muscles for the last time with Moro. Buscati was right, at least that far. It didn't have the stomach to resist again. The squabbles had already begun, the recriminations and finger-pointing, the accusations over who was responsible for the sacrifice of Moro. He smiled as he thought of Detective Felice rehearsing his speech to the ministers...

Now a stocky man edged his way down the row of wooden chairs. "*Permesso,* signore."

"*Prego,*" Massi responded.

"*Grazie, grazie tanto.*"

Massi glanced at the man settling himself in the next seat. He was dressed formally in a dark suit cut with all the style of a cardboard carton—white starched shirt and narrow black tie. His florid face was beaming in a grateful smile. He was about five feet seven with a fatty cyst, also florid, on his left cheek just below the eye, and with thinning black hair which he combed forward in an effort to hide a bald spot.

Massi knew the face well. Vladimir Vishnevsky, consular assistant for cultural exchange at the Russian embassy, KGB colonel specializing in external subversion—his operator. Every time they made contact, Massi wondered why a master Kremlin spy could not find a more convincing way to disguise his baldness, and thereby his vanity.

Vishnevsky riffled through his program like an interested spectator. "*Permesso,* signore." He beamed at Massi again. "Would you tell me, have I missed many mounts?"

Massi smiled back less warmly, but enough for a casual observer to conclude that the seeds of an afternoon camaraderie were taking root. "*Soltante due. Questa qui é il terza.*"

"*Abbene.*"

They sat watching the performance, exchanging occasional comments about the horses and their riders through the next two contestants.

The Russian pulled a large grayish handkerchief from his pocket and wiped his mouth. "I think I will pay a visit to the refreshment tent. May I get you something?"

"No, *grazie.*"

"Perhaps, then, you would like to accompany me, just to stretch your legs, have a little promenade," Vishnevsky said. "I would be honored by your company."

Massi felt his stomach turn over. The invitation was too drawn out. A contact should be swift and clean—not so abrupt as to garble orders nor so prolonged as to risk a passerby remembering the two faces together.

"A splendid idea." Massi got up stiffly. A shared meal would appear to seal their new-struck friendship. They threaded their way through the crowds that were heading for the green-and-white tents set up to the rear of the grandstands. Whatever the occasion, no Italian could enjoy a spectacle, however vivid, on an empty stomach.

The tents sheltered a feast. The smaller one held a full bar—wine, American whiskey, Perroni, Coca-Cola, *limonata*. Vishnevsky exchanged a crumpled five hundred lire note for a carafe of red wine. Beyond the bar a larger tent covered a cold buffet of mortadella, salami, prosciutto *cruda*, salads of every variety, bread and cheeses. Beside it on a longer table was the *tavola calda:* steaming cauldrons of pasta, lasagna, chicken sautéed in wines and herbs, cacciatori and lamb stew. At the far end was a smaller stand, surrounded by children pushing their coins up, fighting each other for the next *gelato*.

Balancing a full plate and the carafe of wine, Vishnevsky led the way back to the stands. He passed the row where they had been sitting and chose two seats to the right and farther in front, where the view was poorer and the privacy greater. Massi followed warily. He sat in silence, watching the Russian's plate as maccarone after maccarone disappeared, the chicken stripped from the bone, a thick slice of bread wiped over the entire surface of the plate, sweeping it clean.

The two hadn't spoken since they returned to their seats. Eating had completely occupied Vishnevsky. It was a bad sign, Massi thought. Balanced on his lap was a paper plate with a single chicken leg untouched. Vishnevsky pulled out the soiled handkerchief again, blew his nose and wiped his porcine lips in a single gesture. His mouth was still stained purple with wine.

"You should be honored, comrade. Your report was taken to the highest authorities. Beyond the KGB." He spoke heartily.

Massi suppressed a smile of pride. He was more human than

Felice knew, than, as Cenci, Massi would allow him to know.

"The answer came this morning." Vishnevsky paused to stuff the cloth back in his pocket. "Moscow knows nothing of this plot, and wants to know nothing."

"You're going to let us...let Buscati proceed then?" Massi asked incredulously.

"Have you lost your senses, comrade? The Fisherman must not be touched. Moscow is unequivocal. True, Paul hates us." Vishnevsky smiled. "Even a Roman Catholic pontiff is allowed to feel hatred so long as it is directed against a devil. But it is also true that he is a shrewd political realist, a pragmatist. Power and its delicate balance is like a game of chess. You sacrifice a loss for a gain, carefully considered and measured. An exacting sport. This Fisherman is a chess master. Moscow can understand, even respect, his ambitions for his Church. So long, of course, as he does not cause us undue problems. His predecessor, Roncalli, so much loved and so much the fool, understood nothing—not even his own impulsiveness or the chaos it created. No, this chess master must not be touched. We do not want another Roncalli. Most especially we do not want Cardinal Zanelli."

Massi nodded. "Just as I imagined from the first. It is madness, utter madness, and counterproductive as well."

"Exactly."

"I told them as much, but they don't want to know. Our new leader, this bourgeois Buscati, protégé of Berlinguer, believes we Italians are independent. Believes that when the deed is done Moscow will applaud the daring blow he has struck for international revolution. He is a political child, so naïve. He wants the world to wait on his command."

"We know about Buscati. A hothead, impulsive like his father. Too bad he didn't inherit more of his mother's deliberate coolness." Vishnevsky smiled benignly as if he were commenting on the grace of the contestant who was clearing the privet hedge. "What a sight, what form, what color! So much for exhibitionists. Your Buscati, he is an exhibitionist, is he not? But no matter. Moscow has confidence. He can be controlled."

123

Massi picked up the chicken leg and bit into it. It was cold and greasy. The oil had coalesced, forming a thick glaze. He wasn't particularly hungry anyway.

The Russian considered the cold chicken leg. "*Mangia, mangia,* you will need all your strength. Moscow is pleased with you, Comrade Massi. Very pleased."

"I have tried to serve faithfully and well—"

"So you have, comrade. That is why Moscow has put the safety of the Fisherman in your hands." Vishnevsky leaned close and whispered harshly. "Buscati must be stopped—now."

"Yes, yes, I couldn't agree more."

The change in the Russian's tone was abrupt and unexpected. His breath was heavy with the smell of the wine. Massi's throat felt dry. He wished he'd ordered a cold drink.

"That's easily accomplished," he rushed on. "An anonymous tip to the director of the Antiterrorist Squad warning that Moro's successor has been chosen and that he wears the shoes of the Fisherman...it can be done tomorrow..."

The Russian smirked. "A simple matter with many drawbacks." His eyes were fixed on the intense young fräulein clearing the last obstacle.

"Twelve seconds ten, three errors," the announcer proclaimed over the thronged piazza. The girl wept.

"Moscow would not be amused by your proposal. First and most obvious, you would be compromised immediately, and then you'd be no further use to us. You are replaceable, naturally. We all are. But, between us, why deliver your own death sentence?"

Massi grimaced.

"But there is a more important fact to consider than the length of your life. We don't want any alarms sounded. You must convince your *covo* to abandon this plan before anyone suspects it was ever conceived."

"And if it is not convinced?"

It seemed to Massi that Vishnevsky waited too long to respond.

"Moscow would not understand such a question."

Massi steamed. Vishnevsky couldn't have conveyed his message correctly. "I told you to make it clear, Buscati is a megalomaniac, intoxicated by all the attention. He wants to outdo himself. The next strike must be even bigger, more dangerous, more shocking than before. More, more, more. That's all he understands. He insists we must strike again, now, while the world still cowers in fear. And our blow must make the Moro slaying seem like an act of mercy. We must bring Italy to a halt—and not just Italy, as he puts it, but the whole corrupt imperialistic Western world.

"Do you know what the fool said? 'We pierced the heart of Italy's political system, now we must strike the organ in its sanctified, mysticized, counterrevolutionary bourgeois soul. Who is more important to Italy than Moro? Not Fanfani. Not Andreotti. Not Berlinguer. No, there is only one, and we must seize him as we seized Moro.'"

"Why haven't you taken charge of your own *covo*? That is what Moscow ordered."

"He caught me by surprise while I was preparing to make my move."

"You don't like Comrade Buscati?"

Massi snorted, "Buscati will always be the aristocrat playing down to the masses. Though he tries hard to disguise it his arrogance betrays him in subtle ways—in the accent of his speech, the imperiousness of his manner, in his ignorance of poverty and pain and the anger they breed, his indifference..."

Vishnevsky's florid face reddened more. "You are jealous. You lose your judgment before Buscati. That is perhaps why you weren't sufficiently convincing."

Massi flared at the charge. "But..." Vishnevsky held up a hand to caution him, to remind him he was in danger of calling attention to them. "No matter, remember...we're here to judge the performance of the English lord and the Irish officer. Not of Comrade Massi."

Massi concentrated on the course to calm himself. The Irish army captain in full uniform, ramrod straight on the back of a chestnut mare, was vaulting the first hurdle. The captain, his face grimly set in the warm Italian sun, flew into the air, horse and rider one, clearing the fence cleanly. But it wasn't a gain he could afford to celebrate. The next hurdle was only a stride away. Each hurdle had to be met and mastered in the briefest possible time. The test was not of form alone, nor of speed, but of the two—a double challenge.

Massi enunciated each word. "You must make it clear, Vishnevsky. It is too late to dissuade the *covo*. Buscati has divided us so that he alone has control. The operation must be stopped by some other means. The first steps have already been taken. The boy Franco Mirabella has penetrated the Vatican to collect information about the pope's regimen, to inform us of his movements. Taglia and I have begun staging the usual incidents to divert the police. Domenica and Di Voto are already stockpiling weapons, commandeering vehicles—"

"We know. The PLO has made reports. So have Germany and Czechoslovakia. If your comrades are as stubborn as they are industrious, then you must find other... other more decisive ways to stop them."

"Are you asking me to betray my comrades?"

Vishnevsky's smile was indulgent. "Of course not, comrade. Moscow does not ask you to give the kiss of Judas... unless, of course, there is no other way. I surprise you that I know Judas Iscariot? Don't judge so facilely, my friend. I am not the ignorant, strong man that you think. That too, but not only. No matter. The Fisherman's safety is in your hands. Moscow has left the details to you, to show the faith we have in your skill and loyalty."

"You are asking me to prove my loyalty to you by being disloyal to my closest comrades if necessary?"

"That is perhaps one way of looking at the matter."

"You are asking me to choose," Massi persisted.

Vishnevsky shook his head. "The naïveté you display today does not become you, comrade. It insults your intelligence, and my own. You *made* that choice a long time ago."

In the grandstands around them there was a collective catch of breath. The Irish captain's mare had stumbled on the horizontal bars, catching her left rear hoof on the top rung and somersaulting over. Two men in khaki uniforms rushed onto the course and lunged for the loose reins. The horse bared her teeth and whinnied.

The captain picked himself up, bruised and muddied, and walked toward the frightened horse, murmuring softly as he approached. The animal whinnied again, then quieted and allowed her master to lead her limping off the course. To what fate? A warm compress, ointment, rest and then another show? Or a quick bullet to the brain—no more pain, no more challenges? Piero Massi considered the fate of the animal as if it were his own...

"You must make them understand, Vishnevsky, this is no time to play games. Buscati is not a total fool...he knows the Vatican is impregnable. So he plans to make the Fisherman come to us...willingly. He'll be taken—"

"Moscow knows nothing," Vishnevsky cut in harshly. "We know only Piero Massi. And we will not forget him. So you see, my friend, how trusted you are." He reached over and squeezed Massi's thigh. "We won't meet again. Not until the Kremlin is satisfied that the Fisherman is safe in his summer dacha."

Across the course the cypresses and umbrella pines shuddered as a cool breeze filtered through them. Mama, mama, mama. For the first time that he could remember Massi yearned for the smothering embrace, the stifling bosom, the hollered commands, the total control. In the tradition of Italian mothers she had manipulated him at least as skillfully as his KGB officer. But she was no Abraham. She would never sacrifice him on her sacred altar, as Vishnevsky was doing now.

Massi felt his glasses slip down the bridge of his nose as the clammy moisture of fear gathered. He took them off. The white horizontal poles striped with brilliant vermilion and stacked horizontally two abreast, the white lattice fence and the dark green of the privet hedge, the yellow-and-green barriers, the squares of black, yellow and white, alternating like a checkerboard—all the vibrant colors of the course and its obstacles, the riders and their horses—blurred like a watercolor in a flood. Without his glasses Massi was helpless. Edges dissolved, colors ran together. He polished the lenses carefully, wiped the frames dry and dabbed the sweat from his face. "The sun is growing more intense," he said.

Vishnevsky smiled as Massi put his glasses back on. He wasn't deceived. The glasses began to slip slowly down the bridge of Massi's nose again. He quickly pushed them back with his thumb.

"Don't fail us, comrade." Vishnevsky squeezed Massi's thigh again as he got up. "I don't have to tell you what the cost would be, even for one who has served as faithfully and well as you."

CHAPTER NINETEEN

The sun sets in the west in Rome as it does everywhere, but in Rome it sets behind St. Peter's. One may sit on the Pincio, as they did in the old days, at the Caffe Valadier, take an aperitivo and enjoy the spectacle in Technicolor and Cinerama. Sandro and Paola leaned against the wall at the top of the Pincio and watched. It was the perfect place to be in love.

"It's more beautiful each time, don't you think, Sandro?"

"Like you." He took her hand.

She glowed as gloriously as the city spread out before them. "I wonder how a tourist feels, seeing it for the first time. I can't remember my first time, can you?"

"Yes. She was the mother of my best friend in Fiesole." He brushed her fingers against his lips. "I was fourteen. I'd forgotten, or maybe I only pretended I'd forgotten, that he was going hunting with his father. She was at home alone, except for the servants. I knew she liked me in a way no mother should, because she was always caressing my head or hugging me so that my face was against her breasts..."

Paola was blushing. "I was talking about the sunset, here on the hill."

He laughed. "I'm sorry...but tell me, who did you make love to the first time?"

Paola turned away. "I should be getting home. My mother will be worried if I'm not back by eight-thirty."

"You mean you can't remember that either?" he teased.

She shook her head. "There has never been a first time."

Sandro turned her around so that her back was against the wall and she was facing him. He was no longer laughing. "I was hoping you would say that, because I want your first time to be with me. Don't look so frightened. I'm not going to drag you into the bushes and deflower you. I'm in no hurry. I'll wait until you're ready. You'll want me someday, Paola, you know you will. Maybe you already do?"

She tried to get away but he caught her and drew her against him. He felt her tremble in his arms and knew it wasn't the light breeze over the Pincio that had caused it. "Tell me. How many boys have stolen kisses, Paolita?"

"Only one, at Mardi Gras. We were both only nine. His name was Enrico..."

"Then this will make two."

"Please don't," she whispered.

He smiled. "I don't remember how I did it when I was nine, but I'll try." His last words were lost as his lips grazed her forehead. "Was I as nice as Enrico?"

She felt his breath, cool on her face, and then he was kissing her eyes and her hair. She put her arms around him and he held her closer. They swayed together, while the sun, like a huge tangerine, dropped behind Michelangelo's dome.

"Franco hasn't mentioned us," he said finally.

Paola lowered her eyes. "He doesn't know, neither does my mother. No one knows."

"It's best that way, *carina.*" He caressed her cheek with the back of his hand. "Your mother wouldn't approve of a vagabond like me."

"I thought you were studying law."

"I'm a vagabond nonetheless."

130

"I'm twenty-three years old and they still don't let me have a life of my own..." Paola hesitated.

"What is it? You can tell me."

"Franco warned me to keep away from you," she blurted out. "I was teasing him, asking him what other handsome friends he was hiding. Then all of a sudden he turned on me. 'Don't have anything to do with my friends if you know what's good for you,' he said. 'The best friendships are broken when a sister interferes.' I've never seen him so nasty."

Sandro held her closer. "Let's always keep it just you and me. If no one else knows, then no one can come between us—no one and nothing, except love." He smoothed her hair and watched the streaks of coral and mauve fade in the sky. "It's easier for me, because I have no family to confide in. My parents both died in the war when I was three. My mother wanted to give me a brother or sister, but the baby died stillborn with her." He went on stroking her hair until the sun was a golden sliver on the horizon.

"May I see you tomorrow?"

"I have to work."

"When then?"

"Wednesday is my day off..."

"Good. I'll claim you for the whole day. We'll take a drive...to the Alban Hills. It's beautiful there, especially this time of year."

She looked up at him, her eyes shining. "We used to go there to the papal palace at Castel Gandolfo, but not since my father died."

"You still miss him, don't you?"

Paola nodded. "Very much, though I think Franco needs him now more than I do."

"Your mother must be pleased that he's moved back home again."

"She is, very pleased. We'd almost given up hope. But something about him is different. I can't explain. If *babbo* were here..." Her voice trailed off.

"If you like I could talk to Franco and tell him what's bothering you and your mother. He's my friend. He'll listen to me."

Paola shook her head, but he could see that she was pleased by

131

his offer. "I shouldn't be bothering you with my family's problems. Every family has them, I suppose, only they seem so much worse when they're your own."

Sandro tilted her face up so that he was looking into her eyes. "I want to help you, Paolita. You can trust me."

CHAPTER TWENTY

Massi sat impassively, watching the remaining contestants take the jumps. He heard the winners announced and watched them approach the judges' stand. The victory parade, led by a division of *carabinieri* in full-dress uniform, red-and-white plumes of their cocked hats swaying, astride white mounts, circled the ring. Through it all he still felt the pressure of the Russian's fleshy hand on his leg, reassuring and menacing, encouraging and threatening.

"We won't meet again. Not until the Kremlin is satisfied that the Fisherman is safe in his summer dacha."

In his mind Massi went over every detail of the *covo*'s meeting that followed the mass for Moro. Cumulus smoke and fear had sealed the room in a bluish pall. The stench of anxiety thickened the air. He heard his own voice, rising: "Your plan is brilliant, Buscati—brilliant and impossible. Paul is beyond our reach. He lives like a prisoner in the Vatican. Even my contacts would be useless."

Buscati's cold smile had punctuated his reply: "I couldn't agree with you more, comrade. The Vatican is a fortress and a labyrinth.

133

It would be difficult if not impossible to slip through its security screen. And even if we succeeded in penetrating the Apostolic Palace we could never hope to escape with our prisoner. So, we won't even attempt it. Instead, we will wait for Paul to come to us..."

Massi watched until the last red-and-white plume was a dot in the distance, then got up and followed the crowd out of Piazza di Siena, beyond the refreshment tents where the waiters, their white aprons splattered and stained, were emptying the remains of the *tavola calda* into large vats and collapsing the bar.

The days had begun to lengthen. Afternoons were lingering beyond their allotted time, encroaching on the evening hours. He walked through the Borghese Gardens, passed strolling lovers, arms wrapped around each other's waists. He'd always thought it was an awkward position and wondered idly how they managed it. He never could. Either the arms were uncomfortably entwined and the walk was even, or the arms were embracing and the walk was more like a stumble. One arm around one waist worked well, he'd found. But arms around each other's waists was an impossibility, you couldn't concentrate on anything except trying to keep in step...

So much for young lovers. He walked on blankly, passing families devastated by Sunday outings, listening without hearing to fathers shouting their annoyance at the children trailing on their mothers' arms, dripping ice cream and tears. They weren't deceived by the afternoon light. Whatever the sun said, it was past their suppertime.

He walked west to Piazza delle Canestre and into the broad shaded avenue, Viale delle Magnolie, leading toward the Pincio, a favorite promenade since the nineteenth century when the hillside where the villas of the Roman aristocracy once stood was turned into lush public gardens. He saw everything—every stroller, every exasperated parent and petulant child, every tourist, every tree and blade of grass with the clarity of unclouded vision. But none of it registered on his brain. His eye photographed the scene like a Nikon, perfectly focused, perfectly exposed, the shutter set correctly for the fading light; yet the film remained blank. Was he so dispensable? Were the Russians the new emperors and he the fool—the Christian—being tossed to the lions? Was this his punishment for allowing his *covo* to get out of hand? Or was he being rewarded with a difficult mission? If it was a reward, why was Vishnevsky abandoning him until the road was safe? Both were links in the same chain. If one link could be removed, so could a second.

Massi walked on, not even noticing that he'd passed from the broad avenue of the magnolias onto Viale dell'Obelisco, oblivious to the palm trees that lined the narrower road or the Egyptian needle that Hadrian had brought from Egypt and that gave the street its name. Every road in Rome, even a gravel path in a park or a mean alley, bore a grandiose name disproportionate to its width, length or state of repair. We're a nation strangling on our history, he thought. All that must be changed. Will be changed...

He hesitated, then crossed the road and went into a small bar. Oily pizzas and mozarella *in carozza* were piled at one end of the bar beside a toaster oven. A cellophane covering served as a deterrent to the flies. Massi ordered an aperitivo and carried it out to the terrace, where white metal tables were arranged. The tables at the far end stood in front of canopied gliders, wide enough to seat two. Massi sat down in one and allowed himself to be lulled by its gentle motion. Cradled in mama's arms again. He sipped his drink and rocked slowly, almost dreamily, although he was not a dreamer. He was a pragmatist, swift in action, swift in thought. He'd been entrusted with a delicate mission, which he dared not fail in. He steeled himself, erasing the sentimental pictures that had been clouding his brain, turning him into a coward, forcing him to tighten the sphincter muscles of his anus.

He'd warned the *covo* against the explosive scheme. He remembered the rain that had begun as they argued, drumming against the kitchen window, grating against the dirty glass. Everything else had seemed to stop. Then Buscati's angry voice had ripped through the silence.

"You all know what the newspapers and television have been

saying. Moro's kidnapping was too precise, too surgical, too well planned for the bungling Italians to pull off. The masterminds had to be foreigners—Germans, Palestinians, anyone but us. We were merely the lackeys who took the orders and did the dirty work...It's true we couldn't have executed Moro alone. But now we are stronger. We have money and contacts. We must prove to everyone that we are masters in our own house. Massi has said that the Soviets will try to stop us. But how will they discover it? Only six people know about it. The six in this room, in this *covo*, at this table. Will one of us turn against his comrades...?"

Beyond the terrace of the *caffe* the elongated palm leaves cast eerie shadows across the busts of the illustrious Romans that lined the road.

Massi walked languidly back to the bar like a man with nothing to do and nothing to think of except the evening, ordered a second Campari and returned to the swing. He had confidence. He could outwit the bourgeois showoff Buscati. And no one—except Vishnevsky and his Kremlin bosses—would ever suspect that the operation had been sabotaged from within. He sipped the Campari slowly. The Soviets spent two hundred million dollars a year exporting terrorism. Guerrilla fighting, sabotage, street fighting, assassination techniques, undercover operations. They exploited all of it as a calculated instrument of foreign policy. But they knew better than to favor this madness.

"Moscow is unequivocal," Vishnevsky had said. "The operation must be stopped before it jeopardizes our own plans." Vishnevsky didn't have to spell it out. Massi understood.

Darkness settled firmly over the gardens of the Pincio, where Messalina, third wife of the Emperor Claudius, had hosted orgies so licentious that they shocked even her fellow libertines. If Buscati believed the operation had been compromised, he'd be forced to abandon it. There was only one course of action. One of the six would have to be made the scapegoat. By the time Massi had drained his glass, he had determined who would be sacrificed.

CHAPTER TWENTY-ONE

Officer Nino Messina was driving east on the coast road just outside Genoa when he saw a white Renault with French plates pulled over on the shoulder. Two girls in shorts and halters were attempting to change the right rear tire. One was trying to jack up the car while the other looked on helplessly. When they saw his police car approaching they ran out into the road and started waving. Messina passed them, then pulled up ahead and walked back. He liked what he saw. They were both pretty blondes with assets their brief shorts and tops did little to hide.

As soon as he picked up the jack to change the flat himself, they began to thank him profusely, leaning over him as he worked, anxious to help. It would have taken a stronger man than Officer Messina not to look up when they bent down. In view of the distractions, it took him longer than usual to change the tire. When he finished, and they'd thanked him again, giving him their names and addresses and promising to give him the time of his life if he ever got to Lille, they said good-by.

Messina began to walk back to his car. He had gone several strides before he realized that it was gone. The girls were as shocked as he and full of apologies. They gave him a lift back to the station, even though it was out of their way.

When the chief insisted on running a routine check of the girls the next day he found that their names and addresses were fictitious. He couldn't trace the Renault. Officer Messina had been too distracted to take down the license plate number.

Two days later, up the boot in Bergamo, Officer Dante Allegra answered a call reporting a child trapped in the elevator of an apartment building, one of the few ever built in the town. He checked both elevators—they were operating normally—and searched the building. There was no sign of a child in trouble. When the puzzled officer came out of the building, his car was gone. An elderly neighbor, who had been watching from his window, insisted that he saw the officer come out the back door of the building and drive away. When Allegra swore he had never left the building, the old man became very confused.

In the Cassia section of Rome to the northeast of the central city Ciro Iacono wiped his mouth on the sleeve of his jumpsuit and closed his lunch box. He strolled down the road, checking the repairs his work crew had made that morning. They had another hour of work, if they didn't tax themselves. It was too hot a day to overdo. He put his lunch box on the front seat of the truck and crossed to the shadier side of the street to join his men. Enzio and Lorenzo were stretched out on the grassy road bank and, judging from the snores which greeted him, they were sleeping soundly.

Iacono lay down a little distance from them and closed his eyes. He and his wife had been up most of the night with their infant son. They'd waited three years for the baby and now the doctors were saying that he was going to die. Iacono didn't understand the medical talk. All he knew was that little Ciro couldn't breathe.

He closed his eyes and held the tears in. A motor revved. Enzio raised up on one elbow and looked down the road. Iacono didn't hear him shouting, "Ciro," until he'd called three times. Screaming, "*Alt! Alt!*" the three men ran out into the middle of the street and chased the truck. Enzio and Lorenzo stopped after a few paces, but Iacono kept running until the truck had disappeared from view. Then he sat down at the edge of the road and let the tears flow.

CHAPTER TWENTY-TWO

The Alban Hills rose on all sides, encircling Sandro and Paola in a verdant embrace. The volcanic lake shimmered silver and blue in the brilliant sunlight. It was the siesta hour and it was off season; they had Castel Gandolfo to themselves. The town sat perched on the lip of the crater of Lake Albano, on the very spot where the citadel of Alba Longa once stood. Legend had it that the ancient city was founded by Asacanius, son of Aeneas.

They were breathless as they stood hand in hand and looked back down the steep hill they had just climbed to the square below. Behind them loomed the palace of the popes, sun-baked yellow stucco, built in the style of the Renaissance with its insistence on purity of line, balance and symmetry. It was more like a castle than a summer cottage. Beside them a fountain by Bernini cast a fine cool spray. All fountains should be by Bernini, Sandro thought. A breeze from Lake Albano swept their eager faces and fluttered through the flags that stood at half-mast, three in the square below and three in front of the castle—the yellow-and-white flag of the Vatican, the red, white and green colors of the state of Italy, and the blue-and-white ensign of the commune of Castel Gandolfo.

"It will be easier going back, and more fun." Sandro brushed a wisp of Paola's windswept hair from her cheek.

"I liked the climb," she said smiling.

He still held her face in his hands. It was full of wonder. She had never been alone before for an entire day with a boy, and she had never really cared until today. She'd lied to her mother to go with Sandro. What else would she do? She was afraid the answer would be anything...anything for Sandro, just to be with him. He made her feel alive—interesting, and pretty. She'd never thought of herself as either interesting or pretty before.

He bent toward her and kissed her upturned lips. She looked startled but she didn't turn away.

"Sandro! In front of the pope's own house!" She tried to sound properly outraged.

He grinned. "What better place to steal a kiss, and then another?"

He drew her close. She was soft and supple, shy and yielding at the same time. She wanted it more than he. He could feel it in the way her body shaped to his, naïve yet knowing instinctively.

"Don't be ashamed because you want to kiss me. Take what you want, I do."

She hesitated, embarrassed that her desire was so transparent. But it wasn't diminished in the slightest by her embarrassment.

"Kiss me, Paola." She felt his breath like a warm breeze on her forehead and did what she was asked as she always had, only this time without reluctance or regret.

Lips, tongues, bodies came together, and when he drew away she clung to him as though once she had known his touch she couldn't bear to relinquish it. She reached out to him, just to feel his hand, his sleeve. They kissed again. Then, arm in arm, they walked around the palace, pausing now and then to kiss again.

A special pass was required to visit the palace. Paola wanted to go inside, but Sandro had no need to see the interior. She wanted to stay in Castel Gandolfo, find a quiet trattoria and have lunch. It was so serene and beautiful, and they were so alone. She feared they might never come again, or have such a day again. But he insisted on getting back. He did not want to be there once the town awoke, and he had already gained everything he could from the trip.

The drive back to Rome was leisurely. The radio played the popular old songs from fifteen years before—"Non ho l'eta," "Da una lacrima sul viso." Paola hummed along, her hand resting on Sandro's arm, drifting in and out of reveries, thinking of the remembered taste of his kisses, the flavor of his lips, the sweetness of his breath on her face. She closed her eyes. She had never been happier.

Sandro drove carefully, remembering to reach over occasionally to stroke Paola's hair. But mostly his eyes were fastened on the road—three and a half kilometers from the town of Castel Gandolfo, then a right turn onto Via Appia and twenty-one more kilometers to Rome. It was not his first trip from Castel Gandolfo to Rome, nor would it be his last. He was testing himself, piling detail upon detail; the narrow road to the left, leading to the ruins of the ancient town of Bovillae; the still awesome remains of four towers—the first three square-shaped, the fourth, the cylindrical Torraccio; remnants of tombs, too many to try to count; then on the right the Trappist monastery, originally the Palazzetto della Sirene, built by Cardinal Colonna; and finally the juncture with Via Nettunense that veers off to the left for the shore towns of Nettuno and Anzio. The five kilometers, from the turn onto Via Appia to the juncture with Via Nettunense, was the critical stretch. They would meet the Fisherman there just after dawn, when his limousine turned off Via Appia for the town. He should go by helicopter to his summer palace in Castel Gandolfo, but he refused. Buscati had learned that this summer more than ever Paul was looking forward to the extra hour of tranquillity and meditation the drive would provide.

Paul was an early riser. Buscati was assuming he would start out after he'd said his daily mass and finished his breakfast. Somehow it amused him to think of the pontiff sitting down to a cornetto with his espresso, and he made a mental note to be sure to have plenty of them stocked up. Buscati was growing more curious about the man with each new scrap of information Franco fed him. He seemed to be a model of order in his personal life, so far as it went. He would make an ideal terrorist, Buscati thought ruefully. A theoretician, though. It was difficult to imagine Paul storming the barricades. Perhaps they should try to convert him. A novel idea, and entertaining. But he would make a difficult convert. He'd probably welcome his kidnapping as an opportunity to bring lost sheep back to the Light. Buscati thought back to the letter Paul had written in his own microscopic hand on his personal notepaper embossed with the miter and crossed keys of Peter, offering himself as hostage in exchange for Moro. He wanted to be a martyr. He would insist on it. Ah, it was beautiful. The Fisherman would do their work for them.

Sandro reached over and brushed Paola's cheek. She caught his hand and pressed the open palm against her lips. He considered pulling off the road but decided against it. He didn't want to frighten her away when they were just getting started.

"Will I see you tomorrow?" he said.

"Do you want to?"

He laughed softly under his breath. "Tomorrow and every tomorrow."

Nothing could be left to chance.

BOOK III

Betrayals

CHAPTER TWENTY-THREE

General del Sarto kicked the wastebasket under his desk and sent it flying across the room. "Get me Felice," he bellowed through the intercom. "Now. I want him *now*."

"I'm connecting you, general, as fast as I can."

Del Sarto's face was as purple as an eggplant. "Never mind, I'll get him myself." He stormed out, thundering as he passed through his outer office, "Have my car at the door." He strode down the corridor toward the minister's office, waving a sheet of crumpled paper in his hand.

Moments later, sirens screeching the urgency of his mission, the general was speeding down Via XX Settembre. The office of the chief of the antiterrorist squad was in the massive Defense Ministry. The rest of the squad was housed a kilometer away in the Questura Centrale, Rome's police headquarters. Cars slowed; pedestrians stopped to watch the white bulletproof Alfetta maneuver through the traffic at suicidal speed, craning their necks as it disappeared around the corner onto Via delle Quattro Fontane. Fear clouded their faces. Ever since Moro, you could feel the city tense at the first blast of a siren.

The driver turned right into Via San Vitale and braked sharply in front of the vast stone edifice known as the Questura. The gray pigeon-soiled building with the red, white and green flag hanging limply from the central archway was not one of the splendors of Rome.

General del Sarto pushed aside his bodyguard and charged in, still waving the crumpled paper. He commandeered an elevator to take him to the seventh floor, swept out, passed the rows of faceless secretaries and burst into Felice's office. Felice leaped to his feet at the sight of the general, overturning his chair.

"Goddammit," del Sarto raged, slamming the paper down in front of the startled detective, "I won't have it. Do you hear me? I won't have it. These hoodlums have got to be stopped. No one is safe anymore. Not even the general of the Carabinieri in his own office."

Felice picked up the paper and examined it. His sleepy eyes blinked as he devoured its contents. Though the message was brief and to the point he lingered over it as if there were intractable passages to ponder. Finally he handed the note to Cenci, who skimmed it in a moment and gave it back. Again Felice read it, while the general fumed:

> Left-wing hooligans will attack Marco Petri, vice-president of Fiat International, as he emerges from his office at 7:00 o'clock tonight.

The terse note was signed "Prima Linnea," a right-wing terrorist group.

Felice looked up at his furious superior, cleared his throat, asked innocently, "*Mi scusi, mon* generalissimo, but how did you come by this... this communiqué?"

"I found it in the goddamn wastebasket underneath my desk, where I rest my feet every day. It could have been a bomb as easily as a letter. A bomb in the private office of the Carabinieri!"

"A most distressing occurrence," Felice said. "But, generalissimo, if I may ask, what were you doing searching in your wastebasket?"

"A phone call, imbecile. Anonymous of course. It couldn't be traced. Now you listen to me, Felice, we put together the biggest manhunt in postwar history and what did you come up with? Copies of our own secret reports on kidnappings." His eyes narrowed. "I let you get away with that one. But now the bastards are operating freely in my own office. This time I want results. And if I don't get them, by God I'll find someone to nail for this. And, when I do, I'll crucify him."

"I'll give immediate orders to evacuate the area around Fiat. No pedestrians, no vehicles will be allowed to enter a twenty-block radius. The offices will be closed early from Via Veneto to Via Barberini..." Felice spoke hurriedly, blocking out the area on a wall map of the city as he talked. "Signor Petri will have round-the-clock protection for the next forty-eight hours, or until we are certain that he's no longer a target."

"One moment, generalissimo," Officer Cenci interposed deferentially.

"What is it, Cenci?" Felice snapped. "We don't have time for any of your hairsplitting now."

Cenci ignored the curt words and shifted his focus to the general. Although del Sarto occasionally consulted with Felice directly, he usually sent his orders through Cenci. He found the officer's crispness, efficiency and subtle flattery preferable to Felice's natural state of chaos. Cenci put order into his boss's life and kept out what he wanted. Felice willingly left the paperwork to him. Just the sight of the massive files stacked on the desk each morning depressed him. If nothing else, he was indebted to Cenci for relieving him of that burden.

"If we evacuate the area as suggested and alert Petri we will succeed in preventing the attack, at least for the time being. But it will be a Pyrrhic victory. The terrorists won't be apprehended, nor will the danger, which has now reached our most august generalissimo himself, be lessened. Instead of evacuating, perhaps we should consider an alternate plan."

Officer Cenci took off his wire-rimmed glasses and as he spoke polished them with a white tissue he'd extracted from his trouser pocket. "We infiltrate the area with police, guard the offices and person of Petri and wait for the strike. If we clear the area we tip our hand, and the terrorists wait for another day and another target. If we surprise them at the scene we have them in our grip."

"But the innocent people," Felice protested, "passersby on their way home to dinner, people enjoying an evening stroll, tourists admiring our city. They could be caught in the crossfire. No, no, Cenci, we can't jeopardize them for the sake of apprehending a few *brigadisti,* no matter how much we'd like to have them in our hands."

The general listened impatiently to Felice's objections. "If we're going to save Rome we have no choice but to do it Cenci's way."

"Generalissimo—"

Del Sarto cut him off. "Before I sit down to dinner tonight I want to know those terrorists are jailed or dead. One's as good as the other. That's an order, Felice. The commander of the Carabinieri will not be made a fool of by a bunch of *brigadisti.*" He turned and marched out, even angrier than when he'd arrived.

Felice felt his throat constrict. "So the few are risked to save the many, the innocent are sacrificed to keep the general's wastebasket clean. So be it, Cenci." He sat down heavily at his desk. "Make the arrangements. Police in plainclothes deployed on every rooftop, in every alley and doorway within five blocks of the Fiat offices. Move them in yourself. Send a detail to Petri's office. He shouldn't change his routine—just increase his guard. I'll meet you at the corner of Via Bissolati at six-thirty sharp. By then I expect all units to be in place."

"Yes, sir." Cenci stood awkwardly in front of the desk, as if he had something else on his mind.

"That will be all," Felice said. "And," he added with a coldness Cenci had never heard in his voice before, "you have countermanded me publicly for the first and last time."

Cenci left quickly...having already risked a good deal to set things up for his own purposes...

When he was alone Felice leaned back in his swivel chair and shut his eyes. Maybe, he thought, I'm getting too old for this job.

Good food, sound sleep and an occasional scrub of the back, right in the center between the shoulder blades where it's difficult to reach...that's not so much to ask out of life.

He went to the window and looked down at the street below. The siesta hour was over and the streets were beginning to fill again with Romans and tourists, old men and young, saints and hustlers, women carrying the ubiquitous string bags filled with the evening meal, children searching for some entertainment in the rubbish-strewn gutters. The people don't want mercy, they want revenge, he thought. They want to see death come to those who have brought fear and confusion into their lives. And they have history on their side. Didn't Romulus execute his own brother Remus for disobeying Rome's first law?

Felice opened the window. The steady rush of water from the city's three hundred fountains mingled with the voices of the passersby. Would any of them be among the few he must silence that night to make the many safe?

CHAPTER TWENTY-FOUR

Lisa curled up on the bed with the copy of *Il Messagero* Massi had brought with him. When she came to "Il Servizio in Cronaca," the section describing the terrorist strikes of the previous day—what friends had been taken, enemies hit, where the Molotov cocktails had landed in the night—she grinned delightedly. They were responsible for every incident reported, and not one of them had been taken.

"We work well together, Massi," she called out. "We're entitled to crow a little after such a performance."

Massi looked back at her, one eyebrow raised in a question.

Lisa laughed. "Professionally, I mean."

"I thought so." He was pulling his undershirt down over his genitals to catch the dripping as he padded toward the bathroom. There was a hole the size of a hundred lira coin in his shirt, and his buttocks were bony. He donated the salary he earned as a police officer to the movement, keeping only pocket money for himself.

Lisa tossed the newspaper on the floor beside the bed and stretched languidly. Her body was supple and golden brown, except for a white triangle that her bikini had shaded.

"Buscati will be pleased."

"The hell with Buscati," he said. "Do you think we're doing this for him?"

"It's his operation. It was his idea, and you said yourself it's a brilliant one—"

"I did, and I also said it was impossible."

Lisa watched him. "Are you still opposed?"

"I voted with the *covo*."

"Yes."

"And I am doing my part, aren't I?"

"I didn't mean to imply any lack of commitment. But you're still afraid we'll fail."

"We can't win, it's impossible." He shouldn't have said it again, he thought.

"Will you try to stop us then?"

"I have tried for the good of the cause only, you know that..."

Massi closed the bathroom door and turned on the water to drown out her next words, cutting off a conversation that had gone too far already. He should never have let her draw him in. It was dangerous, a foolish risk even now. Sentimentality was not a weakness he allowed himself.

Still, she could have been anything she wanted, had anyone, he thought. But it's too late now. She was bright and beautiful, and so coolly elegant, radiant in sex, a patrician to her cracked, roughened fingertips. She was more alive than anyone he'd known, more licentious and, at the same time, more reserved. He had never brought her to climax, though she seemed to enjoy whatever he did to her. She initiated sex as often as he, more often, but he'd never possessed her. Although she drove him to wild orgasm, when it was over he felt betrayed, as if he'd been brought to the highest peak and dropped over the cliff, and when he thought about it afterward it always seemed as if she'd been playing with him, almost mocking his passion. It angered him, made him feel inadequate...

"So Buscati was better in bed, more of a man? I'll show you.

153

This time I'll show you," he'd said, and forced himself on her. She had resisted, and when he became more insistent, she grew more aloof. He'd lost his temper. The afternoon session ended as it always did, only this time Massi felt guilty. He had wanted to make it especially good for her, it was the least he could do...But Lisa didn't much care for sex in the afternoon. She liked it at night or in the early morning—especially the early morning. Often he wasn't sure whether he'd had a wet dream or she'd drawn back the sheet and left him drained and elated. If he asked her later, she'd laugh at him and refuse to answer. He wanted to try again. He knew he could satisfy her if only she'd let him. But now it was too late...

Lisa lay flat on her back, arms folded behind her head. She would have to watch Massi more carefully. She was no longer sure he could be trusted. He was getting edgy and secretive. She wanted to have him again. The first time she'd been sulky and disinterested. But they had work to do. Later, when it was over, they'd do more, lots more. She'd want sex then. She'd require it.

There was hardly a man in the movement whose weight hadn't crushed her, except Franco. Shy, intense little Franco. An *innocente*. She would have him tonight, too. Buscati would be furious if he found out, but why should he know unless she wanted him to. She would search Franco out and give him his dream. He would never muster the courage to take her himself. Lisa knew that Franco wanted her. He stared at her surreptitiously and, if she caught his eye, he reddened like a tomato sauce and stammered. She laughed at his awkwardness and his desire. It was mean, she knew, but tonight she would make it up to him a thousand times...

Massi came back, a thin towel wrapped around his waist, and sat down on the bed beside her. The humid air from the bathroom began drifting into the cramped, dreary room. Dampness clung to his skin like mildew.

"It doesn't have to be this way, I can make things different for us if you'll give me a chance..."

She stiffened as he began to stroke her hair and got up. Flaunting her nakedness, she bent over in front of him, pulled a shopping bag out from under the bed and started checking its contents. A soundless laugh full of anticipation rose in her throat.

"I think I'll initiate Franco tonight. What do you bet our little comrade is a virgin? Well, not for long."

"We'll see," Massi said, as he began to dress to meet Detective Felice.

CHAPTER TWENTY-FIVE

At 6:30 P.M. Guido Felice shambled up Via XX Settembre Largo, crossed in front of Santa Susanna and paused at the corner where it's joined by Via Bissolati. Officer Cenci was waiting. The two men exchanged a few words as they strolled toward Fiat Direzione at number 57, pausing in the doorway of the spacious showroom to continue their conversation. To a casual observer they appeared to be a couple of men—the older, formally if uncomfortably dressed in an ill-fitting dark suit; the younger, neat and well groomed in slacks and an open shirt—discussing, perhaps, the purchase of a car.

On the third floor of the Fiat Building Marco Petri glanced at his eighteen-karat digital watch. One minute later, at precisely 6:55, as he did every evening Monday through Friday—he was a most precise and organized man whose life was as carefully timed as a bomb—Petri stood up from his desk and went to his private washroom. He washed his manicured hands with the lily-scented soap that was the exact sea-green hue of the bathroom tiles, dried them on a sea-green linen towel deeply edged with lace and combed his sparse gray hair carefully over his bald pate.

Signor Petri was ready to meet the phalanx of bodyguards and carabinieri who waited in his outer office to escort him to the private elevator, through the lobby of the rococo building to the main entrance. For three strides, the distance between the ornate front doorway and the security of his bulletproof limousine, he would be vulnerable. If Petri was apprehensive, he showed no trace of it as he opened the door to his outer office.

"Gentlemen," he said cordially to the two dozen burly, heavily armed men, "after you."

On the street Detective Felice checked his watch as a gleaming gray limousine rolled around the corner and eased into the reserved spot directly in front of the building. It was 7:05, give or take a few minutes. Felice's watch was always a little fast or a little slow. What was time, after all, except an artificial creation of northerners and accountants who wanted everything measured in seconds and centimeters, even the time from a glorious sunrise to a startling sunset.

Felice looked carefully in both directions. He saw nothing to alert him, nothing to give him a hint of danger. It was a miraculous Roman evening, the kind that natives savor before the stultifying summer heat sends them rushing to the mountains and beaches, for once willingly surrendering their town to the hordes of hapless tourists. The sun setting over St. Peter's was turning the orange tones of the city to gold. The evening traffic was just beginning to congest; the streets were filling again with Romans imbibing the last breath of a glorious day.

A young girl in a peach silk blouse and white skirt passed by with two companions. Judging from the shopping bags they carried, hers with the chic red-and-green band of Gucci, they had been on a spending spree. The girl was tall and lithe with stylishly bobbed auburn hair. But there was something about her—the way she carried herself, the brightness of her smoky eyes perhaps, or her flashing smile—that reminded Felice of Elena. The three strolled down the street aimless and carefree, enjoying the fading day. Felice was almost sure he'd seen the girl somewhere before, or was it only in his dreams?

He heard one of the young men whisper something in her ear that made her smile. Why can't all young people be as effervescent as the girl, he thought. Even his own children lacked the spark that made youth so precious and at least provided a memory to look back on with nostalgia. He thought of his eldest, Giovanni, brooding and moody, and of the terrorists they were waiting to trap and kill—youths probably no older than that happy trio, cold as a Swiss winter and consumed with misplaced bitterness.

Felice looked up and down the street in both directions, then shrugged at Cenci. "So much for the generalissimo's private communiqués. One or two minutes more and we can have a good dinner and a little peace, both of which I could sorely use."

Officer Cenci did not turn a hair. His attention was fixed on the Fiat Building entrance. The plate glass doors were opening. A wedge of police and bodyguards pushed through, so thick that Petri was completely obliterated from view. The door of the limousine opened. The guards dropped back slightly to allow him room to enter the car. In that instant the pretty girl who reminded Felice of Elena and her companions dropped their shopping bags and swirled, submachine guns firing. Two policemen fell under the spray of bullets.

A powder-blue Fiat screeched around the corner from the same direction that the limousine had come, rounding the curve on two wheels. The back door flew open. The girl ran toward it, firing a final salvo as she went. Her companions fell, but she showed no fear...she expected to be protected.

Felice was caught off-guard but Cenci was ready. He was crouching, legs splayed, both arms extended, gripping his revolver, unblinking, his entire body concentrating on the accuracy of his shot. Sight, shoot, kill. And if the target happens to be a beautiful girl he had just shared a bed with...so be it. The enemy came in many forms. Lisa did not try to duck, certain that Massi was just playing his part as Officer Cenci. He squeezed the trigger. One shot was all he fired. It ripped into her chest and brought her down beside her fallen comrades. The impact of her fall loosened the auburn wig she'd been wearing, revealing close-cropped blond hair.

Slowly Felice raised his vast bulk from the sidewalk, where he'd sprawled when the terrorists opened fire. He was filled with the revulsion that rose in his gut each time he looked on such a messy scene. He had killed more than once through the years, but he'd never learned to accept it as just another part of the job, like filing a report or cuffing a thug. He felt the sour, sickening taste of vomit rise in his throat and knew without waiting for a ballistic report that Cenci's bullet had reached its mark. He admired his assistant's coolness under fire, at the same time he hated the cold-blooded way Cenci had aimed his revolver at the girl as if she were no different than a bull's-eye or an empty beer bottle.

Italy had changed. Once the cuckolded husband, the father whose daughter had been violated, the insolent *papagallo* whose pride had been damaged publicly—once these had been the defiant few who filled the police records. Now they'd been replaced by organized terror—unpredictable, arbitrary, ruthless violence executed in the name of some vague collective good. The new crimes were a message to the country at large that any means were justified to provoke a crisis of democratic institutions and replace the law of the state with the law of the gun and of the people's kangaroo courts. No wonder the new detectives were bloodless too...

Felice walked over and touched his assistant's shoulder in a gesture that Cenci recognized as one of respect, even admiration. "Call the ambulances," he murmured.

Officer Cenci was glad of the order. He had performed his job with efficiency, but he didn't want to face the measure of what he had done. Not yet.

Felice walked over to where the bodies lay strewn, feeling every kilo of his excess weight. One of his men was dead; a second was severely wounded, his shoulder and stomach riddled with bullets. Petri lay in the door of the limousine, moaning. His custom-tailored trousers were soaked in blood. He'd been shot in the knees, and probably crippled for life. There was nothing Felice could do for any of them except wait for the ambulances to arrive. He moved on to where the terrorists lay. One of the men had been thrown back by the force of the answering fire. He sat in a pool of his own blood, his body crumpled against the wall of the Fiat Building. His eyes stared vacantly. His hands still clutched the Skorpion. The other lay sprawled in the gutter, half-on and half-off the sidewalk. Felice touched him gingerly, whether in a gesture of condolence or to see if any life remained, even he wasn't sure. The body had already begun to stiffen.

Finally he turned to the girl. Her chest looked like a Sicilian blood-orange. The fine, peach-colored silk was stained through with rich red juices. So much life snuffed out. He knelt down heavily beside her and took her hand. She was a terrorist, a sworn killer. But she reminded him of Elena. Was he getting too old and sentimental for the job? He thought of her as she'd been just moments ago, rounding the corner, full of promises yet to be discovered. Cenci's bullet had been aimed at her heart. He felt her pulse flutter.

Ambulance sirens, at first vague and distant, grew louder until they blotted out every thought by their insistence. A hushed crowd of passersby stood docilely behind the police line formed to hold them back, absorbing the grisly spectacle in stunned silence. The traffic from Via Veneto began to snarl and knot as other police moved to cordon off the block.

The stretcher-bearers worked swiftly. Felice stepped back and watched the girl's body hoisted into the back of an ambulance beside the wounded carabinieri. A second ambulance carrying Signor Petri was already moving out. The three dead still lay on the pavement, their corpses zipped into body bags for delivery to the morgue.

General del Sarto could sit down to dinner now and feast on the delightful news of two dead terrorists and a girl hanging onto life by a thread.

He picked up the discarded shopping bags. They were splattered with blood. The one she'd carried her weapon in was empty. The other contained a dozen little fragmentation grenades about the size of tennis balls, V-40s so nice and light you could throw them much farther than an ordinary grenade.

CHAPTER TWENTY-SIX

Felice and Cenci sat on either side of the narrow hospital bed waiting for the girl to regain consciousness. The surgeon, still dressed in his blood-splattered cap and gown, had given his prognosis: "After four hours in surgery her condition is critical. There is the slimmest chance that she will survive, and even this will be shattered if she is subjected to police questioning."

Studying her face, as chalky as the hospital gown that now covered her, Felice didn't doubt the doctor's assessment, or his own duty. The girl had to be questioned. They would go easy on her if she cooperated, otherwise they would do whatever they had to do. What difference? They'd probably be doing her a favor. Better a brief if too strenuous interrogation now than years in jail. If she lived, they'd send her to the Regina Coeli first, where the rats outnumbered the prisoners. In the damp cells by the Tiber fungus would grow on her clear skin and the dim light would dull her eyes. Regina Coeli—Queen of Heaven—at least the name should be changed. It was an insult to the Virgin. After the trial she would be transferred. Probably not to Asinara, the maximum security island prison. Her sex alone would keep her out of there.

Mussolini used Asinara to contain the opposition. Now it had been refurbished to house the most dedicated male urban guerrillas. No one had ever escaped.

Felice sighed. *Grazie Dio,* we Italians are chauvinists. Even our justice is machismo. The girl would probably be sent to Messina for life, soul rotting with the body in a barren cell... Felice tipped back in the too narrow hospital chair, prepared to wait until morning if he had to.

"I'll wake you up if there's any change," Cenci offered.

Felice grunted and closed his eyes. The girl's labored breathing sounded like a reproach. Even though he knew she'd been acting, he couldn't dispel the picture of her swinging down the street so full of life. He saw her laughing eyes when he shut his own, then thought again of Elena. His wife would be keeping his dinner warm through the night until it was as dry and tasteless as their sex. She was unyielding—they couldn't afford to waste a meal no matter how long it had to wait. Wastefulness was a luxury for the rich. Although a detective's salary was a fortune compared with the provincial police pay he had been earning, she couldn't change the frugal habits she'd perfected over fifteen years of marriage. He wanted to bring her presents now that their circumstances were improved—nothing elaborate, a box of chocolates or maybe a sheer nightgown—but he knew better. First there would be the happy surprise in her face, but before the package was open disapproval would begin to tighten the corners of her mouth. Nothing would be said, but for the next three days they'd have nothing but polenta or *brodo con riso* to make up for his extravagance.

Felice tried to put the depressing thought out of his mind by concentrating on the undiluted joy of spaghetti *alla amatriciana* and veal chops at Nino's—simple food exquisitely prepared, the tomatoes freshly picked and just warmed with the *pancetta,* the chops as tender as a mother's kiss, served with a trace of lemon. With a dinner like that before him now he might even think fondly of Officer Cenci. He opened one eye. Cenci was sitting exactly as he had been for the past hour—bolt upright in the straight chair, his attention locked on the unconscious girl. Felice sighed and closed his eye again. Such vigilance exhausted him. There was no question that Cenci's ambition would take him far. Felice would be dismissed as ineffective and Cenci's diligence rewarded. He'd seen it happen many times before. Perhaps his wife was right to blame him for the life they'd endured. If he'd been more like Cenci ten years ago, who knows? She might not choke at Nino's prices.

At the windows the white curtains billowed like sails, filling the high narrow room with a draft of cool air. Victims of these incidents were usually taken to the Policlinico beside the university. But the clinic was overcrowded, so the ambulance had rushed the wounded across the city, wailing up the Gianicolo to the newer Ospedale Salvator Mundi.

On a clear night the hospital afforded a splendid view of the city. To the east the dome of St. Peter's loomed silver-white in the moonlight. To the west Castel Sant Angelo squatted, round and stolid. Since the Middle Ages a covered way had linked Castel Sant Angelo to the Vatican so that the pope could take refuge there if he was under siege. Two popes before Paul had escaped capture that way. Beyond Castel Sant Angelo and the dark line of the Tiber stretched the main thoroughfares and monuments of Rome. To the northwest, out of view, stood the Questura, where on the fifth floor the computers gorged like sharks on the data the police analysts poured in.

Cards in the girl's purse identified her as Sandra Bassiglio, Via Joia, Brindisi. But before the doctors had extracted the bullet from her chest her true identity was certified. Every scrap of information on her family, friends, schools, social contacts, habits, acquaintances and lovers was being gathered. The same was being done for her two comrades, and the weapons they'd fired were being traced through the new data bank at Wiesbaden, repository for ten million items of information on the lives, tastes and habits of terrorists around the world. Queries on the three were being relayed to the Paris SDECE, the U.S. CIA, the British MI-5, the West German Landswehr and the Israeli Mossad, as well as to the maze of Italian police units—the Polizia, the Finance Guard, the Service for Information and Democratic Security, the Service for Information and Military Security, the Directorate for General Investigations and Special Operation. Felice suspected that whatever help they received would have to come from the foreign forces, thanks to the dismantled security system and the scattering of key agents.

Felice couldn't dispel the picture of a golden girl on a golden day, a young Juno. Such a foolish sacrifice, such wasted ideals. What had driven her to that desperation, he wondered. He looked at her again. Had he dozed? He wasn't sure. Her eyes were wide, smoky gray and eerily bright, and she was staring at Officer Cenci. Her lips were drawn back in a ghastly smile. Triumphant or trusting, he couldn't be sure. Felice watched the spectral scene as if it were a movie.

She raised her arm, frail in the hospital gown, in the familiar clenched-fist salute. As she did the IV needle was pulled loose, ripping the iridescent skin. She didn't seem to notice. A trickle of blood oozed down her arm. She moistened her lips, trying to find her voice. From somewhere deep in her throat a strained whisper escaped. "*Al pesc...*" Cenci leaned forward, so close that he hid the girl from Felice's view. His hands disappeared in the whiteness of the sheets, and the whiteness of her neck.

Felice sprang to the side of the bed with surprising agility to hear her words. He was too late. Cenci sank back and stared at his hands, which lay limply on his knees. The girl's burning eyes were now glazed. Her mouth hung slack.

"What did she say?"

Cenci looked up and stammered, convincingly. For the first time Felice felt simpatico. He reached across the bed and put an arm around the officer, an act of intimacy he'd never presumed before. "Never mind, when your mind clears you'll remember her words."

Cenci trembled visibly, and moved away.

Felice rang the bell on the bedside table. He'd done Cenci an injustice thinking he was as cold-blooded as his quarry. A nun in white and soundless shoes floated in like a cloud. Her beatific face darkened as she looked from the two men to the girl and back.

"We didn't question her," Felice said woodenly. "She died before we had a chance." He was embarrassed by his own words. He didn't have to explain his actions, but nuns and priests always made him feel defensive, like a boy caught masturbating.

The two officers were going down the Gianicolo slowly, almost lethargically, as if the driver understood their mood and was manipulating his vehicle to conform to it.

Cenci had regained his usual control. The show of emotion in the hospital would not be referred to again by either of them. Still, Felice needed to know the girl's last words. He began to question Cenci, closely but kindly.

"She said *al, al pes*... I'm not sure what she was trying to say"— Cenci hesitated—"but I think she was saying Pescara." He took off his glasses and rubbed his eyes. "Yes, sir," he said more confidently, "I'm sure that's what she said, Pescara, *a* Pescara."

Felice frowned. "But you just said *al.* I heard that much too— *al* something. Then her voice faded and I couldn't hear her anymore."

"What difference? She said Pescara. That's the important thing. I was very close, how could I be mistaken?"

"It's a minor point, a quibble really, but if she was saying Pescara she would have said *a, to* Pescara, but we both heard *al*—to the Pescara makes no sense."

"Am I a liar?" Cenci challenged. His voice rose.

Felice was surprised by his uncharacteristic outburst. "*Calma,* Cenci, *calma*. What is Pescara, after all, a town on the Adriatic, not too big, not too small, that attracts a few tourists in the summer months. The girl reminded me of Elena when we first met—the way she looked when I fell in love with her. That's why I'm pressing you...too hard I suppose."

Cenci closed his eyes. He didn't want to listen to more of Felice's erotic secrets. He was the worst kind of Italian—he lived for his stomach and his balls. He didn't even care about the soccer team.

But he was deceptive for all that. To underestimate him would be the fatal mistake. Cenci had to guard against this natural tendency. Felice wasn't as stupid, or as slow as he pretended.

"Do you remember how she looked when she passed us?" Felice was saying. "A shopping bag and a boy on each arm? Do you remember her eyes, laughing, and the way she moved—"

"I remember it clearly," Cenci broke in. Felice could try to sink back into myth and fancy. Not him. Dreams could become nightmares, but it didn't work the other way.

"Ah, I thought you must. Any man would—enough." He stopped himself abruptly. "I'm getting sentimental about an assassin, a murderer. She would have killed you or me as effortlessly as she shot Petri. Then why, Cenci, do I feel her loss here?" He clasped both hands into his ample belly. "Is it just me, or do you feel it too?"

Cenci didn't answer immediately. In the darkness of the car Felice couldn't see his face clearly. He could only hear his breathing, so careful, as if the process of inhaling and exhaling oxygen required deliberate thought. It had been a long difficult day for Cenci—and it was far from over. He hadn't expected Lisa to linger as long as she did, but she was dead now. That was the important part. No one could reach her. She couldn't tell Buscati the name of the pig who shot her. He knew how vindictive the *brigadisti* were, as unforgiving as the Cosa Nostra...

"She knew what she was doing," he said finally. "She knew the risks. She was challenged at her own game and she lost. There will be others to take her place."

"I must be getting too old, or too soft for this business," Felice murmured wearily.

"A week in the mountains with Elena and you'll be able to put all this behind you," Cenci told him in a tone of uncharacteristic sympathy.

"I just took a week, Cenci."

"No, sir, it was only a couple of days after months of working night and day, eighteen hours at a stretch. It wasn't enough time."

"And when will you take a break? You must be exhausted too, although you never show it."

"I'm not so tired. Not yet."

Felice slumped down on the seat. "Yes, Elena and the mountains. Did I ever tell you about that first time when the poppies were in bloom...? But of course I have. Too many times. *Pazienza,* Cenci, I can't cut my heart out of this dirty business of ours any more than I could cut off my balls."

They drove the rest of the way to the Questura in silence, broken once or twice by Felice murmuring "*a* Pescara" to himself, and still wondering. Well, in any case the police in the Adriatic port town would have to be alerted at once to the possibility of a terrorist attack.

CHAPTER TWENTY-SEVEN

Massi hurried across Piazza della Republica. The water gushed unseen. The city was sleeping—no rallies, no protesters, no travelers bustling by on their way to the Stazione Termini. The last note of the last chorus of "Arriverderci Roma" had died away from the outdoor bandstand at Caffe d'Italia. A lone motor scooter with a pair of helmeted, blue-jeaned riders circled the fountain.

Massi knew exactly what he was going to say. Just the facts. They were damning enough. He would give them tersely and let Buscati draw his own conclusion. There was only one. He would have to abandon the operation. Massi could afford sympathy, even encouragement. I will say we can try again when we have more time to plan, he thought.

A dim light shone through the grimy window of the all-night trattoria on Via Giovanni Giolitti on the south side of the train station. It stayed open twenty-four hours to accommodate travelers. He wouldn't tell Buscati how long Lisa had held on. It was like her to confound him to the very end and force him to kill her with his bare hands, right in front of Felice, before she talked. She should have died instantly. The bullet had gone straight to her heart. Massi took a morbid pleasure in that. Something had touched her heart at last. There was a certain justice in it, but he wasn't a philosopher. He was a party man. Party men couldn't afford the freedom of philosophy, its limits unknown and unknowable.

He pushed open the door of the trattoria and scanned the small dining room: a dozen rectangular tables with soiled cloths; four wooden chairs at each, two to a side; a gray tiled floor that had once been white; a molded plastic ashtray, black with "Cinzano" written in white on the rim, on ten of the twelve tables. Bread crumbs, a few stray pieces of lettuce, a dandelion green or two, a cork and a napkin littered the floor. One man, middle-aged, overweight and overtired, slouched behind the hot table. The food, like the floor, had assumed a grayish pallor. There were three customers. Two men occupied a corner table. The older, who had graying temples and a deep vertical worry line that formed a crater between his eyes just above the bridge of his nose, glanced furtively toward the door when it opened, then turned back to his companion, evidently satisfied with what he saw, leaning forward and talking intently, taking up where he'd left off. The other, a bored, insouciant boy, turned to see who had entered. Unlike the older man he didn't hurry back to their conversation. While his companion discoursed sotto voce, he continued to watch Massi. He wasn't interested really, merely passing the time until the bumbler across the table had worked up enough courage to go across the street with him to the men's room of the Termini.

The third man sat alone at a table by the window. It wasn't the table a customer would choose who wanted attention; on the other hand it wasn't an inconspicuous corner table either. That was one of the first lessons they learned: never to go out of their way to be noticed yet never to look as if they had something to hide, even if they found themselves in a swarm of carabinieri. They should appear in public as innocuous as the landscape or the furnishings.

Buscati looked up from a half-eaten plate of manicotti. A smile of recognition lit up his face. "I thought you would never get here." He glanced at his watch and tapped the crystal warningly.

"Eighteen minutes to catch the rapido." He stood up as Massi approached, wiping his mouth with the napkin that was tucked in his collar, and drew the other man into a quick embrace. If anyone was interested in checking, the express train to Naples was scheduled to depart at 2:48, exactly eighteen minutes from then. A worn valise was tucked under the table at his feet.

Massi returned the embrace. "Plenty of time for a coffee then," he said.

"Not plenty, my friend, but just enough."

Massi didn't miss his meaning. "You'll take one too, then?"

"Prego." He pushed the pasta to the side and reached in his pocket for change. Massi raised a hand to stop him and went over to the counter. Buscati was only allowing him a few minutes, he thought worriedly. Time was running out on them. There was no use taking an unnecessary risk of being seen or remembered together now. Massi mulled this over as he carried the espresso back to the table.

Hunching over the small thick cup, Buscati allowed the steam to warm his face. *"Che successo?* What's happening, my friend? The train won't wait, you understand that."

"I'm sorry I'm late. It was my girl—she's left me."

Buscati yawned. "Tell me what happened. It will make you feel better to unburden yourself."

"There's not much to tell. She said she had a business appointment today—with a man. She never came back."

"Don't worry, she will. They always do."

Massi shook his head. "Not this time. She can't."

Buscati scorched his lips on the coffee. "Are you sure?"

Massi nodded.

Buscati stood up and tossed a coin on the table "Come on," he said, grabbing the valise, "the rapido won't wait for anything— even a guy who's lost his girl."

Once outside they headed across the street toward the terminal, ignoring the persistent calls of the taxi drivers.

"Who was the Judas?"

"It looks like Malaverde," Massi said. "We used him on several of the last jobs—"

"Malaverde! Why would he do that?"

"Jealousy. Lisa was a provocative woman. Dangerous, too. She was too easy to fall in love with, and too cruel to the men who were fool enough to fall. Malaverde was her newest victim. He was especially bitter. But we'll never know."

"Dead too?"

"The first bullet is always reserved for the informer."

"And you?"

"I've been careful."

They circled the terminal, walking behind it, down narrow non-descript streets, then veered to the south, neither wanting to walk toward the university on this night of all nights. For a few blocks each man was lost in his own memories of Lisa.

The last time, just before she went to her death, Massi thought she had loved him a little, even though it hadn't been good for her. Had she softened, or had he? "There is no way to link me to Lisa," he said, "but you will be easy to trace. You were her lover all through the university. Everyone knew it. It's only a matter of time." With a precision that marked all of his actions from the most mundane to the most significant, he took off his wire-rimmed glasses and began to polish the lenses. "I told you the risks would be a hundred times greater now but you wouldn't listen. We can't operate freely the way we did in the past. The political climate has changed. The full power of the state has been rallied against us. Every police unit is already out hunting us, waiting for another false move. I don't have to remind you that I speak with some authority on these matters." He put his glasses on again and re-placed the handkerchief in his pocket.

For an instant a streetlight lit Buscati's face. He seemed to be smiling, a cold smile. Then the darkness erased it. "It's only a matter of time for us too. After that the cops can track me with satellites and radar and squads of carabinieri. They can put their noses to the ground and sniff away to their heart's content. It will be too late. We will be holding our venerable hostage, and the world will kneel down and beg."

"I hope you're right, because if you're not there's nothing I can do to help you."

"I understand. So what do you propose we do? Abandon la Rete del Pescatore, now that we're so close?"

"Exactly, before we're all compromised."

"No, we've come too far."

"We could scatter the *covo* until the scent grows cold, then regroup—even try the operation again if we like. In my opinion it's time to act the mosquito not the lion—to sting here and there with small annoying strikes, keeping the fear and our cause before the people. It's not the time to stage a grand theatrical production, even if it were possible."

Buscati took a short item he'd clipped from *Il Tempo* that morning out of his pocket and showed it to Massi. It was difficult for him to read in the darkness, but he could make out that according to a reliable Vatican source, a secret meeting was scheduled at Castel Gandolfo on July 17 between Pope Paul and an envoy from Czechoslovakia. "We need two weeks—two weeks at the most. I say we go ahead."

Massi looked down the empty street. It was dirty and deserted except for a few parked cars. Perspiration had begun to form under the bridge of his glasses. He felt them slip down his nose. The pupils of his eyes dilated until the irises were little more than a hazel border. "There's something I haven't told you. Lisa talked before she died."

Buscati grabbed him by the throat and spun him around. "Liar. Lisa would never talk. Never."

Massi's glasses were askew. "She talked, I swear it. She said, '*Al pescatore.*'"

"I don't believe it. Not Lisa. Anyone but Lisa."

Massi shrugged. "I thought the same. But she didn't have a chance. It was a setup. Malaverde tipped off the cops. The place was surrounded when they got there. Malaverde and Scorso died on the spot. Lisa should have died there too but she hung on long enough to be questioned. She was in no condition to refuse."

Buscati pushed him away in disgust. "They could have pulled out each hair of her cunt one by one and she still wouldn't have broken…just to show me."

172

"Think whatever self-pitying bourgeois thoughts you need to, Buscati, but don't be an ass. You're still in love with her and would jeopardize the whole network out of some absurd sentimentality. Open your eyes, Buscati. She wasn't *your* girl. She was the *covo's* whore. She went down on every one of us, and tonight she was going to initiate young Franco. Only the plans were changed on her." His voice was like gravel.

"Be reasonable, for Christ sake. You know that they have ways to make anyone talk, just as we do. They could break you like that, if they got their hands on you." He snapped his fingers sharply.

"What did you do to her?"

"In spite of the amazing new medical equipment and techniques the police often find that the old, primitive methods are the most effective for their purposes. You don't need the graphic details spelled out. In her condition one needed to do very little—a shot of phenobarbital, a little pressure with the fist, a finger applied to the open wound. There are so many ways, and who can resist when all it takes are a few words to make the torture stop? The pain...no anesthesia, no pain-killers. You're not yourself. You know as well as I, and what you don't know you can imagine."

Buscati turned away. He needed time to think. If Lisa did talk, even Detective Guido Felice would be able to track them down with a few days time. But if she didn't, then Massi was lying...

"So you think we should abort the plan," he said slowly.

"We have no choice. It's doomed."

"Not doomed—uncertain. Franco must get us the departure date immediately. When he does we'll decide whether to take the Fisherman or abandon the operation—"

"Don't be a fool, Buscati. How many fishermen do you think there are in Rome? Felice may be slow but he's not retarded. How long do you think it will take him to put it together?"

"Divert him. Give him a different scent to follow."

"It's too late for that. Don't you understand. Lisa talked. We can't win this one."

"Have you forgotten, Massi, we have it on considerably higher authority than you that we will succeed? Moro, himself, wrote that his execution would lead to a spiral of violence that would overturn the government. Who understands the workings—and weaknesses—of the state more? You or the man who created it? Moro knew the corrosive illness that is rotting our country from inside. We have to feed that sickness. We can't let ourselves become timid. We can't become cowards because our work is harder now. Paul won't whimper, why should we? He'll ask to be martyred, and so they'll be forced to meet every demand to save him. He won't beg them to compromise. He'll insist they hold firm, and so force them to give in. They can't abandon a saint to the devils. They'll be afraid of bringing the wrath of God and the people on their heads."

"You're a dreamer, Buscati. A dangerous romantic. We saw with Moro, the humiliating strike only serves to strengthen their determination. True, we made our name and our cause known the world over. But even if we could succeed, which is impossible, what would we gain by a second, even more shocking kidnapping? More publicity and more attention? Is that our goal, or do we want to break the back of the state? To bring on the revolution? They gave up Moro, they must give up the next one—yes, even if it is the Fisherman himself. We've tied their hands and their feet. They *can't* give in. Don't you see that?"

Buscati stopped walking and faced Massi in the street. "You've been against the operation from the first."

Massi paused and pushed up the glasses, which had slipped down his nose again. "It's true, I've had reservations from the start. But I put aside my personal misgivings and accepted the decision of the group. Can you say that I haven't done my part?"

Buscati didn't answer. He couldn't deny the truth of Massi's words and yet..."Damn that Judas, Malaverde. He's dead—you're sure?"

"Absolutely."

"And you have no doubt he was the traitor?"

"None."

"The bastard. I wish he were alive so I could make him pay for this."

Massi allowed a brief smile to crease his lips. "At least we agree on something."

CHAPTER TWENTY-EIGHT

Buscati walked on, mindless of the dawn that was beginning to color the city. The only sounds were the rush of the fountains, the eternal sound of the Eternal City; the roar of an occasional motorbike, the cough of an occasional car. He remembered how his teacher at the university, had put it... Too much is compressed in a single place, antiquity and Christianity, emperors, popes, martyrs, butchers, philanderers, gladiators, clerics, consuls. There was no room for the twentieth century. Blame it on the she-wolf. She and the suckers, Romulus and Remus started it all. Blame it on Caesar for being an imperialist. You couldn't breathe. Couldn't even build a subway. Every foot excavated turned up another relic. While the present went down in a conflagration of exhaust fumes and mind-shattering horns, the past was exhumed to live on in the city where everything was eternal. It was intolerable...today the poverty of the proleteriat, the corruption of the Christian Democrats, the impotence of the Communists held no import. *"Ce sempre domani. Magari.* Things will be better," he told himself. He couldn't bring back Lisa, but he could make them pay. He would net the Fisherman. Yes, and then they would pay...

Buscati circled back, drawn against his will to the front door of the Policlinico, where the wounded were brought after a strike. The neon lights of the *pronto soccorso* sign glared at him like a whore's lips. Lisa had passed under that sign hours before, he thought. Massi hadn't told him that the clinic beside the university was overcrowded, that the ambulance had rushed the wounded across the city, wailing up the Gianicolo to the Ospedale Salvator Mundi.

It wasn't a lover or a husband Lisa had needed...it was a mother. She'd loved her superficial, hedonist mother, and never understood her own need. Lisa and Paola, motherless and mothering. Lisa, the black sheep, Paola the ewe. Lisa sacrificed, betrayed, slaughtered. And he was the wolf in the fold. He wanted to look at her again, even though her body would be cold and rigid. But Massi had been right about one thing. He couldn't afford to be emotional now, just because a girl was dead.

He hurried away. His plan *would* succeed, a plan so bold that it could determine not only the future of their organization but the future of Italy, maybe even of the Western world. He was depending on its very audacity to carry him to power. With Renato Curcio and the other Red Brigade leaders dead or imprisoned he would emerge as the new leader of the radical left. It would be the nucleus for a new European movement, replacing faltering bureaucratic Communism that had become a useless institution in a single generation. It was the PCI and Berlinguer he was determined to destroy—the compromisers, the men who'd made a mockery of the Communist idea for the appearance of strength. They'd been easily coopted, bought by the crafty Moro for a sliver of corruptible power. Lisa would not die in vain. The next victim would be his choice...

It wasn't the Church he wanted to destroy. It had already destroyed itself. Look at how many in Italy alone, under the Fisherman's very nose, flouted its rulings. Many might still call themselves Catholics, it was a comfortable nomenclature, but they didn't believe and they didn't practice. Look at how many divorced, how many fornicated, how many committed adultery, how

177

many married in civil services, how many aborted their children. No, he didn't need to bring down the Church, the Catholics had done it themselves. And he didn't want to bring down Paul. Only use him. He could already feel il Pescatore taut in his net. He even knew what he would say to him...

"Try to understand, old man, it's nothing personal. We're seizing Peter, not Paul. Our enemies may be Pilates in their hearts, but they can't publicly deny the Fisherman of Souls. We won't hurt you unless we have to. And we'll let you pray." He grinned sheepishly. "We'll need all the help we can get."

He'd heard Paul was steeped in French culture and in private quoted from Verlaine and Rimbaud. Well, he'd have plenty of time to display his talents. Buscati made a mental note to ask Franco if it were true. Franco...he'd have to decide what to do with the boy. Time was running out and Franco was failing them. Each day he had a different excuse. He kept insisting that the information they needed was guarded as closely as the pope. Paul's itinerary used to be published in *l'Osservatore Romano*. Now only his personal secretary, the Vatican security chief, the cardinal secretary of state and three or four ranking Curia cardinals were informed in advance. Not even the nuns in the kitchen knew with certainty on what day the pope would travel to his summer palace at Castel Gandolfo. The reign of terror had moved even the impassive Church. Franco seemed terrified, even though Buscati had never asked him for anything more than details of the Fisherman's schedule, repeatedly assuring him that his role would begin and end there. Franco was too nervous.

The metal doors protecting the storefront from vandals were being raised. Matteo was arranging the Cinzano umbrellas and plastic chairs in front of his espresso bar when Felice started home. The rising sun was turning the cement walls a warm peach, softening the dour faces of the storefronts. He loved it all like a woman—the peeling facades, the smell of bread baking, the cigarette-stained tables, the wash lines strung across the alleys of his *rioni*. It was shabby and comfortable, like pants worn at the knee and seat. He sank into it when he returned each night, inhaling its sounds and sights and smells, and somehow the tension eased. But not this morning. This morning he was bringing Lisa Taglia home as surely as he had once brought his wife to meet his parents. A dog barked angrily at him, he wanted to bark back. What killer dream did she die for? Or was it something else? The question gnawed at his gut like hunger.

Felice climbed the steep, slanting stairs to his apartment. The shutters were closed tightly, staving off the new day. Three hours to sleep. The Virgin smiled down from her shrine as he climbed into bed. His wife groaned but didn't move or open her eyes. Had she always groaned when he touched her or had sounds of pleasure gradually altered in tone and inflection, until they signaled only annoyance, or resignation? It did nothing for a man's ego, or his performance. And it didn't help either to know that the Virgin was always watching. In the beginning Felice had felt her painted plaster eyes boring into his ass every time he mounted his wife. He'd begged, threatened and commanded her to move the shrine, but she was stubborn and devout. It gave her solace. Through the years, he'd begun to turn to the statue for solace too, and encouragement. Lying on his back afterward, he would ask the Virgin how he'd done. His wife would warn against blasphemy and cross herself.

Felice closed his eyes and pressed his body into the folds of her warm flesh. His flaccid penis was lost in the avenue of her behind. Others had died, young and old, and he was always touched. Tonight, though, he felt devastated, unable to block out the sight of the girl, a cold slab on a mortician's table, curling lips being stretched into a final smile.

CHAPTER TWENTY-NINE

Felice opened a fresh pack of Nazionali and considered the dossiers on his desk: Pietro Scorso, Stefano Malaverde and Lisa Taglia. "Ah, the wonders of the computer age. A dead girl's life can be dug up and dissected before her body is cold. Marvelous, Cenci. Will I find anything of interest here?"

"Possibly," Cenci replied noncommittally, "and possibly trouble. They all had the usual left-wing radical connections at the university. Beyond that, not much—except that the girl comes from a very wealthy family."

"Not uncommon is it in your experience?"

"This wealthy, yes. Her father is Enrico Taglia."

Felice blew a cloud of rancorous smoke through his nostrils. "*The* Enrico Taglia of Taglia-Montemercato?"

"The same."

"*Porca miseria,*" Felice swore, slamming his open palm against his forehead. "What have I done?" He raised his eyes to heaven. "Why am I cursed so? Do you know what this means, Cenci? Of course, you know. Del Sarto's phone is already ringing with orders to let the family bury the girl in peace. I bet five hundred lire you won't read a line about it in the papers after this morning's edition. We feed our children lire instead of love and wonder why, like the young Jesus, they're hell-bent on driving the money lenders from the temple. Was her father next on the list of kneecappings? Or was it her mother?"

"The mother is in the United States. The father is in Brussels on business. His office is trying to locate him."

"So then we have a few hours anyway, before the wall of official silence rises up around us." Felice opened the dossier, transforming himself into a paradigm of efficiency. "Cenci, you follow up the lead to Pescara. Try to find out if the girl was ever there. Wire her photo, see if anyone recognizes her. I'll handle this end myself." He picked up a red pen and began to read the file. It was there if he could see it. He felt it in his bones.

The cards in the girl's purse had identified her as Sandra Bassiglio, Via Joia 19, Brindisi. They'd been stolen in a raid on the town hall there, and her Uzi submachine gun had been traced to an attack on a Swiss armory. Her identity was now certified as Lisa Taglia, the wealthy, pampered and once dangerous daughter of a Milanese industrialist and an American heiress.

Felice shook his head as he read through the cold facts that identified but said nothing really about her. Just the shell, a cannellone without the filling. How would he find the meat and cheese, the egg that held it together, the herbs and seasoning that gave it zest? He warmed to the task ahead of him. He would track down every friend, every enemy, every lover. By the time he was through the cannellone would bulge. He delved into her dossier.

Sandra Bassiglio, nee Lisa Taglia. Born Dec. 24, 1952. Father, Enrico Taglia, president of Taglia-Montemercato Tires and a member of the board of directors of IBM Italy. Mother, Mary (Babe) Gaynor of Richmond, Virginia, and Rapallo, Italy; U.S. citizen, heiress to a tobacco fortune. Parents divorced 1966, amicably. Mother remarried and divorced, 1966. No siblings. Educated at the American School in Rome; Ecole Moreau, Zurich; Radcliffe College, Cambridge, Massachusetts, and the University of Rome. Political affiliations: *Studenti per una pa-*

tria libera (SPL). Fidanzato: Allesandro Buscati, Fiesole, 1973 – 76. No known address...

Felice pictured the poor little rich girl, searching for a family and a place to belong. It was corny and a cliché—but probably not so far off the mark. He hoped there was more to the girl than that...A dream couldn't be so banal without diminishing the dreamer.

CHAPTER THIRTY

There was no funeral mass for Lisa Taglia. An official from Montemercato, a professional flack, came to Rome to handle the arrangements. He requested a private meeting with the detective handling the case. He was not prepared for Guido Felice.

"The body is being flown to the States at her mother's request for burial there. Signor Taglia is too grief-stricken," the representative assured Felice somberly, "to come to Rome and view his daughter's body. She was so young, so impressionable..."

"Ah, on that point I quite agree. It is a tragedy when a girl that sheltered, that innocent gets swept up in a dangerous business like this. She was a victim, in her way, as much as the man from Fiat."

"Her father's sentiments exactly. You must be a father yourself."

"Three children, but younger."

"Of course."

Felice reached in his hip pocket and produced a leather wallet with a yellowed photograph inside. Two sallow boys and an overweight, sad-eyed girl faced the camera with frozen smiles and blank eyes.

"Beautiful," the Montemercato man murmured. His voice was dipped in olive oil. His hair too. He must swallow Bertolino by the quart to have a voice as smooth as that, Felice thought. He was dapper and supercilious, with the manners of a mortician. Taglia's troubleshooter, paid handsomely to smooth the waters.

"Did Signor Taglia love his daughter?" A foolish question.

The man from Montemercato bestowed a condescending smile on the detective. "No man loved a daughter more. Or gave her more. Wealthy men have the same paternal feelings as you or I, my friend. Money does not affect the heart."

"Then I imagine his grief is so intense that he has secluded himself on his estate."

The man from Montemercato uncrossed his legs. "Signor Taglia cannot shut himself off at a moment's notice, anymore than the prime minister could suddenly take to his bed. He is a very busy, very important man. He has commitments months ahead. You must understand, my friend, it is not like you or I. With power and position comes grave responsibility. Poor Signor Taglia, grief-stricken though he is, must carry on as always. His grief is a private matter, and that privacy must be honored."

"You mean you want no publicity?"

"None whatsoever."

"Unless I've been missing something in the papers, you've succeeded very well, so far."

"Thank you. But it isn't just the publicity. Signor Taglia wants this unpleasant matter dropped. There's no need to rake up dead leaves. Nothing will be gained—and much could be lost. He was hoping we could arrange something...just between us."

Felice let the implied threat float over him. "I'm not sure I understand what you mean."

"How plain must I be, sir?"

"Signore, I am a simple man, doing my job to the best of my limited ability, a public servant. As much as I would like to leave a father to his grief, I can't let personal considerations influence my public duty. She was a beautiful, privileged girl, full of life. I would like to know how she came so far from home...And why

184

are our children our enemy? It is very disturbing—a civil war of generations unparalleled, I think, in the history of a nation even as ancient as our own..."

The Montemercato man waited impatiently, wondering what all this had to do with the detective's role, as he put it, of "a public servant." "I will be blunt. Signor Taglia wants the investigation dropped. He is very grateful for your concern but he believes you have gone far enough. There's nothing to be gained from turning every pebble in his daughter's life over and over. I put it to you as one reasonable man to another."

"Ah!" Felice raised an eyebrow and began to search through his crowded ashtray for a butt that could be retrieved and re-lighted.

The Montemercato man watched him with disgust. *"Prego."* He flipped open a gold monogrammed cigarette case in which a dozen English Ovals were aligned and held it out to Felice. "Forgive me for not offering you one before."

"Grazie, but I believe I have found what I was looking for." The Montemercato man's nostrils flared when Felice lit up, as if he'd just caught a whiff of cow dung. "So then, if I understand you correctly, you are advising me to stop my investigation into the death of Lisa Taglia, alias Sandra Bassiglio."

"Suspend the investigation might be a more suitable way of phrasing it," he replied, "until time has softened the family's sorrow."

"How long would that be?"

"The indefinite future. Naturally, your discretion would not go unnoticed."

"And if, much as I would like to accommodate a grief-stricken family, I must put the good of the state first?"

"In that case, I'm sure you know Signor Taglia has many influential friends. It could prove to be a very shortsighted decision on your part."

"You make it difficult to refuse such a reasonable request."

"I pride myself on being a reasonable, and accommodating, man."

185

"Just as I hoped. I can see that you are and so you will appreciate my situation." Felice leaned across the desk, exhaling a gust of smoke in the other man's face. "Confidentially, just between us, my investigation has gone about as far as it can. We've pursued every angle we could find and come up with a dead end. Still, there are several questions that perplex me."

"Although I would like to help, of course, I don't think I could be of much assistance. I never saw the girl and really know very little about her—"

"You misunderstand me. I didn't imagine that you and she were confidants. I would like you to arrange an introduction for me with Signor Taglia. There are a few details of the case I'd like to discuss with him, father to father, before we consider the case closed. I had hoped he would come to Rome himself."

"I told you, Detective Felice, Signor Taglia is a very busy man."

"I do remember you saying something like that. And so I am willing to go to Milan to meet with him at his convenience. I would only take an hour or two of his time. I could go back with you directly, if that would be agreeable."

The man from Montemercato felt the perspiration gathering along the back of his neck, behind his starched collar. He had never before dealt with a more pigheaded, dull-witted man. No wonder the terrorists operated freely. "I'm afraid that's impossible, out of the question. Signor Taglia isn't even in Milan."

"He's still in Brussels then? I thought that was a three-day meeting."

"So it was," he conceded grudgingly, "but the signore is still out of the country."

"Let's see. He's not at home and he's not in Rome. And he's not at his plant in Milan or the conference in Brussels."

"Correct."

"Of course. He has sought refuge in some secluded retreat to be alone with his memories of his daughter."

The man from Montemercato smiled. "Exactly, sir. You have a father's understanding heart."

"And I don't suppose Signor Taglia would want to be disturbed by a mere police detective."

186

"You are *most* understanding, sir."

"Yes, I am. But unfortunately the terrorists are not so understanding. They won't wait for a father's heart to heal, and just between you and me, we have reason to believe that Lisa Taglia was implicated in a larger plot than the shooting of one middle-level Fiat executive."

"Signor Taglia would know nothing about that, I can assure you."

"Of course not, but he might possibly know something about his daughter that you and I do not know. Where can I find him?"

"Detective Felice, let me warn you, a man can be too persistent. Duty, like everything, carried to an unreasonable degree can prove counterproductive, even dangerous."

"I take it you enjoy threatening people."

"A word of friendly advice should not be construed as a threat."

Felice stood up and held out his hand. "The way I see it, Lisa Taglia was too sheltered, impressionable. When she went to the university she was taken in by the radicals. Once she was—how should I say it?—compromised, she couldn't see any alternative except to go along. They are a very violent, very dangerous group she was dealing with—as tough with one another as they are with their victims."

"Her father's thoughts precisely."

"I would like to have the opportunity of discussing them with him."

"As I have told you, that is out of the question."

"And her mother? Could I talk with her?"

"She's in the States and isn't expected to make a trip to Italy again in the foreseeable future. She was here just a few weeks ago."

"Then of course she saw her daugher on that trip?"

"I would have no way of knowing that."

"Were they close, mother and daughter, since the divorce?"

"The divorce was amicable, as I said before."

"Of course, I remember now. And neither has remarried?"

"I believe the signora did remarry—briefly."

"Who was he?"

"An employee of the family."

"A Montemercato executive, you mean?"

"Not exactly."

"She married a member of the household staff?"

The man from Montemercato stiffened. "It was an unpleasant incident, all round. But it's over."

"The newspapers must have been full of it. I believe I can find out easily enough all I want to know about the lucky groom."

"I may as well save you the trouble," he said unhappily. "Signora Taglia had a brief liaison with a gardener on the family estate, a young man by the name of Mario Russo. Of course it didn't last."

"And he received a very generous gift for his discretion."

"You are an understanding man, as I said before."

"I try to be...yet with all that, that scandal, the divorce was amicable?"

"As amicable as could be expected in view of the unfortunate circumstances. The boy was young enough to be her son."

"Or her daughter's lover."

"The girl was only fourteen at the time."

"Unfortunate."

"Yes."

"Is the mother as beautiful as the daughter?"

The man seemed momentarily flustered. "What an unusual question for a police investigation. I wouldn't be able to answer that. I wouldn't know."

"You wouldn't know? Why wouldn't you?" Felice lowered his voice as if he were about to reveal a deep secret. "Your boss will never hear your answer. It's strictly between us, man to man. You must have seen them both. The mother is beautiful too, I can see the answer in your eyes. You're in love with her, or why would you hesitate. It isn't wrong, you know. It's natural for a man to find another woman—even his boss's wife—desirable."

The Montemercato man looked about the office as if he were afraid of being overheard, then leaned across Felice's cluttered desk and said huskily, "Signora Taglia is the most beautiful woman I have even seen. She used to sunbathe on their yacht in the

Adriatic. I remember a day in August—I was just beginning my first year with the company. I was little more than a courier really, sent with papers for the signore to sign. I flew to Rimini, then motored to the yacht in an open skiff. I arrived in the middle of the siesta. Everyone was in the cabins below deck resting or playing cards. I went up the ladder to the deck. It was empty except for a woman sunbathing. She was lying on her stomach, asleep I supposed, and she was toasted a shimmering golden, like white grapes that have been left on the vine. I thought she was asleep. I prayed she was asleep as I stared with a gaping mouth. I was young and gauche then, and I had never seen a naked woman except my wife. Here this golden goddess was lying in the open, bare and unashamed. I thought I was dreaming. I had no idea who she was. I should have waited until the noon hour was over before making the boat trip. The sun had gone to my head, done things to my brain. While I was standing stark still, thinking this, my mind reeling, my mouth open, she turned over and raised herself up on one elbow to get a better look at me. Everything I was feeling must have been written on my face, because she laughed. And still laughing, she dropped down on her back and raised her leg, running her bare foot up my trouser until it reached the obvious bulge in my pants. 'You like what you see, don't you?' I nodded dumbly and she laughed again. 'It would be foolish to deny it in your condition. It is always foolish to deny the self-evident. That's a lesson for you to remember—especially as long as you are working for my husband, *giovanetto.*' Every inch of her was golden, even the curls between her legs...At that moment Signor Taglia poked his head up on deck. To this day I don't know how long he had been watching us. He said, 'Forgive my wife. She likes to tease, but little else. She only promises what she will not deliver.' I might still be rooted to that spot on the deck of their yacht if he hadn't interrupted us. I was sure my job was lost, my career ended before it began. I was young and foolish enough to think that it was worth it. But Signor Taglia never mentioned the incident again."

"Taglia is either a very reasonable man or a damn fool."

"The very rich are different about their women—and their men."

"You must have seen the signora again after that."

"Yes, many times, but she never remembered me."

"She's a bitch, then."

The man from Montemercato ran a hand over his slick hair, as if to reassure himself that he hadn't disturbed anything except old memories. "No," he said, "an American."

CHAPTER THIRTY-ONE

Detective Felice had been pursuing the ghost of Lisa Taglia like an exorcist, when orders came through from two ministers, one senator and General del Sarto to close the Taglia case. "The hell with it all," he cursed and indulged himself at lunch with a plate of macaroni, veal *piccato*, greens boiled with lemon for a *digestivo*, washing it all down, including a loaf of bread, a hunk of asiago, with a full liter of wine. The Frascati and the heavy meal had made him drowsy. When he got back to the office he swept the stacks of files aside and stretched out for a siesta. After all, he shrugged to Cenci as he closed his eyes, "No one wants us to work."...

The dead girl was smiling up at him from her bed. Instead of a clenched fist, she was waving gaily. The blankets were turned back just below her bare breasts. They were round and pointed, like spring buds. She was calling to him, mouthing something. He thought she wanted him to suckle her, but the words kept fading so he couldn't catch them. When he went over and knelt beside her, the waving hand turned into a clenched fist and the pink nipples began spurting blood. He tried to wipe away the startling red that splattered on him but only managed to spread it, until he was covered with her blood.

He sat up, rubbing his arms and face, trying to clean off the liquid that was drenching him....

Three thousand miles away in the rolling hill country of Kentucky, where thoroughbreds blossom as naturally as lilacs, two men waited politely in the living room of the Gaynor mansion. It was an inviting room...the draperies, sofa and overstuffed armchairs were covered in the same flowered chintz print; the straight chairs were upholstered in peach-colored moiré, a few shades lighter than the carpet.

There was nothing striking about either man, nothing memorable that seized one immediately and fixed the face and person in the mind of a stranger. There wasn't even anything to distinguish them from each other, or from countless other men of their age and size. They looked to be in their mid-thirties, clean-shaven with sandy hair and conservative summer suits (one khaki, one blue cord), blue Oxford-cloth shirts and striped regimental ties.

Outside the living room windows, as far as the eye could see, lush lawns, broken only by white picket fences, still sparkled with the morning dew. Although it was only quarter to nine you could already feel the promise of the sun. It was going to beat down all day long.

"May I help you gentlemen?" The men's attention was drawn from the view by the slurring, honeysuckle voice. The sweet smell of fresh-cut grass drifted through the open windows. "I'm Mrs. Rachel Shields, Miz Gaynor's housekeeper and companion."

The men replied by showing their badges.

"I know you're from the FBI. The maid told me." She looked at them with curiosity. "I don't recollect ever setting eyes on a real life agent before, outside the television set that is, let alone two of them. I can't imagine, though, what the Federal Bureau of Investigation would want, coming around here, looking for Miz Gaynor." As she talked, Mrs. Sheilds was appraising the two men. She was shrewder than she looked.

"We'd like a few private words with Mrs. Enrico Taglia, née

Babe Gaynor." The cord suit cleared his throat. "It's concerning the death of her daughter."

"Lisa Taglia of Rome, Italy," the khaki suit echoed.

Their voices were crisp and businesslike. Hers droned like a lazy summer day. Rachel Shields' age was a closely held secret. Her black hair, which she pulled back off her face in a tight bun, was just beginning to show the telltale signs of gray, but her figure was lithe as a schoolgirl's.

"It was a terrible shock for Miz Gaynor, poor dear. The girl was her only child. She'd been in Rome recently with friends and arrived home positively glowing. All she talked about was her visit with Lisa."

"Did you know the girl?"

"Sad to say, only from photographs."

The khaki suit stepped forward. "We'd like to talk with Mrs. Taglia now. You've been most helpful."

"I am sorry, gentlemen. She has been under sedation ever since she received the news and is unable to talk with anyone. If you need further information you might want to contact her physician, Dr. Robby Walker. Now, unless there's something else, gentlemen..."

"We just want to ask Mrs. Taglia a few questions. We won't upset her," the blue cord persisted.

The soft, lilting voice took on a hard edge. "It's out of the question. You see, gentlemen, Dr. Walker was forced to put Miz Gaynor in a private sanatorium two days ago. Dr. Walker's office is right here in town. I'm sure he'll be able to help you more than I can." She was already herding the agents toward the front door.

"Rachel, are you talking to yourself again, and at this ungodly hour not fit for man or beast. Can't a person get a little peace and quiet anymore?" The petulant voice came from the top of the stairs.

"Who's that?" the cord said. Both men were craning their necks up to see the woman.

"Oh that, that's only my sister Sarah," Rachel replied. "She's come to keep me company, what with Miz Gaynor gone and all.

But just between us, she's turning out to be more trouble than companionship."

The agents caught a glimpse of a tousled golden blond head as the door of the Gaynor mansion shut in their faces.

An afternoon hush had descended on the bar and grill of the Ritz-Carlton, dowager queen of Boston's Back Bay hotels. It was the lull between the bustle of lunch and the influx of drinkers stopping in after work for the happy hour, although no such common name would cross the lips of the Ritz clientele.

"Another Manhattan before the place becomes a dreadful crush, dear?" Ingrid Taylor-Martin said to her husband Steve, plucking the cherry from her empty glass. "I'd be happy to get the waiter for you." Ingrid stopped with the cherry poised at her lips, and looked up startled. Two men—one heavyset with thick-rimmed tortoiseshell glasses and a wash-and-wear suit; the other, considerably younger and trimmer—were smiling pleasantly down at them. The fleshy one tapped the shoulder of a passing waiter and slipped into the burgundy leather banquette beside Ingrid.

"Manhattans for my friends here, and two large Cokes with a twist of lemon for us." He waved a finger across the table at his companion, who was sitting down beside Steve. "Mind if we join you?" he asked, draping his large frame across the table.

Ingrid smiled sweetly, and bit off the cherry with her small pointed teeth. "Not at all, if you're buying."

Babe Gaynor had dropped the couple unceremoniously ten days before. Overcome by a sudden case of homesickness, she'd gone back to the old plantation, leaving them high and dry. Their bill was soaring even faster than inflation, and all they could do was sit pretty until they found someone else to pick up the tab.

"You folks wouldn't be Ingrid and Steve Taylor-Martin by any chance, would you?"

"The two and only," Ingrid said brightly. Although it was only a little after three, she and Steve were already well fortified.

The big man grinned and reached in his pocket. "FBI," he said, passing his badge across the table. "We'd like to ask you a couple of questions about some friends of yours. We know you were in Rome about two weeks ago with a Babe Gaynor, formerly Mrs. Enrico Taglia—"

"What's all this about?" Steve interrupted nervously. As long as he thought they were prospective patrons he'd been content to let Ingrid handle the two men.

"Nothing serious, as long as you're willing to cooperate. We always like to give our foreign colleagues a hand, if they ask us. And they have a few questions about the daughter, Lisa Taglia."

"Wouldn't it be more to the point to question the family? We don't even know the girl. We're acquaintances of her mother, nothing more."

"No one is suggesting an involvement on your part. But I'm sure you understand, we talk to everybody. It seems this girl, Lisa Taglia, died in a terrorist attack on Fiat headquarters in Rome."

Ingrid let out a high little shriek and covered her mouth with the blunt tips of her pink-lacquered nails. "How terrible! To be cut down like that for no reason. Poor Babe! What are these young people trying to prove? I can understand envying the rich. It's difficult not to, especially when you're at their mercy, as we all are, aren't we? But to shoot down a beautiful girl like that in cold blood just because of her name..."

The big man shifted his bulk around to look at her squarely, pressing Ingrid deeper into the corner of the banquette. "I think you have the picture confused, little lady. Lisa Taglia was shot by the Italian police." He smiled warmly. "She was *one* of those young people you were just talking about."

"There must be some mistake, you don't expect us to believe..." Steve's voice trailed off as he watched the agent across the table shaking his head.

"There's no mistake. I double-checked with Interpol. You folks wouldn't know anything about the girl's activities, would you?" The big man droned on affably, as if he were asking about a new movie.

Before either could answer, the waiter interrupted with their order. Steve blessed his arrival; it gave him time to compose himself. Ingrid's face was still ashen as she clutched her fresh drink like a lifeline. She seemed to have shrunk into herself, become even smaller. An aging child who might crumble altogether at any moment.

She pictured Lisa lying on ancient pavement somewhere, splattered with blood and begging for mercy while some hard-mouthed cop poured bullets into her lovely body. An old desire, in spite of herself, came over her. She even wanted the girl in death. She should have taken Lisa home instead of Steve. She wouldn't have been so heavy-handed. What a quartet they would have made, if Babe didn't balk. Lisa wanted mothering. It seemed everyone did...

When the waiter was out of earshot Steve took a drink and began to answer. His voice was more controlled. "We hardly know the Taglias. They're social acquaintances, nothing more. I wish we could be of more helpful."

"We have information that you traveled extensively in Europe with Babe Gaynor, mother of the deceased."

"Why do only cops say 'the deceased'? Do they teach you to say 'the deceased' in cop school?" Ingrid giggled naughtily. Her face looked oddly awry, as if she'd been wearing a mask that had slipped out of place.

The agent studied her. "Where do you two live?"

"Here at the Ritz—indefinitely."

He arched a bushy eyebrow. "Pretty high living isn't it? What do you do?"

"Search for the secret of life. Enjoy ourselves and others—the stars, the gods, the almighty omnipotent booze bottle." Ingrid was waving her delicate hands, making empty circles in the air.

"Please, darling, I believe the agent was questioning me." Steve stared intensely at his wife, trying to will her into submission. "I'm sure you'll have your turn soon enough, so try not to interrupt again."

"I was only trying to *help*."

Steve turned to the man across the table from him. If he monopolized the agent he might succeed in keeping the man's attention away from Ingrid. "If you mean are we gainfully employed, the answer is yes. We're consultants."

"Consultants in what?"

"Investments, mainly. I'm afraid if you're looking for a tip, we can't help you though. We limit our advice mostly to friends. It's a choice we can make, since we have independent means."

It was clear enough to the big man what they were...social parasites, leeches. It was none of his business. He didn't care what the Taylor-Martins' invisible means of support was. His job was to gather information on a dead girl. "Babe Gaynor was one of the friends who sought your services." It was a statement of fact, not a question.

Steve inclined his head slightly. "You could say that I suppose."

"When was the last time you saw or spoke to her?"

"Ten days ago."

"You flew together first-class from Fiumicino Airport in Rome to Logan International Airport here in Boston, on TWA flight 736 thirteen days ago. A limousine drove you directly here to the Ritz-Carlton where you checked into Suite 1110."

"My compliments to Mr. Hoover or whoever it is now. I had no idea you boys did your homework so well."

The big man ignored his sarcasm. "Mrs. Taglia checked out ten days ago. Any idea where she was going?"

"Home to the old plantation," Ingrid broke in with a thick Southern drawl.

The big man looked at her sharply. "When was the last time you saw Babe Gaynor?"

Steve answered quickly before Ingrid had a chance to say anything more. "We said good-bye to her right here at the Ritz when she was leaving."

"You haven't spoken to her since then?"

"Not a word."

"I thought you were friends."

"Not friends, acquaintances."

"Acquaintances who were close enough to travel through Europe together? Would 'travel companions' be accurate?"

Steve nodded. "You have our full itinerary, I suppose."

"We're only interested in the time you spent in Rome," the big man said. The younger one, who sat beside Steve, was like a rock...the only sign of life he gave was to sip occasionally at his Coke. The big man hadn't touched his.

"We were there a week. We stayed at the Grand." The younger man took out a notebook and ball-point pen from his jacket pocket and jotted a note.

"Do you remember the dates?"

"We flew back to the states thirteen days ago. We were in Rome seven nights. You figure it out. I'm sure you're better at math than I ever was."

"You must have seen a lot of the girl in a week."

"To the contrary, we only saw her once. The night before we left she met us for drinks at Harry's Bar on the Via Veneto. Later we went across the street to Jackie O's for a little supper. I saw her home in a cab. The next day we flew back. And *that* is the extent of our knowledge of Lisa Taglia."

"Did Mrs. Taglia make any effort to see her daughter before that?"

"I wouldn't know, she has a full social calendar."

"An intimate relationship. Mother and daughter must be very close."

"I think they were, in their own way," Steve said. "I'm sorry we can't be of greater help to you. The whole business is quite shocking. Horrifying, really. We had no idea, of course. How could we?"

"Where did the Taglia girl live?"

"I haven't the slightest idea. I dropped her off at her father's apartment near the Palatine Hill. I don't remember the exact address."

"Do you remember her talking about her friends, any names she might have mentioned, anything unusual in her behavior? I appreciate that this is unpleasant for you, as it is for her family. In view of her father's position the Italian government is trying to avoid turning the case into a public sensation, as we are on this side. But we can only keep this ugly business quiet if we get every-one's cooperation. I hope you understand what I'm saying."

"I wish we could be more help," Steve said. "It was just the usual small talk—nothing sticks in the memory. Ingrid and I will rack our brains, of course, trying to remember, but it was really quite a commonplace meeting—a mother and daughter chatting about family matters for a couple of hours. We just happened to be there—along for the ride, so to speak. If anything comes back to us, though, we'll be sure to contact you." Steve signaled to the waiter and started to get up. "Ingrid?"

Ingrid looked up suddenly. She seemed to have floated away into some world of her own, created by the Manhattans she'd been consuming at a prodigious rate, and a little by the shock. "Of course, there was that business with the Arab ambassador, or whoever he was, and the mysterious gift." She leaned over to the young agent across the table as if he were an intimate friend. "I was dying of curiosity to see what was inside, and Lisa knew it. I could see it in her eyes, but she was so mean. She refused to open it and never let it out of her sight for a second, so I didn't have a chance to sneak a peek. Now I'll never know." A small sob caught in her voice. "It's not as though everyone you know gets a present from an Arab sheik."

The waiter came over but the big man waved him off. "The last round's on us."

"No, just put it all on my tab—"

"Ed, take him with you and get the check business squared away." The young agent placed a powerful grip on Steve's arm. "May I give you a hand, sir?"

"No, *thanks,*" Steve said, "I think I can manage."

As they walked away, the big man was putting a protective arm around Ingrid. "Now then, Mrs. Martin, tell me all about that mysterious gift. I'm wondering with you what an oil sheik would be giving a rich young girl like Lisa Taglia."

CHAPTER THIRTY-TWO

"Have you ever been to Pescara, Cenci?"

Officer Cenci looked up sharply. His boss was standing over his desk. His face was as innocent and sleepy-eyed as ever, but he was in too early. That should have warned Cenci that something was afoot.

"No, sir, I never have."

"An inexcusable oversight on your part. We must make the trip then. You can't imagine what you've been missing. A still un-spoiled fishing town on the brink of the Adriatic...And while you're there, drinking in the sea air, you might find out what connections Lisa Taglia had."

"But we received the full cooperation of the carabinieri in Pes-cara. They turned up empty-handed."

"That's all the more reason for us to make the trip. These locals sometimes can't find their own noses unless they sneeze, if you understand me."

"Certainly, sir. But they may not react kindly to such an infer-ence."

"You're the soul of tact, Cenci. I leave it in your capable hands how best to proceed so as not to antagonize our provinical compatriots. I'll continue up the coast to Venice. We can leave today and be back at our desks tomorrow before anyone misses us." He winked.

Cenci considered him warily. "I thought del Sarto said the case was closed."

Felice ignored that. "You read the report too, then? Enrico Taglia is in Venice, drowning his sorrow."

Cenci nodded.

"I should have known. You're always a step ahead of me. Don't worry though," he said with a broad smile. "You can bring your box of tissues and we'll buy a toothbrush for you on the way. You see, Cenci, I have a theory which I will confess to you in the strictest confidence. The kneecapping of Petri was just the tip of the iceberg. I put myself in the place of these hoodlums...I am proud and a little cocky after *la cosa di Moro*. I've created, after all, an international sensation. I'm heady with power. What am I doing, then, shooting at Fiat executives, judges—petty bourgeoisie all of them—and at the same time if the reports we've been receiving are right, stockpiling weapons? Only one thing—gearing up for something even more explosive than Moro...It's human nature, we're never content with our last success. We must always challenge ourselves, top ourselves. Look at the daredevil or the athlete. Are these guerrillas any different? They have the same human nature, and when they stumble because they've reached too high, we must be there waiting...

"Lisa Taglia will bring us to them. She must. We have nothing else to go on. If we follow every lead about her, however slim, we'll come to another clue, and then another. Somewhere in the Taglia case is that blasted American needle, and del Sarto, the minister, the senator, the president himself be damned."

Officer Cenci listened with mixed feelings. Maybe he should have told Felice what Lisa had really said—*al Pescatore*...to the Fisherman...instead of thinking that Buscati could be frightened off. But he'd been trained to distrust everything—especially the truth. Now time was running out. How could he stop the operation

201

without compromising himself? The *covo* would turn against him and his usefulness to Moscow would be over.

"Can't you think of anything to say? Is my theory so foolish, so farfetched you can't find words to reply?" Felice was growling. Cenci had the knack of making him uncomfortable.

"We have orders, sir, from the minister himself." He had to maintain his dual role while he planned his next move.

"Yes, and we shall respect them, of course. But if I should happen to bump into a certain Signor Taglia while taking the sun in Venice and we fall into conversation as fathers do about their children, then it can't be helped, Cenci, can it?"

CHAPTER THIRTY-THREE

Guido Felice stood on the veranda of the Hôtel des Bains, feeling as out of place as a mussel in an oyster shell. So this is the Lido, he thought. Small tables covered with blue linen cloths and white wicker nineteenth-century armchairs with matching blue pillows were set up along the veranda that stretched the length of the rambling hotel. Tuxedoed waiters hovered close by, ready to leap to answer a raised finger or respond to the nod of a head. Half a dozen or so tables were occupied.

"*Cameriere*," a woman called to him. Her coloring and accent were English.

"I don't work here," he said with an awkward bow. "I am a...a guest. But perhaps I could be of some assistance anyway?"

"Thank you, no," she said brusquely with a backward glance at the squat little man. "I would have sworn you waited on me yesterday."

"We swear too easily, especially women, these days."

She seemed not to hear him.

Across the macadam road, cramped in double rows along the narrow sandbar of beach, were straw cabanas built like tropical paradises. Down the road at the Excelsior the cabanas were imitations of sultans' desert tents.

Felice started down the steps of the hotel in the general direction of the Tahitian huts. He would have liked to stop at the bar for an aperitivo to cool his body and fortify his spirit, but he was afraid of what it might cost. Pound for pound the Lido of Venice probably sported even richer flesh than Cannes or Cap d'Antibes. And the prices made it even more exclusive. It had already cost Felice more than he dared think to get there. There was parking for his car; the *motoscafo* ride across the lagoon of Venice to the Lido; the ride from the dock to the hotel, not more than a kilometer or two but too hot to walk, and the outrageous tip the bellhop had insisted on to steer him to Signor Taglia, even after he'd sworn he'd come from Montemercato on a matter of security.

The man had looked disdainfully at the five thousand lira note Felice slipped into his hand. "It can't be that important. You say you're security for Montemercato? Everything must be tight as a virgin there."

Felice didn't want to flash his police badge unless he was forced to, so he slipped another bill to the bellhop.

"Signor Taglia is a guest here, but where he might be now— in his suite, at the casino, on the mainland, in Venice, swimming, sailing, on the tennis courts, he is an enthusiastic player..." The man shrugged, overcome by the value of such possibilities.

"I see. Your memory..." Felice handed over another note.

"He's in his cabana, 4C to the left, the front line, closest to the sea of course."

"Thanks." Felice turned toward the cabanas again.

If the porch of the Hôtel des Bains made him feel out of place, the Lido itself was even worse. He'd never been more acutely aware of the ludicrous figure he cut in his black suit and black shoes, his starched white shirt now limp and crumpled from sweat, not to mention his overweight body. He felt like a priest in a nudist colony. The sleeve of his jacket looked as though it contained more material than the combined clothing of everyone on the beach. The men all seemed to be bronzed and muscular, with tight stomachs and haunches. And the women...

Felice drew in his breath. Nubile, near-naked mermaids, one more beautiful than the next as far as the eye could see. They were bare except for small disks the size of their nipples, and a bikini bottom that consisted of a single string that slipped between rounded buttocks. He gaped, blood began to rush to his head, his ears rang. Absurdly, he felt as if he might faint. A ripple of musical laughter came to him, it seemed, from a far distance. Two girls not ten feet away were pointing at him and laughing. *"Cameriere,"* one called.

Too much sun, Felice told himself, shaking his head to clear it. He turned down the beach as fast as he could, away from their laughter in the direction the bellhop had indicated. His shoes sank in the sand and filled with the annoying granules. He hated sand. Sand was why he and Elena always went to the mountains. But for this, he thought, taking in the burnished expanses of bare female flesh, he could put up with it.

Just ahead, a mixed group of a dozen or so people clustered on the sand. In their center a man sat in a canvas sling chair under a striped umbrella. A magnum of Dom Perignon languished in a silver ice bucket at his side. A silver tray of canapes gathered sand beside it. Felice recognized Enrico Taglia from his newspaper photographs. He was wearing a robin's egg-blue bikini emblazoned with the Montemercato crest. A full-length hooded terry-cloth robe of the same color and marking hung across the back of his chair, billowing in the breeze like a sail. Felice didn't have to interrupt the party. The entire group had been watching his ungainly progress with undisguised amusement.

Signor Taglia beckoned with a restrained toss of his head, and a bevy of girls crowded around him, like concubines in a seraglio. He didn't look much like a grieving father. Drops of perspiration, as big as prayer beads, were standing out on Felice's forehead. His shirt and undershirt were stuck to his chest and back like a second skin, and his shoes were so weighted with sand that the motion of putting one foot in front of the other was becoming as laborious as a child taking his first steps.

Felice shook his head at his own stupidity. Why had he expected to find Taglia alone, just because his daughter was lying in a Roman morgue? A few moments of your time, signore, as one grieving father to another... He was losing control, the dead girl was making him behave like a fool, but he stumbled forward, he couldn't stop himself.

The girls gathered closer around Taglia, giggling and pointing down the beach, then began running, bare breasts bouncing. Still laughing and chattering, they surrounded Felice, closing in on him. He raised his hands in front of his face, as if he were warding off a blow. He was afraid to push them away. Their bare flesh intimidated him.

"You are hot, signore, in your silly black suit. What you need is a refreshing swim. The water is cool and inviting."

"We'll help you," another said. "*Ragazze!*"

The girls crowded nearer. The sea and sand, the straw-roofed huts and striped parasols swam before his eyes in a mist of sweat. They pressed closer. Dear Lord, it was every man's dream to be enveloped by so many beautiful available girls, and it was his nightmare. They were pulling at his clothes, working with obvious experience on buttons and buckles. He tried to fend them off but his hand grazed a soft brown nipple and he pulled back. He felt himself shrink, useless as a eunuch. He was panting and pleading sotto voce, "*Basta, ragazze! Basta con la scherza!* Your little joke is over. Enough!"

But they were as persistent as buzzards. His cheeks burned; his penis shrank. All he could hear was Taglia's raucous laughter, so loud it seemed to drown out the roar of the sea. Felice tried to cover himself with one hand and reach into his pocket with the other. He stumbled forward three short steps, like a prisoner with cuffs around his ankles.

"Taglia, *sono il capo della* Squadra Anti-terrorismo. *Io proprio.* Police! Police!" He was shouting now, waving over his head the badge he'd finally managed to extract from his pocket.

Taglia's laugh broke off. Beneath his dark tan his face paled with anger, and he started for Felice. The girls began backing away, abruptly silenced. Even their breasts seemed suddenly still, Felice thought. He stood alone in the middle of the Lido, his trousers and shorts bunched around his legs, his shirt soaked with sweat and opened to expose his ample hairy paunch, his tie, loosened but still knotted, flapping against it.

Taglia didn't stop until he was standing directly in front of Felice. He grabbed the identification from his hand and read the name.

"Felice. Guido Felice. F-E-L-I-C-E." His voice was a light whisper, more dangerous than a shout. "I would hurry back to Rome, if I were you Guido Felice. My daughter's case is closed, or did General del Sarto forget to inform you?"

CHAPTER THIRTY-FOUR

At a lively bar in Trastevere, near Piazza Mastai, Piero Massi waited in line to pay the cashier, flipping a five hundred lira coin nervously between thin calloused fingers. There were two men ahead of him, both in business suits with short, spreading collars and black knit ties. They looked slick and shiny, like freshly simonized cars.

The cashier had a pleasant, open face. Her hair was rinsed an auburn red, the color of a certain type of hen, and set in stiff waves, as though rigor mortis had set in. Her ample chest, bundled in a blue V-neck sweater, rested against the edge of the booth. A silk scarf, splashed with brown and white, was tucked in at her neck, suggesting a certain modesty befitting a woman of her age. Massi judged her to be in her mid-fifties but he couldn't decide whether the brown-and-white design on her scarf was intended to be floral or geometric.

When it was his turn he slapped the coin down in front of her, covering it with his hand. "*Un* cappuccino *per favore,* signora."

The woman never even looked at him. She slipped her hand over his to scoop up the coin and the scrap of paper beside it, to an onlooker a crumpled bit of cigarette wrapper, perhaps, that the customer had mistakenly dropped. She raised an eyebrow when she saw the paper. It was the first time in months that he'd used the emergency underground network, but direct contact was too dangerous to risk now and he had to reach Buscati.

"*Scusi,*" he apologized.

She waved him away as he attempted to retrieve it, and she picked up both the paper and the coin. For an instant, before ringing up five hundred lire for the coffee, her hand went to her bosom to rearrange the scarf. Massi watched with approval. He had done all he could. The next move was Buscati's. He knew that the paper had found sanctuary in the cashier's ample chest. She gave him change and a receipt.

"*Grazie,*" he murmured, dropping the coins into his pocket. He crossed the narrow crowded room and tossed the receipt on the bar. "Cappuccino, *per favore.*"

The barman was lean and serious-faced. Not a motion was wasted as he made the coffee, steamed the cream and poured the two together into a glass held in a gold-colored metal holder, then swung around without spilling a drop and slid the coffee across the bar.

Massi drank it slowly. It was thick and satisfying. He thought of Lisa drinking Irish coffees on the Via Veneto..."If any decadence is worth preserving, it's the Irish coffee at Harry's." He could hear her saying it, cool and offhand. He wondered if it had ever occurred to her that she would die. It must have. But he was sure she never really believed it. Having things given to her was a part of her nature that no revolution could change. She couldn't imagine something might be taken away—especially something she took as much for granted as her life. She was immune to reeducation. Buscati too. Scratch the surface and they were both oligarchs. It was easy to say I'm prepared to die, easier and much more exhilarating to challenge death and destroy others—but the *fact* of death was something else.

Massi swirled what remained of his coffee in the glass to catch the foam that had settled around the rim, then finished it in one long drink.

"*Buona sera,*" the barman called politely as he went out. Through the cloudy window of the bar he saw the cashier talking animatedly with a woman who had just gone in. He crossed the street slowly. He hadn't realized how profoundly tired he was. He would like to have gone back to the dingy room he'd once shared with Lisa and make love to her, even if he had to force himself on her. Instead he'd have to go to his other apartment, clean and desolate.

The cashier waited until Massi was out of sight, then motioned to the bartender and went back to the small supply room behind the bar. She dropped a *gettone* into the pay telephone and dialed a number from memory. She listened to it ring twice, hung up and dialed again. While it was ringing a second time she reached inside her sweater and retrieved the note that Massi had passed to her.

"*Pronto,*" she said brightly, smoothing out the paper. She read the message crisply. "Piazza Risorgimento at five o'clock. The fat man is gaining."

"*Abbene,*" a breathy female voice replied.

The cashier didn't know to whom the voice belonged or even what the message meant, but she never doubted that it would be relayed and would eventually reach the person for whom it was intended. She was just a conduit, a thin spoke in the wheel of revolution, but she believed what she was doing was important— and safe. She was a foot soldier in the irregular forces—an army of hundreds who wanted to do their part for the cause without endangering their comfortable middle-class lives. Sometimes when she read *la Cronaca* she wondered if she'd played a part in the shooting being reported, and she felt a flush not unlike what she felt when the barman, so skilled behind his counter, so crude over her in their bed, demanded more from her than receipts for coffees and aperitivos.

Vishnevsky fell in step with Massi as he walked through Piazza Mastai. He walked briskly, a newspaper folded under one arm, his florid face even redder than usual, although it wasn't an exceptionally hot day.

"Comrade, our friends are worried. They're afraid you've forgotten them. You can speak for a moment. We're not being observed. Have you truly forgotten us?"

Massi's breath constricted in his chest, making it difficult to breathe, nearly impossible to speak. He kept looking straight ahead. "No," he managed to get out, "but it is a difficult assignment, it can't be done overnight—"

"We appreciate the difficulties. You newcomers forget, terrorism was our invention." The Russian's voice warmed but he didn't look at Massi. They walked up the street, one a step ahead of the other. "I said you could be trusted. I will tell you again, don't disappoint me, my friend. Or them."

Vishnevsky quickened his pace as they came toward the corner and turned up Viale Trastevere. Massi didn't watch him go. He turned toward the river and kept walking.

Massi strolled through Piazza Risorgimento, a paperback stuck in the back pocket of his French blue jeans. Through the perimeter of trees that sheltered the small rectangular square loomed the shadow of the Vatican. How many before them had challenged its immeasurable power and been crushed, he wondered. He circled the square a second time before he found an empty bench. It was pleasantly cool there beneath the leafy canopy. Taking Calvino's *Invisible Cities* out of his pocket, he began to read. A young man came along with a slice of watermelon he'd bought from a vendor on the corner. Settling himself on the bench halfway down from Massi, with a muttered "*Permesso,*" he began slurping the watermelon and spitting the slippery flat seeds, playing a game with himself, trying to spit each one farther than the last.

Massi cleared his throat. Buscati grinned, then laughed. It was a sound that seemed to gurgle in the back of his throat. "In the south, in Naples, they have a saying, *O mellone cchiene 'e fuoche mange, veve, e te 'llave 'a facce.* With the watermelon, you eat, you drink and you wash your face." He wiped the sleeve of his shirt across his face as he spoke.

Massi glanced over, then went back to his book. He squinted at the page of small black type that swam before his eyes in wavering

211

lines like a school of fish. Until he was nine, the tip of his nose was always black. His mother used to swat him for it. No matter how often she scrubbed his face, the next time she turned around his nose would be smudged again. She cursed him, and herself, for having borne "*una talpa.*" His fourth-grade teacher was the first to realize the cause of *il naso negro.* He held his books so close, the print rubbed off on the tip of his nose. Massi got glasses. He'd kept his nose clean ever since.

Although his wire-rimmed glasses were squatting on his nose he still raised the book up, as he had when he was a child, until it was only inches from his face and began to mumble as if he were reading aloud to himself. "*Basta.* We've gone far enough. This is my last warning. I wouldn't give it if I didn't have absolute knowledge that this thing is about to explode in our faces. Believe me. Felice's breath is on our necks. He's countermanding orders to stop the investigation and pressing ahead. Since Lisa, he's been like a man possessed. He'll stop at nothing. He seems stupid— perhaps it's an act, I'm not sure. But he's also persistent. He's taken Lisa's death like a personal affront. Right now I have reason to believe he's in Venice, grilling the mogul Taglia himself."

"Is he an idiot?" Buscati spat a black seed across the square. "Di Voto's mother swore to him that the senator made the call."

"Not only the senator, the interior minister, the minister of defense...Felice will pay dearly for his insubordination, but that won't help us. By then it will be too late. Call it off, I beg you for the last time. If you have to prove you're a man, go find some woman and show it to her."

Buscati wiped his mouth on his sleeve and spoke through it. His voice, muffled by the material, sounded almost pleasant. "This Felice was never a threat before. He's a fool, *un pagliaccio grosso.* Just put him off if he's getting close."

"He knows about you and Lisa and about SPL. The police are hunting for you, Buscati." Massi tried to keep the desperation out of his voice. He couldn't, say that Moscow was anxious. And that, ultimately, Moscow would have to be served no matter what.

Buscati spit another seed with such force that it flew across the path and landed on the bald pate of a man sitting on the grass. He pointed and laughed. "Perfect shot! The trouble with you, Massi, is you have no faith." He took a large bite out of the melon and spoke with his mouth full. "Everything is in place. One more week—that's all I need. One more week. Even you can spare me that."

Massi watched the red fruit pulverize in Buscati's mouth. "Each day brings Felice a step closer—"

"He's a family man, isn't he? Give him a scare. You know what to do." Buscati stood up and aimed at the nearest trash basket as if it were a basketball hoop. The rind hit the rim, wavered and fell in. "And, Massi, don't contact me again unless it's important. No more of these false alarms."

CHAPTER THIRTY-FIVE

Felice nodded curtly to the officer at the desk and walked quickly down the corridor to his office. Each footstep echoed with unnatural loudness in the cavernous hall. He wondered, with the detachment of a condemned man considering someone else's fate, if Taglia had reached the minister yet, and the minister had reached the general. He hesitated at the door of his office. Fear seized him and forced him to tighten his sphincter muscles. He'd seen prisoners tremble and defecate in their pants, grown men he'd arrested. Now it was his turn. He turned the knob slowly. If the general were waiting for him it would be in a flood of lights. His office was black.

Felice flicked the switch and sat down at his desk. The fear began emptying out of him like water through a sieve and he was left with nothing but exhaustion. He was drained, and he hadn't eaten since morning, but for once he had no appetite. All he wanted to do was go home to bed. It seemed as comforting now as his mother's womb.

Felice went through each sheet of paper as if it were a dead-weight, feeling as weak as a man recovering from a serious illness.

Among the messages, all routine, was a report from Cenci—one paragraph, neatly typed, exactly according to departmental regulations, and phrased with admirable discretion. The interviews he had conducted provided no additional information and of course there was no mention that they had taken place in Pescara.

Felice let out a thin plume of air. At least he could count on Cenci to keep his own counsel...not that it would matter when Enrico Taglia got through with him. *"Cafone,"* he cursed, lit a cigarette and wondered how Cenci had gotten back from Pescaro with the time and energy to write his report. He went through the remaining papers in the same mechanical way he made his penance after confession, though he couldn't remember the last time he'd been. Probably before his daughter took her first communion. His wife had insisted they all receive the sacrament together that day, and so she had dragged him to the confessional with her. She went faithfully every week, although he was sure she didn't confess what he considered her major failings. He wondered occasionally what she did say. That she overcooked the spaghetti? Or served her husband dried-up dinners? Or had submitted to his lovemaking...?

An hour later he was walking through the narrow cobblestoned streets of San Lorenzo. Every peeling facade, every step of the neighborhood was familiar and comforting. He felt the tension drain. At least he was safe for a few hours. He stopped at the bar for a Campari...he could use a drink, and here at least he wouldn't feel like a buffoon.

"Buona notte, Matteo," he called to the bartender.

"Buon giorno. It may be night for you, Guido, my friend, but it's the start of a new day for me. *Scusame,* but I follow the sun, not the police."

Felice rested one foot on the brass rail that ran along the bottom of the empty bar. "A Campari, and have one yourself."

"It's too early for me, but I'll take a coffee with you."

Matteo placed a stemmed glass of Campari in front of Felice and made himself an espresso. He was a tall sturdy man with dark swept-back hair—quite handsome by neighborhood standards in

215

his white coat and slick hair. His wife was the cashier days, but in the evenings she chose to stay at home with her children and look the other way.

"Before I forget, I have a note here for you. I haven't seen you in a week. I thought you were working too hard but now I know just what kind of work you've been doing." He winked at Felice.

Matteo started to make himself another espresso while Felice opened the note. It was printed in the large awkward script that a child might write. Felice drained his Campari in one gulp.

"*Che successo?* You look as if you just saw the ghost of your dead mother." Matteo brought a small white porcelain cup of steaming coffee and placed it on the bar.

"Where did you get this?" Felice's voice had a flat professional tone that Matteo had heard other police use but never his old friend.

"A girl left it for you."

"Do you know her?"

"No, but I know the type as well as you do. Let's say she wore her illegal profession plastered on her body like a sign."

"Would you recognize her again?"

Matteo shrugged. "One *putana* is like another. After a while they all look the same and feel the same. But if your wife caught a glimpse of her and knew she'd been in here leaving notes for you, *she'd* recognize her again." He reached across the bar and nudged Felice.

Felice pulled away and threw a bill on the table. "*Buon giorno,*" he said curtly.

"What's wrong, Guido? I was only joking. I won't breathe a word, you can trust me..." Matteo called after him but Felice was already at the door.

He thrust the note deep into his trouser pocket, kept his fist clenched around it until he'd walked the three blocks and climbed the steep flight of stairs to his own home.

He pushed open the bedroom door with the feeble gesture of an old man. In the darkness he stumbled over to the bed and began shaking his wife.

216

"*Lasciame da solo.* Leave me alone." Her speech was slurred with sleep but the irritation came through clearly. She thought he was an animal when all he was was a normal husband. She tried to push him away.

"Shut up." He switched on the light. Elena covered her eyes, sheltering them from the glare. "I'm sending you and Luisa to the mountains for a holiday."

"A holiday! *Sei pazzo.* It's five o'clock in the morning and you're talking about a holiday."

He opened her armoire and began tossing clothes onto the bed where she lay. "Here, hurry up and start packing."

His wife raised herself and started shouting at this further invasion of her privacy. "*Basta,* Guido, *basta.* Stop it or I'll call the police. I don't care who you are, I swear on the immortal soul of my mother that I will." She blessed herself hurriedly.

Felice stopped emptying the armoire and stared at her. Without another word he dug the note out of his pocket and handed it to her, then sat down heavily on the bed while she read.

"*Dio mio.*" She crossed herself again. Her face had turned the color of the bed sheets. Then, sobbing, she fell into his arms.

"*Calma, calma,*" he muttered into her shoulder, which was warm and humid from sleep. "At least the boys are safe in the country for a while."

"But why Luisa? She's just a child."

He held her tighter. "To stop me. I must be closer to something than I know," he said as much to himself as to his wife. It was the first time he'd allowed himself to think it. An hour ago that thought would have warmed him all over. Now it chilled him.

His wife was still moaning as he helped her pack. When the bags were standing at the door, stark and undeniable proof of their fear and the terrorists' power, they went into Luisa's room and woke her up. Though still half asleep she maintained a steady drizzle of complaints as they dressed her and bundled her up for the trip.

Luisa was not what Felice had once imagined his daughter would be. She was fat and lethargic, a whiner. Still, he loved her, however unreasonably. She was, after all, his. And it didn't even matter that his love was unrequited. He hugged her close and tried to kiss her. But she pulled away.

His wife paused only long enough to light another candle before the statue of the Virgin. At the door of their dark, compressed apartment, the only home they'd ever known together, she looked over the room as though she thought she'd never see it again, then hurried Luisa down the stairs, leaving her husband to carry the bags.

Felice swore under his breath that he would blow out the candle when she was gone. But of course he wouldn't dare. Who knew what curses it might bring on his unhappy, overweight daughter.

CHAPTER THIRTY-SIX

Felice put Luisa and her mother on the train, settling them in a first-class compartment, and for once Elena didn't complain about his extravagance. He then walked the kilometer and a half from the Stazione Termini to the Questura and showered there. Standing in a stall with tile that looked as ancient as the city, he watched the sand from the Lido that had hidden in the creases of his flesh gather around the drain. For once he scarcely noticed his penis. Overnight it had become a useless apparatus, good only for emptying the bladder. He pissed in the shower, aiming the line of urine at the granules of sand, trying to force them down the drain. Finally he got out, put his grimey, travel-worn clothes back on and walked with unusual briskness down the hall to his office, where Cenci was already at his desk.

"We have work to do," Felice barked to his crisp assistant.

"A report on the Taglia case from the FBI." Cenci held out a computer printout. "It just came in."

"Anything else?" Felice scanned the printout, then without waiting for an answer tucked it under his arm and started out again.

"*Che ce?*" Cenci called. "What's the matter?" Felice always prefaced each day with a litany of pleasantries that would sour the sweetest disposition. This morning he hadn't even said *buon giorno.*

Felice stopped, grimacing as if he were in physical pain, and turned to study his assistant like a stranger. "I have reason to believe that today may be the last judgment, and if it is I will be cast down much farther than hell. My only chance is to get to the general before anyone else does this morning."

Felice hadn't slept in thirty-six hours. He'd long since passed the point of normal tiredness and was operating on a surplus of nervous energy, caused by the flow of adrenaline that rushed through his body after it had been denied rest. He knew from experience that the adrenaline would last only a few hours; then he would be hit by an exhaustion so complete that the simplest motion, like lighting a cigarette, would demand a conscious exertion of strength. He had no time to waste, even on the most cursory pleasantries. If his head was going to roll anyway, he might as well make sure it bounced like Saint Paul's.

When General del Sarto arrived in his office Felice was already waiting like a humble plaintiff. He looked terrible. His clothes were disheveled and black circles rimmed his eyes. Del Sarto greeted him with disdain, but for once Felice appeared unaffected.

He cleared his throat. "I have one request, generalissimo. Give me another day on the Taglia case."

Though startled by his lieutenant's uncharacteristic abruptness, del Sarto was already shaking his head. "It's a very delicate situation, Felice. The family has been embarrassed enough. Surely you're not so dense that I have to spell it out for you. I have it on the highest authority. The girl was looking for adventure and she fell in with the wrong crowd." He made a dismissive gesture of wiping his hands. "*Basta.* Next case, lieutenant."

Felice's eyes opened wide. "*That* is what you call these terrorists who have turned our country into a warren of frightened rabbits—'the wrong crowd'? *Mi scusi, generale, ma...*" He threw up his hands.

"*Calma,* Guido, *calma.* You're romanticizing this girl." Although he was younger than his deputy del Sarto replied paternally...he didn't like being criticized by a subordinate but he couldn't risk letting the idiot detective go off upsetting everything he touched. "Who was this Lisa Taglia, after all—a rich bitch, beautiful and bored. You've seen that type before. They have everything—fast cars, their pick of men to wait on them and flatter them from the moment of puberty, pills, American whiskey. Only something forbidden, something truly dangerous can satisfy them, the way a man should satisfy a woman. She wasn't a Mata Hari or even, *grazie* il Signore, a Joan of Arc. She was a foolish girl who let herself be used. If it would satisfy your romantic nature, imagine that she fell in love and the young man turned out to be a *brigadiste*. She became a pawn in his hands. A girl in love is putty. You remember how it was. Imagine whatever you like, Felice, just close the case. The girl is in the morgue. She paid the price. There's no reason to make her family pay again. Have some compassion. Think of her as if she were your own daughter."

"I am, sir. That's why I came to plead with you." His voice was little louder than a whisper. "You see, with due respect, she was not just a pawn. I was there. I watched her. She was neither an *innocente* caught up in a terrible chain of events or a rich bitch going along for a new adventure, as you suggest. She was one of their leaders. The young men killed with her were her subordinates. It was clear she was used to giving commands. These machines the Germans and Americans have devised, these computers, are so efficient. It's incredible. They are not like me. They never make mistakes. They've traced her identity cards to a raid on the Brindisi town hall, and her weapon, an Uzi, to a terrorist attack on a Swiss armory. There's also evidence that she may be linked to the bombing of the movie house in Naples."

The general's face darkened with every word his deputy spoke. "Goddamn you, Felice. How dare you disobey my orders. I told you to *forget* Taglia. I'll handle the case myself. Have you no sense? There is nothing more to investigate."

"*Mi dispiace, generale.*" Felice raised his shoulders, signaling his helplessness in the face of the bureaucratic quagmire that controlled the life of every Roman. "You know how these things are done. The corpse is not cold before the routine tests begin—the fingerprinting, the dental impressions, the analyses of blood and urine, the hair and clothing—the results chewed up, swallowed, digested and spit back by the computers with more facts and figures than any man might want to know. I envy the digestive systems of those machines. If I could digest a bowl of *penne all'arrabbiata* with such ease I would be a happy man. But about this matter—the Taglia girl. The computers' appetite is voracious. Once they have begun to eat, we mortals are helpless to do anything except watch them belch and burp until they spit back their reports. Would you care to look at them? I have them here in my pocket." Felice's voice and expression were as bland as polenta. Without waiting for a reply he reached inside his jacket and took out a sheaf of folded papers, the sides lined with perforations, and offered them to the general.

Del Sarto accepted them grudgingly. He was trapped. Whichever way he turned could prove politically disastrous. Felice went on in the same even voice, as if unaware of the distress that was making his superior's breath come short.

"On the top you will find a report from the American FBI. I just received it this morning. Most interesting, most interesting." He waited until del Sarto had scanned it before making his request. "I want to find that box, with your permission."

Del Sarto stared over the top of the paper. His face registered the shock of someone who found a gun unexpectedly jammed between his ribs. "And where do you propose to look for it?"

"In Taglia's apartment on the Palatine." The silence in the general's office was more oppressive than the heat of a Roman August. Felice plunged on. He had nothing more to lose. Del Sarto had instructed his aide to take all his telephone calls, but Felice knew that the president of the Republic was never put on hold. He expected the roof to cave in at any moment. "Imagine, if you will, sir, that these violent incidents from Naples to Milan are not random acts as they appear at first glance but part of a much larger plan—an operation that would make the Moro affair look like child's play. We know nothing, except that the dead girl received an anonymous gift in a crowded bar from an Arab diplomat. It might be nothing more than that, or it might be the clue we need. Lisa Taglia went back to her father's apartment with the brass box described by the FBI still in her possession. For all we know it's still there. I am only asking permission to look for it. We could make it seem like a simple robbery. It could be done easily. If the box is not there the thieves escape with nothing and the illustrious Taglia, the minister, the president—all will be grateful to the police for stopping a burglary. If it is there, it disappears. If anyone misses it, he won't dare to admit it."

Felice allowed himself a faint smile. He'd made his point well. If del Sarto squelched the investigation now and the girl turned out to have been involved in a much bigger operation, his head would be delivered as splendidly as John the Baptist's, on a china platter from Ginori, and the minister and the president, who were sending him cautious warnings, would be the very ones to order it.

Del Sarto sat in silence, eyes closed, rubbing the lids in circular motions. Physically he was Felice's opposite—slender in build and precise in his movements.

"How do I explain to the minister if you bungle it?" he asked finally.

"With my ass in a *panino*. With my neck in a noose. Do I have your permission to search the apartment?"

Del Sarto's nod was almost imperceptible. "If you find something, I want to know. If you're discovered..."

"I understand, generalissimo. A word from on high and Abraham was willing to sacrifice his only son."

Del Sarto started to reply, then stopped himself. He wasn't sure if the detective was mocking him or trying too hard, as he usually did, to be accommodating. He leaned across the desk until he was as close to Felice as he could get. Tinted contact lenses made his hazel eyes appear blue.

"The case of Lisa Taglia is closed. Have I made myself clear? What you do now is out of my hands, but you know the penalty for disobeying a direct order."

CHAPTER THIRTY-SEVEN

Columns of lost palaces rose in uncompromised beauty from fields of wildflowers, purple wisteria and the dust of history. Ilex and pines and bay trees framed views of what was left of imperial Rome. Before the emperors departed, the entire Palatine had been one vast palace. Now it was the domain of hundreds of cats.

Felice stood on the crest of the hill—the Palatine before him, Enrico Taglia's apartment behind him. There was no need to rehearse their story again. Cenci would pose as an associate of the PR flack from Montemercato who had been sent to Rome to do Taglia's dirty work—to bury the girl and clamp a lid on the ugly embarrassing story. Felice was his bodyguard. He'd sent Cenci home to put on a suit and tie. Now he waited, not impatiently. He was past impatience. He felt removed from such mundane emotions as aggravation. He had only hours, perhaps minutes, left before Taglia's complaint would resound through the halls of government, shock waves bouncing from Quirinale to Ministry to Questura; only hours before the exhaustion his body was refusing to admit would reduce him to a useless mass.

Felice inhaled deeply, not the acrid fumes of a Nazionale but the sweet fragrance of the wisteria that clung in the air like a narcotic. Turning, he glanced up at the windows that he thought should be those of Taglia's apartment. He swayed back and forth on the balls of his feet and craned his body upward. If he were building up an arsenal he couldn't imagine a better place to house it than the elegant apartment of one of the girder's of postwar industrial Italy. He hoped the terrorists appreciated their own irony. He tried not to think about Luisa, but one corner of his mind was constantly worrying if she had arrived safely. If the *brigadisti* been studying him, then they knew he loved the mountains...

Felice had filed a routine report saying he'd received a threat that his daughter would be kidnapped and tortured if his investigation continued. He wasn't sure if either del Sarto or Cenci had seen it yet. He said that he'd sent his wife and daughter to the mountains. He hadn't, of course. He'd sent them home to his in-laws in Civitavecchia. Who would expect him to trust the police bureaucracy with the welfare of his own family?

Felice took long, deep drafts, filling his lungs with wisteria. He felt giddy, light-headed, and it occurred to him without much surprise that he hadn't thought of Elena in days. A fine drizzle was beginning to fall. He turned back toward the Palatine.

A yellow van had been pulling away when he arrived. Since then only one person had passed him—a tourist, unmistakably, from the camera slung around his neck, the guidebook in his hand and the way he walked. His feet were obviously sore from tramping over the stones and shards of imperial Rome. He needed a chariot. If I had lived then I wouldn't have been an emperor or even a courtier—a jester perhaps, they had them then too. Or more likely a slave, barefoot and sweating... He was thankful that he hadn't lived in a time when grown men wore togas and short tunics.

A figure small and vague was starting up the hill. Felice squinted through the mist. His hair was damp from the drizzle and plastered down on his forehead. The lone figure was climbing toward him, growing larger and clearer with each step. He raised his arm to wave, sure that it was Cenci. Just then a deafening blast exploded at his back, lifting him off his feet. Automatically his hands went to his ears to protect them from the roar and he fell face down on the pavement. Shattered glass rained down on him. A second explosion, smaller than the first, shook the street again. Chunks of metal, pieces of furniture, scraps of material and human flesh swirled down. He lay in the gutter under a sheet of debris.

The silence after the explosion was what the second after death must be like, he thought numbly. The rancid smell of smoke smothered the scent of the wisteria. He tasted warm liquid on his lips and knew it was his own blood. There was something warm and thick clouding his eyes as well. Wiping them, he tried to get up. He was still struggling when he heard footsteps behind him. Someone was running from the building. He called out to Cenci to shoot. The officer fired and missed. Not like him...

Still lying on the pavement, Felice raised himself up on one elbow and aimed carefully at the back of the fleeing figure. The man took three more strides, then fell forward. In the distance Felice heard the wail of sirens as he lurched forward again onto the cobblestones of imperial Rome.

CHAPTER THIRTY-EIGHT

The early Christians buried their martyrs in niches cut out of the walls of subterranean tufa quarries beyond the walls of the city and the reach of the law. The maze of underground tunnels and galleries is still filled with their skeletons.

In an irony that only a Roman who cloaked himself in anticlericalism as if it were sanctifying grace could enjoy, the gleaming, stainless steel room at EUR was also called The Catacomb. No man or woman, however hard-boiled, had ever come out of it without giving a full confession, even inventing more if necessary to satisfy the technicians who interrogated him. Beefy guards brandishing bats and chains had been replaced by subtle bullies—inconsequential-looking men dressed in green surgeon's gowns.

"He's just a lackey, a punk. He knows nothing. If you even look at him he shits in his pants and starts puking out everything he knows or can imagine. He's worthless, *mi scusi*. You can see for yourself. He broke before I'd even warmed up."

"*Che peccato*," Felice murmured. He could hardly blame the boy for that.

"A coward. Chicken-livered. No balls." Marcus Andresca spewed out his verdict contemptuously. He was clearly a disappointed man. Andresca was small in stature, slight in build with the quick nervous movements of a ferret and the face of an angel. A new moon of black hair encircled a bald globe. Shrewd brown eyes blinked out at the malevolent world beneath perpetually beetled brows. There was a Jesuitical cast to his face. In fact, Felice thought, he could have been a Jesuit, if he'd chosen another form of confessions.

"A pity the boy has neither courage nor valuable information. It's always a challenge to reduce the one and extract the other." Andresca's smile was beatific. He was a man who clearly enjoyed his work. "The beauty of my methods is that it leaves no scars. No visible scars, that is. It is a matter of science and skill. Unfortunately I rarely have the opportunity to practice my techniques fully. I'm like a heart surgeon. Imagine Dr. Christiaan Barnard with nothing but murmurs and not a cardiovascular infarction among them." He raised his hands in a gesture of frustration, the fingers transparent within the surgical gloves.

Involuntarily Felice's hand went up to the bandage on his forehead. Removing the splinters of glass and metal that had lodged in his scalp had been pain enough for him. The butt of a Nazionale clung to his lower lip.

"*Permesso,*" Andresca said, indicating the cigarette with a forward thrust of his chin. He was a fastidious man.

"*Mi scusi.*" Felice was about to grind out the offensive butt on the floor of The Catacomb, then thought better of it and looked around for an ashtray among the gleaming instruments. Beside them Faustus's vials and beakers of colored glass were child's play. Ah, the glories that are Rome!

Andresca came to Felice's rescue, accepting the cigarette with tweezers. Felice tried not to think what more repugnant uses the tweezers had been put to. He'd never asked how any of the equipment was applied, holding tight to his ignorance.

The Catacomb looked like an operating room or the gym of an elaborately equipped health club. Machines for stretching, shrinking and testing every part of the anatomy waited in the spotless, windowless room. Spotlights glared their hot white light at the young man strapped to what resembled a dentist's or barber's chair. His legs were belted around the arms of the chair; his hands, against the headrest. His body was drenched in sweat, his head hung down like a dead weight. He was naked except for the small metal disks still attached to his genitals.

"Untie him, please. I can't question him like that." Felice looked away, his eyes roaming around the room, searching for something to focus on so that he wouldn't have to look at the prisoner.

Andresca unstrapped Carlo Cardi and slapped him to bring him to. "*Alzi, alzi,*" he commanded. He prodded at the boy with an electric rod, forcing him to his feet. Cardi swayed uncertainly. The skin of his buttocks and back was still on the chair.

"I'll call you, Andresca, if I need you," Felice said.

Andresca nodded curtly and started out.

"And the lights please. I'm not as strong as you, my friend." He tried to speak easily to hide his revulsion.

When they were alone Cardi fell at his feet. "I will tell you anything you want to know, only get me away from that devil. I'm innocent."

The bullet had been removed but the wound was unbandaged and the leather strap had cut into the open flesh. Blood ran down his leg. Felice pointed to the wound. "Who do you think you're talking to? I gave you that when you ran out of Taglia's apartment."

"I'm not one of them. You have to believe me." He was grasping Felice's knees. "What have I done? Grabbed the *borse* of rich American women on Via Veneto, peddled stolen cigarettes. Petty things, small-time."

Felice took his arm and led him over to what looked like an operating table. He lit two cigarettes and gave one to Cardi. "So you have discovered that your friends aren't the only ones who understand terror tactics."

Cardi leaned against the table, grateful for the support and the cigarette. He inhaled deeply, drawing the smoke into his lungs, then slowly letting it escape through his nostrils. "I was nothing—

just a moving man. How did I know that I'd be moving weapons?"

"Where did the guns come from?"

"I didn't ask. Two men contacted me at dawn yesterday. I'd done a job for them once...carrying guns north from Naples. They wanted me to help them again. I rented a truck—"

"Where did the guns come from?"

Cardi shrugged. "Everyone understood they came from the Middle East, from the Libyan Qaddafi. This time there were five of us. We went to this fancy apartment and said we were delivery men. The place was empty except for servants, an old man and his wife. We gagged them and tied them to chairs in the kitchen. It was all too easy, too easy," he kept muttering to himself. "We had a van outside. We filled it with weapons, but there were so many more. I was left behind to guard the place until the others came back for a second load. They told me not to touch the stuff, just to watch the servants. I'd never handled anything more than a stiletto and there I was with all this stuff I'd never dreamed of." He shrugged. "I was curious...What did they expect? I lit a cigarette and opened this beautiful box...it was brass or something...to see what was inside. That's all I remember until you shot me."

Felice took the butt from Cardi, squashed the embers gingerly between nicotine-stained fingers and dropped it in his jacket pocket. He didn't want to give Andresca any reason to work the boy over again.

"What were the weapons for?"

Cardi began to weep. "I swear I don't know. They never told me anything. They were bragging about something—something even bigger than Moro. That's why we had to get the weapons out. They knew you were raiding the place and there was no time to get more. They never told me anything, I just heard them talking. They never told me anything..."

"What were your friends names?"

"I told that *sadico* I didn't know any of them except Di Voto— Michele Di Voto, Michele Di Voto..."

Felice left him weeping. Andresca was right. Carlo Cardi was a petty criminal not worth bothering with. A braggadacio and the first to wet his pants. He'd betray his own mother. The antibomb squad was still sifting through the ruins of Enrico Taglia's apartment when Felice walked out of The Catacomb into the futuristic square of EUR, il Duce's dream city. The newspapers were already plastered with the grisly story. Children sailed model boats in the oblong pool and shouted to one another. Their mothers sat on the benches and shouted at one another. The outer wall of the apartment had been blown out completely, twentieth-century debris to add to the dust of Imperial Rome. Among the rubble were rifle stocks, splinters of furniture and human limbs, bits and pieces of the elderly servant couple. Inside, what remained of the apartment was a heap of scrap metal.

Taglia's complaint on Felice had come through. But in the wake of the explosion the minister could do nothing more than advise the general to issue a severe reproach and curb his deputy's excesses in the future. In the meantime, the government was forced to reopen the Taglia case. Officer Cenci received special commendation for his part in the shooting and an all-points bulletin was put out for Sandro Buscati, wanted for questioning in the case.

When he got back to the office Felice fed the information Cardi had given him to the computers. Two more dead. The toll was mounting. While he was breathing wisteria and worrying about Luisa they had driven the van away under his nose. The terrorists were ahead of him again. All there was left to do was mop up the blood. An arm had been found in the rubble, believed to be female, and a straw hat with a net veil and still jaunty yellow rose, miraculously unharmed. Nothing more to indicate that a man and a woman had lived and died because once again he was too late.

CHAPTER THIRTY-NINE

"Uno, due, tre, quatro, cinque."

Sandro Buscati counted aloud to give her a head start, then sprinted up the hill after her. Paola ran faster than she ever thought she could, the excitement of being chased giving her extra speed. She felt as if she were flying, but at the crest of Monte Mario, he caught her and wrestled her to the ground, pinning her hands over her head. One minute they were panting and laughing, the next they were kissing in a way he'd never kissed her before. When he withdrew, she lay back oddly calm and touched his cheek as if it were fragile.

"Sandro," she whispered again and again.

His answer was to kiss her eyes, her hair, her forehead, her chin, the shallow hollows of her throat.

Below them at the Olympic Stadium the last seconds of the soccer game were being played. Fans were already beginning to stream out to the cars that lined both sides of Viale degli Affari Esteri. The wide avenue that swept pretentiously up to the white marble Foreign Ministry building was quiet, except when there was a soccer game at the stadium. Then it became a parking lot.

232

The roar of the crowd merged with the sound of her own heart as Sandro began to undress her. She closed her eyes. He opened her blouse wide and unfastened her bra, releasing her breasts. She trembled, startled by her own nakedness.

"You're beautiful, Paolita..."

"No, you are," she whispered, stroking his forehead.

He rested his face on her naked breast and she held him there pressed against her. He began to stroke her, kissing the valley between the rise of her breasts, his lips reaching up for her musky nipple. Then he took her in his mouth and she closed her eyes again, her whole body yearning up to his. She felt his hand slide under her skirt.

"No, Sandro, we can't," she said as her legs opened wider to him.

He stroked the inside of her thighs, tracing the line of her panties with his finger. She prayed he wouldn't stop. Her mouth felt dry, her lips were parted, she was breathing deeply. Her cheeks burned. She'd never imagined anything could be like this. She moved on the grassy slope, hungry for more.

"Don't stop now," she begged.

A laugh gurgled up from somewhere deep in his throat, and he reached inside her pants, opening her gently with his hand.

"I love you, I love you, I love you..." She said it over and over.

"Do you want me too?"

She nodded.

"Tell me that you do. Tell me how much you want me to take you."

Paola looked up at him, her eyes full of love and desire, and suddenly she began to scream. Over his shoulder she could see a wizened man standing on the ridge of the hill. His fly was open and he was masturbating. Sandro jumped up swearing and ran at the man, who disappeared in the bushes as soundlessly as he'd come.

By the time Sandro got back, Paola was already buttoning her blouse. He held her tight in his arms.

"They're harmless, men like that. Don't worry, he couldn't see

233

anything that far away, he was just imagining.—"

"It made me feel dirty." She shuddered.

"Has he spoiled everything for you?"

Paola snuggled against him. "Nothing could do that."

He looked at her for a while, then said, "Will you make love to me the next time, Paolita?"

She nodded, looked away. "If you show me how."

He kissed her cheek. "Next time I'll bring something—some protection. I can't take any chances with you, *carina.*"

The soccer game was over by the time they walked back down the hill. The avenue was empty again, except for the ministry building constructed by Mussolini and the two low buildings on either side of it, built for the 1960 Olympics and now used for an international student center. Ponte Milvio lay a few steps to the north.

Sandro kissed her again in front of the Foreign Ministry, his lips and tongue promising what would happen the next time. She started home, then ran back for a last kiss. Started a second time, and turned back again. He watched her go for the third time until she was out of sight.

The apartment was empty when she got home. Signora Mirabella had gone to Brescia for the day to visit her mother. Paola opened the door to Franco's room, thinking he might still be taking a siesta. Sleeping was his main occupation since coming home. She threw up her hands and laughed out loud. "What a mess!"

Franco had become obsessive about his privacy, not allowing either her or her mother into his room, even to clean. The closeness of the shuttered room was oppressive. Opening the windows, Paola went to work. The sheets were the color of soot. She stripped the bed and turned the mattress, humming all the time to herself—saw a small black notebook taped to the springs.

Paola hesitated, then pulled it off. She knew she shouldn't pry but the temptation was irresistible. She'd just glance at her brother's diary, then put it back and Franco would never know the

234

difference. Still humming, she sat down on the arm of a chair with the notebook. It seemed more like a timetable than a diary. She'd just started reading when she heard her mother come in.

Slipping it into her skirt pocket, she made the bed the way it had been, putting the soiled sheets on again, though she wasn't exactly sure why. She intended to ask Franco what the notebook meant when he got home, but instead she fell asleep and never saw him until the following evening.

She was watching television with her mother after dinner when he burst out of his room.

"Which one of you has been in my room?" He was as white as a cloud.

"I'm the guilty one," Paola admitted brightly. "I was going to change your sheets—"

"Where did you put it?" he demanded.

"I won't give it back until you tell me what it means," she teased, not thinking that there was anything to his cryptic notations ...she'd only taken the notebook to ask him what it meant, she intended to give it back...

Franco turned on her with a look that sent shivers up her spine. "What's the matter?"

"You are." He lunged at her, grabbing her by the hair. Though slight, he was wiry and strong for his size. Paola burst into tears.

"*Basta*, Franco. Your sister likes to tease you, that's all. Have you forgotten how the two of you used to be—holding hands one minute and wringing each other's necks the next?"

"Where *is* it? Where did you put it? I'll kill you if you don't give it back, I swear I will."

Paola wriggled away from him and ran toward her room. "Leave him, mama, there's something eating at him inside." She slammed the door shut but he burst in after her.

Paola had tried to make the dim, cramped room as pretty as she could. Her mother had been swaddled in grief when they moved to the new apartment, so she'd decorated it herself, afraid to appear frivolous by asking for help. The results were amateurish and only partially successful. The hand-stitched curtains and matching chair cover were a polished cotton of full-blown yellow roses against a sky-blue background. A yellow eyelet spread that she'd bought with her employee discount covered the bed. Propped against the pillow in splendid isolation sat a porcelain doll, the finest thing Paloa had ever owned; it wore a white satin evening dress with a miniature gold cross around its neck and a black lace mantilla in its hair secured with a pink flower. Her father had presented it to her on her tenth feast day, the only one he'd ever remembered. Opposite the bed was a painted wooden bureau, originally designed for a child's room. A low bookcase containing a few books, framed photographs and useless mementos ran under the window. The floor and walls were still bare except for a mirror hanging over the bureau.

"Where is it? I'm going to find it if I have to tear this room to shreds and you with it." Franco started emptying drawers and sweeping things onto the floor.

Paola revolved around him in desperate circles. "Are you crazy, Franco?" She lunged for her treasured possessions—the blue-and-white crocheted box with the little good jewelry she owned, the picture of her father holding her on his shoulder when she was three, the silky pink chemise from Sandro. "It's just a little notebook, *stop* it." She grabbed for his arm but he turned on her, pushing her down on the bed.

"Where is it? Give it to me!" He was beating her head against the baseboard, hysterical now.

"*Lasciame* and I'll tell you," she screamed. "I...I hid it in my bra." She thought that would stop him, but Franco couldn't or wouldn't stop. He began pulling her blouse, clawing at the thin cotton. The doll rolled off the bed and shattered against the bedpost as it fell.

"No, Franco!" Paola gasped. She tried to cover herself but she was helpless. The material ripped.

Paola lay back, suddenly still. Her breath came in heavy waves. A red scratch mark ran across the mound of her breast to the nipple. Franco, suddenly still too, stared at the naked flesh rising and falling.

236

He stared, unable to turn away, as if he were hypnotized by the motion. Tears began to stream unchecked down his sallow cheeks.

Paola reached up for her brother and laid his wet face against her.

"Let me help you, Franco..."

"You can't help me now. No one can." He nuzzled deeper into the soft pillow and wept, helpless to stop....

At first he'd been excited by Buscati's plan and proud to be included for the first time in the innermost *covo*. If they kidnapped Paul, he kept telling himself, they could insist as ransom that the Church divest itself of all its wealth and distribute it to the true faithful, the suffering proletariat. All *he* had to do was supply information. He'd be a conduit, playing no part in what might follow. He wanted to belong so badly he'd forced his doubts and fears aside. But the memories of Moro's humiliating trial and even more humiliating death would not be forgotten. The contrast between the celebrant proceeding painfully through the solemn mass for Moro and the vibrant priest he'd once loved as much as his own father had shaken him. Paul had looked very old and very sick. Each step, each motion seemed agonizing. He was seventy-five...eighty? What if he was too weak to withstand the ordeal? What if he refused to be ransomed? Buscati wouldn't answer...

A tear rolled down Paola's breast and clung to her nipple. Franco caught it with his tongue. Salt trickled into the scratch, stinging her, but she didn't flinch. She pressed his face tighter against her and continued to stroke his head, making maternal sounds, until he took her nipple in his mouth and began to suckle. Only then did his crying stop.

In the living room the signora smiled fondly. It was just like old times again. The children fighting over some foolish little notebook, as if there wasn't enough paper around the house for both of them. From the quietness now she knew they were making up, as they always had. She dropped off to sleep watching television, the smile still on her lips.

* * *

It was just after dawn when Paola went into the bathroom and locked the door. Franco was still asleep. She emptied out the hamper and found the skirt she'd been wearing the day before. Franco's notebook was still in the pocket. She sat down on the toilet and read it again, this time with more care.

La rete del pescatore, it said in his neat script. The net is cast and we wait impatiently for the catch. What could it mean? A five-pointed star was drawn on the inside back cover. She thought of Franco at Moro's mass and began to tremble...

Getting up heavily, Paola went to the medicine closet, took down the adhesive tape and fastened the notebook securely inside her pants. It was the only place left that she could think of that might be safe. She left for work early to avoid seeing her brother again, and that evening she called to tell her mother she'd be working late and was going to spend the night at her friend Gabriella's...

CHAPTER FORTY

The Berlinguers' apartment in the Prati section was modest though comfortable and as heavily guarded as an artillery post. The Communist chief couldn't afford any display of wealth or class. Only in the USSR were private dachas admissible.

Signora Berlinguer received Detective Felice in the formal parlor. She'd just come home from mass, which she attended daily, her husband's position and philosophy notwithstanding, and she was still wearing her hat, a stylish navy straw skimmer with a veil that she pulled back when she went to make lemonade for him. She served the drinks herself. No servants were visible in the home of the Communist chief.

"My husband should return shortly. Was he expecting you?"

"Yes, he was, signora, but it is my good fortune that he has been detained."

She accepted the compliment with a gracious smile. She was a handsome woman, courteous, composed and somehow sorrowful. She didn't ask why he wanted information about Sandro Buscati. Maybe she didn't need to ask, or maybe she just didn't want to know. Felice guessed it was the first. She was clearly an intelligent woman.

"Sandro was like a son to us—he always will be. He lived with us when he attended the university. Those were happy days. But the young like their freedom. Sandro was no exception." She smiled fondly. "I can remember once wanting desperately to be independent. My family always seemed to be blocking my way—with the best of intentions. Young men feel it even more strongly, I think, don't you? By the time I realized how foolish I was it was too late. It always seems to be too late for those who really love us. But you came to talk about Sandro, Detective Felice, not to listen to me reminisce. Forgive me. We don't see as much of him anymore as we'd like."

Berlinguer strode into the room before she could say more. "My apologies, I was unfortunately detained but I see my wife has been taking care of you. Why are you looking for Buscati?"

Felice lumbered up and shook hands. "For questioning only, in connection with the investigation of the terrorist Lisa Taglia. I imagine you're familiar with the case. We have information that Buscati was engaged to her."

"They were at one time. They met in school in Switzerland, I believe, when they were both very young. Too young to know their own minds. Beyond that..." He raised an eyebrow and shoulder, indicating the futility of Felice's visit. He'd only agreed to it to quash the viperous rumors circulating within the government. Although he'd condemned the *brigadisti* publicly, he knew many people still blamed him for the Moro tragedy. A faction among the Christian Democrats persisted in accusing him of withholding vital information—clues to the identity of the kidnappers and the whereabouts of their prisoner. Even a growing number within his own party worried that his independent line had so provoked Moscow that in retaliation the Soviets had bankrolled the terrorists.

"I assured your general that I'd cooperate, but there is little more I can add to your file. We took the boy in because his parents had been dear friends. They were both killed in the Resistance. He has no family left, except a sickly grandfather and an aunt in Fiesole. Beside them the Fascists look like anarchists."

240

"And the young Buscati is a Communist like yourself?"

"He is a Marxist—but not like me." Berlinguer's lean, angular body was taut. Through the years he'd kept in occasional touch as young Sandro was sent from one exclusive boarding school to another. It seemed the least he could do for Alessandro and Claudia. Sandro had obeyed his grandfather until the day he came of age, then he'd gone off to Rome, determined to be true to his father. He was brilliant, uncompromising and totally committed—the successor Berlinguer had been looking for to take his place one day. He had trained Sandro, and loved him like a son. It wasn't enough... "Buscati left here the day I agreed to join the Moro government. Neither my wife nor I has communicated with him since." He smiled thinly. "Compromise is not in the vocabulary of a young ideologue. It was an unfortunate breach, my wife had grown fond of the boy."

"Can you tell me if he was a member of the *Studenti per una patria libera?*"

Berlinguer paused. "I don't know that he was a member, but he was interested in the group. Those ideas are very popular at the university."

"*Permesso,* signore, but are they also your ideas?"

"They are the ideas of Professor Marcus Rose's. He professes to be a philosopher and the club's spiritual leader. You should talk to him. I regret I can't be more helpful. If I receive any information on Sandro I will notify you at once."

Berlinguer was brusque and to the point. Felice would not question him or his wife more closely. He had to walk a delicate line.

The signora showed him to the door. "If you do find Sandro, Detective Felice, tell him his room is waiting."

"Not just his room, I think."

"You are a kind man," she said as she closed the door. "I wish I could pray for your success."

CHAPTER FORTY-ONE

The road wound up from the riverbanks of Florence through the foothills of the Apennines toward the Etruscan town of Fiesole. "Look back, my friend," Felice urged Cenci, "the view will take your breath away."

The flowering of the Renaissance stretched out beyond the sweep of poplars and pines and olive trees. The sun glinted off the crowns of the trees, threading the green with silver webs. Orange-tiled roofs spread across the city of Florence. Rising through them towered Brunelleschi's ribbed dome of the Duomo, which, according to specifications, had to reach such a height and power that no one thereafter could expect to see anything more magnificent from human handiwork.

"It isn't Rome, of course, but it's not bad for Tuscany," Felice said.

They found a *pensione* in Feisole and took two rooms, spare and clean, for the night. Felice would have liked a bowl of soup and a glass of wine, but the afternoon was already half spent and they hadn't come all that way to admire the view or linger over lunch. The *patrone* directed them to the Villa Buscati. Cenci seemed anxious to reach their destination. If it had been anyone else Felice would have ascribed his attitude to normal curiosity, but Cenci could never be accused of such an understandable reaction.

Felice ran over in his mind what they'd discovered about Sandro Buscati. He was the most promising clue they'd gotten from the Taglia girl's thickening dossier. She'd been engaged to him once. On the surface it seemed like a glorious match—she with her new industrial wealth and striking beauty, he a scion of the old Tuscan aristocracy. Felice wondered what had gone wrong. The list of known or suspected lovers that followed Buscati made his stomach turn. Lovers or violators. In her case he wasn't sure there was a difference.

They found the Villa Buscati without difficulty. The *patrone*'s directions had been clear. Everyone, it seemed, knew the place— and why not. From the looks of it, it must have been sitting there for centuries. The meanest imagination could picture what Villa Buscati must have looked like once. Now the walls that surrounded the vast property were crumbling. Weeds and saplings stuck up arrogantly through the cracks. No one answered their calls, so Felice got out and opened the high iron gates to allow Cenci to drive through. The gates were heavy and needed oiling. Inside the walls the once formal gardens had gone to seed and sprawled over their beds into the gravel paths like unkempt rebels.

A round, worried-looking woman bustled out of the villa, wiping her hands on her apron and shouting at them as they approached to get out. The villa was private property. Even after Felice had identified them the woman still shook her head, her suspicion only deepened.

"Signor Buscati can't talk to you. He is ill and very old, withered up like a fossil. Only Signorina Buscati and I are here. The others have all left or been let go. How can you expect me to keep up an ark of a place like this alone..." Her hand swept behind her and over her head in an encompassing circle of despair.

Felice clucked sympathetically. Cenci stared, his computer-gaze devouring every detail of the place—memorizing it, compartmentalizing it, filing it, storing it.

Signorina Buscati granted them an interview in a square frescoed room across the courtyard that once must have been a music room. The furniture included a harp and pianoforte and was covered in heavy yellowed sheeting. She sat stiff-backed and tight-lipped on a straight chair with lion heads curling around the back. It was the only seat that wasn't covered. Beside her in a wheelchair a vacant-eyed old man with flowing white hair mumbled to himself, punctuating his interior monologue with hoots of raucous laughter, as if he were goosing himself or recalling some ribald joke, which seemed totally out of character with the place and with his classical face.

Signorina Buscati spoke brusquely, her voice as empty as an echo. Bitterness soured every word. "*Communists!*" She spat out the syllables like cherry pits. "There is nothing more to say. I ask myself why we expected more from the son of a whore? It was in his blood. Bad blood. *Povero,* Alessandro, not the son, the father, my brother—*un innocente* led astray like a sheep from the fold."

She folded her arms across her vacant chest as she spoke. Long bony fingers, thin violet veins like the tendrils of a plant spreading across the hands, clutched at the sered flesh encased in black crepe.

That evening, on a terraced garden with Florence dim below them in the distance and the Tuscan skies an inky blue overhead, Felice and Cenci sat encased in the blackness of the night. They had dined alone. In spite of the excellent dinner—a risotto in a light cream sauce with wild mushrooms and a thin broiled beef-steak with a full-bodied Chianti—neither man felt satisfied. A pall hung over their table. The beautiful spot, the pleasure of being away from the Questura even on business—nothing helped. Both men felt vaguely apprehensive. They couldn't escape the specter-like Buscatis. Death hovered around them, making it difficult to swallow.

Felice brooded. The meeting at Villa Buscati was an omen. They hadn't spoken about it, except briefly on the drive back to Fiesole.

"Let the dead bury the dead," Felice had said.

Cenci did not answer.

244

CHAPTER FORTY-TWO

Via del Mare leads past the ancient aqueducts of Rome and bill-
boards advertising Jantzen swimsuits, to the bloody beaches of
Anzio and Nettuno and to the bustling confusion of Leonardo da
Vinci International Airport. The road was crowded and Massi
drove with caution, although the heavy traffic parted like the Red
Sea at the sight of his white sedan.

At the intersection, where the road converged, the beaches to
the left, the airport to the right and the sea straight ahead, he
turned right and drove to Fiumicino. He parked in one of the
spaces marked *riservato* in bright red, block letters. The guards at
the entrance of the airport saluted as he passed, a leather shoulder
bag slung over one shoulder. He went directly to the private office
of Dottore Ettore Guardi, director of the airport. Dottore Guardi
was a worried man in the best of times. He gazed out at the world
with deep reservations from behind thick-framed tinted glasses.

The two men went over the schedule of arrivals and departures
and reviewed the tightened security measures effected by order
of the Consiglio dei Ministri. When they were through, the director walked Massi outside where a carabiniere waited on a mo-

torcycle to escort him around the airport. Massi shook hands with Guardi and climbed into the sidecar.

Alitalia Flight 179, Rome to Boston, was preparing for takeoff. He watched the ground crew work, even checking the baggage hold as the last piece of luggage was loaded. As he leaned into the hold he swung the leather bag forward and pulled a tab on the side, opening the bottom of the bag. A smaller bag, containing what looked like a tape recorder cassette, dropped into the luggage compartment. He snapped the tab shut again and turned back to the crew. Shouting a few words of praise over the firing of the engines, he climbed back into the sidecar to continue his check.

The passengers were lining up at the gate to board Flight 179 when Massi turned back onto Via del Mare. He looked at his watch. Two hundred eighteen passengers were scheduled on the flight. In nine minutes, when their seat belts were securely fastened and the plane started its ascent, the change in pressure would cause the barometric bomb he had deposited in the baggage hold to explode, engulfing the 747 in an inferno.

He accelerated swiftly and the traffic, which was lighter now, again parted to let him pass. Through the rearview mirror he saw the flames silhouetted against the sky—brilliant orange streaked with vermilion. It was three minutes early, still the fire was spectacular.

Massi drove slowly, watching through the mirror all the way. He hadn't wanted a woman since Lisa. Now he experienced a resurrection, and it had been only fourteen days, not forty. He remembered them all—every girl he'd had or ever wanted. His mother, who didn't know how to love him except by carping at him and criticizing everything he did. (She went to work as a maid after his father left them...he couldn't make her understand that he'd rather go hungry than have her clean other people's dirt for him.) The pretty cousin he'd forced down behind the church when they were supposed to be hearing mass. The bovine Czech instructor at the training camp in Karlovy Vary who'd forced him to perform with a bayonet at his throat. His Japanese classmate at "The Center," 2 Dzerhinsky Square, Moscow. They'd looked on themselves as the chosen few, elected for special, advanced training at KGB headquarters, and when they mounted each other it was in deadly earnest, as if they were performing for the greater glory of the Party.

He unbuttoned his trousers and gripped himself. He'd never been bigger. Lisa, of course, would have laughed at him. His foot pressed down hard on the accelerator as he came into Rome.

CHAPTER FORTY-THREE

"I have agreed to every request, no matter how tenuous, or dangerous to me personally. Do I get even one arrest in return? No, I get a phosphorous bomb planted at Fiumicino—a million, two million in damages, a 747 demolished, three dead and eighty-four wounded. Where was the special security the Council of Ministers authorized on your request? Who is to be held accountable?"

Felice stood on the carpet in front of the general's long desk like a schoolboy for whom a licking was overdue. His whole body, from his heavy eyelids down, seemed to droop. Cenci stood at military attention at his side. Felice wished del Sarto would turn red and pound the desk as he usually did. His carefully measured anger was somehow more menacing.

"What can I say?" Felice shrugged. "You are a patient man, *grazie Dio,* and you must be even more patient. An arrest would look good in the papers but it would mean nothing. There is no shortcut. All we can do is inch along, putting one and one and one together and hoping, *magari,* we get a five, an eight, even a two. We are investigating the airport bombing but there is no reason to think the pattern will change until—"

"Until we have another *cosa di Moro* on our hands." Del Sarto was leaning across his desk so that, although spoken softly, every syllable was enunciated. "Moro, Moro, Moro! *Basta con la cosa di Moro.* It's the rope that will strangle us all. It was a tragedy. A national humiliation, but we can't keep beating our breasts and responding to each new case with our guilt. Aldo Moro is dead. Why can't we let him rest in peace at last?"

Felice's body seemed to rise above the fussilade. "Because we're facing something as big or bigger than Moro. I can't prove it yet, but I sense with everything in me that all these incidents, no matter how serious in themselves, are only a prelude to something else. The question is what? It's foolish to worry about another kidnapping, because there is no other Moro. Whom would it be— Andreotti, Berlinguer, Fanfani? *Mi scusi,* all fine men I'm sure, but they're not the heart of Italy, the bread and wine of our country—at least not in my opinion. You may well differ."

Del Sarto's office was as inhospitable as a desert. He wasn't accustomed to having his officers answer back. They might curse him behind his back but none had ever contradicted him publicly before, and he would make sure none dared to again. Ignoring Felice, he turned to Cenci.

"And you, Cenci, what is your opinion?"

"As Detective Felice has said, sir. *La cosa di Moro* was as much a symbolic act as it was a foul murder. He was the cement that was holding the country together. One can argue that without him Italy would be a broken dish. If you don't have the cement, then the pieces will fall apart, the nation will collapse."

Del Sarto drummed on the desk impatiently. "Do you agree with that thinking, Cenci?"

"It's one way of looking at the national crisis, sir. I don't necessarily concur but I see the validity of the argument—"

"Generalissimo..." Felice's anger was fanned by frustration. "If we rule out kidnapping then we're left with a puzzle with many pieces that we keep shuffling around on a board. They all seem to fit together, yet no picture emerges...We have a flurry of underground activity, an arsenal that explodes in our face—the work it now appears of Michele di Voto who has a long history of subversive activity—and a dead girl, a seasoned terrorist. All leading us where? To Pescara? Hardly. The girl's former fiancé, this Buscati, may be able to point us in some other direction, if we can find him in time. We have information—although it's still very tenuous—implicating him in the Moro kidnapping. Officer Cenci is personally organizing the manhunt for Buscati."

"*Abbene,* then I can expect him to be apprehended swiftly."

Cenci accepted the compliment with a slight bow. Felice didn't acknowledge the barb.

"Buscati apparently intiated Lisa Taglia in sex, and we can only surmise what else. He is a PCI member. His parents were Resistance workers, both killed in the war. The family is very patrician and wealthy. They've disowned the boy, as they disowned his father. The grandfather is the closest remaining relative—an ancient patriarch now sunk in a torpor of senility and guarded by a maiden aunt. You know the type—stiff-backed, thin-lipped and shrouded in black, as if she'd died years ago and was just waiting to be buried. The home is a mausoleum."

"You've been there?"

"Cenci and I made the trip to Fiesole. We returned yesterday. The report should be on your desk."

Del Sarto grunted. He didn't look through the papers stacked in a neat pile in front of him. "What did you get from Berlinguer?"

"Nothing substantial. The signora was very protective, and he was closed-mouthed. Evidently Buscati lived there until Berlinguer agreed to join the government, then he moved out in a pique and hasn't been heard from since. Or so they say. He and the Taglia girl were both involved in a radical university club, SPL, organized and enlightened by Marcus Rose, a Marxist philosopher who advocates the violent overthrow of the state. It all fits together, but leads nowhere." Felice paused. He had given his report accurately and without emotion. The general listened but made no response. A stalemate has no winner or loser, Felice thought.

"Maybe I'll have a talk with Professor Rose," Felice said. "If I understood how these radical children think, I might see where they are leading us."

The General shook his head. "Talk is cheap, detective...Don't you agree, Officer Cenci?"

CHAPTER FORTY-FOUR

A single ray of light escaped from the wooden confessional and bisected the side aisle of the Church of Madre di Dio. Otherwise it was dim and cool. Outside the sun was dropping, bringing Romans relief from its blistering rays. The evening cacophony of traffic—blaring horns, quarrelsome drivers, the roar of motor-bikes—was just beginning, but the thick stone walls formed a noise barrier. Inside the church the only sounds were the nervous rustling of the girl who knelt rigidly in a back pew and the occasional cough of the priest who waited patiently to forgive the sins of the faithful, even though most of them had forgotten that he was keeping his solitary vigil.

Hearing confessions was Monsignor Giacomo Vecchione's personal penance. He shouldn't complain, though. It was the only pastoral duty he was called on to perform. Once a week he dragged himself away from the manuscript he was writing. It would be the true story of how Pacelli responded to Hitler, exposing once and for all the lies and distortions that had been publicized so widely. He had been first assistant to the nuncio in Berlin, yet he refused to speak publicly. In the privacy of his study in a secluded convent on Monte Mario he was painstakingly transcribing the truth in longhand, locking each sheet in his safe as he finished it. It was his last will and testament, not to be published until his death.

Monsignor Vecchione was a canon of St. Peter's, although he'd been retired for five years because of failing health. He was short and voluble, with a surfeit of nervous energy. His skin was pasty white, as if it had rarely been exposed to the sun in seventy-odd years. His sparse hair, which he kept the same rich brown color of his youth, was combed over his scalp in a vain effort to camouflage its bareness. A brilliant canonist, an arch-conservative, a disciple of the feared and powerful potentate of the Church, the now blind and bedridden Cardinal Ottaviani, he was that rare combination—a gregarious scholar. His tongue tried valiantly to keep pace with his febrile brain. As a result, he spoke as rapidly as a machine gun and in half a dozen languages, frequently lapsing from one to the other absentmindedly. He spoke each with a thick Italian accent, so that while his vocabularies were remarkable the language—whether German, French, English, Spanish or Greek—invariably sounded more like Italian.

The only duty delegated to Monsignor Vecchione since his retirement was to hear confessions at the Church of Madre di Dio. The church sat at the center of Ponte Milvio—the tobacconist, *gelataio,* post office, *trattoria,* meat market with the fresh carcasses of chickens and rabbits hanging in the window to attract the shoppers, bar, *alimentari* and gas station all arching in a semicircle around it. There was little else to the village, except the ancient bridge, which had spanned the Tiber since Constantine.

Monsignor Vecchione closed his breviary and reached up to flick off the reading light in the confessional. As he did, a figure crossed through its beam. He hesitated a moment, listening. Then turned the light off with a sigh. Why did they always wait until the last moment? Only two confessions all day and now that he was ready to leave, here was a penitent who more than likely wanted counseling on her entire life, and the lives of her husband, her children, her cousins and neighbors.

Paola Mirabella knelt in the cramped confessional and made the sign of the cross. She had been kneeling in the back of the church for over an hour, praying fervently to the Virgin Mary for help. But the Virgin seemed not to be listening that day, or not to know the answer. Paola wished there was someone she could turn to. Her father would have known what was right for his son. He would have been able to read the cryptic notebook she'd discovered. Franco was easily led astray by his own dreams and delusions. She knew him better than anyone in the world, and she loved him. She could never betray him, any more than she could abandon him now. Was she doing the right thing? The priest was leaning over, his face half-buried in his hands, his ear close to the grating that separated them, waiting for her to begin her confession.

"Bless me, father, for I have sinned," she whispered. Her voice was so soft that the priest leaned even closer until his ear was pressed against the grid.

"Speak up, my child."

Paola began again. "Bless me, father, for I have sinned."

Although she wasn't here to confess her own sins, she didn't know how else to start. She would never confess her love for Sandro. In the eyes of Mother Church, it might seem wrong. Fornication was an ugly word, forbidden in thought and deed. But in her heart she knew that no love as deep and full as theirs could be bad. God was love. Christ was love. No, she would not confess her love for Sandro. She wouldn't diminish it by even considering that it might be sinful. The priest was still waiting.

"It is not my own sins I have come to confess," Paola began awkwardly, "although I did take a...a..."

Her voice was so soft, and tearful, that Monsignor Vecchione turned and squinted through the dark grate, trying to see her more clearly. All he could make out was a bowed head. "What did you take, my child?"

"A small black notebook."

She must be scarcely more than a child to be distraught over such a minor theft, he thought. Why he himself had lifted a pen from a *tabaccaio* when he was a boy, then felt so guilty he'd returned it.

"Who did you take the notebook from?"

"From my brother, Franco."

"Ah, your brother. Well then, the solution is simple. Give the notebook back to your brother and the Lord will forgive you." He smiled at the innocence of her transgression. "Now that will be penance enough for you." He raised his right hand. "*Absolvo te*—"

"No, *no,* father, I can't return it, although he says he will kill me if I don't. It's so…so secret, so mysterious—" She broke off, wishing that she'd never come yet not knowing how to end her confession. She should have confided in Sandro. He was Franco's friend. He'd know what to do better than an anonymous priest.

"What is troubling you, my daughter. It can't be just a notebook, no matter how secret it is. You shouldn't be afraid to tell the Lord. You are His child, He is your father. You must never be afraid to bring your troubles to Him."

Paola wasn't sure herself what she'd thought the priest could do. She didn't recognize him, although she and her mother knew all the padres at Madre di Dio. She'd only come because the seal of the confessional would preserve her secret. Franco would still be safe.

"It's not just that my brother is a Communist, father. It's worse, I know it," she whispered. "It is all written out in the notebook but I can't understand it—" Her voice broke. "What can I do? I can't go to the police. How can I save my brother? I'm so frightened for him…I'm afraid he has joined *i brigadisti.*"

"That is a matter for the police then, not the priest."

"No." Paola said.

"What would make you do your duty, my daughter? If you had known that Moro would be slain, would you have sacrificed your brother?"

Monsignor Vecchione's voice was gentle, but the moral dilemma he posed struck Paola deeply. She looked up and her eyes met his. "Franco is my brother. Before everything else, he is my brother. How could I betray him—no matter what he has done or plans to do?"

"Then why have you come here seeking guidance?"

"I thought the priest would know how to help him. That was my hope and my prayer."

Monsignor Vecchione stared into the darkness. Why was he baiting a simple girl, agonizing her further with moral choices she probably couldn't understand and would never need to. Undoubtedly the boy was harmless enough and she was letting her imagination run away with her. He should try to ease her mind instead of burdening her with philosophical conundrums.

"We shall see that no harm comes to your brother," he comforted her, "if you will only tell me what it is that gives you such cause for alarm."

Under the seal of silence and the careful probing of the priest, Paola found herself confessing everything. "He was a good boy, father, so pious and devout. He was going to be a priest. But then..."

Paola's fear rushed out in a flood of memories. She told how Franco had turned away from the Church, embittered by its wealth and unable to accept the poverty he saw even in the shadow of the Vatican. At the university he joined a Communist youth group. He argued with his father about it and left the house. He didn't come back until his father's funeral. He began to stop by on a Sunday for dinner after that, but with each visit he seemed more withdrawn, even contemptuous. Gradually even those visits became more infrequent, until six months ago when they had stopped entirely.

Paola confessed how she had searched for her brother, even going to the Questura because she was afraid he'd been arrested. Then she saw him, as clearly as if he were in the room with her, on the television set at the mass for Aldo Moro...

"I was afraid, father. I knew my brother wasn't mourning Moro's death. The next week he came home. It was almost as though he'd never deserted us. He was devoted to my mother, affectionate toward me. I couldn't forget the face I'd seen on the television, but whatever he'd been, whatever he'd done, it was enough that he had come back. Sometimes a dark cloud seemed to come down on him, but Franco was always a moody boy, and he does have

255

some wonderful new friends. I buried my fears and accepted my brother, until I found this notebook..."

Monsignor Vecchione listened closely, occasionally asking a question, encouraging Paola to unburden her soul. Something in her confession touched him—her love for her brother, her earnestness, her confusion. "If you bring your brother to the sanctuary next week, then I will do what I can to help him. Now I will give you my blessing. Go in peace to love and serve the Lord."

The old *monsignore* took off his stole, kissed it and folded it. The girl's confession was his last for the day. After the spring of terror Rome had endured, it was surprising that more women weren't rushing to the confessional with wild stories about their sons and brothers. Even so he would talk to the boy, if it would ease the girl's mind. She seemed so gentle, so tortured, and opportunities to perform pastoral duties were rare for a priest like him.

He hurried up the side aisle toward the sacristy. In the flickering candlelight he saw the girl praying before the statue of the Virgin. Her dark, thick hair fell loosely to her shoulders, and her eyes were closed tightly in prayer. A rare sight these days, he thought.

CHAPTER FORTY-FIVE

It had been easy for Felice to track down Marcus Rose: A few threats and coins, judiciously balanced, to the concierge of his apartment and he learned that the professor was attending a party at Villa Foltrina in Tivoli. The party was already in high gear when he arrived alone and uninvited in a sporty yellow convertible, borrowed from a friend in the Secret Service. He passed uncontested by the guards, who watched at the gates with snarling Doberman pinschers on four-inch leashes, by saying that he was a guest of Professor Rose.

A long gravel drive lined on both sides with umbrella pines curved into a half-circle in front of a majestic stone villa, bathed in a glow of pale blue light. A liveried servant opened the car door for him and another met him at the steps and escorted him into the huge marble foyer. Miniature yellow and magenta lilies filled the granite urns on either side of a circular pool and floated in the shallow water. Felice imagined himself floating beside them. The servant, who would have been more convincing as a sumo wrestler than a butler, stood uncomfortably close and eyed him skeptically. Beside him Felice felt svelte for the first time in his life.

"I'm a friend of Professor Rose. Do you know if he has arrived yet?" He'd taken off his tie and opened the first two buttons of his shirt in an effort to appear inconspicuous, but he'd forgotten to remove the cross.

Grunting a reply, the butler clomped across the entrance hall to the door of a long frescoed room. A string quartet was playing Mozart. The music had been such a dim echo in the foyer, Felice thought he might be imagining it. Now it swelled, soaring above a wave of raucous laughter. There must have been fifty or sixty people gathered in small groups, but the dimensions of the room were so vast, it looked empty. The butler pointed toward the far end, where a tall man with stooped shoulders, half a head of carrot-colored hair and a full reddish-brown beard was holding court before a dozen or more rapt listeners.

It was impossible to mistake Marcus Rose. His lank red hair hung to his shoulders like tassels; bare patches, the result of uneven pigmentation, interrupted his beard, giving it the appearance of molting feathers, and that part of his face unconcealed by hair was covered with freckles.

Felice hovered by the door waiting for the disciples to disperse before approaching. "*Permesso, professore,* I am a student of your students." Felice bent his ample middle in the suggestion of a bow. "Your *Studenti per una patria libera,* that is. You see, I too want a free country."

Rose studied him as if he were a rare specimen to be dissected. "A free Italy or a liberated one? The difference is not mere semantics. If these subtleties are overlooked, history grinds to a halt and society atrophies." He warmed at the chance to lecture. "And to liberate our country we must make history happen."

"By violence?"

"By whatever is necessary. Unlike Aquinas, I hold that the means do justify a worthy end. Have you ever heard of Thomas Aquinas, signore?" He peered at Felice like a god looking down from Olympus on a mere mortal.

"He was a dumb ox—like me. But I can't stomach this violence...so many hurt for so little—"

258

"A small price when you understand that violence creates revolution, and revolution is the only true force of history."

"*Permesso, dottore,* you misunderstand me. It's the game of revolution our spoiled children play that I have no stomach for. Of course I would prefer change to develop naturally, like a woman's body. But I'm not against revolution itself."

"You are a poet."

"No. A scientist of the state of Italy, and a humble detective." Felice handed his badge to the professor, who waved it away.

"Go on, my friend, tell me more of your ideas. I don't often hear the opinions of an average Roman. I'm like a hermit in the university. I sit in my solitary cell and do nothing except think and write and talk about the national condition."

Felice shrugged. It was difficult to imagine a hermit—a Saint Jerome for instance—at Villa Foltrina. "Half the men in Italy do the same, in cafés from Brindisi to Turin, but they don't get paid for it."

"A not inconsequential difference."

"There is another, even more significant. They can't be held responsible for their views."

"And I can?"

"Inciting violence, treason, undermining the state. There could be many charges."

"Or simply freedom of expression? What the Americans call First Amendment rights?"

"You abdicate responsibility too easily, *professore.* If you stand in the classroom every day and call for the violent overthrow of the government, then one day your students pick up the guns and go out shooting, aren't you as guilty as they—or guiltier?"

Professor Rose smiled indulgently at Felice. "Tell me, signor carabiniere, have you ever seen a man shed a drop of blood from the force of a word?"

"Intent can be more dangerous than action. The Church, wise mother that she is, teaches that action without intent is mere accident, but intent even without successful action is a heinous offense."

"And would you have me bow in submission to the outmoded teachings of that moribund institution? The Church would be a joke if its hold on the people were not so pernicious. It's a masterful twister of words, and mortal sin, which is what you're talking about, is as absurd today as a missile beside a cannon. So, my urban poet, don't preach the doctrines of the Church, writ in lead and marble, to me. Talk to me more about revolution." He leaned close to Felice, exhaling a plume of dark smoke with his words, and flicked the ashes of the Havana on the parquet floor. "I wonder what you'd be without the cross around your neck and the badge in your pocket? I'm beginning to suspect that stripped of those precious talismans you might be an anarchist."

"And Pope Paul is a soccer star!"

Professor Rose scooped two flutes of champagne from the tray of a passing waiter and gave one to Felice. "To once and future soccer stars and to our local constabulary." He sipped the wine. Felice emptied half his glass in a swallow.

"I have some understanding," Felice said. "When you're young and your blood is boiling and your balls bursting, you're always on the brink—hungry for a woman, and if not a woman then something else to embrace. What makes me so angry it sours my appetite is the lie of revolution, the game of terror you teach our children. They talk tough and strike like cowards. Moro was old, probably weakened if not insane from his weeks in captivity. But they had to bind him with ropes and handcuffs before they dared to shoot him. I should believe *this* is the hope of Italy—the saviors who will bring a new state of glory, or even justice? Ah!" He brushed his chin with the back of his hand in a gesture of disgust. "They're not for me, *dottore*, not for me. 'Even in destruction there's a right way and a wrong way, and there are limits.'"

"Yes, my friend, Camus, *The Just Assassin*. I *am* impressed. But he was a romantic and we are realists, like Lenin. 'The purpose of terror is to terrorize.' So simple, so direct. It erases quibbling distinctions, useless sentiment, immutable morality."

Felice drained the rest of his champagne and jabbed a finger into the professor's open shirt. "I know you, Marcus Rose. You are the brains behind the *brigadisti*. Your little club, *Studenti per una patria libera,* is their nursery. Your books are their bible. And what do you preach? Violence, violence, violence against everyone without distinction—political enemies and innocent men, women and children. You would even destroy a little girl who has done nothing worse than answer her father back. She knows nothing..." His voice had risen until he was shouting so loudly that even Mozart couldn't compete for his attention. The other guests were turning curiously in their direction. "You're a learned philosopher and I am just a simple man but I personally hold you responsible."

The professor dusted off his shirtfront where Felice had jabbed. "Champagne makes you churlish, my friend. Some fresh caviar might restore your good humor." Taking the detective's arm familiarly, he leaned close. "The party's livelier outside. You'll enjoy it, if you let yourself."

Without giving Felice time to reply he propelled him through French doors out to a marble terrace where a bar and buffet table were set up under a black-and-white-striped awning.

Rose had to shout to make himself heard. Inside, the atmosphere had been subdued. On the terrace the air was charged with gardenias and drugs. Bodies—nude bodies, partially clad bodies, bodies swathed in Halloween-like costumes—spilled down the terraced steps and sprawled through the formal gardens, coupling and uncoupling in orgiastic displays. Sunk at one end of the garden was an Olympic-size pool. Gardenia petals floated amid the slippery swimmers. A woman, her body punished into unnatural slenderness by a diet of greens and spa water, posed at the edge of the diving board, her body jackknifed, a flower blooming in her anus. Behind her a rock band pulsated, obliterating conversation.

The professor pointed across the terrace to a man with a wreath of white hair clipped short. He was wearing a purple toga and held a Russian wolfhound on a silver leash. "Our ingenious host," Rose shouted. "Shall I introduce you?"

Felice shook his head. Roberto Foltrina was an art dealer specializing in antiquities. He was also a grave robber and worse—part of the cutting edge of Rome's radical elite who filled the

261

coffers of the *brigadisti*. They had passed light-years beyond sophistication. There was nothing they wouldn't try, the more bizarre the more enticing.

"His entertainments are always diverting," Rose was saying. "I wonder what he has planned for us tonight."

As if on cue, Foltrina raised a dog whistle to his lips. On the lawn behind him an elderly man in a gladiator's tunic was spearing a boy who crouched naked on all fours. He started at the piercing sound and looked up, his scrotum dipping below his skirt like a scalloped hem. For an instant his eyes locked with Felice's, then the guests crowded around their host, obliterating him from view. They were all looking toward the pool.

A gypsy girl with thick black curls dripping water was springing through the gardens. A small, hairy creature clung to her breasts, his bandy legs too short to reach around her waist. At first Felice thought it was a monkey, but as she drew closer he realized that it was a dwarf dressed in a red monkey's cap and jacket. The guests parted to let them enter the circle around Foltrina.

The dwarf slid down the girl's slick body and began an awkward sort of dance around her knees, using her legs like Maypoles. Each time he pranced through, he jumped up trying to reach her pubis. Laughing at the dwarf's antics, Foltrina knelt beside the wolfhound and unfastened the silver leash. The dog bounded forward with an excited yelp. The little man screamed and tried to hide behind the gypsy but she drew him out through her legs and introduced him with elaborate formality to the panting beast...

Felice turned away. He was past embarrassment or disgust. Nothing could surprise him anymore, and everything could.

"What's the trouble, my friend?" the professor called.

Felice kept on walking. "Nothing. I wouldn't want to spoil your party by stringing up Foltrina and strangling his dog, that's all."

"Our little entertainment is not to your liking? No matter, I'll find some girls for you. Or would you prefer a boy? You look like the paternal type."

Felice swung around. Contempt and anger were clear on his broad face. "Is this what's become of the political genius that built an empire that was the envy of history? My condolences, Marcus Rose." He seemed to balance on the balls of his feet, rocking back and forth as if deciding whether to level the professor or leave quietly. Finally he chose the latter course.

The professor started after him, then changed his mind and went over to Foltrina instead. Felice looked back just in time to see him start into the house with Rose—in search of the sumo wrestler, no doubt. Quickening his pace, he rounded the corner of the house and broke into a trot. He stayed in the shadow of the trees, skirting the front entrance, and headed for the field that had been converted into a parking lot for the evening. The thick grass muffled his footsteps. The canary-colored Alfa was easy to spot, even in an ocean of fabulous cars. Heaving from the exertion of running, he sank into the car and revved the engine. As he came up on the clutch, the Alfa bucked and spluttered. He jammed it back into neutral and turned the ignition again. The sumo wrestler and the car attendant were running down the marble steps when he veered into the crescent, radials skidding, shards of gravel flying, hitting the fender with the staccato ping of hail. He blew them a kiss and flashed on his high beams as he swung into the drive. He was driving fast, but not so fast as to demand attention if the guards hadn't been alerted. They were growing larger and clearer, their uniforms, a more oblique gray than the night, giving distinction to their blurry silhouette. Their forms arched like bows from the strain of gripping the Dobermans. Felice couldn't see the leashes—only the bared teeth of the dogs and the curved bodies of their masters. He raised a hand to wave as he passed. Just then one of the Dobermans charged the car. The automatic gates began to close, slowly, evenly. Sharp canine teeth sank into his shoulder. He gunned the engine. The dog was thrown back by the sudden acceleration and the car shot through the gates, so close that they grazed the sides, scraping off a line of canary paint from each door.

Felice walked into the bar stiffly, holding his left arm close to his body, trying to hide the tear. The shoulder of his shirt was ripped through to the undershirt where the Doberman's jaws had clamped like a staple gun. He went up to the counter and asked for a coffee and a *gettone*. The barman studied him suspiciously.

"*Scusi*, signore, I'm in a hurry." Felice's always thin supply of patience was nearly exhausted.

Reluctantly, the barman shoved both over to him and pointed to a telephone near the door. "Make it quick," he snapped, "same with the coffee."

Felice palmed the telephone token and gulped the muddy coffee. "No one would want to stay in a hole like this, except rats maybe," he said. Only his voice was mild.

On his way out he stopped to make a call. He could hear the barkeep raining curses on his mother, his wife, his wife's mother, his mother's mother... but he didn't turn back.

It was three o'clock before he reached the office and stretched out on the springless couch, using his jacket for a blanket.

He didn't want to go back to the empty apartment, not this night.

Driving back to Rome shortly after three-thirty, Marcus Rose was stopped by a patrol car and charged with drunken driving. In spite of his heated protests, boisterous remonstrances, humble pleadings and blatant attempts to bribe the arresting officers (who accepted without compunction), he was taken into custody, transported across the city to EUR and delivered up to the gleaming Catacomb where Andresca waited to receive him.

Although Felice had gotten him out of bed with a personal favor that fell somewhere on the shadowy side of the law—something potentially sensitive, even politically dangerous—Andresca wasn't annoyed. To the contrary. He was anticipating a rewarding morning's workout. Business had been slow.

Felice was snoring when the phone jarred him back to consciousness. He'd pulled it over on the floor beside the couch so that he'd be sure to hear it. He was accustomed to being awakened at all hours, and answered with a gruff, "*Pronto.*"

"Why didn't you send me a real man—someone who'd be a

challenge? I'm sick of cowards, especially when I have given up my sweet dreams for one," Andresca complained. "They're insulting to a professional of my expertise."

Felice was now wide awake and fully alert. "So our friend the professor is only brave in talk—as I suspected."

"He didn't last ten minutes."

"I trust you were gentle and discreet."

"A lamb in wolf's clothing."

"Did you make sure he'll keep silent?"

Andresca laughed. "He doesn't have so much as a bruise to remember our rendezvous by, but we have an interesting list— everything you asked for. Your professor is no fool."

"*Grazie,* Andresca. You're an artist—and a most persuasive man." Felice replaced the receiver and curled up like a fetus. He was wondering how long he'd hold out if he ever became one of Andresca's guinea pigs.

CHAPTER FORTY-SIX

The syncopated music that blared over the amusement park faded into the background the higher Paloa and Sandro swung. The strings of flashing colored lights from the rides flickered like fireflies below them. An occasional laugh, clearer or more raucous than the others, floated up from the din. Otherwise the people below, mouths full of candy and confections, hands clutching loved ones, looked like an army of ants as they swung even higher.

Sandro bent his knees and leaned his body against the horizontal bars of the cylindrical cage. His face was set grimly. The sweat was pouring down his neck, onto his shirt.

"Please, Sandro. It doesn't matter whether we turn over in full circle or not. I like riding like this, swinging through the sky in our gilded cage, just the two of us together where no one can touch us, no one can see us, and the night so cool and peaceful..."

Paola looked down through the bars. It wasn't true what she'd just said. She wished she were down there with the ground firm beneath her feet and the crush of the crowds surrounding her— insulating her from her fears. She'd never seen Sandro like this, and it frightened her.

"We're going to stay here all night if we must and all day tomorrow," he said, "until I get this goddam cage to go over the top the way it's supposed to. Maybe by then you'll let me help you."

Paola could feel the violence in him as surely as if he'd struck her. She looked down. EUR stretched flat and clean and well-planned below them. She should never have begun to tell him about the notebook. It was selfish of her. She'd wanted some of his confidence to seep into her. Now she wished she'd kept her mouth shut. There was no point in dragging Sandro into her family's troubles.

"Push, push," he began to shout.

Paola leaned into the cage with all her strength, tears and sweat mingling and streaking her face. The shell-pink chemise was plastered to her body. She'd worn it to surprise him.

Paola hadn't seen Sandro since their afternoon on Monte Mario. She wondered if he'd brought the protection he'd promised. She was eager and apprehensive at the same time. She wanted very much to please him.

He groaned like a gored matador. All of a sudden the cage turned over. Paola screamed and Sandro laughed without humor. It was a grating sound that only added to her anxiety.

The cage swung wildly as the people on the ground cheered. When it finally stopped he grabbed her arm, pushing her out ahead of him.

"Let's get out of here," he said.

"Please, Sandro, you're hurting me."

He forced himself to smile at her. "I'm sorry."

The amusement park was crowded with flushed, dazed and grinning faces. He swam through them, propelling Paola at his side. She had to run to keep up, he was walking so fast. It was only when they reached the quiet outside the park that he loosened his grip.

"Let's see the notebook now. Did you bring it with you?"

"Yes, but there's really nothing to see. I shouldn't even have mentioned it to you. It's just that Franco got so upset when he discovered I'd taken it. It's really silly..." Her voice trailed off. She tried to think of something else to take his mind off it.

"Give me the notebook, Paola," Sandro told her. "If Franco's in trouble, then I'm going to help him. What else are friends for?"

"You don't have to get involved, *carino*. The monsignor said to bring him to the sacristy tomorrow. I'll make him come with me somehow."

"Let me talk to Franco. He'll listen to me more than to some pious phony priest. You know how bitter he is about the Church and everything connected with it. Give me the notebook so that I can read it first. I have to know what I'm talking about. Where do you have it, in there?"

He snatched at her bag, but she swung it to the other side, out of his reach. "Really, you're as bad as my brother." Paola tried to keep her voice light. "Have you forgotten what you promised tonight?" She reached up as they walked and kissed his neck, just below the ear.

Sandro stopped and pulled her against him, kissing her mouth deep and hard. "Does it feel like I've forgotten?"

Her breath caught in her throat and she shook her head. She couldn't speak. He wasn't the same Sandro she'd known, even his kiss was different. He'd always been so gentle before. Now she felt a harshness in his touch, in his lips, as though he wanted to punish her. It frightened her and at the same time drew her to him.

"Kiss me again," she whispered. Her lips were so close to his that she could feel his breath on her mouth.

"You want it don't you, my hot little virgin."

"I want *you*, Sandro," she whispered. Her body was shaking as she reached for his lips.

Sandro pushed her away. "The notebook first, then I'll give you as much as you can take and more."

Paola turned away and burst into tears. "I thought tonight would be special. I even wore the chemise you gave me."

She was sobbing so he couldn't understand what she was saying. He shook her by the shoulders, gently at first, then violently, but she only sobbed louder.

"Stop it, Paola," he demanded. "Keep the damn notebook and let your brother rot. I only want to help you, you and your foolish brother. What else do you think I want with you?" He slapped her hard across the face to make her stop.

"What have I done except love you?" She was holding her cheek where he'd hit her.

He tried to soothe her, but she broke away and started to run as fast as she could, as far as she could. She wanted to get away from all of them—from him, from Franco, from her mother. Through a blur of tears she saw the bright red sign with the white M for Metropolitana. She ran for it. At the steps she could hear the train roaring into the station. The darkness and her tears made it difficult to see and she tripped on the stairs.

The last blue car was disappearing in the tunnel when she reached the subway.

The platform was deserted. Obscenities, swastikas and five-pronged pointed stars were scrawled on the wall. Paola huddled against it, as still as a corpse. She thought she heard his footsteps on the stairs, but the only sound was her erratic breathing. She waited for what seemed a lifetime, then sure he wasn't following her, she went to the ticket machine and dropped in fifty lire. She was reaching for the stub when she saw him. There was no place to run. She looked down the tunnel. There was no light in the distance.

Sandro came toward her slowly, talking quietly as he approached. "What's the matter, Paolita? Why are you running away from me tonight of all nights?"

"Don't come near me."

He stopped and held out his hands to her. "Forgive me, Paolita, I didn't mean to hurt you. I only wanted to make you stop crying. You were hysterical. I'd never hurt you. I love you and I want to make beautiful love to you. I want to kiss you again and hold you and caress you. Come back, *carina*. Don't leave me now, when we've just begun to love."

Paola hesitated, still uncertain, and he began walking toward her again. Her heart was thumping when he took her in his arms. She searched his face. "Do you mean it, do you really love me, Sandro?"

He touched her lips, just brushing his against them, then they were kissing urgently, as if they could never stop. He raised her skirt and pressed her against him, his hands tightening around her buttocks. She felt him hard and demanding and moved against him.

"Do you *really* love me, Sandro?" she whispered again.

"More than you'll ever know, Paolita..." His breath was hot in her ear.

She leaned back and he kissed her throat, her hair. Nothing else mattered. "How can you love me when I've behaved so badly? I don't know what came over me. I've been frightened for Franco ever since I saw him at the mass for Aldo Moro. But I know you'll help us if you can. Of course I'll show you the notebook. Maybe you can make sense of it. It says something about...about a fisherman's net. I know Franco doesn't care anything about fishing, he doesn't even know any fisherman...except Saint Peter." Paola tried to make a joke of it.

She felt Sandro's fingers move up from her shoulders to caress her throat. "You're too curious, and too clever, *carina.*"

Full recognition came suddenly. *"Dio mio!"* she gasped.

She stared, unable to believe.

"Povera Paolita," Sandro murmured. *"Che peccato."*

CHAPTER FORTY-SEVEN

"Lisa's dead two weeks. The police are closing in. They're one step away and gaining every hour. Yet you come to me again with your tail between your legs. You've given us everything—rises at five A.M., mass at five-forty, breakfast at six-twenty-five, coffee, a cornetto and a piece of fruit, perhaps, washed down by more prayers. At eight o'clock he goes to his third-floor office to look over the international reports that have been brought up to him from the secretary of state." Buscati ticked the schedule off on his fingers event by event. "He likes a little wine with his meals, reads the European and American papers at night, watches television and goes to bed at two A.M. *Everything except the one thing we need.* About this you say each day, 'impossible.'"

"I'm trying, you have to believe me," Franco said. "I'm doing my best. What do you want me to do? Say to the secretary of state, 'Pardon me, *eminenza,* but would you tell me when the pope goes to Castel Gandolfo?' or go into Paul's study and say, 'When are you leaving, your Holiness? I would like to send you a *buon viaggio* card.'" His voice was rising. "Since Moro everything there is different. Not even the nuns know. Only his secretary, his doctor, the secretary of state—"

"*Stai zita!*" Buscati warned. "You want me to believe that the date is guarded as closely as a nun's virginity. But when more than one person knows it's as tight as a sieve. You can always find someone willing to talk. It's a subtle kind of boasting—a way to show how important one is to have such information. I'm beginning to think you're holding back on us. You've brought us this far and now you're getting cold feet. I warn you, Franco, you can't hold out on us any longer."

"It's impossible, you're asking the impossible—"

"Five, six, seven people know and you can't convince even one to talk?" Buscati's impotence made him especially cruel. "All we need is a moment of indiscretion. I don't have to tell you what it means if you fail us now."

"You think I'm a coward, Buscati." Franco turned away. "You're not the first." He wished he had the strength of his father. Franco wanted to tell Buscati that Paul was a good man. He wanted a promise that The Fisherman would be safe in their net. They could hold him as a prisoner of war, with all his rights spelled out under the Geneva Agreements. Franco wanted to say all this and more, but he didn't have the courage.

He remembered Sunday afternoons, sitting around the dinner table listening spellbound as his father and Monsignor Montini reminisced about the years under Mussolini when they first met. His father had been a philosophy student at the University of Rome and the young Montini, then Pacelli's secretary, had been spiritual adviser to the Federation of Catholic University Students. When the Fascists banned their organization Montini had held clandestine meetings in the catacombs. "If today we cannot go forward with flags unfurled, we will work in silence," he'd vowed to the students.

Franco remembered the intensity of Montini's deep-set blue eyes, glowing from beneath the bushy black eyebrows, which always seemed an incongruity in his aesthetic face. His eyes had been his dominant feature. But at the mass for Moro, Franco had only seen pain and sorrow in them. The fire seemed to have burned out.

Now it was his comrades who had to work in silence, who could not yet go forward with banners unfurled. And it was another pair of fiery eyes that were galvanizing him, boring into his mind and heart.

"We're all cowards. But if we force ourselves to go ahead anyway, then it is bravery. I only think you're indecisive, Franco. There are times when indecisiveness is good, then it's called caution or prudence. But not in this operation."

Franco looked up and for a moment his eyes fixed on Buscati's. Unaccountably, he thought of *il gatto*. Through all Montini's years in the Vatican under Pius XII the big gray cat had enjoyed the run of his terrace. It had been his private domain which none ever entered without paying court. When Montini was named archbishop of Milan he gave *il gatto* to Franco and Paola. They tended him lovingly, catering to his every whim, but the cat never adjusted to life away from its private terrace and never seemed to reconcile itself to the loss of its master and friend. One day it simply disappeared without a trace. Franco asked his father if it was a miracle, because he couldn't figure out how the cat had escaped from their locked apartment while he was in school. His father had laughed at him, saying it must have slipped out unnoticed when the door was opened. But Franco secretly believed *il gatto* had been spirited to Milan and was even then settling itself in the archbishop's residence. Of course, he knew that was nothing more than a foolish boy's dream. Were the dreams he was being asked to share with his new comrades just as foolish? His eyes and throat stung from the smoke that clung like cobwebs in the air of the *bottiglieria*.

Buscati drained his wine. He wanted to goad Franco into action without pushing him so hard that he destroyed the boy before his usefulness was over. He gripped Franco's arm. "Your comrades are depending on you. Don't fail us. We've come so close, and still we're helpless—armed, drilled, deployed and impotent. You've got us by the balls, Mirabella. It's not a pleasant position to be in. Remember that."

Franco got up from the table without looking at Buscati. He'd take his failure out on Paola and his mother when he got home. He'd be sullen and short-tempered and close himself in his room refusing supper. He'd intended to tell Buscati about the notebook and Paola, but he was too afraid. Now he had one more worry to gnaw at his gut. He knew he should have confessed but he couldn't get the words out. He envied Buscati's courage and confidence. His father had been that way—assured, easy, worldly. He'd never been afraid of anything except, maybe, himself. At their next meeting Franco promised himself he would own up, and prayed that Paola didn't figure it out before then. He'd been avoiding her—and she him—unable to face each other since the night they'd shared. It hadn't been difficult because the signora had been called to Brescia to care for her ailing mother.

Buscati ordered a second *quartino* of red table wine. It was only 11:30 A.M., but in Rome not too early for a glass. The old barroom with its vaulted ceiling and thick stone walls was cool even in July. Giuliani was one of the last of a venerable species, the Roman *bottiglieria*. There were only a few left, cheap, inconspicuous establishments tucked away in the city's medieval alleys. He met Franco at Giuliani because everyone minded his own business there. Also it was convenient—just a ten-minute walk to St. Peter's.

Buscati studied the frescoed walls, trying to gain control of his temper. Cherubs, who looked as if they knew whereof they spoke, sang the praises of the grape in poetry and proverbs. The room was smoky, the wine rough and robust. The police must be having difficulty identifying the body, Buscati thought. Otherwise the family would have been notified already.

If Franco ever suspected...but then how could he? The secret Franco was keeping worried Buscati even more than his failure. As for Paola, for all her innocence, she had been wily. All women were, even the most naïve. It must course in their blood, he decided.

CHAPTER FORTY-EIGHT

Monsignor Vecchione didn't wait for Paola to bring her brother to the sacristy. He didn't even go to Madre di Dio that day. He was miles away in the Reichstag. It was dusk when he finally stopped writing. He knew he'd worked too long because his eyes felt the strain. He locked the papers in his safe and lay down on the couch to rest. He wondered what supper would be, not that he cared what he ate. The next morning when Sister Isabella brought his breakfast tray, he was still lying on the couch.

Since his retirement Monsignor Vecchione had lived in a convent operated by an order of Spanish nuns. He had a study, bedroom and bath on the second floor; the solitude he needed to finish his writing, and the care he required as his glaucoma grew worse each year. The nuns served him meals and handled his correspondence. He'd lost almost total sight in the right eye and the left was deteriorating rapidly. He was frightened by it. His vision of the world was growing blacker every day, and he knew that his thinking reflected his personal darkness.

The old monsignor sat up and tried to pretend an alertness he didn't feel. He looked through his mail, then opened up the morning paper. All he could read without the aid of a magnifying glass -were the headlines. He looked them over, more out of habit than interest. He had little use for the world of today. His world was in the past. A young girl's picture was on the bottom of the front page. He glanced at it, then stopped and looked more closely. He brought it over to the window where the light was better and looked at it under the magnifying glass, then he read the story, and studied the picture again. *Madre di Dio...*

Felice adjusted the earphones and lit a cigarette, although he knew such weakness was frowned on in The Catacomb. The soundproof booth where he sat was linked to the interrogation rooms so that Andresca could hear everything that happened and watch it on a recessed 19-inch television screen. Alone in the glass-walled booth Felice felt as if he were sitting in the center of an ice cube. He shivered as the cries of the professor reverberated against his eardrums. The unedited tape made sweat stand out on his face even as chills shook his heavy frame.

"*Porca miseria,*" he muttered again and again.

He covered his eyes and imagined he was Marcus Rose, his naked hairy body bathed in acrid sweat, his speckled face washed in tears. He was glad he'd declined Andresca's invitation to monitor the interrogation.

The professor was begging, gasping. The arrogance of power belonged solely to the other side now. Andresca explained that he was about to inject a solution in the veins that would send the blood rushing to the head until it felt as if the skull would burst open. "Don't worry though, it's not lethal. I have many more inventions to test. I've been waiting for a patient like you. You can't imagine how eager I am to test you thoroughly. Regrettably, a man of your caliber rarely comes to my attention. Still," he went on pleasantly, "if you happen to recall the names of members of your club—what is it called?—then perhaps I could be persuaded to wait for the next patient." Andresca was an unfailingly courteous torturer.

Felice was glad that he was sitting down. He legs felt like wet

276

toilet paper. He had to fight back the waves of nausea that threatened him. He was in Andresca's power now—as unequivocally as Rose. The tape he was listening to was a copy. Andresca would never hand over the master.

"Well, *professore?*" Andresca persisted. His voice was sharper.

"My head. I can't think." The professor was gasping. Felice adjusted the volume.

"The name—last names first. We want a complete list."

"No more." Rose began vomiting names. Each time he paused Andresca pressed him for more, until he'd given up thirty, forty. Felice only recognized two—Taglia, and Buscati.

"Bravo, professore. Your friends should be proud of you," Andresca told him.

For a full minute the only sound on the tape was Rose's labored breathing, then Felice heard a strained whisper, an eerie, ghostlike sound. "You can't get away with this—you and that pig Felice. I'll call a press conference the moment I get out of here. The world will know what you are—"

"That's your prerogative, of course." Andresca spoke as if he were discussing a technical point of order. "But then you'd leave me no choice. I'd be forced to swear that you are an informer and publish the list of names you've just provided. The decision is yours, *professore.*"

"Bastard."

Andresca was generous in victory. "I never doubted you were a reasonable man. At this rate, you can be home in time for breakfast—I'll even have one of my men drive you. You may feel a little weak. There's just one more thing though—"

"Basta."

"Lisa Taglia."

"You killed her, why do you ask me?"

"Was she involved in something beyond that unfortunate incident?"

"I don't know, I swear it. Buscati took the money we raised and vanished. He's evasive. I lost touch."

"She was still with Buscati then?"

"*Per sempre.*"

"Lovers?"

"No. Enemies."

"Enemies? But united for the cause?"

"I don't know, I can't remember."

"Another shot might jog your memory—"

"No, my head...what do you want me to tell you?"

"Everything, of course."

Professor Rose began in a low stammering voice. "She and Buscati joined my club when they came to the university. They were already lovers, engaged to be married. In our meetings we discussed true brotherhood, which means equality in all things— goods, ideas, possessions, husbands, wives, lovers. Everything shared. To each according to his need. Buscati resisted until I accused him of hypocrisy in a public meeting. Then he had to prove himself. Every man in the room wanted her—and the women too. She was beautiful. Impassioned in our meetings but an ice queen in bed. A disappointment. I fucked her every way I know how. She merely submitted, to everyone. She did it for Buscati, I suppose, but not for the ideal. And he never wanted her after that."

CHAPTER FORTY-NINE

One of the utilitarian yellow cabs that have replaced the old green-and-black Roman taxis drew up in front of a centuries-old building on the south side of St. Peter's Square. Monsignor Vecchione pressed a bill, double the amount of the fare, in the hand of the bewildered driver and, with a glance at the Apostolic Palace across the street, entered the arched portal and hurried across the inner courtyard of the old monastery, now seat of the Holy Office. The morning paper was stuck under his arm like a furled umbrella.

The monsignor never walked. He always moved in a half-run as if he were late and, at the same time, managed to convey the impression that he was proceeding in opposite directions simultaneously. Permanently harried and hurried, he performed the necessary functions of daily life—putting food in his mouth, dressing, paying taxi drivers—with a total lack of awareness. On one memorable occasion he decided an American niece who was studying art in Rome looked too thin, so he took her to the first Yankee place that came to mind—the American Bar, a nightclub on the Via Veneto. That in itself was an arresting sight, but then he insisted on ordering hamburgers for both of them, totally forgetting that it was Good Friday and he was in cassock and clerical mushroom hat.

Vecchione went directly to the office of Cardinal Zanelli and pushed right in without waiting to be announced. He slapped the newspaper down in front of the curial chief.

Zanelli glanced up from the thick leather folder he'd been reading. "What intriguing news have you brought me today, Vecchione?"

Zanelli and Vecchione had known each other for years. Both had once been protégés of Ottaviani but their careers had diverged. Still, the cardinal's opinion of the monsignor hadn't changed with time. Professionally and intellectually, he respected him. Vecchione had been second to the nuncio in Berlin when Hitler was carving out an empire and second to the nuncio in Madrid when Franco was forging his Fascist version of Spain. He was no fool, though he sometimes played the part. Personally, though, Zanelli found him distasteful. Thick steel-rimmed glasses magnified his opaque brown eyes. Stains ran the length of his rumpled cassock, and his clerical hat was angled forward on his low forehead.

"I bear no news. I come as a humble confessor, seeking guidance. A girl is dead and I, in my selfishness, may be responsible. She came to the confessional asking for help, and I failed her." Tears came into his eyes. "I never thought she was in danger. Women are so hysterical—"

"*Calma*, Vecchione." The cardinal motioned him to sit down, but he was too agitated to keep still.

"She found a small notebook belonging to her brother, with the five-pointed star of the *brigadisti* drawn in it. He'd embraced the Communists some months before, now she was afraid he'd gone further."

"And what dire thoughts did the notebook hold?"

"She could only understand a few words, '*la rete del pescatore*. The fisherman's net is cast'..."

The cardinal listened, with more interest than he showed. "My advice is to go back to your books and your papers. Your imagination is running away with you. You've always been more interested in politics than in priestly duties—a failing of our generation, perhaps, don't you agree? Go back to your convent with a clear conscience. The girl's death was a coincidence, nothing more. You can't be held responsible for every accident of life, no matter how tragic or personally unsettling."

The day was sticky and slow. Zanelli reached into his cassock, took out a monogrammed white linen handkerchief and daubed at his forehead where beads of perspiration were beginning to form. A fastidious man. "I envy your role as a confessor. A man in my position has no opportunity to perform such humble duty. Don't you find that the simple pastoral act gives a satisfaction like no other—a sense of priestliness one rarely feels here in the curial offices of the Vatican where I have labored so long?"

Years before as a young monsignor Zanelli heard confessions in a church in Trastevere. He would listen to the contrite words of the penitents, begging forgiveness for a stolen orange, for refusing a drunken husband, for cheating a neighbor, rough hands clasped and unclasped in their distress, and envied the simplicity of their sins. If they only knew it, their immortal souls were far safer than his own. Zanelli wasn't fool enough to be taken in by the easy flush of piety. Hearing their confessions was a balm to his own conscience—the mighty man absolving the pathetic transgressions of those poor people of Trastevere. It was part penance for him, part a purging of his own deeper guilt and hunger.

The cardinal looked at his watch, an elegant instrument and family treasure passed on to him from his father. The crystal face was enameled with small Roman numerals in the style of an illuminated manuscript. In the center was a tiny golden lion, symbol of Venice, the city of the Doges and Zanellis, of romance and centuries of trade, of canals and gondolas and tender baby octopi. The hands were spit from the lion's mouth in the shape of two fork-tongued snakes which at that precise moment were pointing to noon.

"I read the report this morning. This girl you're talking about—

281

she was Mirabella's daughter. Do you remember him, Vecchione? You didn't like him any better than I, as I recall. Still, it's strange what extraordinary coincidences give shape to our lives..."

Costanto Zanelli strolled in the shade of the Vatican gardens. The olive and chestnut trees that offered a cool canopy on such a sticky day murmured in the evening breeze like old friends sharing confidences on a summer's night. The classical sculptures cast their ancient shadows along the gravel paths. The cardinal's head was bowed over his breviary, but he couldn't pray.

Paola Mirabella leaves a mother, Maria, and a brother, Franco. Although he'd brushed by the boy once in haste, Zanelli had not let him pass unchecked. No one with access to the private floors of the papal palace was too insignificant for his attention. The cardinal recalled Suor Marianna's glowing words: "A mother is blessed who has a son like Franco Mirabella. The boy is devoted to our Holy Father. It is rare to find such dedication in one his age today. There is nothing he won't do for us—for il Papa. He is thirsty for news—he says every detail of il Papa's day brings him closer. I pray he will hear the call of the Holy Spirit, it has always been his mother's fondest dream that Franco become a priest, you know..."

But his sister had said he was a Communist, and worse. After Vecchione departed, Zanelli had reread the article on the dead girl but he hadn't begun to make the puzzle until now. The pieces fit with a stunning logic. *"La rete del pescatore,"* the girl had confessed.

And to think Vecchione had almost dismissed her as an hysterical female. Where would it lead Holy Mother the Church and her faithful servant? If his suspicions were true, the possibilities were infinite. The idea was mad, but then so were the *brigadisti*— bloodied, amoral, zealous children, mad and bold. Anticipation clutched the cardinal like icy fingers.

Books, libraries, cities, countries, continents could be filled with the "what ifs" of history. Still, he couldn't refrain from considering them. The immaculately maintained Vatican gardens were as for-

282

mal as Paul's manners. Cardinal Zanelli looked at the yuccas and cactuses planted among the olive trees like thorns in a crown of jewels, and dared to think the unthinkable. Destiny, it seemed, had called him to give succor to the enemy in order to save the Church...

It could be a positive step—what the Church needed to awaken it to the danger of continued rapprochement with the Communist bloc. Look at Cardinal Mindszenty. After so many years of patient suffering to be called back to exile in Rome and to know that it had all been for nothing, that the Vatican was now embracing ostpolitik. It could be the shock treatment the Church needed to put it on its true course. Much could be gained, and little lost— except an old Fisherman. Well, nothing of value comes without some price.

CHAPTER FIFTY

The fifth floor of the Questura was a maze of gleaming computer consoles linked to international data banks and police headquarters all over the Western world. Ever since Felice had fed them the professor's list, he'd hovered close to the machines like an expectant father, studying each report as it appeared. Already the printouts formed a stack on his floor high enough to make a chair. It was about all they were good for.

Just when Felice was beginning to think that he'd bartered his soul to Andresca for nothing, Baby Doll began flashing and burping. He rushed over to watch the message form on the massive Honeywell. Baby Doll was spitting up again. The computer had picked up a link that both he and Cenci had overlooked. Another girl was dead, and her brother was on the professor's list.

Felice cleared the screen and turned to find his assistant at his elbow. He exhaled forcefully, making no effort to direct the smoke away. Cenci had begun to stick by his side as though they were cemented. Looking back, he thought that it had started immediately after the debauchery at Foltrina's. Cenci went everywhere with him now except to the urinal. Felice had taken to making frequent trips. His guilt over how he'd come by the list made him short-tempered. He'd tried to keep the entire episode a secret, but Cenci had put him on the spot by asking bluntly, "I understand you met Marcus Rose. What did he say?"

"He's a sycophant—with information. I got all the SPL members. The computers are checking the names." He wondered how Cenci knew. Andresca? Possibly. He couldn't think of anyone else except Salvi in the Secret Police who'd loaned him the Alfa. Felice couldn't remember if he'd said where he was going when he borrowed the car.

Cenci was friendly, even expansive, making him yearn for the indifference that used to infuriate him. He was sure Cenci was suspicious. It was bad enough knowing that Andresca had something on him. If he had to deal with Cenci too, his life would be unbearable.

"You stay here," he said, "in case Baby Doll burps again."

"Where are you going, sir?" Cenci asked.

Felice only patted the big Honeywell and walked away.

Downstairs in the Homicide Division Detective Rico Mosca sat erect behind a spotless desk, shirt-sleeves rolled neatly to the elbow, silk tie knotted tightly at the neck. The toe of a glossy black loafer shone through the desk hole. He was small and compact with features an edge too sharp for his round face. Lines as deep as trenches ran down from the corners of his mouth enclosing a chin that receded to nothingness. His glasses were tinted amber, a few shades lighter than his hair.

Detective Mosca was the only dapper man Felice had ever known who didn't make him feel like a slob. Still, he tucked in his shirt and hiked up his trousers at the door. Although they'd worked together as rookies, their paths rarely crossed now.

"Guido!" Mosca jumped up at the sight of his old friend and embraced him. "What brings you down to my cave? It's too much to hope that you've come for a friendly visit."

Felice gestured with upturned palms. "It's just as easy for you to come up as for me to come down."

"Getting up becomes more difficult every year"—Mosca laughed—"for me anyway. You always were a randy goat though."

They joked together, trying to recapture their old camaraderie, but somehow their humor felt forced. As if by mutual, though tacit, agreement, they gave it up after a couple of minutes and settled down to the business of murder.

"The death of Paola Mirabella." Mosca sighed when he heard which case had brought his friend down to homicide. He pushed his chair back, pulled out the bottom drawer of the desk and propped his feet up on it. "That one's got me stumped. It's a strange case. Officially it's listed as an accidental death. We had no witnesses, no evidence of foul play—no evidence at all really. We had to peel what was left of the girl off the tracks, her body was so badly mangled. The motorman didn't see her until he was almost on top of her, and then it was too late to stop.

"At first I thought a kid probably tried to snatch her purse, she panicked, ran into the station, lost her balance and fell off the platform in front of an oncoming train. Then we found her pocketbook tossed behind some shrubbery several blocks away. It had been wiped clean. No fingerprints at all. As far as we can determine, though, nothing had been taken."

Mosca held a pencil extended between the tips of his index fingers, brushing it against his lips. "What was a girl like Paola Mirabella doing at EUR all alone at night?"

"A boyfriend?"

Mosca shook his head. The sounds of the shifts changing filtered through the closed door—muffled footsteps, boisterous greetings. "No. From what the coroner could determine she was probably a virgin. Her mother is very strict."

"Suicide?"

"It's possible, of course. You can never rule it out absolutely in a case like this. On the other hand we have no reason to assume that she was suicidal. She could have been upset over her father's death, but that was almost a year ago, and everyone we've talked with said she'd adjusted well to the loss. You remember the father, Guido? Giovanni Mirabella, the journalist?"

Felice nodded, Mosca went on. "No one has any idea what she was doing out there. Her mother was away at the time visiting her family in Brescia. By all accounts she was a conscientious, level-headed girl devoted to her family, very religious—your classic good girl. I'd take you to the morgue to have a look at her, but we returned the body to her mother for burial yesterday along with her personal effects."

"Do you have a list of them?"

"Sure, but I can spare you the eyestrain." Mosca began ticking off the items from memory. "A purse with wallet, keys, handkerchief, tissues, perfume, sunglasses—the usual, what we could salvage of her clothing, a silver bracelet broken in two and flattened like a patty, and the remains of a notebook. She must have had it somewhere on her body. Her dress had no pockets."

Notebook? "Could you read it?"

"No. It was hard even to tell it was a notebook. What's your interest in the case anyway?"

"Curiosity, mainly. Her brother may be a *brigadiste*. He's flirting with them anyway, we know that much."

Mosca whistled. "Giovanni Mirabella's son! That's rebellion for you. We haven't talked to him yet..."

The business of Ponte Milvio went on undisturbed by the violent death of Paola Mirabella. The large number of people who attended the funeral mass at the Church of Madre di Dio made a sharp contrast to the mourners—one weeping woman leaning heavily on the arm of her slim, nervous son.

The mother and brother of the deceased. Felice checked off the category in his brain through force of habit. But the cold definitions didn't describe the pair of lonely mourners. Signora Mirabella shuffled up the center aisle like an old woman, clutching with both hands the black-banded arm of her son, the only possession she had left—a boy with the dazed glare of a lost child. A choir of schoolchildren sang the *Dies Irae,* pure voices like angels calling the girl home. He thought of his own Luisa...

Felice blessed himself and slipped out of the church. He'd pay a call on the signora in the morning. Cenci could pick up the boy then too. They should be allowed one day at least alone with their grief.

Massi waited by the rear door of the church—like any one of the hundreds of curious spectators. He felt light-headed, almost giddy—the police were closing in, and still Franco hadn't gotten the date. Surely Operation Fisherman was as good as aborted. Buscati had no choice now but to let it die stillborn. He'd make the contact to meet Vishnevsky in the morning.

CHAPTER FIFTY-ONE

A low murmur of *"eminenza"* proceeded Costanto Zanelli as he passed through the tide of mourners, red cassock standing out like a flame against their black dresses, ringed hand outstretched to receive their kisses. One by one the mourners dropped to their knees, their grief damped by his awesome presence. Zanelli admired his own skill. He was an expert at this, moving through a crowd without ever breaking stride, yet managing to convey the impression that he had touched each one personally.

He found Signora Mirabella in the eye of a storm of women who were raining laments on her. Although she was a big woman, she seemed shrunken. Her eyes were bloodshot from lack of sleep, her face blotched from weeping. He couldn't help wondering how many hours and days she'd been crying.

"Signora Mirabella, I hope I'm not intruding." He beamed beneficence on the grieving mother. "Your husband and I had our differences, but they were never personal. We respected each other as men of conscience and honor. He was"—Zanelli raised an eyebrow quizzically—"a respected adversary."

"*Eminenza,* you honor my family by your presence—what little is left of it, only my son and I." The widow's face reflected her surprise at seeing Cardinal Zanelli in her apartment. She was accustomed to receiving princes of the church...when Giovanni was alive they'd been frequent guests...but never Zanelli. He had been a vociferous critic of the views her husband championed in his column. Privately the signora had agreed with Zanelli as often as she'd agreed with Giovanni. But who was she to say? She kept her mouth shut and her rosary turning.

"Ah, yes, you have a son—Franco, if my memory serves me well." He took her arm under the elbow and eased her back into the chair as she pressed her lips to his ring. "You must rely on him. That is good. We should lean on our young, but not so heavily that we crush them. They are the bulwark of our future, but not our crutch."

"You remember Franco?" The signora flushed with pride and she called to her son, "Franco!"

A young man turned from the window where he'd been standing apart, his back to the room of mourning women, his very posture discouraging anyone from approaching.

"He refuses to be comforted." She shook her head. She didn't understand her son's behavior but that never stopped her from making excuses for him. "They were so close, my Franco and Paola. When he was a little boy he was always running after her, trying to keep up. She always waited for him. And now, now he mourns alone. His grief is locked inside him unable to escape. He won't speak of Paola. He didn't even want to come to the mass or the graveyard..." Her tears flowed. "Forgive me, *eminenza*. Finally I became so upset, he relented and accompanied me..."

Cardinal Zanelli squeezed both of the widow's hands in his. "I will talk to the boy, signora, and try to ease the burden of sorrow he carries on his young shoulders."

"You are too kind, *eminenza*." A fresh flood of tears engulfed her. Zanelli knew that Paul would hear about his gesture to the Mirabella family and be touched by his generosity of spirit. He crossed the room and laid a hand on the boy's shoulder.

"We meet again, Franco, only this time we enjoy the luxury of time and share a bond of sorrow." He'd recognized the boy as soon as he turned at the window. Today the face was gaunt and white. Fear peered from his dark eyes and held the muscles rigid, the fear of an animal under chase? His fingers twisted the cord of the drape like worry beads. "Do you remember when we last met—collided would be more accurate?"

Franco looked at him blankly. "I recognize you from Vatican ceremonies I used to attend with my parents and from newspaper photographs, but I don't believe we ever met—"

"So much the better," Zanelli murmured under his breath. He studied Franco's distraught face.

"May I ask why you have come here, *eminenza*? You were not a friend of my father."

"No, but I knew your sister in a way, and our sorrow today— the sorrow of all these good people—is for her."

Franco looked at the clusters of mourners. "They gossip about Paola behind my mother's back. They all whisper that she was murdered for sex. They talk as if she were a whore—Paola who blushed if two people kissed on the television screen. *'Putana'* they say to each other and then they come here and pretend to be grief-stricken. I'd like to kick them all out, but my mother wouldn't understand."

He sounded very angry, on the edge. No young man with respect for the cloth or what it represented would speak of such delicate things to a prince of the Church. Even in the privacy of the confessional he would hesitate to speak so crudely. So, Zanelli thought, our Franco is still a zealot but no longer a believer. He must find a new Christ to die for—if he hasn't already... "Grief can be suffocating to those who are left behind. You can't push yourself so. See me to the door, Franco, and stroll a way with me. You must think of yourself a little, if only for your mother's sake. She worries about you."

"She always has, and she'll worry more if I go out. I can't leave her now, surrounded by these hypocrites."

"It isn't going out that worries her. It's the company you keep. In my case I think I would be found acceptable enough for a walk through the village. She won't mind, Franco. Trust me." He smiled.

Franco shrugged. At least the cardinal was a way to escape from the miasma that pervaded his mother's house.

They walked down the hill of Via di Farnesina in silence, passed the Church of Madre di Dio, from which Paola had been buried a few hours before, between the row of small shops and the open stands of vendors. Nothing changed in Ponte Milvio. It appeared untouched by the turmoil that had buffeted the nation through the spring. The rabbits and chickens freshly slaughtered that morning hung in the window of the butcher. The men with eternal faces—too old ever to have been young, still too young to fear death—lounged in front of the bar. The old women stood at the open stalls selling nylon stockings, children's sweaters, ball-point pens and stilettos. An ice cream vendor peddling lemon ice was wedged between them.

Directly ahead the Tiber flowed yellow and mawkish under the narrow bridge that gave the village its name. Ponte Milvio possessed none of the grandeur of history that marked other Roman landmarks. Yet Helen's prayers had been answered on that innocuous bridge. Her son the Emperor Constantine saw a cross appear in the heavens above it, accepted Christ on the spot and led his forces to victory.

"The village seems timeless, and yet it is very much of our time— a unique blending of the past with the present and the hope of the future. It isn't often that I have the freedom or inclination to stroll like this." Zanelli spoke warmly, nodding to the men who bowed and the women who made awkward curtsies as they passed. He wanted Franco to see him as a man of the people. Not that he expected a confession.

"Take that bridge, Franco. It is not a feat of engineering nor a wonder of architecture. Still we look on it with reverence, not for its intrinsic value but for what it represents—a mother's faith in the supreme, inestimable power of prayer to bring her son to Christ."

"Have you ever considered, *eminenza*, that it might work the other way—to turn him away?" Franco asked.

"You must explain the meaning of such harsh words."

"Harsh idle words of no consequence." Franco backed down hastily.

"A most appropriate subject then for an idle conversation like ours. I'd like to hear your theory—purely as a theory, of course."

Franco shrugged. He had nothing more to lose. "When a mother's faith is very strong, she teaches her son to believe—more than that, to love Christ's Church. To go through the world begging for souls, to strip himself bare, if necessary, to clothe the naked, to go without a meal to feed the hungry, to give up his own home to shelter the homeless—all in the name of the Holy Mother the Church. The boy believes fervently when he is young, and as he grows up, he is inevitably disillusioned."

"Inevitably," Zanelli agreed. "While he is humbling himself, he looks at Christ's Church and sees that it is dressed in cloth of gold. Her princes eat like kings and live palatially. And so he turns from the Church, which he once embraced so passionately, to look for another faith in which he can believe as fervently. There is nothing new or shocking in this. It's as much a part of history as Constantine or the cross over Ponte Milvio. Four hundred fifty years ago the Anabaptists thought that both Church and state were impediments to faith—stumbling blocks to God. They taught that authority was evil because it stood between man and his Creator. So both Church and state had to be destroyed and a new order established, pure and untainted by the lust for power. They believed, very much like today's *brigadisti*, that violent destruction is a purgative, and they dreamed of building a new social order from the ruins of the old. The inevitable occurred then, as it will today with these new Anabaptists. The terror they spread led not to the destruction of Church and state but to the creation of a counter-terror of unbelievable fury. The cult and its leaders were annihilated. Out of their dreams of a just new order the Inquisition was born. It is a source of continued surprise to me that none of our journalists or our intellectuals have considered the historical parallels—the parallels within the Church itself—in their consideration of, say, the Moro slaying..."

293

"You look skeptical, Franco. It's not something the Church likes to boast about. You won't hear Paul discourse on the topic in his Sunday homily to the faithful in St. Peter's Square. But it is no secret. One of the largest and best organized terrorist groups in history was the Jesuits. The Society of Jesus—or 'the little batallion of Jesus' as it was known—was in fact the shock troops of the counter-Reformation. They made today's urban guerrillas look mild. When the Society felt it necessary to eliminate a king or prince, the chosen assassin was prepared in a ceremony called the Blessing of the Dagger. The Jesuits' terror tactics were so feared that, one by one, they were expelled from France, England, Venice, Spain and Naples. Clement IV suspended them as a religious order until they vowed to renounce their terrorism...Our angry young men and women today are lambs by comparison. They strike symbolic blows—shooting a capitalist here, an executive there, an unimportant judge or police officer easily replaced. And no one remembers that we, the Church, gave the world its first organized band of terrorists."

Zanelli placed a paternal hand on Franco's shoulder. "So much for the ironies of history, my son. If nothing else they serve as a distraction from our present grief. In this temporal world, and perhaps in the hereafter, everything seems destined to come full circle. The Church has conveniently forgotten that it was once the instigator. Now it regards itself as a likely target—some think with good reason. The Vatican was always a cloister, shutting out the larger world across the Tiber. Now it is an armed camp."

The cardinal stopped at the corner of Lungotevere and turned to look at the boy. "You can imagine my surprise, Franco, to find that a young man, you, was passing unchallenged through the papal apartments themselves. When I learned you were the son of Mirabella, all my questions were answered." Zanelli favored Franco with one of his rare smiles. "Your father and Montini were closer than many brothers. It is heartening to see that you remain loyal to our Holy Father. So often the sons and daughters whom we loved the most become unappeasable foes. When we are elevated to a powerful position they believe we can right every wrong, turn around every injustice. They expect more of us than we can deliver, and so they turn against us."

He paused to give Franco time to digest all that he'd said. The boy's face was taut, his eyes as guarded as a vault. "You are surprised that I know you visit the Vatican from time to time? You shouldn't be. We met, or should say, brushed shoulders one morning outside the papal apartments. You don't remember. There are so many men in red robes there, our faces and figures meld into one, I suppose." He laughed easily to show no offense was taken. "I have a reputation as the most curious—some would say nosiest, but I prefer intellectually curious—man in the Vatican. I inquired about you. You would blush to hear the good sisters sing your praises. But enough. I don't want to embarrass you, and I have talked too much already."

They had crossed the road that ran along the Tiber and leaned over the bridge watching the river. The boy was so unlike his father. For all their differences, Giovanni Mirabella was a delightful man to spend an evening with, as witty as he was brilliant. Although you could almost see his brain spinning, you could never be sure if he would deflect you with an erudite pun or confound you by twisting your argument to his advantage. He was a man to reckon with. Franco seemed to have inherited little of his father. He was grave and deadly serious. A literal mind and single-minded. God save us from the humorless and the righteous, Zanelli thought. The water below them was stagnant and opaque, like the boy beside him. Except for a nod once or twice, he'd offered nothing to their conversation. Zanelli tried again. He wasn't ready to admit that it was his own invention, nothing more...

"It is a difficult time to be alive, my son, so few possibilities and so many conflicting loyalties—to family, new comrades, old friends." He chose his words carefully. "Even within the Vatican we feel a tension. Vatican II shook the foundations. It made us fear the loss of our spiritual power. Now the threat of violence makes us fear for our temporal power as well. The belief is that anyone looking for something irreplaceable to destroy would be too easily lured by the art, the books, the wealth of treasures in the Vatican. It cannot be denied. They must be a temptation. Think for a moment, my boy—to deface a Raffaello or cripple a judge, to destroy a Michelangelo or murder some Fiat executive? Which would be the greater crime?...It is a question for the epistemologists, the metaphysicians, the seminary students. From a humanitarian standpoint the destruction of a human life, no matter how insignificant, is the more deplorable act. But is it in truth? Death is a daily story, even violent death—and inevitable. But the destruction of a masterpiece of Western civiliza-tion...think of the outcry from around the world. You can argue that one is the work of God, the other the work of man. But that is too facile. For all we know a work of God and a work of genius are one and the same. If one by one our national treasures were systematically destroyed, the state would be forced to act. The world would demand it."

Franco fidgeted. He regretted ever leaving his mother's house. Zanelli's talk made him uncomfortable. He felt as if the cardinal was amusing himself, and somehow he, Franco, was his toy. He'd refused to be drawn into the conversation, but now he felt com-pelled to reply. If he let Zanelli's argument stand it would be like admitting that their own plan was mistaken...

"*Eminenza, mi scusi ma,* you give perhaps an unbalanced argu-ment. You weigh a Michelangelo against a petty judge. Your equa-tion is unfair. A petty judge against a della Robbia, perhaps, and a Moro against a Michelangelo..."

"But we have only one Moro and so many Michelangelos. There may be other men his equal, but in this case the symbol is more important even than the substance of the man. So what other life would you weigh against a Michelangelo to balance the scale?"

Franco hesitated. He'd said too much already. But Zanelli was just warming to the subject. "You disappoint me, Franco. You pose a delicious argument and then you back away. Why, the possibilities are endless—and so diverting. A Berlinguer or a Fra Angelico." He laughed, delighted by his own wit. "A Fanfani or a Piero della Francesca. Of course, one would have to know the minds of the *brigadisti* to predict their final choice—a Leonardo or Andreotti, the Sistina or the pontiff—"

"But that would be impossible...out of the question," Franco said too quickly.

"I have shocked you profoundly. I am sorry. You are too literal minded, my boy. We are merely weaving tapestries out of whole cloth. It's idle speculation, like the number of angels that could fit on the head of a pin."

The cardinal put an arm around Franco's shoulder. *"Non farci caso,* the Holy Father is in no danger. The Vatican is as safe as a mute's silence. Paul is a prisoner in his own home. Security won't let him out. The poor man, I don't envy him. Even if his health permitted, he couldn't move beyond the Vatican and Castel Gandolfo—from one palatial jail to another and back."

Franco felt his heart racing. He didn't dare to look at Zanelli. He felt as though his thoughts were transparent. Maybe the plan was possible, though he doubted it, his fear outweighed his hope. Still, Buscati was waiting...

"The change should be good for the Holy Father. They say the mountain air is good for one's health and I know Suor Marianna is concerned about his. She says he has never slept well and now he doesn't eat well either. Like a sparrow, she says." Franco knew he was talking too rapidly, gathering speed like a runner going downhill. But he couldn't stop himself. "I remember he always used to go to Castel Gandolfo in July but I haven't read any word of the trip in *l'Osservatore...*"

Cardinal Zanelli pressed Franco's shoulder lightly, then removed his arm. "He leaves very soon, Franco. On Thursday, after his morning mass. It should still be cool at that hour. Paul doesn't like air conditioning in the car. He is old-fashioned. It gives him chills, he says. One could argue which is more uncomfortable—chills or overheating—but that would be like the question of life versus art, and we would be starting all over. I have kept you from your mother too long already.

"I have enjoyed our conversation, Franco. It brings your father back. He and I had our differences but we shared one passion. We loved to debate the hypothetical, to construct elaborate scenarios with rococo embellishments. It could be anything, as nonsensical as our own just now, as long as it was good exercise for the mind. I called it cerebral calisthenics. We were both intellectual show-offs. You are not so vainglorious as we were at your age."

He held out his hand. Franco hesitated, then knelt down on the Ponte Milvio and kissed the ring. The cardinal placed his hand on the boy's head. "I came to comfort you, and I have done all the talking. From the terrorists to il Papa—you must forgive an old man's wandering mind."

CHAPTER FIFTY-TWO

Franco didn't go back to the apartment in Ponte Milvio. He couldn't face his mother. All her hopes, her dreams, were invested in him. Now in her grief over Paola he felt she was looking through her tears to him, waiting for him to be the son she had fashioned out of pride and love and conceit. She always said that he was more like her, and Paola was like her father. She wanted to boast a little. It didn't seem like much for a mother to ask.

He had ten thousand lire in his pocket. He didn't know what he could do to waste the sixteen hours until his meeting with Buscati. He didn't know any cheap *pensione* where no luggage was required and a room for a night was given without question. Anyway, he didn't think he could stare at the same four walls for that long. He thought of taking a bus, but the routes were too short. He'd have to keep riding back and forth. He found himself in the terminal, studying the schedule of arrivals and departures. The longest trip at the cheapest price. A train ride seemed like an inspiration. He could sleep on the train. The rocking motion would calm him. It would lull his conscience and soothe his grief. He needed to be moving and at the same time cradled, contained.

He bought a round trip ticket to Verona and boarded the train.

Franco was still stunned. He wanted to shout and to weep, to celebrate and to die. At Paola's funeral he had decided to go to Buscati the next morning and admit defeat. Her death had made him reckless. Who could have attacked her—trusting, loving, selfless Paola? The scum didn't deserve to live, although he'd done as much to her himself and never stopped to look back until now. And Lisa, lovely, unattainable Lisa, she too had died for nothing. He would confess to Buscati that he had failed and the mission was lost. Franco knew he wouldn't be forgiven. His comrades were not the Church. But he would be purged. He wouldn't have to choose between his friends and his father any longer. Confession was his catharsis. Failure was the perfect solution...

Then, just when he'd accepted it, even embraced it, he was given this gift, if that was the word for it. He couldn't believe his luck—or his misfortune. If the cardinal only knew what he had done...

CHAPTER FIFTY-THREE

"Shall I pick up Franco Mirabella this morning?" Officer Cenci stood at attention waiting for his orders. He was as bright and crisp as the morning.

Felice raised his eyes from the morning newspaper and fumbled for the ashtray he knew was somewhere in the debris on his desk. Not finding it, he ground out his cigarette butt in the top drawer. "Is that the brother's name?" he asked blandly.

He'd made a point of keeping the report on Mirabella to himself. He didn't want to explain how he came by the names of the SPL members, if he could possibly avoid it.

"The newspaper accounts were quite detailed," Cenci answered. "I remember his—"

"Go ahead. Pick him up," Felice cut in, "and if he doesn't cooperate, give him a tour of The Catacomb. That should loosen his tongue. I'll follow you out there. I'm going to have a talk with the mother."

Signora Mirabella was still weeping when Felice rang her bell. The blackness was pervasive. A black ribbon was draped across the door, and a birdlike woman, swaddled in black, ushered him into the living room where a coterie of other women, without a spot of color except in their eyes, surrounded the signora, milking her tears.

Felice bowed. "*Permesso,* signora. May I speak with you alone for a moment?" He didn't want to show his badge in front of the other women.

She looked at him blankly and nodded without even asking his name.

"*Permesso,* signora. I am Guido Felice, carabiniere," he said when the line of scavenging blackbirds had filed out. "You've probably met too many of us already but I only ask for a few minutes."

The signora continued to sob as if she were alone.

"Detective Mosca returned a package to you," Felice pressed on as gently as he knew how, "containing your daughter's personal effects."

"No!" The signora shouted suddenly, startling him. "They were not my daughter's. Paola was a good girl. A good girl. There was something pink—a piece of torn cloth, silk or satin with the lace still on it, but I knew what it was. She *never* owned such a thing, where would she get it?"

"Perhaps there was some mistake and you received the wrong package. If I could see it..."

"I threw it away. I won't look at such things or listen to their talk. Paola was a good girl, I swear on her father's soul. *Un'innocente, veramente un'innocente, dolce, pura, sensitiva.*" She sobbed convulsively between each word.

"*Calma,* signora, *calma.* We too believe she was blameless. That's why we're trying to find out what she was doing out there—why she died. There was a notebook in the package that she carried with her."

"...A small black book?"

Felice nodded. "I believe so. Do you know what was in it?"

"Some childish foolishness. It was Franco's, her brother's. Paola found it one night and wouldn't give it back to him. He got so mad. She could be a terrible tease when she wanted to be. If I'd known it was in that package I would have kept it. For the memories."

Felice was nodding his head sympathetically. He hoped it was all a terrible mistake and Franco Mirabella had nothing to hide. "Where is your son now? Is he at home?"

Signora Mirabella burst into a fresh bout of weeping, even worse than before.

"We've lost the boy. He skipped right after the funeral." Felice leaned in the window of Cenci's patrol car. "His mother's hoping he'll call at least. She said he was very distraught over his sister, and bitter."

Cenci's fingers locked around the steering wheel. "I'll put a tracer on the phone, check the airport and stations, the usual."

"Good." Felice slapped the car door. "I'm going to get a coffee, then I'll be along."

He watched from the curb while Cenci drove away, then went around to the back of the apartment house, moving quickly. Two dozen garbage cans—all full—were lined up ready to be collected. Felice started to riffle through them. Some people are pigs, he thought, they don't even wrap up their garbage. He tried to hold his breath and worked faster, thinking how carefully his wife always tied up theirs, making sure no one ever got a whiff of their life. The noise of a disposal truck grinding up the hill galvanized him. He plunged into another can and overturned it. There was no time to worry about neatness. He didn't want to be caught rummaging through garbage and have to explain what he was doing.

He overturned two more cans and kicked through the debris. Eggshells and coffee grounds stained his cuffs. Under a pile of withered gladioluses was a soggy and stained package, the brown paper partially torn open. He scooped it up and carried it back to the car as gingerly as if it contained a time bomb.

Mosca hadn't exaggerated. There was almost nothing left of Paola Mirabella except for her pocketbook, a few pieces of ripped, blood-stained clothing, and a small, misshapen object, also torn and stained, that might once have been a notebook. Felice tried to open it, but the covers were welded together with congealed blood and flesh.

303

CHAPTER FIFTY-FOUR

Via San Francesco di Paola was actually a flight of outside stairs constructed on the site of the ancient Via Scelerata, so named because on that spot an impudent girl named Tullia ran her chariot over her father's dead body. An imposing seventeenth-century palazzo at the top of the stairs housed the Instituto Centrale del Restauro. Paintings, sculptures, frescoes and bronzes were brought there from all over the country to be restored by Dottore Enzio Berneschi and his hand-picked staff. Dottore Berneschi was an exacting master of an exacting craft.

The top-floor laboratory where he worked was a long vaulted room with a clear view of the Colosseum and a clutter of artifacts in varying states of decay. Felice bore the doctor's scrutiny, balanced on a wooden stool in the shadow of a decapitated marble woman, his generous behind encircling the seat like the rings of Saturn. Berneschi had waved off his two assistants when the detective arrived but continued working on the Etruscan fresco he was restoring. A chemist, a surgeon, an artist—Berneschi was all three, and a magician as well. From broken bits and shards he reconstructed the history of art.

Felice couldn't disguise his surprise on meeting the famed restorer. A small almost fragile frame was encased in fat, like a filet wrapped in suet. Beneath a wreath of black hair sprinkled with gray, the edges of small, round features dissolved in a fleshy face. He chain-smoked, spilling the ashes onto the floor, his shirt, his work, and wiping them away like the dust of history he so painstakingly erased. He was awkward and nervous—a bumbler, to all appearances, inclined to spill a drink or break a hostess's prized crystal. Yet he was the best restorer in Italy—and probably the world. He could take a shattered figure and reconstruct the sculpture, bring back a fresco from a darkened wall, wipe away a mediocre painting and reveal a masterwork. He'd once brought forth a Raphael, painted over and forgotten for centuries.

Felice shook his head. "Where would one ever acquire the confidence and the audacity to paint over a Raffaello?"

"We're all egotists," Berneschi laughed, "though we may not admit it. And artists are supreme egotists. The worse one is the more highly he esteems himself. But what brings the police to my studio—grave robbers or art forgers? A visit from the carabinieri is an unnerving honor I'd just as soon not have conferred on me."

"Relax, *dottore*," Felice said. "I was hoping to persuade you to do a little work for me." He took an envelope from his pocket and handed it to Berneschi. "It's not an antiquity, not even contemporary art. But as you can see, it could stand some restoring."

Berneschi took out the remains of the notebook and examined it under a high-intensity magnifying light. The blood and hair and particles of flesh that clung to it showed clearly. He slipped the book back in the envelope, wiping his hands on his trousers, and reached for the cigarette he'd left balanced on the edge of his work table, inhaling deeply to settle himself. The sight of blood—even the thought of it—made his stomach somersault.

His face was like moss as he handed back the envelope. "This isn't exactly my line of work. I'm sorry."

Felice made no move to accept it. "I know, *dottore*, but I was hoping you'd make an exception. A girl died with it—maybe even for it. We don't know because we can't see inside it. She was a

305

lovely girl, I'm told. If you could restore it even partially..."

"Why did you come to me? I don't do police work. You must have your own people—"

"Your skill is renowned, Berneschi. And the notebook is all I have. It may be nothing at all—a waste of your precious time. Or it may be of great value to us."

"What branch of the carabinieri did you say you were with, Detective Felice?"

"*La Squadra Anti-terrorismo,* and I didn't say."

Berneschi fingered the envelope uncomfortably. "Can I refuse?"

"Of course, *dottore.* But I don't believe you will. You are employed by the state. If your sympathies lie elsewhere..." He shrugged and eased his weight off the stool. "I'll leave the notebook with you while you make up your mind. *Arriverderla, dottore.*"

The envelope fluttered in Berneschi's hand as he watched Felice lumber toward the door. "When do you need this, commisar?" he shouted at the retreating figure.

"A week ago, a year ago. Who can say? I'll come back tomorrow for your answer."

"Tomorrow's Sunday. I don't work on Sundays."

"Neither do I. Does anyone care?"

CHAPTER FIFTY-FIVE

"You are sure of the date? There can be no mistake, no misunderstanding. It's better to know now if you're uncertain than to expose the operation to failure."

"I have *told* you, Sandro, a thousand times. He leaves for Castel Gandolfo on *Thursday, the thirteenth of July, after mass.*"

Buscati persisted. "Who told you? How can we be sure? If you have some confirmation—"

"It came to me on the highest authority, from a prince of the Church, one of the most influential men in the Curia—the name would mean nothing to you." Franco's voice was tired. He was weak from fatigue and from hunger. Still, he stubbornly refused to identify his source, guarding Zanelli's identity with a special single-mindedness. Franco didn't understand himself why he was reluctant to reveal how he'd gotten the information. Probably because it had come to him by chance. He'd failed and been handed a reprieve. Absolution. He wanted his comrades to believe he had succeeded. He'd been given a mission and had carried it out like the best of them. Even more, though, he wanted to keep something for himself. "What more do you want of me?" Franco's voice broke. He couldn't hold on much longer.

"*Calma,* Franco. Of course the day has not been posted on the walls of Vatican City."

Buscati was alarmed by Franco's appearance. His skin was the color of dust. His eyes were a study in pain. His fingers were in perpetual motion. He had to be jiggling, touching, fingering something, anything—his hair, his sleeve, a matchbox. If he wasn't, he bit his nails with a vengeance. The sound of the snapping, nail against porcelain, nail against porcelain, had the same nerve-wracking effect as a dripping faucet.

Buscati made the decision. As long as he lived, Franco was a risk. If he were caught in the cross fire Thursday it would be a regrettable accident, and no explanation required. If he survived, he could be used to break Paul. They could make him a martyr in front of the Fisherman. It would be interesting to study Paul's reaction.

Buscati smiled warmly. "You have done your job well. I'm proud to be a comrade. You know, Franco, I must confess that I was worried. I wasn't sure you were strong enough. For the rest of us Paul is just a symbol. For you it is more personal—intensely personal—or I have misjudged you. You know the Fisherman first as a man. I defended you when the others questioned you. But when you brought us so close, then seemed to be backing off from the final step of your mission, I became suspicious. Forgive me. How wrong can a man be. You are exhausted, physically and emotionally, yet you still brought us this prize. You have earned special consideration, comrade." Buscati put his arm around the boy and embraced him. "Now tell me, Franco, what would you rather do first—eat or sleep?"

Franco managed a weak smile. "Eat a little and then sleep a lot."

Buscati laughed and slapped him on the back. "Good. There's a trattoria around the corner and a spare mattress at my place. Your job is over now. You will stay with me until the operation is complete, and then we shall see..."

"But my mother. She'll be so worried, on top of Paola—" His voice broke. "I left her in the middle of the funeral without a word."

308

"Don't worry. We'll take care of your mother. In the morning we'll call her. You can tell her something to keep her from worrying—something she'd like to hear. We'll decide together what to say. You had to get away for a few days, you were so overcome..."

"I can say I've gone to the Alban Hills with some friends...?"

"This is no time for joking. Somewhere as far from the Alban Hills as possible...Is there a place where your family would go when you were young? A place that would mean something to your mother?"

"My father took me to Elba once when I was small. I always wanted to go back. He used to make a joke about it. My exile, he called it."

"*Perfetto.* From this moment you are on the island of Elba. Enjoy your stay. You will say something like this. 'Forgive me, mama, for causing you added worry, especially now. But the sound of weeping became too much for me, I couldn't stand it another moment. I had to get away. I'm on the island of Elba where I went with *babbo,* you remember. I think I'll stay here for a few days, I have to be alone. For the first time I realize how precious life is—my life. It's truly a gift of God, I have to decide what to do before I waste any more of it. Give me a few days to think and pray for direction, then I'll be home to look after you. Lay a flower on Paola's grave for me.'"

Franco looked at his friend, and for the first time since he had known Buscati, he truly feared him. Deceit came so effortlessly to him. He wondered where Buscati had buried his conscience.

"You make it sound so easy. But for me it is very difficult to live a lie the way I've been doing these past weeks—to deceive and fib to people who love me. I don't deserve their love—"

"Jesus would have been on our side, Franco. He was a revolutionary. That's why the authorities killed him. He was telling the poor they were as good as the rich. He was preaching social justice to the masses. Look at the men he chose for his disciples, his twelve comrades, workingmen, proletarians, and the woman he loved was a whore."

"The Church magisterium has never accepted that interpretation—"

"The Church doesn't need to accept it. Only you do. Did you consider not bringing me the information because it seemed... how shall I say it? Because it seemed to you like a betrayal of the Fisherman?"

Franco nodded.

"You struggled with the decision all night alone?"

He nodded again. It was as if Buscati could see into his soul. "I felt like Judas Iscariot pointing out Jesus. That's the one, seize him."

"Why did you tell me, then? You could have gone on pretending it was impossible to find out the date."

"We're comrades, you were depending on me..."

"That's the only reason?"

"No, but I can't explain it. It's because of my sister Paola, and Lisa, just days apart. I didn't want them both to die for nothing. One is bad enough, but not both..." He turned away so that Buscati wouldn't see the tears that filled his eyes.

Buscati looked at him in surprise. "You were fond of Lisa Taglia?"

"She was a comrade..." Franco felt embarrassed.

"And very beautiful."

He nodded.

"So you feel like you have lost two sisters, Lisa and Paola, in just a few weeks. But in time you'll get over both of them and you'll find other sisters to care for, and even have fun with. Many other sisters. You and I are warriors, Franco. You must be prepared, even eager, to kill. To do that, you have to face the reality that your friends', your family's, *and* your own death is inevitable... It's nothing more than a necessary consequence. I'm sorry about your sister though. The one time I met her, she seemed simpatica."

Franco couldn't look at Buscati. Talking about Paola only made it worse, and he didn't want to cry like a baby in front of his friend and comrade.

Buscati put an arm around him and led him toward the door. Giuliani's was beginning to fill up with the noontime crowd, many of whom brought their lunch from the trattoria around the corner. Outside the air felt heavy with rain.

CHAPTER FIFTY-SIX

When Felice returned to the institute he was informed that Dottore Berneschi was away on holiday.

"When did he leave?"

"I'm not sure, sir." His assistant was obviously a bad liar. "But he left a package for you."

"What are you doing here? Don't you know it's Sunday?" Felice asked gruffly as he accepted a manila envelope with his name scrawled across the front.

Inside were the notebook and a sheaf of 5 x 7 pages. A note attached to the front sheet read: "Doesn't look like code—just simple shorthand. A cryptologist would know better. *Auguri*."

Felice smiled. Wherever his sympathies lay, Berneschi was taking pains to conceal them. His restoration was a work of art.

Using X rays and special chemicals, he'd reconstructed each page, enlarging the scraps of paper he could salvage and piecing them together with the precision of a surgeon. The missing parts were filled in with blank rag paper, cut to fit exactly, just as the missing parts of a sculpture are filled in.

* * *

"What do you have there, sir?" Cenci inquired.

The sky had faded to gray but the day was still light. Felice reached across the desk and flicked on the overhead light. His face was an eerie, bluish white under the fluorescent tubes. He was glad that his wife was in Civitavecchia. At least she couldn't complain that he didn't care about his children because he was working another Sunday...

"What do you make of this? It was scraped off the subway tracks with the body of the Mirabella girl." He handed over the black book but kept the enlargements firmly planted on the desk in front of him.

Cenci took it gingerly and spread out the scraps of paper that drifted down when he opened it on the coffee table. Kneeling on the floor in front of it, he tried to fit the pieces together. All he could make out were two words. He stared at them until the letters dissolved and swam on the paper. Felice's voice seemed to be coming from a great distance.

"For two weeks I've been thinking, wracking my brains, lying awake nights wondering...Pescara? Pescara? What could there be in Pescara besides sea and fish and a little coarse sand?"

He'd picked up the receiver while he was talking. "Get me Vatican Security."

"But I was sure the Taglia girl said "Pescara'," Cenci said.

Felice was shaking his head. "It would be 'a Pescara'—to Pescara. But remember? You told me she said 'al'—to the...to the Pescara? No. She must have said, 'al Pescatore.' to the Fisherman. I've wracked my brain all day. There's only one fisherman our brigadisti would want to destroy, and he fishes for souls."

He put his hand over the receiver while he waited for the call to go through. "Go home and get some sleep, Cenci. There's nothing more you can do tonight."

Cenci had taken off his glasses and was polishing the lenses abstractedly, trying to hide the relief, and terror, that churned inside him.

BOOK IV

The
Net
Closes

July 13, 1978

CHAPTER FIFTY-SEVEN

A Swiss Guard in dress uniform waved the black Fiat 128 through the gates of the Apostolic Palace and watched as it turned right onto Via di Porta Angelica. Felice didn't look back at the fifth-floor windows where the lights from the papal apartments still burned brightly. The traffic was light and he drove fast, choosing his route carefully through the colonnade of St. Peter's onto Via della Conciliazione and along the river past Castel Sant' Angelo and the palatial Ministry of Justice. There was no time to lose. He rolled down his window as he drove, pulled a cigarette out of the half-empty pack on the dashboard, extracted a red-tipped wax match from the box beside it with the picture of Piazza Navona on the cover and struck it with one hand. He lit the cigarette, flicking the match out the open window, then rested his elbow on the rim. He moved with economy and skill, never losing speed. It was a technique he'd mastered through years of practice, a small ritual perfectly executed. Its familiarity and the sureness of his movements comforted him, in the same way thoughts of Elena once had.

He sped along the Tiber. The river was black and murky. The

air, heavy. It felt oppressive, though it was only the second week of July, and a cool July by Roman standards. His body was thick with sweat. The enlargements reconstructed from Franco Mirabella's notebook lay on the seat beside him. The director of Vatican Security and the pope's personal secretary had identified them immediately. The timetable was precise, and deadly accurate. Every detail was filled in except the final date. And the papal secretary had just supplied that. In approximately five hours, the Fisherman was scheduled to drive to Castel Gandolfo.

A stray dog loped along the river below the road. Felice crossed the river at Ponte Cavour and sped along, turning down the Corso, wheeling left onto Via del Tritone, then right into Via delle Quattro Fontane. The Corso was quiet. It was a daytime street. But at Piazza Barberini the whores were still filtering down from Via Veneto, there were still couples in evening dress and tourists still clutching their cameras, high on *vino di tavola* and the Eternal City. He didn't turn into the Questura but sped along and braked in Piazza del Viminale. He opened his door as he turned off the ignition and rushed out.

Nodding brusquely to the guards, he went upstairs. For a fat man, he moved fast when he wanted to. Minutes later he emerged, flanked by General del Sarto and the minister of defense. The Fiat 128 circled the piazza and turned back onto Via delle Quattro Fontane. It was heading for the address of Pomponius Atticus, with whom Cicero corresponded so frequently.

The Quirinale is the highest of Rome's seven hills. The spacious piazza that stands at its summit affords an arresting view of the historic city, with the dome of St. Peter's casting its shadow in the distance. The Palazzo della Consulta and the stately Palazzo del Quirinale face each other across the square. Between them loom the eighteen-foot statues of the Dioscuri, Castor and Pollux, signed on the bases—"opus Phidiae" and "opus Praxiteles." The Greek sculptors were ignorant of the statues. The inscriptions were carved by order of Sixtus VI. There is also a basin of dark granite in the piazza once used as a cattle trough in the Roman Forum. The Palazzo della Consulta is the seat of the Supreme Court. The

318

Quirinale is the official residence of the president of the Republic. Previously it was the royal residence of Victor Emmanuel and before that the summer palace of the popes.

How much simpler a security task they'd have if it still were, Felice thought as the black Fiat eased up the hill. *La manica lunga* passed on their right—the long sleeve of the palace. The president, like his predecessors and the kings before them, preferred to live in the homier *palazetto* at the far end. An audience had been requested and granted. Within minutes, the president, bleary-eyed and incredulous, would be briefed on the plot to ensnare the Fisherman. The car drew up to the majestic entranceway. The guards pointed their submachine guns down and saluted smartly as General del Sarto and the minister of defense swept by and hurried up the grand staircase. Felice was a step behind them, still debating with himself. Should he reveal his plan and request authorization, or carry it through on his own and risk the consequences? I have the cooperation of the Vatican. How can they refuse me?...A magnificent fresco of Christ surrounded by an entire choir of angels shone down on him. He wiped his hands on his trouser legs. He'd never met the president and was understandably nervous.

Running a damp hand through his hair, he followed the others into a paneled library. "*Al Pescatore, a Pescara*," Felice mumbled to himself. He'd realized almost too late that there was nothing in Pescara except sand and fish and endless sea. He should have seen right away, followed his first instincts. But loyalty had blinded him—or was it laziness...? He'd been so close, he couldn't or wouldn't see. Some things go beyond politics. That's what he would say to the general and the minister and the president, if he had to. The enemy sits among us. Takes an *espresso* with us. Risks his life with us. Infiltration. It was a cold word that didn't describe what had been done. An act of betrayal. He felt like he'd been raped. Right down to his soul. His person. His privacy had been violated. How many rape victims had he seen? And just now he'd begun to understand something of their anguish, their embarrassment, their sense of defilement.

CHAPTER FIFTY-EIGHT

As soon as Cenci came through the apartment door he saw the wedding picture. It stood in state in an ornate gold-toned frame on the coffee table. The couple was posed awkwardly before the camera. Except for the gray in her hair, Elena hadn't changed as much as her husband, who in the picture possessed a full head of wavy black hair and the broad-shouldered, muscular build of an athlete. A Perugina candy boxtop, cut out and covered with transparent plastic wrap, was tacked to the wall above the sofa. The scene, in full color, was of mountains, green and flowered, with a crystal lake in the forefront.

Their eyes met for a moment, then Felice's lids drooped.

Cenci winced. He didn't want to be drawn into the private passions behind Felice's public poses. He didn't want to see the fat man stripped naked. He preferred the antagonist he knew.

"Why did you send those goons to break into my apartment and bring me here?" he said. "To watch you change your clothes at three in the morning?"

"I had no choice," Felice said.

"Of course you did. I'd be in the office in a couple of hours—"

"Perhaps, and perhaps not. I couldn't know for sure. But I wanted to face you here...where I have no secrets, and now neither do you. You're not alone, you know. We're all dreamers and fools. But you—you are a Judas."

Cenci's eyes were fixed on the wedding picture that captured in sepia the union of Guido and his wife. She was fat, and he resigned, and they hadn't even begun. "Elena?" Cenci murmured under his breath.

Felice shrugged.

"And the mountains?"

"You can see for yourself, there, on the wall...on the candy box. I get a new one each year for my feast day."

Felice went into the bedroom to change his shirt. It was a quarter to three in the morning. The apartment was empty. Elena and the children were still away. Outside two carabinieri stood guard at the apartment door.

He came back, buttoning a clean shirt. Black hairs curled over the straps of his undershirt.

Cenci took off his glasses and breathed slowly on each lens. "Whatever you're planning, it isn't necessary. I've located Buscati. We can pick him up in a couple of hours with a roadblock on Via Appia Nuova. He's going to try to get out of Rome before dawn."

Felice laughed harshly. "I've already arranged an appointment for you in a couple of hours—on the same Via Appia Nuova. It's an ingenious plan, I can say in all modesty, approved by the general, the minister, the president himself, and the Fisherman's own secretary. You know, the Fisherman, Cenci, don't you, but you were planning, perhaps, to know him better. You're about the same size, I judge. You see, we need a scapegoat to catch Buscati, so I volunteered you, *scusate*. Come on, I'll explain it to you on the way. You'll enjoy it."

CHAPTER FIFTY-NINE

In a modest house just off the main highway to Castel Gandolfo Antonio Bartoli cursed roundly and fumbled for the switch to turn off the alarm clock. It was 4:30 on the morning of July 13. He'd consumed the better part of a gallon of wine the night before and the incessant alarm pierced his hangover like a stiletto. Bartoli reached across his sleeping wife for the telephone. She wheezed and pulled the sheet higher around her shoulders. No man with a head as large as his was that morning should even consider the possibility of work, he thought, as he dialed his brother's number to tell him not to pick him up for work. He slammed the receiver down, swearing so vehemently this time, heaping curses on his brother's sow of a wife, her ignorant mother and gypsy grandmother, that he interrupted his wife's snoring.

"*Madre di Dio, Antonio, a quest'ora! Che successo?* You'll wake up the children."

"The children, the children. They've kept me awake often enough."

"They are babies. You are a man—or you're supposed to be."

"Watch your tongue, woman." Bartoli jabbed a knee into his

wife's rump. "They may as well hear me. Nobody else can. The goddamn phone is dead."

Three kilometers to the west, Marcello Donato closed the door of his farmhouse and, whistling softly to himself, climbed into the cab of his pickup truck. The day was going to be a fine one. The first traces of sunlight were filtering through the darkness, bringing the promise of a successful day. The back of the truck was filled with the produce he and his family had picked and loaded the night before to take to the market in Castel Gandolfo—arugula, kale, fennel, broccoli, zucchini and dandelion greens.

He turned on the ignition and sat there, his low whistle merging with the idling motor. The truck was like an old friend. Marcello understood its moods and its needs. It didn't like to be rushed into action in the morning, much like himself. He always got up earlier than necessary so that he could take his time. He enjoyed his early morning ritual—grinding the fresh beans, brewing the coffee, breaking up a crust of yesterday's bread in the oversized cup he only used at breakfast, pouring the steaming coffee over it, and sitting down alone at the kitchen table. In winter he bent over the cup to catch the warm steam on his face and hands. It was the only heat in the farmhouse. The hot coffee ensured a full evacuation, then he could go to the market without worry.

This morning was no different from the others. He'd looked at his wife and twin daughters before he went out. They were all sleeping peacefully. He whispered good-by and blew a kiss to each of them. How he loved his three beauties. He'd always wanted a son—until he had the twins. Then he couldn't imagine why he hadn't wanted a daughter—two daughters. And there was still time. Angela was delicate, but she might yet bear him a son to help on the farm.

Marcello sat patiently, letting the motor idle before releasing the brake and putting it in gear. The truck hadn't moved two feet before he realized something was wrong. He turned off the ignition and climbed down from the cab to take a look. His jaunty tune turned into a low whistle of amazement.

323

Pushing his hat back and scratching his head behind his ear, he circled the truck slowly. All four of the tires had been slashed. He walked around the farm in a daze. There was no one in sight and no sound except the chirping of the birds and the low rumble of the cat who'd followed him out of the barn and was now rubbing against his leg.

Marcello bent over and scratched the cat's head. He only had two spares—one good and one barely serviceable—which he kept for an emergency. He could walk out to the highway, try to hitch a ride to Castel Gandolfo, buy a new set of tires on credit, hitch back, change them, and hope to get to the market before noon. Or he could go back to bed and worry about the truck later. The vegetables would keep in the cool stone barn until tomorrow, and his family would be glad of a day's respite from picking in the fields. He imagined slipping back into bed and pressing his firm body against the warm curves of his wife and knew that if he did, before dawn he'd be thanking the fates for keeping him home that morning. On the other hand he should do his duty. They could ill afford to miss a day's income, especially with the unexpected expense of a new set of tires, even a used set.

On a day like this promised to be, it seemed that whatever he chose would be right. The almost ceaseless rains of the winter and spring seemed like a dim memory. Marcello Donato didn't know it, but his life depended on his choice.

Bruno Triano braked his Alfetta sharply. He was speeding north mechanically, his mind and body still heavy with sleep, and he didn't see the roadblock until he was almost on top of it. "What a morning," he grumbled to himself. Nothing had gone right. He'd nicked his face shaving, spilled coffee on his fresh shirt, misplaced his keys and now this—the last straw. A roadblock from Castel Gandolfo at five-fifteen in the morning. He drew up beside the carabiniere who was standing in the middle of the road waving him down.

Triano stuck his head out the window. "I suppose you're going to tell me that Moro's assassins are sneaking out of Castel Gandolfo at five o'clock on a summer's morning?"

The carabiniere touched his hat respectfully. He seemed neither amused nor angered. "The road is temporarily closed for repairs. It will reopen by ten o'clock. We regret the inconvenience."

"Ten o'clock is no help to me. I'm due in Naples by nine-thirty."

"*Mi dispiace,* signore. But that is impossible." The policeman's tone remained friendly but firm. He wouldn't budge.

Triano reached for his wallet. It was worth a few extra lire to keep his appointment.

At the first movement the carabiniere's eyes hardened. "The road is closed," he repeated.

"This is the only road. How can you close it?"

"It's for your own safety."

"I'll pass at my own peril."

"If I arrest you, you will never reach Naples. Do I make myself clear?"

Triano made a gesture of disgust at the stone-faced policeman, slapping his shoulder and raising a straight arm. A black-and-white barrier blocked the road. He could drive straight through. There was no police car in sight to give chase, only this lone, determined man in gleaming white uniform. Triano was mostly hot air and bluster. When it actually came down to it, he didn't have the nerve. Grinding the gears like a hurdy-gurdy, he stepped on the gas and circled around, leaving a squeal of rubber and a plume of black exhaust.

The man in the police uniform spat at the receding car. *"Brutto cafone!"* Such people didn't deserve to live. There would be no place for them in the new Italy. He watched until the Alfetta was out of sight, then turned and waved the checkered flag he carried in a wide arc, three times.

Five kilometers down the road toward Rome, Luigi Domenica stood on the back of a gray truck marked "Road repair." Through high-powered binoculars, he saw the carabiniere give the all-clear signal. Then he looked at his watch—5:19. So far everything was proceeding exactly according to Buscati's schedule.

Marcello Donato didn't notice the road crew until he reached the intersection of Via Appia. Typical, he thought as he headed in their direction. There were half a dozen men and not one of them was working. That's what's wrong with Italy. Then he caught himself. Who can blame them on a day like today, and since they weren't working, maybe they'd agree to give him a lift into town. He waved to the foreman, who was coming down the road toward him.

"This road is closed to all traffic, vehicular and pedestrian, signore," the man called. A large yellow sign, "Danger—Men Working" stood in the middle of the road.

"Then I'm out of luck, unless you'd be willing to help me... The strangest thing happened to me this morning. I have a farm back there, just over the hill." He gestured over his shoulder with a thumb. "I woke up to find all the tires of my truck had been slashed. At first I suspected thieves, but none of the vegetables had been stolen. I was hoping to hitch a ride into town to buy new tires. Mine are beyond repair. I could pay you in vegetables. But if the road is closed..."

"I wish I could, but we have to get on with the job. The road will reopen at ten."

"Your crew doesn't look like it's in much of a hurry." Over the foreman's shoulder Marcello could see the men in the distance. Their uniforms were familiar—their jumpsuits, their caps, the color and markings on the truck. He squinted to see them more closely. Instead of picks and shovels, they were carrying semi-automatic weapons—

"You caught us at our first break this morning," the foreman was saying affably. "My advice to you would be to go home and catch a few extra hours of sleep." His voice was easy but his steely eyes never strayed from Marcello Donato's face.

"Who are you?" Donato didn't recognize the high, shrill voice that asked the question. He felt the fear begin, like a terrible urge to urinate, and he had to control his hands from reaching for his groin.

"It's your misfortune to have such excellent eyesight. A little myopia..." The voice trailed off.

"I'll forget that I've seen you—"

"Yes, you'll have to forget. We didn't count on a man so dedicated to his work. We thought you'd be glad of the extra sleep. You've worked so hard these weeks. We thought you'd welcome a day off."

"You've been watching."

The foreman only smiled.

"What about my wife and children?"

"We have no quarrel with them, unless they come looking for you too soon."

"They're still asleep, they don't even know anything happened—"

The foreman raised a hand in what would have passed on any other day of Marcello Donato's life except the last one as a friendly gesture. Four workmen began advancing rapidly toward them.

Donato had to concentrate all his attention on controlling his bladder. It felt ready to burst.

The foreman read his fear. "Believe me, if there was anything else I could do, I would."

"Who are you?"

"The future of Italy. The neglected soul of our nation."

"*Brigadisti.*" Donato's throat was so dry, the word came out in a whisper.

"It's an ugly word, don't you think? And inaccurate."

"What are you going to do with me?"

"You've left us no choice. Don't try to run. You couldn't go fast enough, and you'd only make it more painful for yourself."

"But my wife, my little girls, they need me. I've seen nothing, I remember nothing..."

The foreman stepped aside. Donato felt his knees buckle. He wouldn't run and be shot in the back like a coward. They'd get him one way or the other. Better to die with dignity if he could. He thought of his father in the war. He'd come home a cripple, with medals to attest to his bravery. At least his daughters wouldn't have to live with the memory of a father who died trying to run away.

Marcello Donato held his water and his ground as three belts of semiautomatic fire ripped through the clear morning air, cutting through the swallows' song and through his body. He didn't think about his wife and his twins then—his three beauties. He thought only that it was too glorious a day to die.

Pope Paul turned to give his benediction. The chapel was empty except for Monsignor Macchi, who was serving the mass. Paul hadn't changed his private chapel. There was no utilitarian table facing the open room.

He raised his hands. "The mass is ended."

"Go in peace," Monsignor Macchi responded.

Paul's cavernous eyes wandered around the chapel and came to rest on the painting of Michelangelo's "Death of Saint Peter," which hung on the wall to his left. Peter didn't feel worthy to die as Christ did and so they nailed him to the cross upside down. A shudder of empathy shook Paul. It was a terrible way to die. Now the popes were no longer martyrs for Christ. Instead, they crumbled a little more each day, each year.

Peter had been a mountain of a man. A fisherman. A laborer, passionate in his work and in his faith. A man of flesh and blood, not intellect. Yet he followed Christ and brought others to Him. And died for His glory. Paul wished he had Peter's simple faith. Even when he denied Christ, he did it with conviction, insisting not once but three times, "I know Him not." Intemperate, yes, but decisive—the way he cut off the soldier's ear with a blow, not waiting to consider every side of the issue.

The rock, Simon Peter. "Thou art Peter and upon this rock I shall build my church and the gates of hell shall not prevail against me." Paul felt more like a reed. He wanted to cry out with Christ crucified, "*Lame, Lame*, why hast thou forsaken me?"

"The mass is ended, go in peace," Paul murmured.

As Paul was finishing his benediction, Marcello Donato fell, bloodied and lifeless, to the macadam pavement.

There was no one to hear the shots. The workmen stuck their guns in their jumpsuits and dragged Donato's body back to the truck. The foreman looked at his watch. Except for the unfortunate farmer, everything was running perfectly. He stripped off his uniform and tossed it to one of the men.

328

"Don't look like you're working too hard. It's unpatriotic," he called brightly. "Any questions?"

"Any more surprises, Buscati?" Domenica said.

"None we can anticipate." His tone was cold, checking the impertinence in the other's voice.

They raised their fists in salute. "*Ricorda* Lisa," Domenica called.

"Yes, to Lisa!" Buscato clenched his fist in solidarity, then jogged away toward the clump of trees where he'd parked the dark blue Opel. He checked his watch again. 6:05. Paul would be having breakfast. Soon they'd have breakfast together. Easing the car into gear, he pulled back onto the road. He had time to circle the area once more. At each checkpoint, he ran through the steps with the waiting men.

At 6:28, Buscati was ready. He made a wide U-turn in the road, waved to the carabiniere, Michele Di Voto, standing guard at the roadblock, and started back toward Rome for the rendezvous with the Fisherman. He would be a supremely easy target. Even if Paul were stronger, he wouldn't resist. He wouldn't want to hurt anyone to save himself.

Three minutes later in Vatican City a black Mercedes-Benz limousine, license plate SCV1, drew up to the front door of the Apostolic Palace. A slight figure in a white cassock, cape and skullcap emerged from the shadows of the ornate portico. Instead of Secretary Macchi, a paunchy *monsignore*, Felice, in a cassock and wide-brimmed priest's hat hovered at the white-cassocked figure's side like a great black bird. The *monsignore* ushered the papal figure into the back seat, closed the door and slipped in front beside the driver with surprising agility.

Costanto Cardinal Zanelli watched from a fourth-floor window as the limousine pulled away. He'd put two and two together and come up with five. If his calculations proved correct, in just a few weeks white smoke would be curling up in the heavens over Vatican City proclaiming a new pope. The roar of the expectant crowd as he stepped out onto the balcony for the first time dressed in the white cassock and cape enthralled him. Yet he felt no satisfaction. He was a classicist, too familiar with the lesson of Faustus to savor his victory. There was still time to alert the minister of defense, but how would that make him look? He would be ruined, and worse—disdained, dishonored, even branded a traitor to his Church and country. Martyrdom held no appeal for this prince of the Church. Yet he couldn't pretend he was innocent. If he'd guessed right, he was as guilty as they. He'd fed them the bait.

"Eternal rest grant to him, O Lord, and let perpetual light shine upon him," the cardinal murmured, and crossed himself.

The Mercedes limousine rolled down Via della Conciliazione and across the Ponte Vittorio Emmanuele, following the same route it had taken two months before when Paul had gone to San Giovanni in Laterano to officiate at Moro's mass. Across the bridge, it picked up a motorcycle escort and sped on, gathering speed once it was outside the walls of the city. In the front seat, the beefy *monsignore* appeared to doze. Behind him his companion sat erect, lost in his own contemplation.

Cardinal Zanelli crossed the Vatican gardens and walked slowly to his office. A copy of *l'Osservatore Romano* lay folded and fresh on the tray beside his double espresso, as it did every morning. He glanced at his watch to check that his secretary wasn't becoming lax. 6:45. He opened the paper on the desk, scanning the headlines as he sipped the espresso. He swallowed suddenly and felt the steaming coffee burn the roof of his mouth. The cup clattered to the tray. Zanelli pushed it aside and reread the short notice in the lower lefthand column of the front page:

> His Holiness Paulus Sixtus has been advised by his physician to cancel all appointments for the next three days. "For some weeks the Holy Father has suffered from an acute worsening of the degenerative arthritis that afflicts him," a Vatican statement released this morning said. "His personal physician, Dottore Mario Fontana, has advised a few days of complete rest." Thus the Pope will be unable to leave for his summer residence at Castel Gandolfo as was planned today.

CHAPTER SIXTY

Twenty-one kilometers to Castel Gandolfo—plenty of time to make a full confession Felice thought. He the *monsignore* took a revolver from the folds of his cassock, checked the cartridges, then placed it on the seat beside him. He took the clerical mushroom hat off and laid it on top of the gun. Shifting his substantial bulk so that he was half turned toward the back seat, he slid open the bullet-proof window that separated them.

He inclined his head deferentially. "Your Holiness, is there something you'd like to tell me? I am not Christ who forgave the lost sheep seven times seven. I am not so good, nor so understanding. But I will try. Perhaps we might consider—not complete absolution, that's out of the question—but a light penance."

The papal figure took off his glasses and began to clean them meticulously on the edge of his white cape. Without them his eyes seemed to sink even farther back into his head. They showed neither fear nor defiance, only the familiar calculating appraisal. Looking at him was like staring into steel gray voids wreathed in dark circles. He polished his glasses as if he were considering his answer carefully, but he made no reply.

Two sharpshooters in helmets and bulletproof vests crouched at his feet, and the driver, rather than the regular papal chauffeur, was one of the best marksmen in the carabinieri. Behind them at a safe distance trailed a full detail of the Squadra Anti-terrorismo, and in ten minutes a second detail would begin moving slowly from Castel Gandolfo. They'd been flown in by helicopter just hours before, flying a wide arc from Rome so as not to be detected by the waiting *brigadisti*.

"I am waiting to hear your confession, Your Holiness." The *monsignore* tapped impatiently on the window. Crumbs from his morning cornetto still dotted the front of his red-trimmed cassock. "How many? Where, when, how? Keep it simple."

The papal figure sank back into the plush upholstery and refused to answer. He wore the face of defeat like a mask.

"You tried to play me for the fool, even threatening my daughter under my very nose. No wonder I was always one step behind your *brigadisti*. Would you really have harmed her? A naïve question, I suppose. You thought you were so clever and I an idiot. Who is the clever one now and who the idiot?"

"*Vogliamo tutto e subito.*"

"Amen," the *monsignore* sighed. "You will not save yourself."

As the Alban Hills rose ahead of them, flat against the bright blue sky, he noticed a road repair truck up ahead. He squinted into the distance. A group of men, five or six at the most, seemed to be half-sitting, half-lying on the grassy bank by the side of the road. It looked like they had lunch boxes in their laps.

The *monsignore* cursed under his breath. The road was supposed to be cleared. He'd given the order himself. Those damn provincials, they never get the job done. Then suddenly he felt a wave of nausea. He grabbed the radio to alert the motorcycle escort and the police details converging in both directions. Out of the corner of his eye he saw a dark blue Opel sedan coming up the road from the direction of Castel Gandolfo. He swirled around to look at the man behind him, saw a thin, mocking smile flicker at the corners of his tight lips.

The limousine was approaching the repair truck, the Opel picking up speed as it drew closer. Just as they pulled clear of the truck, it swerved across the road, cutting between the motorcycle escort and the limousine. In a second they were hemmed in—the Opel in front, the repair truck behind them. The workmen opened fire, spraying the car with their AKMs. As the Mercedes screeched to a halt, the rear doors flew open and the sharpshooters rolled out, scrambling behind the car for protection.

The *monsignore* turned back slowly to the man who waited, pale but composed in his papal robes. "*Arriverderla,* Your Holiness. The joyride is over." He motioned with his revolver to get out of the car.

The man flinched. Then with a glance of resignation toward the almighty power of the gun pointed at him, he obeyed . Heedless of the battle raging around him, he walked slowly, almost reverently toward the Opel.

Buscati watched, incredulous. "The man must be an idiot or a saint!" he shouted. He wanted the Fisherman alive, not dead. Running and crawling, he started to zigzag toward the white-clad figure. Three yards from him, Buscati suddenly pulled up short. He raised his P-38 and aimed it between the man's cold, unblinking eyes. A single word formed on Buscati's lips—Judas.

Still crouched on the floor of the Opel where he'd been thrown by the sudden braking, Franco watched through tear-filled eyes as the Fisherman moved unscathed through the barrage of gunfire, like Christ. The grass exploded with bursts of red. Men's heads blew from their shoulders. Curses and prayers rent the glorious morning. Franco saw it all, as if in slow motion, a dance of death. He was sickened and hypnotized. He wanted to die but he couldn't seem to move, and he didn't want to join the killing.

He watched the slight figure in white, the cassock with the small cape across the shoulders turning up in the morning breeze, the white slippers, the jewel-encrusted pectoral cross gleaming like a beacon, reflecting the silver weapons and the golden sun. He watched and something inside him broke. He burst out of the car, a Skorpion held out in front of him like a ticking bomb.

"I'm coming after you, Buscati. Don't shoot or I'll kill you..." His words were lost in the noise of the battle.

Buscati's gun was aimed when Franco opened fire, emptying

round after round into Sandro Buscati's exploding body. Choking with sobs, Franco threw the weapon away hurling it ahead of him, and ran, arms outstretched, toward the papal figure. The bullet that ended his life caught him in the back and sent his body flying into the air. He fell forward, arms still spread, in the form of a cross, his blood staining the hem of the papal cassock.

Piero Massi, alias Massimo Cenci—Moscow informer, *brigadiste* and officer in Rome's Squadra Anti-terrorismo—kicked the boy's body aside with the toe of a white satin slipper. Suddenly he was completely alone. Moscow wouldn't save him from the carabinieri, and his comrades would believe, as Buscati had, that he had betrayed them and have no forgiveness. The only question that remained was how he would die.

He picked up Franco's gun and turned to face the fat *monsignore*. Felice was waiting for him, his red-trimmed cassock flapping around his ankles, his revolver aimed to kill.

In Vatican City, the Fisherman rested quietly in his study. Although he had defied orders, getting up as usual to say mass, Paul was grateful that Dottore Fontana had ordered this day of rest. He was tired, so very tired. In the morning he would go to Castel Gandolfo. The day would be bright blue and sunny, the trip as smooth as the Alban lake.

And he would never return. Pope Paul VI died in Castel Gandolfo on August 6, 1978, of natural causes.